THE ELEMENT

<u>**ANOTHER NOVEL BY DALE C. GEORGE**</u>
The Device 2017

THE ELEMENT

Dale C. George

Idea Creations Press

www.ideacreationspress.com

Published in the United States by Idea Creations Press LLC.

LIBRARY OF CONGRESS CATALOGING-IN-PUBLICATION DATA
Names: George, Dale C., author
Title: The Element / Dale C. George
Description: First edition. | Salt Lake City: Idea Creations Press, 2023.
Identifiers: LCCN 2023904349
ISBN 978-1948804301
Subject: Science Fiction | Historical Fiction | Science Fiction Fantasy

www.ideacreationspress.com

ACKNOWLEDGEMENTS:

First and foremost, I would like to thank my wife Cindy for supporting me throughout this endeavor. As I wrote The Element, she read segments and gave me suggestions that helped shape the storyline. Once again, my love, you will never know the full extent of your contributions.

Many thanks to Libbey A. Hanson for her outstanding final edit, and the rest of my awesome beta-reading team: Scott Hennessy, Dave Avner, Donna Magaña, and Andria Hoyle. I would also like to give a big shout out to Doug and Kathryn Jones of Idea Creations Press, and to the men and women of the League of Utah Writers, Chapter 1: Davis County.

Lastly, a very special thank you to the men and women of the Davis County Parkinson's Support Group for inspiring the plot of The Element. In my eyes, you are all heroes.

To those who have risked their lives to save others –
there are none braver than you.

And to the men and women of our nation's military,
who take those risks every day.

PREFACE

It's been seven years since I put a pen to paper and wrote about the happenings in *The Device*. At the time, I thought it near-impossible for Madison and me to encounter another person as evil as General Berger. Sadly, I was mistaken. The events occurring shortly after the passing of Madison's uncle resulted in us confronting a different kind of malevolent individual; one whose ambition was not to rule the world, but rather to destroy it.

The person we encountered could best be described as a fallen spirit. For centuries he had walked among us but was not one of us. We came to learn he was responsible for the major outbreaks of deadly diseases dating back seven centuries, all in an attempt to end his mortal existence. His plan endangered every man, woman, and child on the earth. I therefore call upon you, the reader, to suppress your disbelief until you have read my narrative in its entirety.

Once again, I debated whether to place my story in a novel and take the chance of subjecting myself to harsh criticism. After careful thought, and with much encouragement from Madison, I concluded this story simply must be told. I have tried to describe what happened as close as possible to how I remember them, but with the progression of Parkinson's disease making me forgetful at times, there may be some inaccuracies with regards to precise actions at exact moments. After an exhaustive study of the trail of evidence, and a thorough examination of the timeline of events, I have also added unknown narrative and dialog of how I *believe* things happened and what the primary players *might have* said.

Even if you deem my story implausible, I sincerely hope you enjoy it.

George d'Clare

PROLOGUE

Roman-held Province of Judea
Friday, 3 April, 0033, 08:35hrs
Outside Pontius Pilate's Residential Auditorium, Old Jerusalem

As the storm clouds rumbled in the darkening sky, the soldiers cleared a path through the crowd of spectators and led the three prisoners to the city's main street. Two of the men had been found guilty of stealing, while the third, a man from Nazareth, had been convicted of a much more serious crime: preaching heresy. With some people shouting insults and others shedding tears, the soldiers forced each condemned man to carry a large wooden cross, which would ultimately be used as an instrument to end their lives. Although these symbols of execution were heavy, they were only a fraction of the burden carried by the Nazarene, who also bore the weight of the sins of the world.

The procession soon made its way to the business district, at which point the man from Nazareth, weak from the injuries he had received in the flagellation, tripped on an uneven rock and fell. The burdensome cross he carried slipped off his shoulder, and upended a table owned by the tailor Lucas. When his goods scattered everywhere, the angry merchant focused his rage on the fallen man.

"Hasten your pace, heretic!" he screamed. "Why do you loiter?"

When the Nazarene replied, Lucas' blood ran cold. It wasn't only the words that chilled him, but also the condemned man's penetrating stare. Images of Lucas' life flashed before his eyes, and he knew everything was about to change.

* * *

Shortly after his birth, Lucas was left on the doorstep of an aged Jerusalem clothing merchant named Isaac, who took pity and adopted him. While growing to manhood and learning the tailoring business, he developed an insatiable thirst for wealth. Over time, this greed transformed him into a cynic, with a deep-seated disregard for his fellow man.

When he reached the age of sixteen, his tall and overly muscular build attracted the attention of many traders and seafarers in need of a strong back and a weak mind. Instead of accepting one of their employment offers, which would have paid him handsomely, he remained working for his adoptive father. From carefully observing Isaac over the years, he'd discovered the old man had been buying and selling stolen textiles. Although Lucas had grown to hate his profession, he bided his time hoping Isaac would die or involve him in the darker side of the business, which in either case would make him a very wealthy man.

A few days after Lucas turned eighteen, he accompanied Isaac to a business meeting to collect a debt from a man named Matthias. When the payment came up short, Isaac knocked Matthias down, handed Lucas a knife, and ordered Lucas to slit Matthias' throat. Realizing it was a test, and if he failed he would be forever shut out of the old man's secretive affairs, Lucas obeyed the instructions.

As he stood over Matthias' body, tears came to his eyes.

"Father, what have I done?"

Isaac walked over and patted him on the back.

"You have done what was needed to keep our business solvent, my son. This also sends a message to others. I will not be cheated nor taken lightly."

"Should we not feel pity for Matthias?"

Isaac grasped Lucas' shoulders and shook him.

"Listen to me! Never feel pity for an enemy!"

"Was he an enemy?"

"Anyone who does not pay you for the fruit of your labor is an enemy! If you are to remain in business, murder is a necessity. You must never show weakness, any weakness at all, or you will end up like Matthias!"

Hearing Isaac talk of *him* remaining in the business resonated in Lucas' ears. Overjoyed at the prospect of becoming rich, his feelings of remorse for taking Matthias' life withered away.

For the next year, Lucas accompanied Isaac to other meetings and murdered other debtors at his father's behest. His increasing participation in these affairs exposed him to a plethora of unsavory characters, one of whom was a shrewd scam artist who called himself "Janus the Great." A flamboyant showman, Janus wore disguises and used hypnosis to swindle unsuspecting noblemen out of their gold and jewelry. Observing Janus use the power of suggestion enchanted Lucas to no end, and he begged Isaac to allow Janus to teach him the tricks of his trade. Thinking it would be good for business, Isaac agreed. Janus, owing Isaac a debt, also agreed and accepted the broad-muscled boy as his new apprentice.

Under Janus' mentorship, Lucas learned the "Ways of the Wind," a secret discipline of hypnosis. When he completed the training two years later, Janus proclaimed Lucas a "master illusionist who has no equal."

Lucas becoming an expert in disguises and hypnosis coincided with the loss of Isaac, dying from causes incident to age. The now-emboldened young man picked up where Isaac had left off with his shady business dealings, and teamed with Janus in schemes to dupe rich people out of their wealth. In a short period of time, they amassed a small fortune, some of which they used to bribe local Roman officials for certain privileges.

Everything was going well for the two skilled con men until one of their previous victims, the rich merchant Avner from Hebron, happened to recognize Janus at the marketplace in Galilee. The ensuing confrontation escalated into a physical altercation, finally ending when Avner stabbed Janus to death. Since Avner and the local Roman garrison commander were good friends, he wasn't arrested, and knowing Janus worked with an accomplice, Avner persuaded the Roman to dispatch his soldiers to find him.

Having witnessed Janus' death from across the city square, Lucas quickly fled Galilee. When he reached his hometown of Jerusalem, he shaved his head, trimmed his beard, and hid out in the clothing shop hoping Avner and the Romans wouldn't find him.

As the days passed, Lucas became more comfortable in the belief he had escaped the fate befallen Janus. Pleased with his good fortune, he began selling his merchandise each morning in the marketplace. While pretending to be a simple clothing merchant trying to make an honest living, he schemed of ways to relieve noblemen of their riches, envisioning himself as one day being the wealthiest man in all of Judea.

Unfortunately for Lucas, providence would intervene and send him down an entirely different path – longer and much more torturous. His journey on this particular route was destined to begin early one

April morning, when a condemned man from Nazareth tripped on an uneven rock and dropped the large wooden cross he'd been carrying.

* * *

When Lucas' thoughts returned from the past, images of his future flashed in front of his eyes. He could see himself walking, on and on, down a long, twisting path with no end in sight.

I'm so tired. When will this end?

Rounding the next bend, he found himself back in the Jerusalem marketplace. Stunned, Lucas stared at the Nazarene for a moment.

"What did you say?" he finally asked, his cracking voice betraying his fear.

Jesus smiled and spoke firmly. "I said I shall stand and rest, but if you do not repent, you shall go on until the last day."

"Who are you to threaten me, condemned one?"

"One who knows."

Lucas laughed nervously. "What do you know about me, heretic?"

"I know you have slain your fellow man in the name of avarice."

"And how do you know this?"

"Your eyes betray your wickedness," Jesus replied. "So I say for the last time, repent now for the sins you have committed, or go on until the last day."

Lucas looked around and was met by the penetrating stares of the townspeople. Suddenly afraid, he turned and ran as fast as he could away from the procession. Later, back in the clothing shop, he worried about what the Nazarene had said to him. He then recalled a story Janus had told him about a fabled element called "carmot."

"Legend describes the carmot as being the one true element that gives us life," Janus had said. "If you were to find some and ingest it, your ability to control people with hypnosis would be virtually limitless. More importantly, whoever possesses the carmot, possesses the power of life and death."

Remembering Janus' words, Lucas had an epiphany: *to escape my fate, I must find this carmot element!*

With his resolve as hardened as his cynical heart, Lucas walked out into the desert and began his search.

* * *

Just after nine o'clock in the morning, the three condemned men arrived at an area outside of Jerusalem known as "the place of a skull," where they were crucified to the large wooden crosses they were forced to carry. Although Jesus' mortal existence came to an end, the story of his extraordinary life and the lessons he taught were destined to live on.

Lucas would also live on but in a different way. Jesus had given him the *Punishment of Endlessness* – binding him to wander the earth without the rest of death, until mankind descends into chaos, and God brings about the Day of Reckoning.

PART ONE:
THE INHERITANCE

THE ELEMENT

CHAPTER ONE: THE SICK UNCLE

Present Day
Outside the Dixie Regional Medical Center
St. George, Utah

The warmer-than-average spring had given way to an early summer in southern Utah, resulting in an onslaught of activity normally reserved for mid-June or early-July. Some of the bustle included flocks of birds swooping in the sky, bees hoovering over blooming cactus flowers, and an overabundance of people jogging alongside the roadways. I'd been taking in these sights while stretching, trying to get the blood circulating in my legs. After the three-hundred-mile non-stop drive down from Layton, I was stiff as a board. Not helping matters were my pronounced symptoms of Parkinson's disease, which make my muscles rigid and slow my movements to a snail's pace.

I followed Madison through the hospital's double doors and proceeded to the emergency room reception area. We soon located the duty nurse who gave us the grim news: the necrosis-like infection striking Madison's Uncle Charlie (Charles Dewhurst) had worsened. Unsure of what was causing the condition, the physician had transferred him to intensive care and placed him in a hyperbaric chamber, where they were treating him with oxygen therapy. Still implementing safeguards from the recent Coronavirus pandemic, the hospital required Madison and me to wear full ensembles of personal protective clothing to get in to see him, including surgical scrubs, facemasks, and disposable paper booties over our shoes.

Entering the room, the small curtains inside the chamber were pulled closed, hiding Charlie from our view. An oxygen line running from the wall to the side of the compartment resonated a faint hiss, as if air were slowly being let out of a balloon. The only other sounds were beeps from a vital sign monitor and Charlie nervously reciting Shakespeare, both of which were coming from a small, built-in speaker on the side of the chamber. Between heavy breaths, he recited the complex passages flawlessly; his hoarse voice sounding like a professional thespian in mid-season form.

"If you prick us, do we not bleed? If you tickle us, do we not laugh? If you poison us, do we not die? And if you wrong us, shall we not revenge?"

Madison slowly approached the chamber. "Uncle Charlie?"

"Maddie?"

He pulled the curtains aside and revealed a truly horrifying sight. His skin was red and swollen, with open sores on his face and neck that were either weeping with infection or bleeding. His lean, athletic physique had withered to an overly fragile frame, and his once-tanned skin now appeared thin and pallid. The pronounced wrinkles and dark spots aged him fifty years from the last time I'd seen him. From his milky, glossed-over eyes and the way he faced the wrong direction when Madison spoke, I could tell he was also blind.

As I looked upon his decrepit and deteriorating body, I thought back to the first time I met Uncle Charlie.

* * *

In the summer of 2001, Madison and I had just started dating. We'd taken a weekend trip down to Cedar City to attend the Shakespearian Festival. Since her uncle was an avid fan of the literary giant and lived merely fifty miles away in St. George, she invited him and he met us there.

He was a thin man, around six feet tall, and much younger than I expected; thirty-five to forty years old by my estimation. He had a charismatic glow about him, exuding a healthy and fit appearance men half his age would be envious of. His hair was unnaturally dark, as were his black beard and moustache, which he kept short and perfectly trimmed. From his slim and toned physique, I surmised he religiously stuck to an exercise regimen. We'd visited him several times over the years, and his dark hair color and fit appearance hadn't changed. He was truly one of the lucky people in the world whose body defied Father Time.

What I found fascinating about him was his penchant for telling stories, which showcased his considerable knowledge of medieval history. He could recount events and quote the famous historical figures who had lived back then like an aged college professor who had taught the subject all his life. Also impressive were the seven languages he spoke fluently, which included Russian, French, Japanese, Bulgarian, Italian, and two I'd never even heard of before: Ancient Macedonian and Crimean Tartar. Dazzled with his intellect, I sat in awe listening to him. I also wondered how anyone could retain such a vast amount of knowledge.

The only things I found strange about him were his overprotectiveness of Madison and the way he kept his private life to himself. When we first met, he subjected me to a battery of questions ranging from how much money I earned to my religious preference, all of which I took as his way of finding out if I was suitable to date her. When I asked where he was from and what he did for a living, he simply replied he grew up in Flagstaff, Arizona, and he worked for the government as a metallurgist. When I inquired further about what his job entailed, he changed the subject altogether.

After this initial meeting, Madison explained why her uncle was so protective of her.

"When I was six, my parents died in an airplane accident. Since Uncle Charlie was my only living relative, the courts awarded him custody of me."

"Is he married?"

"He was, to a woman from Japan named Sara. Just before I came along, she died. He doesn't like to talk about her, but over the years, from some of the things he's said, I can tell he's still devastated."

"He never remarried?" I asked.

She shook her head.

"What about brothers or sisters?"

"No. All he has is me. When I joined the Air Force Reserve and decided to move up to Layton to be closer to the base, he was supportive, but he took it quite hard. The night before I left, I found him crying in the kitchen, staring at an old photograph of Sara he'd taken shortly before she died. We had a long talk, and at one point I asked if he'd like to move to Layton with me, but he wouldn't hear of it. He said he couldn't leave his Great Work." When she said the words, she drew quotation marks with her middle and index fingers.

"His Great Work? You mean as a government metallurgist?"

"He said that, but I got the feeling he was talking about something else."

In the years since our first meeting, I'd grown to like Charlie and he seemed to have accepted me. When Madison and I got married he showered us with expensive gifts, including an all-expense paid trip to Disneyland for our honeymoon, and a gold miniature statuette of "The Kiss" by the famous French sculptor Auguste Rodin.

* * *

I don't know how long I'd been staring at him, stunned and unable to speak. Hearing Madison crying snapped me out of it, and I pulled her to my side until she composed herself.

"What happened to you?" she finally asked, ending the long pause.

"Now, now, Maddie," he replied, "don't be sad. I'm sorry you had to come down here and see me like this. But like the waves make towards the pebbled shore, so do our minutes hasten to the end."

"Don't talk like that, Uncle! You'll be out of here and back home in no time."

Grimacing, he shook his head. "I won't be going home. My past has finally caught up with me."

"What do you mean?"

He hesitated before answering. "I've been poisoned."

"Poisoned?"

"Yes. A poison with no antidote."

"Did the doctor tell you that?"

He nodded.

"Which one? I'd like to have a word with him."

He took a deep breath and smiled. "Though she is little, she is fierce. No Maddie, a doctor *here* didn't tell me that, but another one did many, many years ago."

"Did he tell you what kind of poison it is?"

He ignored her question. "Is George with you?"

"Yes."

"Hi Charlie," I said.

"How are you, George? How is your Parkinson's condition?"

"For the most part I'm doing okay, thanks to Madison. She's become my new right hand."

He didn't need to know my disease had progressed to the point where I had completely lost my sense of smell, and I was considering Deep Brain Stimulation, a surgical option to control the tremors. Feeling useless and irrelevant, I had also been battling depression, a condition people with Parkinson's disease commonly carry with them.

"We all have our burdens to bear," he said, solemnly. "Tell me, are we alone and is the door closed?"

"Yes," Madison replied.

"Please have a seat. I have something very important I want to discuss with you."

"Do you want me to leave?"

"No, George. What I have to say pertains to you."

I scooted a chair up for Madison and slid another up for myself.

Charlie cleared his throat. "Shakespeare once said all the world's a stage, and all the men and women merely players. One man in his time plays many parts, his act being seven ages. And now, as the curtain comes down on my seventh age, I have a confession to make. All those years you lived with me, Maddie, I wasn't truthful to you. I was living a lie and playing a part. But now, before I die, I must impart my secret with you because the Great Work must continue."

"What work are you talking about?"

"Something I've been involved with since I was very young."

"You mean when you lived in Flagstaff?"

He shook his head. "I was actually born in a city called Kaffa in eastern Europe."

"Kaffa?"

He nodded. "It's on the northern coast of the Black Sea. Today it's called Feodosia. My father was of Slavic descent, which at the time, allowed him to attend certain higher institutions of learning and become an alchemist. Do either of you know what an alchemist is?"

Madison and I looked at each other and shrugged.

"No," she replied.

"An alchemist is someone educated in the natural sciences and philosophies of the world. While growing up, my father mentored me and another young man named Lucas, in hopes we would also become alchemists and continue the Great Work. But Lucas betrayed and poisoned us."

"Why haven't you told me about this before?"

"You were too young and wouldn't have understood."

"But why would this Lucas do such a thing?"

"Bear with me, Maddie. It's a long story." He paused for a moment, mumbled to himself, and cleared his throat again. "When my father was a boy, he was mentored by a group of alchemists who called themselves the Order of the Sentinels. These men believed they were put on this earth to protect humanity from the forces of evil. They referred to this belief as their Great Work and dedicated their entire lives to it. Their leader was a blind priest named Vincent, who was also clairvoyant. During his life, Father Vincent experienced many premonitions."

"You mean like Nostradamus?" I asked.

"Yes, but much more secretive than Old Nasty."

His funny name of the famous prognosticator made me smile.

"Believing these premonitions were a divine gift from the Almighty," Charlie continued, "Father Vincent had a trusted assistant, who was a genius at mathematics, transcribe them into symbols."

"Symbols of what?"

"Geometric designs, like triangles and rectangles, but much more complex. To preserve them, he also directed his assistant to transcribe them onto silicate paper so the pages wouldn't burn. When he finished, he had all the pages bound together into what became known as the Wordless Book."

"The Wordless Book?"

"A book with no writing, only the symbols."

Madison nudged me. When I looked, she placed her index finger up to her temple and moved it around in a circular motion.

Intrigued with his story, I held a finger up for her to stop. "Charlie, I don't understand. If Father Vincent wanted his premonitions to remain secret, why document them at all?"

"Good question, George. It all boiled down to faith and beliefs. Father Vincent's faith was strong. He believed the forces of good would someday confront the forces of evil in a battle for the survival of mankind. His premonitions contained the knowledge of not only what was going to happen, but also how the forces of good could emerge triumphant.

"He documented the premonitions and created the Wordless Book so members of the Order could pass it down to their descendants. Or in other words, to those who would be involved in the battle. Much like the Native American code-talkers in World War II used their language to mask communications from the Nazis, Father Vincent shrouded his premonitions in symbols. He believed only the righteous would be able to decipher them, while at the same time, confuse the forces of evil.

"As for deciphering them, Father Vincent knew civilizations and languages would change in the coming years, but mathematics, no matter what the culture, would remain the same. Working with his learned assistant, they devised a truly ingenious method for the future generation to decipher the symbols using mathematics."

Madison let out a long sigh. "If all you have is a symbol drawn on a page, where do the numbers come from? I mean, to do math you've got to have numbers."

He smiled. "As simple as it sounds, Maddie, by measuring the symbol. And by that, I mean every angle, length, area, you name it. The numbers from the measurements are inserted into mathematical equations."

"Which math equations?" I asked.

"All of them."

"All of them?" I looked at Madison, then back to him. "But there must be thousands. It would've taken forever."

He shook his head. "Not really. When an equation is found where all the answers are numbers ranging from one to twenty-six, that's the equation you would use. These numbers corresponded with the twenty-six letters in the English alphabet. Arranged in the proper order, the letters spell out a rhyming parable, and reveal Father Vincent's premonition. As an added layer of security, the math changed with each group of symbols. When Winston Churchill coined the phrase, 'It's a riddle, wrapped in a mystery, inside an enigma,' he could've been describing the rhyming parables hidden in the Wordless Book."

"But why did Father Vincent use English? And why rhyming parables?"

He smiled. "He chose English because it was becoming a dominant language at the time. The parables rhymed simply because Father Vincent enjoyed them."

"You said these premonitions contained knowledge of what was *going* to happen, and how the forces of good could *win* the battle against the forces of evil?"

"Correct, George. According to rumors spread by members of the Order, Father Vincent foretold an evil man would someday try to kill every man, woman, and child to hasten the Day of Reckoning."

"The Day of Reckoning? You mean like the end of the world?"

He nodded.

When I looked at Madison this time, she pulled her facemask down and mouthed the words, "Will you please stop?"

"Father Vincent called this man the Wanderer," Charlie continued, "because Christ had punished him to remain living, wandering the earth, until the final day. In the centuries since, the Wanderer has grown to despise his mortal existence."

"And by killing everyone, he hopes to bring about this Day of Reckoning and end his existence?"

"Precisely, George. Then just before Father Vincent died, rumors swirled he'd foretold a way to *defeat* the Wanderer."

"Did he shroud this premonition in symbols too?"

"Yes. Unfortunately, when his mute assistant completed transcribing it, he also died, leaving no one knowing how to do the math to decipher the symbols. It took members of the Order twenty-seven years to figure out the first rhyming parable. Then things got very interesting."

Completely fascinated, I leaned in. "What happened?"

"The parable told the way to defeat the Wanderer involved using a legendary element called *carmot*. You see, every living thing, be it plant or animal life, has a derivative of carmot inside of them."

"I've never heard of carmot."

"Most people haven't because after Father Vincent and his assistant died, the Sentinels never disclosed their true purpose to anyone outside the Order. Behind the scenes, however, their faith was strong. They whole-heartedly believed in Father Vincent's premonitions. So much so, they constructed a ship called *Conviction*, and set off on a quest to find the legendary element."

"But if every living thing has carmot, why couldn't they just extract some from each member of the Order?"

He shook his head. "The carmot inside each of us can never be extracted. It is the divine substance keeping our hearts beating and our minds thinking. The parable stated only carmot in its purest form could defeat the Wanderer."

I looked at Madison again, and she waived for me to go ahead and ask.

"Did they ever find it?"

"The search spanned many years and crossed the oceans several times without success. On its final voyage, the ship became caught in a storm and was swept toward the south pole. As the *Conviction* foundered, the Sentinels chose the youngest among them to continue the Great Work. Entrusting him with the all-important Wordless Book, they cast him adrift in a lifeboat. That young man was my father, Augustus."

He stopped to catch his breath again. "After many days, he came to a small island. Nearly dead from hunger and frostbite, he crawled up onto the icy shore and found shelter in a cave, where inside he miraculously found a vein of the legendary carmot element. He believed, as I do, he had survived the ordeal and found the element because he'd been *divinely* chosen to continue the Great Work."

"How did he know he'd found the carmot? What did it look like?"

"Frozen, the substance resembles amethyst and emits a violet glow. When touched, it changes to a gel-like state and its glow becomes dark purple."

When Charlie mentioned Madison's favorite color, she sat up straight. "So, what does this carmot element do, exactly?"

"Perhaps the better question to ask, Maddie, is what *doesn't* it do. For lack of a better way to describe it, ingesting pure carmot overloads the natural carmot in one's body, and does many magical things. Imagine, for a moment, you stopped aging."

"No way."

He nodded. "And that's just the tip of the iceberg. It can also heighten one's awareness, intuition, and allow a person to remember everything they've ever read with crystal clarity. It can even enhance a person's ability to control others using the power of suggestion. Even more amazing are its healing powers. If someone contracts a disease, it can cure them. If they become injured, it can heal them. That's how my dad survived all those years ago. But these are only a few minor examples. The most astounding effect occurs when carmot is placed on an ordinary rock, whereby it transforms the rock into pure gold."

Madison and I looked at each other.

"It sounds like this carmot element had a lot in common with the Philosopher's Stone," I commented.

He nodded. "So true, George. As the story was handed down, the stone became the subject of the legend, but the carmot element had actually transformed the stone." He stopped again and grimaced. After taking another deep breath, he continued. "Unfortunately, carmot is as unpredictable as it is magical, like a double-edged sword."

"In what way?" Madison asked.

"If someone ingests the element to prolong their life, they must continue to, like a narcotic. A person can live a hundred, sometimes two hundred years on a handful of carmot. But if they didn't keep ingesting it, at some point they would regress back to their original state."

Sounds a lot like how my Parkinson's medications restore movement to my muscles, but on a much larger scale.

"What if someone used the element to change rocks into gold?"

"The rocks would remain gold, but the transformation would leave a toxic residue on them. To use the gold for barter or trade, they must first be cleaned by immersing them in olive oil."

"Olive oil?"

He smiled. "I know it sounds silly, Maddie, but olive oil contains certain chemical properties that neutralize the toxic residue."

"What if they didn't have any olive oil?"

"If a healthy person's skin came in contact with the toxic residue, it could infect them with a disease. Depending on what type of rock is transformed, it could infect them with a *different* disease."

"*Could* infect them? You mean it didn't infect them every time?"

"Sometimes it would, other times it wouldn't. As I said, the element is unpredictable. Which now brings us to the crux of the matter. The deciphered parables also told of four places in the world where the carmot could be found – each location containing enough to defeat the Wanderer. At some point in the past, the Wanderer learned of the carmot and the existence of the Wordless Book. He's been after it ever since."

"I get it," I said. "By using the carmot to transform rocks into gold, he hopes to spread a disease."

"Not just any disease. He wants to create a virus so lethal, it will kill every man, woman, and child, all in hopes of bringing about the Day of Reckoning. Have either of you ever heard of the Black Death?"

"Yes," Madison replied. "It was a plague in the Middle Ages. George and I watched a TV show about it the other night."

He nodded. "What history failed to record, is that the Wanderer was responsible. He started the plague by using carmot to transform the rocks near Kaffa into gold."

31

"Uncle Charlie, you talk as if these things happening so long ago pertain to you. How does a plague in the Middle Ages..."

"Patience, Maddie, patience" he interrupted. "I'm getting to that."

She strongly exhaled.

"My father placed some of the element in a leather pouch and set off across the ocean to return to Kaffa. At the time, he didn't realize the carmot needed to be stored below freezing. Later, when he opened the pouch, he found it had melted."

"So, what did he do?" Madison and I asked, in unison.

"There wasn't much more he could do, as far as the element was concerned. So when he returned to Kaffa, he set about deciphering the symbols in the Wordless Book. After several years he married my mother. A year-and-a-half later, shortly after I was born, my mother and I became very ill. Knowing the element could save our lives, my father traveled back to the island to recover more carmot. Unfortunately, he returned too late to save my mother. Years later, he went back to the island one last time and recovered all the remaining carmot.

"To anticipate your next question as to why, when I was appointed Captain of the Guards at Kaffa, I met a young man named Lucas who lived in an orphanage. He had a respectful demeanor about him, always helping with the chores and addressing me and my father as 'Sir.' Throughout the next few years, we became close friends. So close, I talked my father into adopting him. Enamored with Lucas, my father began including him in our discussions about the Great Work.

"For the next four years, the three of us lived a rather peaceful existence, but it all changed when my father partially deciphered a symbol telling the magical powers of the carmot. That's when he rushed back to the island and retrieved the remaining carmot.

"On the journey home, he ingested a small amount of it, and his heightened awareness told him something wasn't right about Lucas. To be sure, he spent the entire voyage locked in his cabin, forging a copy of the Wordless Book. After returning to Kaffa, he purposely left the fake book out at night to see if his suspicions about Lucas were warranted. Three days later, my father and I took ill from the poison, and Lucas disappeared with the forgery. To make matters worse, we completely underestimated his next move. To recover the real Wordless Book, Lucas orchestrated one of the most horrific military sieges in the history of armed conflict."

Before I could ask him further about the siege, Madison interjected. "But Uncle Charlie, you still haven't answered my questions. How does a plague in the Middle Ages pertain to you, and why didn't you have this man Lucas arrested?"

He shook his head. "He can't be arrested."

"Why not?"

"Because it happened so long ago, it would be impossible to prove."

"As far as I know, there's no statute of limitations for murder, or attempted murder."

"What if the crime happened in 1346?"

Not believing what I'd just heard, I asked him to repeat what he had said.

"My father and I were poisoned in the year 1346. You see, my real name is Aquinas. I was born April 17th, 1322, and the carmot element has kept me alive for almost seven-hundred years."

Madison looked at me, and back to him. "I want to believe you, Uncle Charlie, but how is that possible?"

He answered her question by quoting Shakespeare.

"From hour to hour we ripe and ripe, then from hour to hour we rot and rot, and thereby hangs a tale. With your gracious patience, I will a round unvarnished tale deliver. And my dear, sweet Maddie, what a tale it is!"

* * *

Fighting off wave after wave of pain, Charlie labored on while we sat listening to his captivating story. In my wildest dreams, I could've never imagined the incredible account he was about to share with us, nor that I would soon be cured (albeit temporarily) of Parkinson's disease.

CHAPTER TWO: THE SIEGE

Tuesday, 17 November 1346, 08:00hrs
Outside Fortress Kaffa
Republic of Genoa

The rising sun highlighted the smoke from the campfires of the Khan's army, casting an otherworldly glow down upon his legion of warriors. They sat entrenched along a grassy hill facing the northern rampart of the fortress, separated from their objective by only a quarter mile of moat water. To the south, more than a hundred ships in the Khan's flotilla also came into view, revealing an arc-shaped sea wall designed to prevent anyone from escaping or bringing in food and supplies. When the Khan's forces had first arrived and encircled the Genoese stronghold, his army numbered well over one-hundred thousand. But now, clenched in the vice of a full-scale epidemic, the able-bodied soldiers under the Khan's command had dwindled to less than half that number.

The disease known as the "Black Death" had arrived at Kaffa in the form of a plague-infected army. Even though the Khan's soldiers still outnumbered Kaffa's defenders, they were being held at bay because of the actions previously taken by the young Captain of the Guards who the king had entrusted to defend the city: Aquinas.

Fourteen days ago, Aquinas had learned of the king's dispute with the Khan and that his army was approaching with their battle flags drawn. He immediately sounded the alarm and deployed his contingent of outnumbered and inexperienced troops to key defensive positions along the northern rampart. In the event of a protracted siege, he also ordered in extra stores of food and water to support the men. So far, Aquinas' strategy had worked: for the last fortnight, Kaffa's troops had repelled numerous attacks, including an all-out assault on the closed drawbridge.

In this exchange, a wave of enemy soldiers had rushed the bridge and thrown their battle axes at it. Since the drawbridge area of the moat was only twenty feet wide, they planned to imbed as many axes as possible, thus gaining footholds for the wave of vaulters that followed. The men who made it across, however, were greeted with boiling-hot pig oil dumped on them from above, which Aquinas had prepositioned before the battle. After several failed attempts, which left many of the Khan's men dead or severely scalded, they abandoned their attack on the drawbridge.

As the standoff continued, Merrick, Aquinas' most trusted soldier and expert with the sword and longbow, returned from his reconnaissance mission. Entering the Captain's chamber, he found Aquinas seated behind his desk, completely absorbed in a map of battle plans.

Merrick cleared his throat several times and spoke. "According to an article I recently read about Kaffan etiquette, if the Captain of the Guards reunites with Nordic warriors returning from behind enemy lines, it is customary to render a handshake."

Aquinas smiled, rose to his feet, and offered his hand. "Welcome back, my friend. Would you like a glass of ale?"

Merrick shook his outstretched hand. "Thank you, sir, I believe I will."

After pouring him a drink and another for himself, Aquinas raised his glass. "To your safe return."

Merrick smiled. "To my return."

After sitting down and settling in, Aquinas got right to business.

"What can you tell me?"

"You were right, My Captain. Lucas is behind it all. In my excursion through the enemy encampments, I was able to breach the inner circle of the Khan's personal security detachment and position myself on a rise overlooking his tent. The vantage point gave me a clear view, and I saw Lucas casting a spell on the Khan."

"I knew it!" Aquinas said, almost yelling. "As reasonable as the Khan has been in the past, I couldn't believe a simple land dispute would drive him to take actions of this magnitude against the king."

"I agree, sir."

"You said you had a clear view of Lucas?"

Merrick nodded.

"Why did you not follow my orders and kill him?"

"I tried sir. I got off a clean shot but…"

"But what?"

"I know this will make me sound as if I have lost my mind, but if I hadn't seen it with my own eyes, I wouldn't have believed it."

"Tell me."

"The instant before the arrow struck Lucas' chest, it stopped in mid-flight and fell to the ground."

"What stopped it?"

"I don't know, sir. It was as if the arrow struck an invisible wall of armor."

Aquinas thought for a moment. "Anything else?"

"Just as our spies reported, the Khan's army falls ill. There is much pestilence in their ranks."

"Very well, Merrick. You may go."

"But sir, how are we going to kill Lucas if he's in control of the Khan *and* is being protected by this sorcery?"

"Let me worry about that. You are not to breathe a word about this to anyone. Do you understand?"

"Yes, sir." Merrick rendered a salute and exited the chamber.

Aquinas immediately proceeded through the inner door and hurried down the long hallway of the citadel to Augustus' quarters. After excusing the matron, he walked to the foot of the bed and looked upon his father. He hadn't moved since he'd seen him earlier this morning, nor had the papers he'd been writing on. Also, on the bed and opened to the same page, sat the all-important Wordless Book.

"Father?"

The old man stirred, opened his eyes, and instantly grimaced. After a moment, he leaned up on one elbow. "Aquinas, I'm glad you are here," he said, his voice raspy and low. "I've deciphered two more sets of symbols."

"More rhyming parables we cannot understand, father?"

By the way Augustus looked at him, with worry and concern, Aquinas could tell he'd betrayed his dour mood.

"Pour yourself a chalice of ale, my son, and tell me what has happened."

Aquinas filled his glass, took a drink, then came to the edge of the bed and sat down. "Merrick has returned."

Augustus' eyes grew wide. "What did he learn?"

"Lucas has cast a spell on the Khan. He has used the carmot to transform rocks into gold."

"Are you sure?"

"Merrick reported the Khan's army is stricken with the pestilence."

Augustus nodded. "What else?"

Aquinas took another drink. "I have failed you. Lucas *is* as you feared, father. Merrick got off a clear shot at him, but an unseen force stopped the arrow."

"He is sure the arrow struck nothing else?"

"Quite sure. Merrick never misses."

"So, Lucas *is* the Wanderer. Damn my poor judgement! If I hadn't been so trusting, we wouldn't be in this predicament."

"But father, it wasn't your poor judgement. I was the one who talked you into adopting him. I should've seen through his shroud of lies from the beginning."

"He deceived us both, my son. I can only thank the Almighty and the sacred carmot for revealing his dishonesty. I shudder to think what would happen if he had stolen the real Wordless Book."

"But without the real book and more of the carmot, will he not be confined to conjuring only magic tricks?"

Augustus shook his head. "Never underestimate the power of the carmot or the cleverness of the Wanderer. Remember the symbols I deciphered last week? The parable foretold the Wanderer as being shrewd with his lies and a master of manipulation. Breaching the Khan's army proves that. It's clear he has discovered the book he stole is a counterfeit. He is using the Khan's army to conquer Kaffa. I can see now, with perfect clarity, how he orchestrated the entire dispute between the Khan and the king."

"But father, what can he gain from conquering Kaffa? There is nothing of strategic value here except the seaport."

"First and foremost, he wants to get his hands on the real Wordless Book and learn the locations of the carmot."

"But if he has ingested the carmot, won't his heightened awareness tell him?"

Augustus shook his head. "Not *all* the time. Remember, Father Vincent said the carmot is as unpredictable as it is magical. If the carmot fails to heighten his awareness, Lucas will need the Wordless Book. By laying siege to Kaffa and blockading the seaport, he believes we are trapped and he can recover it."

"But if an unseen force is protecting him, why does he not just waltz in here and take it?"

"Because he wants to bring about the Day of Reckoning by spreading the pestilence. And by conquering Kaffa first, he'll be able to do that."

This time Aquinas' eyes grew wide. "Of course! He intends to use the ships!"

Augustus nodded and began to say something else, but a wave of pain stopped him. After a moment, he finally spoke. "The poison is working faster than I anticipated. I'm afraid my time is short, and it will fall upon you to continue the Great Work."

Tears welled up in Aquinas' eyes, and he reached out and grasped Augustus' shoulder. "How can I continue without you, father?"

Augustus patted his hand. "You'll do fine, my son, for I have faith in you. But you must move fast and plan your escape."

"Escape?"

"Yes. You must buy yourself time to decipher the symbols in the Wordless Book. The longer you stay here, the greater the chance the Khan's army will overrun Kaffa's defenses. If you are captured, Lucas will have the Khan's men torture you. If he recovers the real Wordless Book and learns where to find the carmot, he'll have everything he needs to bring about the Day of Reckoning."

"But father, what of my responsibility to the king? If I abandon my post…"

"I know you're fond of the king," he interrupted, "and at any other time your loyalty would be praised, but your time here is over. In the scheme of things, the Great Work transcends your responsibility to the king. Remember, Father Vincent foretold the Wanderer will stop at nothing to bring about the Day of Reckoning. To do that, he needs a large quantity of carmot. Somewhere in the book, amid all those symbols, is the secret to defeating him. Whatever this secret may be, it also involves the carmot. From one of the symbols I deciphered last night, I know the answer is in there."

Aquinas thought for a moment and drank the remaining ale in his glass. "As much as you've mentored me in geometry and mathematics, I still cannot make sense of half of those symbols, let alone the confusing rhyming parables you have deciphered from them."

Augustus smiled. "You will have plenty of time to learn the math and interpret the parables. Even if it takes centuries, I have faith you will eventually find the answers."

"Centuries father? I am merely a mortal man with perhaps twenty good years left, if the poison or the pestilence doesn't kill me first."

"You need not worry about the poison, the pestilence, nor any other disease for that matter."

"What?"

"Would you care for another glass of ale, my son?"

As the meaning became clear, tears welled up in Aquinas' eyes again. "You've given me your elixir?"

"The poison should remain dormant in you for the foreseeable future. When you start to feel the pain again, you must ingest more carmot. Lucas believes he stole all of it, but I secretly hid a cache in the basement of the citadel, under the stairs in the meat room. You know where."

Aquinas nodded.

"Remember to pack it in snow, otherwise it will melt."

"But father…"

41

"Please, Aquinas. I'm a sick old man. You are still young enough to carry on the Great Work."

As Aquinas wiped the tears from his cheeks, Augustus raised his head and looked directly into his eyes. "Do everything in your power to keep the Wordless Book away from the Wanderer. Escape in a fortnight when there is no moon and make your way to Amsterdam."

"Amsterdam?"

"Yes. One of the symbols I deciphered last night foretold a vein of carmot can be found in a cave near a dam, under a city founded by fishermen. As the sacred element sustains your life, decipher the remaining symbols in the book and learn how to defeat the Wanderer."

"What if I'm unable to? What if I fail you again?"

"You've never failed me, nor will you now. Pray often and let the Almighty show you the way."

"You've repeatedly told me this ever since I was a child, and I have yet to witness the heavens open up, nor heard an all-powerful voice tell me what to do."

"You must have faith, my son."

"Between us being poisoned, Lucas casting a spell on the Khan, and his army laying siege to Kaffa, my faith has weakened."

"The Almighty works in mysterious ways. Can't you see your faith is being tested?"

"I don't need tests of faith, father. I need you by my side healthy and strong, like the old days."

"The old days are gone forever," Augustus replied, his voice trailing off sorrowfully. "One of the sad unspoken truths about life is at some point we will all die. You must face your future and embrace it!"

When his father winced from the pain again, Aquinas waited patiently for it to pass. Once he was able to talk, Augustus took hold of Aquinas' arm and looked directly into his eyes again. "There is one more thing you must know. The second symbol I partially deciphered last night foretold a weakened man will play a part in defeating the Wanderer."

"A weakened man?"

"Yes, but you must decipher the remaining symbols to learn who this man is and where to find him. Now take the Wordless Book and go."

Aquinas reached over, retrieved the book from the nightstand, and stood to leave. "Would you like me to have the matron fetch you something to eat?"

Augustus didn't respond.

"Father?"

He leaned over and listened for a breath. Not hearing one, he fell to his knees and wept. After saying a prayer, he retrieved the flask of elixir, tucked the Wordless Book under his arm, and quietly exited the chamber.

The next thirteen days passed without incident. With no further attempts to storm the drawbridge, and other spies confirming Merrick's report of the enemy army falling ill with the pestilence, Aquinas began to believe the scales had tipped in his favor – until the morning came when Lucas, using the power of suggestion, ordered the Khan to do the unthinkable.

* * *

The first body struck the north wall before tumbling into the half-frozen moat, cracking the surface ice like a clap of thunder. Aquinas, who had been inspecting the troops along the northern rampart, instantly recognized what was happening.

They are catapulting their infected dead into the city!

The younger, less-experienced men immediately began to break ranks, while the older, battle-seasoned troops tried to stop them. In a matter of seconds fights broke out, at which point Aquinas tried to restore order.

"Remain at your posts!" he screamed. "Defend our home! Defend Kaffa!"

Another body struck the wall, and another, each one impacting higher than the one before it. Although Aquinas kept shouting for his men to remain steadfast, more and more abandoned their positions. When another body sailed over the wall and crashed into a statue in the city square, the older soldiers were overrun, leaving the northern rampart open to attack.

Aquinas quickly summoned his two young aides.

"Find Merrick and have him assemble all the archers along the northern rampart. Once they are in place, he is to report to me in my chamber."

"Yes, sir," they replied, in unison.

"Then form a brigade and cast the enemy bodies into the sea. If the Khan obliges us with more of his dead, cast them into the sea as well." Aquinas instantly saw fear in their eyes. "Didn't both of you recently tell me you have faith?"

The young men nodded.

"Call upon your faith now! The outcome of this siege depends on you ridding Kaffa of the pestilence. Do not to touch the bodies with your bare hands. Cover yourselves with goatskins and shroud your faces. After you dispose of the bodies, you and the brigade are to bathe and change into clean clothes in the stables. Remaining clean is the key to not contracting the pestilence. Do you understand?"

"Yes sir."

"Now go find Merrick!"

Watching the two leave, he knew his instructions might not be enough to save them from the horrible sickness, and he silently prayed they would not become infected.

Back in his chamber, Aquinas spent the next half hour reviewing his escape plan.

Will Merrick believe my story of the carmot and join me in the Great Work?

The answer presented itself less than a minute later, when the fair-haired archer arrived coughing and hacking.

Looking for other signs of the disease, Aquinas noticed an open sore on Merrick's left forearm which he'd tried (unsuccessfully) to hide with his leather archer's guard. The skin around the sore was inflamed red, the lesion itself weeping with infection. Quickly taking his eyes off the wound, Aquinas filled a large chalice with elixir and handed it to him.

"Here, drink this."

"What is it, sir?"

"It will make you feel better."

Merrick took a sip. When the element-enriched fluid reached his tongue, his eyes grew wide. Tipping the glass, he gulped the rest of it down like a man dying of thirst. After taking a deep breath, he ran his fingers through his long blonde hair, cleared his throat, and looked at the chalice.

"Excellent ale, My Captain."

Aquinas smiled. "Please." He motioned for him to take a seat.

Merrick leaned his longbow and quiver against the wall and sat down.

Aquinas pointed to his left forearm. "You're sick with the pestilence."

Merrick immediately covered the wound with his right hand. When he looked up, tears had welled up in his eyes. "I'm sorry, My Captain."

"You caught it when you breached the Khan's security detachment and shot at Lucas, didn't you?"

Merrick nodded. "Are you going to exile me?"

"With your skills? Far from it. I need your help."

"But sir, since you now know I must tell you. I grow sicker each day."

"Not anymore."

"What do you mean?"

"You and I are very much alike, Merrick. Since this siege began, we've lost many people we hold dear. My father hadn't been in his grave a day when you lost your wife to an enemy arrow. I've since heard from the vicar you've taken an oath of celibacy."

"No matter how long I live, my heart will remain with my beloved Bella."

Aquinas nodded. "That is why I have chosen you to accompany me."

"Accompany you where, sir?"

"When I leave Kaffa tonight."

"But My Captain, how can we desert the king?"

"There are many things I haven't told you, my friend, but I want you to know it wasn't because I didn't trust you. Now listen carefully and let me fill your chalice again. You must never repeat what I am about to tell you."

~ The Wanderer ~

The next morning, Lucas woke from his slumber. Rising from his bed, he unexpectedly sensed something wasn't right. With his intuition on alert, he ran outside and looked across the moat at Kaffa.

It's gone!

He silently cursed himself. This was the second time the Wordless Book had slipped away from him. The first occurred four weeks ago, when he poisoned Aquinas and his father. If he'd drank the elixir earlier this morning, his enhanced perception would have told him he had stolen a forgery. Like a naïve choirboy being duped by a seasoned trickster, he had underestimated the old man.

The Khan, who'd been staring wide-eyed at a pot filled with gold stones, noticed his friend's alarmed state and walked over to him. "Lucas, you seem troubled."

"Sound the alarm!"

"What for?"

"I sense Aquinas has escaped with the book."

"I thought you poisoned him and his father."

"I did, but Augustus must've had more carmot hidden somewhere in the fortress and used it to save Aquinas' life."

"All right, I'll do as you wish. But he couldn't have gotten through my men."

Just then, one of the Khan's lieutenants approached and saluted. "Sir, I have just received a report from the flotilla. One of their small boats is missing. The men assigned have been found dead in the water."

Lucas whirled on the Khan. "So, he couldn't have gotten through your powerful men, could he? You are a fool!"

Before the Khan could reply, Lucas quieted him with a wave of his left hand.

The lieutenant stepped in-between them and reached for his sword. "No one insults the Khan."

Moving lightning-fast, Lucas brandished his own weapon and struck first – decapitating the lieutenant in one fell swoop. When the headless body hit the ground, Lucas wiped his sword clean on the dead man's coat.

He focused his attention back on the Khan. "I must leave at once."

The Khan's eyes grew wide and he began to tremble, betraying the fear Lucas had planted in his subconscious with the power of suggestion. "Leave? But what am I to do?"

"I don't care what you and your filthy army do! I intend to find Aquinas, kill him, and recover the book!"

* * *

Without Lucas' influence, the Khan and his army of plague-stricken soldiers eventually retreated from the prolonged siege. Kaffa was saved but at a horrible cost: the disease, carried by rats and mice on the merchant ships, traveled across the Mediterranean Sea to Constantinople, where it spread throughout the continent. In the following six years, the Black Death would kill more than 200 million people – over half of the European population.

Lucas' relentless pursuit of Aquinas to recover the Wordless Book would transcend both time and generations. With the fate of mankind depending on the outcome, the chase for the all-important carmot element had begun!

CHAPTER THREE: THE JUDGE'S RULING

Present Day
Inside the Intensive Care Unit
Dixie Regional Medical Center
St. George, Utah

I looked at the clock on the wall and couldn't believe we'd been listening to Uncle Charlie for more than two hours. When he had started telling us the story, Madison's rolling eyes and loud sighs spoke volumes of her disbelief. As the long-winded account continued, her non-verbal signals changed into repeated head shakes and tears, undoubtedly from believing Charlie had gone insane.

Although I'd deemed his story improbable, it drew me in like a moth to a flame. What intrigued me the most was the *way* he told it, which was different from the other stories he'd told Madison and me over the years. This was the first time he'd ever included himself or told it from the point of view of someone *in* the story; in this instance, Aquinas. In the past, he'd always recounted his tales like a narrator, and had never included himself as one of the primary players.

But it wasn't just the story. His detailed descriptions made the whole thing sound believable. He also revealed his inner thoughts and explained why he'd chosen courses of action, which he'd never done before. When he described his friend Merrick, his words carved an indelible mental image of what the archer had looked like, and when he'd talked about his father, tears came to his eyes.

Pausing, Charlie leaned back and laid his head on the pillow. His eyes, which had been clenched closed, relaxed, and his breathing slowed to the point I could no longer hear it.

"Charlie?" Madison asked.

He didn't reply.

"Uncle Charlie?"

I reached over to Madison, and she took hold of my hand with both of hers.

Warning bells rang out, interrupting the moment with the subtlety of a train wreck. Just as shrill, the duty nurse's voice blared from the speaker in the ceiling, "Code blue, ICU! Code blue, ICU!"

Seconds later, a bevy of doctors and nurses flooded into the room.

Checking the vital sign monitor on the side of the chamber, the lead physician asked, "Are you alright?"

With his calm voice rising to a scream, Charlie replied, "I'd be a lot better if you'd shut off those confounding bells and leave us alone!"

One of the nurses flipped a switch on the chamber's control panel, and the room fell silent.

The doctor turned to us "Sorry, false alarm."

"Get out!" Charlie yelled. "I'm not ready to die just yet!"

Murmuring to each other, the doctors and nurses slowly exited the room.

Once we were alone with Charlie again, Madison stood and motioned me toward the door. "They're gone," she said, "but we really should leave so you can get your rest."

He shook his head emphatically. "I don't need rest, Maddie! I need you to have faith in me. What I am telling you is the truth. If mankind is to be saved, the Great Work must continue. The only way it can is if I pass it on to someone I trust before I die. I never wanted to involve you in this, but now I must."

"Why?"

"Remember I told you how my father deciphered part of a page of symbols in the Wordless Book?"

"Yes, but I don't remember what you said after that."

"I know this is a lot to take in, Maddy, but please pay attention. This is very important."

She sighed. "Okay, I'm listening."

"I finally finished deciphering the rest of that page, which is why I sent for you. The rhyming parable states the secret to defeating the Wanderer will come from a *weakened* man. I believe this parable is referring to George."

I was stunned. "Me? How could it possibly be referring to me?"

"Parkinson's disease has weakened you, hasn't it?"

"Yes, but isn't that a stretch?"

"No, because another parable states the weakened man will be born near a great lake of salt, the same year a young man is chosen to lead the new country. You were born north of Salt Lake City in 1960, which happens to be the same year President Kennedy, one of our younger presidents, won the election."

"So were about fifty-million other people," Madison said sarcastically.

Charlie's voice took on an equally condescending tone. "But my dear Maddie, the parable also states the weakened man will be born on the fifth day of Sextilis, which is August, and he will be sinistro, which means left-handed."

Now I was completely speechless.

"Uncle Charlie, how can you expect us to believe such a…"

His stern voice interrupted her. "Even if you don't believe it, you soon will! As events unfold in the coming days, you'll realize George is the man Father Vincent saw in his premonition. When you two met all those years ago, divine providence brought you together. I was so preoccupied with other things I didn't recognize it. George is the one who holds the key to defeating Lucas. To learn what that key is, you must decipher the remaining symbols in the Wordless Book."

Madison glanced over to me and shrugged her shoulders.

"And if you are to be successful, you must remember the carmot element is as unpredictable as it is magical. You cannot rely on it to save your life or heal your injuries. Also, remember there is an invisible force surrounding Lucas, protecting him until the Day of Reckoning. You cannot inflict a fatal injury upon his body. You can, however, wound his extremities. Keep this in mind when you form your strategy to capture him."

He stopped and winced again. The pain he felt was so strong, it contorted his face. A moment later he relaxed enough to take in a few breaths. Fully enthralled, I sat on the edge of my seat.

"Take note," he finally said, "Lucas has a confederate, an influential woman with a black heart. She's been seduced by the power of the carmot and has no qualms about taking a life." He paused for a moment and took in a deep breath. "From this day forward, keep a watchful eye on those you encounter, for Lucas is an expert in the ancient art of hypnosis known as the *Ways of the Wind*. I have recently learned about this art, and how powerful it is." He stopped and took a few more breaths, before continuing. "He can place you in a hypnotic spell and fool you with his lies. Like a chameleon, he can change his appearance and make you believe he is someone else. His power of suggestion is so strong, he can invade your dreams and learn what you fear!"

"But Charlie," I said, "if he can do all these things and disguise himself as you say, how will we know who he is?"

"Look to his left hand. In a clash with Merrick he lost the tip of his middle finger. No matter what disguise he uses, or what suggestion he places in your mind, he cannot hide it. If his hand is gloved, look to his reflection. Whether it be a mirror, a pane of glass, or a puddle of water on the ground, he cannot mask the echo of his true image. There may be other clues in the Wordless Book, but you'll have to decipher the remaining symbols to find them."

"And where do we find this Wordless Book?"

"I've hidden it in the special place. Maddie knows."

"Wait," Madison said. "I'm confused. Where are you talking about?"

Instead of answering her question, he began reciting Shakespeare again.

"Thou knows 'tis common, all that lives must die; passing through nature to eternity."

"Uncle Charlie?"

"I must go now, sweet Maddie, for my father is beckoning me. I love you."

"I love you too."

He laid his head down and closed his eyes. As the next minute went by, his labored breathing gradually slowed to a stop. Like before, warning bells began ringing and the duty nurse's voice blared from the speaker overhead. A moment later, a physician and two nurses came running in.

Quickly silencing the alarm, the doctor called Charlie's name and checked the vital sign monitor on the side of the chamber. Turning to us, the doctor shook his head. "I'm sorry. There is nothing more we can do."

Madison's facemask couldn't suppress her sorrowful sobs, nor could it catch all the tears streaming down her face.

* * *

Madison took Charlie's death so hard, I spent the rest of the day consoling her in our hotel room. She was so grief stricken, she hardly spoke a word. She finally felt better the next morning, and I talked her into coming down to the hotel's café to eat some breakfast. Over the years, I've learned when she gets in moods like this, it's best to be quiet and let her work things out on her own before trying to initiate a conversation. When we were almost done eating, she finally spoke.

"George, what did you think of Uncle Charlie's story?"

Not to upset her, I thought carefully before answering. "Honestly sweetheart, I don't know. It sounded believable. But if what he said was true, we must believe a secret element in nature can keep someone alive for centuries. And if there is, there is also a two-thousand-year-old murderer out there who was punished by Jesus to remain alive until the last day. And if there is such a man, he hates his existence so much, he is trying to end it by destroying mankind."

She smiled. "It did sound far-fetched, didn't it? It reminded me of Trish at work. When her mom had Alzheimer's, she thought she'd been abducted by aliens from an ocean planet. She even drew out a map of the stars and plotted the location of their world, inhabited by fish people."

I smiled. "So you think your uncle's story was all in his head?"

"Oh George, of course it was. I know my uncle. He was the most-honest man I've ever known. He would never lie to me."

"What do you think he meant when he said he'd hidden the Wordless Book in the special place only you know?"

She shrugged her shoulders. "Beats me. I think he was confused, and his sickness was making him delirious."

Just then, a woman approached us. She was tall and athletic looking, around forty years old, with straight brown hair reaching half-way down to her waist. Her expensive-looking black slacks and overcoat gave her the professional look of a secret service agent. Adding credence to this description, were the small black leather purse she had strapped over her shoulder and the matching briefcase she held in her hand.

"Madison d'Clare?" she asked.

"Yes?"

"You're the niece of Charles Dewhurst?"

Madison nodded.

"I'm Dr. Susan Webster." She set her purse down, retrieved a business card, and handed it to Madison. Looking over Madison's shoulder, I noticed under her name was the title, "Special Investigator, Center for Disease Control and Prevention."

"This is my husband George," Madison said.

She nodded to me. "I was told at the hospital you were staying here. May I join you?"

"Please do."

She sat down, opened her briefcase, and removed a small pad of paper and a pen. "First, let me say I'm sorry for your loss."

Madison's eyes welled up with tears. "Thank you."

"When the admitting doctor at the hospital examined Mr. Dewhurst, he informed the CDC, which is why I'm here. I investigate possible outbreaks to see if they pose a health risk to the public. I understand you used to live with your uncle?"

Madison provided her a brief family history, much like the one she'd given me when we were dating. Concluding, she asked, "Have you found out what was wrong with him?"

"No, not yet," Dr. Webster replied. "But I would like to ask you a few questions."

"Sure."

"Did Mr. Dewhurst have any enemies?"

"None I'm aware of."

"What about chronic health problems?"

"No. As far back as I can remember he's always been healthy."

"Had he taken any trips out of the country or overseas?"

"Four years ago, he traveled to the Judaean Desert in Israel."

"What about more recently?"

"I don't know. Except for the day he died, I hadn't seen or spoken to him since Christmas."

"What did Mr. Dewhurst do for a living?"

"He worked for the government as a metallurgist."

Dr. Webster scribbled a few notes. "With your permission, I'd like to freeze his body and take it to Atlanta for the post-mortem examination."

"With all due respect, doctor, I'm still trying to cope with losing my uncle. I cannot fathom the idea of you cutting his body apart."

"I understand, but we need to take cell samples. The best place to do this is in Atlanta. Our secure lab will contain any infectious agents."

"Agents? You mean there are more than one?"

Dr. Webster leaned in. "Your uncle was suffering from some very serious health problems," she whispered. "He had gangrene in his extremities, swelling of the lymph nodes, and open abscesses all over his skin. These are all symptoms of the bubonic plague."

Madison looked at me, then back to Dr. Webster. "The plague?"

She nodded. "Do either of you have any idea how he might've contracted it?"

We both shook our heads.

"Did he have any friends who are extremists, say far left or right leaning?"

"If he did, he never mentioned them to me. In all the years I lived with him, the only contacts we had on a regular basis were a few neighbors, friends I had in school, or their parents."

While Madison was talking, Dr. Webster jotted down a few more notes.

"I thought the bubonic plague had been cured," I said.

She shook her head. "Many people think that, but it's still an ongoing health hazard. Terrorists have been trying to develop different strains of it for years."

I looked at Madison. "As healthy and in shape as your uncle was, it's hard to fathom he died from the bubonic plague."

Dr. Webster cleared her throat. "I didn't say the plague killed him, Mr. d'Clare."

"Oh? Then what did?"

"Right now, I'm not sure. I'll know more after we get the toxicology results."

She put her pen and the pad of paper in her purse and stood to leave. "Thank you for your time."

"Wait," Madison said. "You asked me if my uncle had any enemies. What did you mean by that?"

She glanced around for a moment and sat back down.

"Mrs. d'Clare, one week ago your uncle walked into the hospital under his own accord, and cool as a cucumber told the doctor he'd been poisoned. Six days later he'd lost his eyesight, hadn't slept, and was ranting and raving like a madman. These are classic symptoms of someone who's been exposed to tincture of Belladonna."

"Belladonna?"

"Yes, Mrs. d'Clare. If my suspicions are correct, not only was your uncle suffering from a plague first appearing in the Middle Ages, but he was also poisoned with a drug used to murder people in medieval times."

* * *

Later in the morning, Madison decided she wanted to go to Uncle Charlie's house. The two-story, one-hundred and twenty-year-old Victorian-era structure, located in the older part of town, had been built by a polygamist settler. A pioneer by faith and carpenter by trade, the settler had built the home like a military fort; its walls and rafters were constructed out of hardwood and fortified with double the number needed.

We'd stayed there when we visited Charlie over the years, and although her uncle kept the inside immaculately clean, its dark wood interior and creaking floors still gave me the creeps. What made it even more unnerving was a gargoyle-shaped stone outcropping at the end of the long driveway secluding the home from the rest of the subdivision.

Approaching, we immediately noticed the front door had been left open. Upon entering, we found the inside completely ransacked. All the cabinet drawers had been opened, the contents thrown on the floor. The front closet had also been rummaged through, and the clothes once hanging inside it were now heaped in a pile in the front hallway.

Madison broke down when she saw the state of things, and I helped her over to a chair in the foyer and called the police.

We sat there for a few minutes until she was finally able to talk.

"Who would do such a thing?"

"I don't know, sweetheart, but I think we'd better stay put. Whoever trashed it might still be here."

A few minutes later, two police officers arrived. One was a big man, muscular, and around forty years old. His partner was a much smaller man and younger, early thirties by my estimation.

"Mr. and Mrs. d'Clare?" the older officer asked.

"Yes," I said, "I'm George d'Clare and this is my wife, Madison."

"Jim Davis," he replied, "and my partner, Steve Hansen."

Madison gave them a teary-eyed explanation of how she was the only relative of Charlie, who had had passed away at the hospital, and how we had found his home broken into. Officer Davis knelt to examine the front door lock and instructed us to stay in the foyer while he and Officer Hansen checked the rest of the house. Ten minutes later, they rejoined us.

"The house is clear," Officer Davis said. "Whoever it was hit every room. There are pry marks on the front and back doors, but the lock in back is a lot stronger and it held. Looks like when they couldn't get in the back way, they came around front."

"We'll need a statement and a list of what's missing," Officer Hansen said.

"We won't be able to tell you if anything is missing," Madison countered. "We haven't visited my uncle in quite some time."

"Would you mind checking anyway? Maybe something will stand out."

For the next twenty minutes, I followed Madison as she went through each room. When we reached the last one on the second floor, she stopped and turned to me.

"I've never been in his bedroom before."

I grasped her shoulder. "It's okay, sweetheart. If you don't want to go in..."

"No, no, I'll have to eventually. I might as well get it over with."

Like the rest of the home, we found his bedroom in a complete state of disarray, with one glaring difference: a large, full-length mirror sitting next to his dresser was completely shattered.

After returning to the officers, Madison completed a short statement, reporting it looked as if nothing was missing.

"Do you plan on staying here?" Officer Davis asked.

"We've got a room at the St. George Inn," Madison replied.

"Good. If something comes up, we'll contact you there."

"But now I'm thinking with Uncle Charlie gone, we should move over here and get this mess cleaned up. What do you think, George?"

"I agree."

"Are you sure you want to do that?" Officer Hansen asked. "Whoever did this may come back, and we can't be here all the time."

I received a silent nod from Madison and answered for us both. "We're sure."

"Not only that," Officer Davis said, "Whoever jimmied the front door screwed up the lock."

"No big deal," I said. "We'll call a locksmith."

After promising they would step-up their patrols in the neighborhood, the two officers departed. Madison and I spent the rest of the day cleaning and straightening Uncle Charlie's house.

* * *

On Sunday morning, Madison received a phone call from the lawyer in charge of Uncle Charlie's estate, Mr. Raymond Edwards, requesting we meet with him. With the lock on the front door now repaired, we secured Charlie's home and proceeded over to Mr. Edwards' office.

Entering the modern-looking red-brick building, a receptionist showed us in. Having never frequented a lawyer's office, I expected Mr. Edwards' office to be large and roomy, but it was just the opposite. The cramped room was barely big enough to fit the office chair, small desk, and two folding metal chairs for clients. Adding to the claustrophobic flavor, an over-abundance of large mural paintings were jammed together on the walls.

Seeing us, Mr. Edwards sprang to his feet. He was a short man, roughly sixty years old, heavy-set, gray hair, and a "combover." (Madison's term for men who grow their hair long on one side and comb it over the top to hide their bald spot.)

"Mrs. d'Clare," he said, "thank you for meeting me on a Sunday. I'm Ray Edwards."

"This is my husband George," Madison replied.

After shaking hands, we scooted in sideways and sat down. Mr. Edwards got right to business.

"I wanted to discuss two items with you, Mrs. d'Clare," he began. "First, you have been named in Mr. Dewhurst's will."

Tears came to Madison's eyes.

"Not only did he leave you his home and property, he also left you a large sum of money. It will all be made official in probate court."

"Probate court?"

"Yes. It was Mr. Dewhurst's instructions I file his will in probate."

"How come?"

"No worries, Mrs. d'Clare. It was Mr. Dewhurst's wishes to have a portion of his money go to a charitable organization. He simply wanted the donation to be noted in the public record."

"I see," Madison said. "What charitable organization?"

"The Parkinson's Foundation."

He must have done it for me!

Tears welled up in my eyes, and Madison took hold of my hand.

"Normally it takes a month to get a court date," Mr. Edwards continued, "but there happens to be an opening at three-thirty on Monday afternoon."

"Tomorrow?" Madison asked.

"Yes. I can send you the transcript if you are unable to attend."

She looked at me. "Do we have anything going on?"

"I don't. But if I remember right, you've got a meeting at work on Tuesday."

She nodded and addressed Mr. Edwards. "I'll let you know on that."

"Good," he replied. "As for the other item, have you given any thought as to what you'll do with Mr. Dewhurst's home and property?"

"Probably sell it."

"Excellent! I just happen to have a buyer who is interested."

Madison shook her head. "I really haven't decided."

"They've made an offer."

"I said I haven't decided."

"The offer is significantly higher than the market value."

"You've already conducted market research?"

"Yes, Mrs. d'Clare. I thought if I could expedite things…"

"I don't believe this. My uncle died only two days ago and you're ready to sell off his home and property without consulting me?"

Madison has a long fuse, but when riled she can launch into full-on "beast" mode. Watching the exchange, I knew Mr. Edwards had awakened her inner creature.

"Forgive me, Mrs. d'Clare, I didn't mean to overstep my bounds."

"You certainly have overstepped your bounds! Who are you to make these decisions?"

She motioned to me and we stood to leave.

"Before you go, I must tell you if we cannot close today the buyer is going to withdraw his offer."

"Let him withdraw it! And as far as the probate hearing goes, we'll be there!"

Madison stormed out the door with me following close behind.

As soon as we climbed into our SUV, she started to vent.

"The nerve of that crooked, ambulance-chasing, son-of-a…"

"Madison!" I yelled.

She stopped and looked at me.

"Which side do you think would look better, right or left?"

"What do you mean?"

"For my combover. Should I grow my hair long on my right side and comb it over, or my left?"

She begrudgingly smiled and started to laugh. "You'd have to do some big-time fertilizing to grow enough hair to cover your dome."

We both cracked up.

Although I'd managed to somewhat calm her, Madison's temper still simmered at a low boil for the rest of the day.

* * *

After enjoying a nice dinner at one of the finer restaurants in St. George, we returned to Uncle Charlie's house. When we rounded the gargoyle-shaped outcropping of rocks, we discovered the front door open again.

"Pull over and cut the lights," I said.

Once we were stopped, I climbed out.

"Get back in here, George. What do you think you're doing?"

"I'm just going to look. Call the police."

Before she could protest, I quickly made my way down the driveway and stepped up onto the porch. Reaching the door, I noticed the new lock we'd just had installed had been pried, and broken pieces of it were scattered across the threshold. Walking in, I looked around and caught sight of a woman calmly walking toward me. Since the lights were out, I couldn't see her face, but in the dim shadow I could tell she was blonde with an athletic build.

I cleared my throat. "The police have been called, so you'd better...."

In a blinding fast move any martial arts master would've been proud of, she spun and delivered a hard round-house kick to my stomach – completely knocking the wind out of me! I fell to my knees, gasping for breath. Looking up, I realized she wasn't alone. There was a man standing behind her in the shadows. From the faint outline, I could tell he was a big man, well over six feet tall and muscular. He stepped forward and touched the temple area on the left side of my head.

Just then, Madison arrived at the front door.

"George?" she yelled.

"Stay back," I croaked, barely managing to gulp in enough air to get the words out. When I looked up, the man and the woman were gone.

"George, what is it?"

"Turn on the lights."

When the foyer illuminated, Madison rushed over to me.

"There were two people, a man and a woman. The woman kicked me in the stomach."

"Can I get you anything?"

"Yes. A pair of handcuffs. The next time I try to do something like that, I want you to lock me to the steering wheel."

Just then, the same two officers, Davis and Hansen, walked in. Since I had been assaulted, they called for backup. Five minutes later, two other officers, Blair and Greyson arrived. Davis instructed them to look outside while he and Officer Hansen searched the interior again. After fifteen minutes, all four returned to the foyer.

Like before, Davis informed us the perpetrators were gone. Turning to officers Blair and Greyson, he asked if they'd found anything.

"Just this," Greyson said. He held up an evidence bag containing a hand-held sledgehammer and a stubby crowbar. "They were in the bushes next to the driveway."

"Now we know what they used to work over the door lock," Hansen commented.

Addressing Madison, Davis asked, "Do you have any idea what they were after?"

"No. Like I told you before, we haven't visited my uncle in quite some time."

"Why don't you go back to the hotel and get a room? You'll be safer there."

Madison's temper immediately flared up again, and she let the officer know (in no uncertain terms) she had no intention of going back to the hotel.

"When I was six years old, my uncle took me in and cared for me when I lost my parents. Now that he's gone, the least I can do is make sure his things aren't stolen!"

"Alright Mrs. d'Clare, we'll continue to step up the patrols. But like my partner told you, we can't be here all the time."

After they took our statements and departed, Madison called the locksmith. While she talked to him, I made my way over to a sofa in the front room and sat down. As I began thinking about the story Charlie had told us before he died, Madison interrupted my train of thought.

"The locksmith will be here in an hour," she said. "Are you alright? What about your stomach?"

"I'm okay."

"George, what is it?"

"What do you mean?"

"You're staring off into space."

I smiled. "I was just thinking about Charlie. He said in the coming days, as events unfolded, we would come to realize I am the man Father Vincent saw in his vision."

"What are you saying, George? His story was true?"

"I'm not sure, but it does make you wonder, doesn't it?"

She smiled. "I have to admit, I haven't stopped thinking about what Dr. Webster told us. But when you take a step back and think about it, Uncle Charlie's story was just too far-fetched."

"What if it's not?"

She shook her head. "George, you said yourself, to believe it we have to believe there is a fabled element out there in nature that can prolong life, and this Wanderer person is a murderer who is almost two-thousand years old."

"True, but ever since your uncle passed away, people have been trying to get us away from this house."

"How so?"

"After the first break-in, Officer Davis suggested we stay at the hotel. Then Mr. Edwards tried to hurriedly sell the house using a high-pressure sales tactic. Now with the second break-in, Officer Davis suggests we stay at the hotel again. Following each break-in, the officers told us they couldn't be here all the time."

"But George, realistically, they *can't* be here all the time. Don't you think they were just trying to protect us?"

I shook my head. "I think they were trying to get us away from here."

"You actually believe the police are involved in all this?"

I nodded. "Your uncle did say this Wanderer is a master at controlling others using the power of suggestion."

"Okay, my conspiracy-theorist husband, for the sake of argument, let's say all these people are involved and they are trying to get us away from here. What do they hope to accomplish?"

"I think they want us out of the way so they can search the house for the Wordless Book."

She thought for a moment. "But if that's true, someone would've had to hypnotize Officers Davis, Hansen, and maybe the other two. How could they hypnotize all of them?"

"I don't know, but it will be interesting to see what happens at the probate hearing tomorrow. If your uncle was telling us the truth, I think someone will contest the will."

"And what if no one contests the will?"

"Then we'll know your uncle's story was just a delusion brought on by his sickness."

* * *

With the air conditioning system broken down and no significant breeze blowing through the open windows, the stagnant air hung inside the courtroom like a prisoner trapped in solitary confinement. Behind the desk sat Judge Taylor. He was a middle-aged balding man who wore his glasses on the edge of his nose and looked over them as he talked. To his right sat the court clerk, whose desk nameplate read "Mrs. Morgan." She was an aged woman who wore her gray hair tied back in a bun. To the judge's left stood the bailiff. A much larger and younger man than the judge, his tight-fitting uniform and rippling muscles cast an authoritative presence over the proceedings.

"The next case involves the will of Mr. Charles Dewhurst," Mrs. Morgan said.

The clerk handed a folder to Judge Taylor, who opened it and began reading. Roughly five minutes later, he looked up from the folder and addressed the court.

"Mr. Charles Dewhurst, recently deceased, wished to leave his estate to his niece, Mrs. Madison d'Clare. Mrs. d'Clare, are you in the courtroom?"

Madison raised her hand and stood. "Here your honor."

"Come forward please."

Madison quickly made her way up to the bench.

"Are you familiar with your uncle's will, and that he wanted five million dollars to be donated to the Parkinson's Foundation?"

"Yes, your honor," Madison replied. "And I intend to do just that."

Judge Taylor smiled. "Very well. If there are no objections…"

From the back of the courtroom, a woman yelled, "I object, your honor."

I whirled around, as did a few other people watching.

"Come forward please," Judge Taylor said.

She was tall with jet-black hair, around thirty-five years of age, and had a toned athletic build. Dressed in an expensive-looking white pantsuit with matching pearl earrings and necklace, she could've easily been mistaken for a high-end fashion model. A gold chain wrapped around her right ankle looked to be of the finest quality, as were the shiny black high-heeled shoes on her feet.

For a moment, I thought she might be the woman who kicked me in the stomach, but I wasn't sure. I hadn't got a good look at the burglar's face. The only thing I knew for certain was the woman who kicked me was a blonde. Of course, if it was this woman, she could've been wearing a wig.

She sashayed her way to the front of the courtroom and stood next to Madison.

"And who are you?" Judge Taylor asked,

"I'm Kathalene Macintyre, Mr. Dewhurst's fiancé."

Madison, who'd been staring her down, folded her arms.

"Could I see some identification?"

"Certainly. I also have some papers I'd like to present to the court." She handed them to the bailiff, who briefly examined them before passing them on to the judge.

Judge Taylor examined them for a moment. "Mrs. d'Clare, please take your seat. I need to ask Mrs. Macintyre a few questions off the record."

Madison returned to where I was sitting. "You've got to be kidding me," she whispered.

"I've got an idea," I whispered back. "If she comes over, ask her something about your Uncle. Something only you would know."

Madison nodded.

Five minutes later, Judge Taylor asked Mrs. Macintyre to sit down, and she strolled over to where we were.

She offered her hand to Madison. "So nice to finally meet you, Maddie. It's alright if I call you Maddie, isn't it? I wish we could've met under better circumstances. Chuck told me so many stories about you."

Madison abruptly looked away without shaking her hand.

Mrs. Macintyre looked at me. "Is there something the matter?"

Following Madison's lead, I looked away too.

Mrs. Macintyre turned and stormed off in a huff.

Once she was out of ear shot, I leaned over to Madison. "Why didn't you ask her something?"

"I didn't have to. I already know she's a liar. Uncle Charlie absolutely hated to be called Chuck."

Judge Taylor called Mr. Edwards up, who explained Mr. Dewhurst had retained him to redraft his will but had died before signing the new documents. Mr. Edwards used a bevy of complicated legal terms and cited similar court cases in hopes of swaying the judgement – in favor of Mrs. Macintyre!

"Can you believe him?" Madison whispered.

I shook my head. "I wonder how much money she promised him."

After hearing Edwards' argument, Judge Taylor cleared his throat and spoke.

"Unfortunately, I've had to rule on many cases like this one, where the will hasn't been updated to reflect the wishes of the immediate family or surviving loved ones. Mr. Edwards, although you've made a strong argument for Mrs. Macintyre, the will duly signed and notarized by Mr. Dewhurst must stand. There's simply no other way around it. Therefore, it is my ruling Madison d'Clare receive title to all of Mr. Dewhurst's possessions, to include his home, property, and bank accounts. The sum of five-million dollars is to be donated to the Parkinson's Foundation. Case dismissed."

Mr. Edwards immediately rose to his feet and attempted to protest the ruling, whereupon the judge struck his gavel down hard on the desk.

"What part of case dismissed didn't you understand, Mr. Edwards?"

Judge Taylor's harsh reaction immediately silenced the lawyer, and he shrank down in his chair like a spineless jellyfish.

Once Madison had completed signing a small stack of official court documents, the bailiff gathered them up and told us we could go. When we reached the parking lot, we were immediately approached by Mr. Edwards and Mrs. Macintyre.

"Mr. and Mrs. d'Clare," Mr. Edwards said, "could we have a moment of your time? We were hoping you might be open to sharing the inheritance?"

Madison's temper instantly ramped up to full-on beast mode. "I don't know what you two are up to but let me make this as clear as I possibly can. There is nothing to be shared. As far as George and I are concerned, you are not welcome in our house!"

"What's with the attitude, Maddie?" Mrs. Macintyre asked. "I loved your uncle."

"If you really knew my uncle, you'd know he hated to be called Chuck. So the next time you try your little confidence game, you'd better get your facts straight! If George or I see either of you again, we're calling the police!"

"Please, Mad…"

"And don't call me Maddie! Let's go George!"

* * *

Following the hearing at the courthouse, Madison and I decided to stay in St. George at her uncle's home. Since we didn't know how long it would be before the CDC released Charlie's body for burial, we planned on using the time to go through everything more thoroughly and decide what to do with his personal possessions. Unfortunately, a catastrophic event would disrupt our plans, and we wouldn't get the chance.

THE ELEMENT

At the time, we had no idea the people responsible for breaking into Charlie's home were desperate. Having failed to find what they were looking for in the two burglaries, and unsuccessful at trying to quickly purchase the home or gain ownership of it in probate court, they were now planning to use a more violent method.

This technique involved using a destructive type of natural element, whose three simple ingredients included heat, fuel, and oxygen.

CHAPTER FOUR: THE FIRE

Eight Hours Later
Inside the Dewhurst Home
St. George, Utah

The flickering pilot light of the gas fireplace projected shadows on the walls, making the oversized outlines of the bulky, pioneer-age furniture appear to be moving. The hardwood floor and ceiling, coupled with the dark and flowery waist-high wallpaper, added to the illusion, framing the rectangular projection like a movie screen.

Madison decided she wanted to sleep in her old room, which was on the second floor of Charlie's home. After climbing into bed, I kissed her good night and rolled over. Ninety minutes later, I woke up feeling tired, but couldn't get back to sleep; a troublesome side-effect of my Parkinson's medications.

Thinking a real ghost might appear if I stared at the eerie shadows any longer, I decided to get up to take a walk. Slipping on my robe and house shoes, I made my way over to the door leading into the hall. When I took hold of the doorknob, scalding pain made me cry out.

Madison bolted awake and turned on the nightstand lamp. "George, what is it?"

"Something's up with the doorknob. I just burned the crap out of my hand."

She sniffed. "Something's on fire!"

Damn! Of all the senses, why did Parkinson's take my ability to smell?

I flipped on the overhead lights, felt the door, and found it hot to the touch. "It's in the hallway."

The wide-eyed look of fear crossed her face. "That's our only way out!"

"What about the windows?" I asked, trying to sound calm.

She ran over and tore open the drapes – the flames outside were halfway up the glass! Not knowing what to do, I looked around and happened to notice the access panel in the ceiling. "What about up there?"

"I don't know," she replied, her voice cracking. "I've never been up there."

"Let's try it. Grab the other side of the bed."

We scooted the bed over until it was directly under the panel, and I retrieved the chair next to the nightstand. Jumping up on the bed, I quickly pulled the chair up, and was soon helping Madison climb into the attic.

After proceeding only a few feet, she stopped and yelled, "There's too much smoke. I can't see anything!"

"Feel around. There should be a gap down the center of the rafters."

A moment later, she replied, "Okay, I think I found it."

Stepping up on the chair, I took hold of the sides of the panel and pulled myself up. I'd no sooner made it through the opening, when a deafening explosion rocked the house. A huge section of the hardwood floor broke away below me, taking the bed and chair with it.

Madison's old bedroom and the dining room below were now a raging inferno.

We shuffled on all fours as fast as we could through the attic until a wall stopped us. After a few hard kicks, I broke a hole through the ceiling and found we were over Charlie's bedroom.

I motioned for Madison to go ahead, and she lowered herself down through the opening. By the time I hit the floor, she'd already made it to the door leading into the hallway. Her shaking head immediately ruled it out as an escape option. I ran to the drapes and tore them open. The flames outside were rising, but not as high as they'd been on the other side of the house. With Charlie's desk chair within reach, I picked it up by the arm rests and heaved it as hard as I could. The impact disintegrated the glass, giving us a clear escape route to the outside.

Before we could jump through, another huge explosion collapsed the floor beneath our feet. Landing on top of the room below, the section of wood we were standing on hit something underneath, causing it to tilt. Like an acrobat jumping on a teeter-totter, the abrupt incline catapulted Madison through the blown-out first-story window, and threw me, left-side first, into the window's hardwood casing. From the audible snaps and lightning-rod of pain, I knew my forearm had broken and I had probably cracked some ribs. Luckily, my bounce off the casing sent me to the right, which placed me directly in front of the broken window. Stepping up on the sill, I jumped through and landed on the lawn. Madison helped me to my feet, and we ran until we were a safe distance away.

"Are you okay?" I asked, coughing and hacking.

"I think so. What about you?"

"My left arm is broken and my side is killing me."

She helped me down to the grass and I placed my uninjured arm around her. Burying her face in my chest, she began to cry.

Looking back at the blazing house, I couldn't believe we'd made it out alive.

A few minutes later, a bevy of firetrucks arrived, but it was too late.

Uncle Charlie's home was a total loss.

* * *

After the ambulance ride to the hospital, the physician's assistant on duty determined I needed surgery to repair my broken arm. Since their lone trauma surgeon was backlogged with two appendectomies and a critically injured victim of a car accident, I had to wait for more than two hours. Finally, an orderly came to take me to the operating room, and after a quick kiss from Madison, he wheeled me away. A short time later, the anesthetist gave me a shot and I slid into unconsciousness.

Unexpectedly, I felt free. Unlike the freedom one would feel getting out of prison, this felt as if I'd been released from the confines of my earthly existence. As I calmly floated skyward, I thought, *if this is what it's like to die, it's not too bad.*

My peaceful demeanor soon changed to a feeling of uneasiness, each foot of my ascension making me more and more uncomfortable.

My injuries aren't life-threatening, so why am I dying?

I looked down on the operating room. Instead of seeing a medical team frantically trying to save my life, the doctors and nurses were standing perfectly still. Looking closer, I realized they were mannequins!

The entire scene appeared foggy, as if I were watching through a steamy opaque lens. A moment later the image sharpened, and I found myself back inside my body – tied to the bed and unable to move. Other than my heart racing in my chest, the only sound emanated from a wall clock, the tick of its hand growing louder with each passing second.

Then the mannequin dressed as the lead surgeon moved! Jerky at first, its actions soon became smooth and fluid; as if its joints had been given lubricant. I wanted to look away but couldn't take my eyes off the macabre sight. It retrieved a large scalpel from a nearby tray, turned its head, and looked at me. The sight of its cold, emotionless eyes sent a quake of fear shooting though my body, and I began to shake uncontrollably. It flailed the scalpel back and forth, simulating slashing motions, and took a step toward me. My deep-seated fear instantly gave way to full-blown panic. I struggled to free myself, but no matter how hard I fought the restraints, I remained in place. When it reached the side of the bed, it leaned over and placed the tip of the scalpel against my throat.

"I'll be coming for you very soon, Mr. d'Clare," it said, in a voice deep and ominous.

A second later I was awake, soaked with sweat and trembling.

"George, are you alright?" Madison asked. "You were having one heck of a dream."

I took in a deep breath, but the sharp pain down my left side stopped me before I could answer. Looking down, I had a cast on my left forearm, complete with a thick, foam-rubber sling around my neck immobilizing it. Underneath my hospital gown, my chest had been wrapped in bandages.

"Where am I?" I asked.

She smiled. "You're in the recovery room."

Her words triggered my memory of being wheeled into surgery. "How did the operation go?"

She shrugged her shoulders. "I don't know. I didn't get a chance to meet the surgeon before they took you in, and he hasn't been out to talk to me yet."

Just then, a man wearing a white doctor's coat and a large, gallon-sized cowboy hat entered the room. When he first walked through the dim-lit doorway, he appeared to be around forty years old, but when he moved into the light in the center of the room, his long gray hair added years to my estimation. He stood roughly six-feet tall with a muscular build, and his thick walrus moustache traveled down to his chin. When he spoke, his deep baritone voice had a pronounced cowboy drawl.

"I'm Doctor Doyle Holliday, Mr. d'Clare," he said, "but everyone around these here parts just calls me Doc."

I smiled. "Doc Holliday? Any relation to *the* Doc Holliday?"

He winked. "He was my Great, Great, Great Granddad. Is this your sweetie?"

"My wife Madison."

"Pleased to meet you, ma'am. I'm the sawbones who put your trail boss back together."

After shaking her hand, he turned back to me. "How are you feeling?"

"My left side hurts."

"I wouldn't doubt it. You looked like you'd been lawn-darted off an unbroken Morgan gelding when they brought you in."

"What about his arm?" Madison asked.

"Jagged break. Took me a while to set. Also, two of his ribs are cracked. But he should heal-up and hair-over. I've worked on rodeo cowpokes who've been stomped by brahma bulls in worse shape. I hear tell both of you were luckier than a riverboat gambler drawing an aces-high flush to get out of that barn-burner alive."

"I guess so," I replied, not knowing how to answer such a description.

He smiled. "Tell me, compadre, on a lumber scale of one to ten, with ten being a full cord, what's your pain level?"

"Nine."

"I'll have the nurse give you something that'll knock it down a button-hole lower. And I'll make sure it's the brand that doesn't get muley with your Parkinson's pills."

"Thank you," Madison said. "That's always a worry."

"Yeah, thanks," I echoed.

"You'll be riding drag for a while. The best thing for you is to rest and get some shut eye. I'll be back 'fore sundown to check on you."

As he turned to leave a nurse came in. He gave her the instructions for the pain medicine and watched her prepare the shot, before disappearing out the door.

Madison and I immediately looked at each other and started laughing.

"Is he for real?" Madison asked.

The nurse smiled and inserted the needle into my intravenous tube. "Don't let him fool you. Doc may be a bit flamboyant, but he's the best trauma surgeon we've got."

"Does he always talk like that?"

"Not normally. He's just practicing."

"Practicing?"

"In the summers he competes in cowboy story-telling contests at the Grand Canyon."

In unison, Madison and I let out a long "oh."

After checking my vital signs, the nurse stepped out. When I heard the door close, I addressed Madison in the deepest voice I could muster. "So how are you holding up, kemosabe?"

Before she could answer, the door opened and Officer Davis walked in, carrying a large plastic evidence bag. Officer Hansen followed, holding a bulging manila folder.

"Mr. and Mrs. d'Clare," Davis said, "We stopped by to see how you're doing and to bring you this." He opened the evidence bag and pulled out Madison's purse; straps burned off, and its tanned-leather color now resembling a piece of burnt toast. "The fire department found it a few hours ago. Would you please check its contents?"

Taking it from him, she quickly zipped open each compartment.

"Are you satisfied everything is there?"

She nodded. "It looks like everything."

"If I could just get your signature on a release form, it's all yours."

Hansen removed a paper from the manila folder and a pen from his shirt pocket and handed them to her.

As she began reading through the document, Davis turned to me. "How did your operation go?"

"I'll be all right."

"When we heard about the fire, we were concerned…"

"I appreciate you bringing me my purse," Madison interrupted, "but we don't need your concern."

From Madison's stern tone, I could tell she was in full beast mode.

She handed the form and pen back to Hansen. "What we need, is for you to find out who broke into my uncle's home, and who set the fire and tried to kill us."

"I'm sorry, Mrs. d'Clare," Davis replied, "but the fire department found no evidence of arson. They determined a leaking gas pipe caused the explosion and subsequent fire."

"The statement we gave to the fire department was in English, wasn't it?"

He nodded.

"So, what part didn't you understand? George burned himself on the door handle *before* the explosion."

"And there were *two* explosions," I added. "How does a gas pipe explode twice?"

"Yeah, explain that one," Madison said, almost yelling. "How does a gas pipe explode twice?"

"I'll admit it sounds strange," Davis replied, "but we can only go by what the fire department tells us."

"What about the burglaries?" Madison snapped. "I suppose you're at a dead end there too."

Officer Hanson, who'd been staring at the floor, raised his head and spoke. "We're not TV detectives who can solve a case in an hour, Mrs. d'Clare."

"Maybe you need to hire some!"

"All right, all right, cool off," Davis interjected. "If there are any developments, we'll let you know."

When they hastily departed, Madison began pacing back and forth. "I've met some idiots in my life, but those two take the cake. And they're cops, no less!"

I reached out. "Come here, sweetheart."

She walked over and sat on the edge of the bed. When our eyes met, tears began streaming down her face.

I patted her hand. "Now, now, take it easy."

"But what if I'd lost you, George?"

"I'll be okay. I'm just glad you weren't hurt."

"I wish the window in Charlie's room would've been wide enough for both of us to…fit…through…"

As her voice trailed off, her face took on the wide-eyed look of stunned surprise. In a trance, staring at me but not seeing me, she slowly stood.

"Sweetheart?"

She turned away and took a few steps toward the door. "It can't be," she whispered.

"What can't be?"

She turned and faced me again. "George, I know where it is."

"Where what is?"

"The special place. It's in the basement under the coal chute."

"The coal what?"

"Where they used to shovel in the coal for the old boiler. Remember? It's red with flowery stickers all over it. You saw it when you helped me move out."

It finally came to me. "I thought it was a slippery slide."

She shook her head. "I painted it and put the stickers on it, but the chute was actually part of the house. When Charlie remodeled and removed the boiler, he found the legs of the chute cemented into the basement floor."

"Who did that?"

"A previous owner. Charlie ended up framing around it and nailing a piece of wood over the top opening. I used to call it my special place because I played with my dolls there. I wish I would've remembered it when Charlie mentioned it, but it's been more than forty years since I've been down there."

"So you think he hid the Wordless Book under this coal chute?"

"There's a small opening below the front lip. Back in those days I could fit through it. When I said I wished the window had been wide enough for both of us to fit through, I remembered saying the same thing to a friend from school who spent the night with me. She

82

was too chubby to fit through the opening. The fire couldn't have melted the chute because it's thick, heavy-duty steel."

I completed her thought. "So, if we can get down there, and the chute is still in place, there's a good chance the Wordless Book survived the fire."

She looked directly into my eyes. When she spoke, it was in the most serious tone I'd ever heard cross her lips. "And if we do find the Wordless Book, we'll know there's a two-thousand-year-old murderer out there who intends to kill every man, woman, and child to bring about the end of the world."

* * *

Not believing a word of the officer's story about the leaking gas pipe, Madison and I decided to investigate the coal chute as soon as Doc released me from the hospital. Even though the home had burned to the ground, the people who set the fire might still be watching the property. If they were, I didn't want Madison crossing paths with them alone.

A short time later, Doc arrived to check on me. When the conversation turned to Madison's uncle, he provided us more information on Charlie's condition, but without the western drawl and lingo.

"When your uncle came into the hospital," he began, "I was the first to examine him. He told me he'd been poisoned, but he wasn't showing any symptoms. Thinking he might have mental problems, I put him in an observation room to keep an eye on him. About six hours later, I stopped in to see how he was doing and found abscesses had broken out on his skin. The next day he'd gotten worse, and his arms and legs were showing signs of gangrene. I treated him with every medication I could think of, but nothing worked. That's when I placed him in the hyperbaric chamber and called the CDC."

"So, you've spoken to Dr. Webster?" Madison asked.

"Yes. She's quite a remarkable doctor. After confirming my diagnosis of the plague, she identified the probable poison. Right off the top of her head, I might add."

"With as many poisons as there are," I said, "I wonder how she did that."

"I did too, so I asked her. Come to find out she used to teach classes on poisoning to new CDC employees. It made me feel good knowing she's not a saddlebag sawbones."

"A what?" Madison asked, chuckling.

He put on his huge cowboy hat and winked. "She's the real dealer in this poker game."

* * *

Drifting off to sleep, I found myself having the same terrifying nightmare I'd had earlier. When the mannequin approached me this time, its mouth opened and it spoke; the deep, menacing voice sending shivers down my spine.

"Mr. d'Clare."

"Who are you?" I asked, trying not to panic.

It stopped and tilted its head, as if it were a scientist examining a laboratory specimen.

"I'm the one Aquinas told you about, Mr. d'Clare. I fashioned this dream from a nightmare you had when you were a child. Do you remember it?"

Not wanting it to know it had uncovered one of my deepest childhood fears, I shook my head. "What do you want?"

84

"You know what I want. That's why I've come to you in your dreams to warn you."

"Warn me of what?"

"You may have saved yourself from the fire, but if you do not surrender the Wordless Book, I will be forced to take more extreme measures."

"I don't know what you're talking about."

"Your wife is a very beautiful woman. I'd hate to see an accident befall her and her face become disfigured."

The threat to Madison made me momentarily forget my fear, while at the same time, sent my temper through the roof.

"If you so much as touch a hair on her head, I swear I'll…"

"You'll do what, Mr. d'Clare? Kill me? Beat me to a pulp?" His frightening laugh reverberated all around me. "Apparently, you've already forgotten what Aquinas told you. Nothing can hurt me, let alone kill me."

"But why are you so obsessed with getting your hands on the Wordless Book? Are you afraid I'll learn the secret of how to defeat you?"

"Surrender the book, Mr. d'Clare! This will be my final warning."

A second later I woke up, breathing heavily and sweating profusely. The sight of Madison curled up and asleep somewhat relaxed me, and I sat on the edge of the bed until my heart stopped racing. With the mannequin's sinister-sounding voice still ringing in my ears, sleep eluded me for the remainder of the night.

Lying awake, I wondered if my medications were to blame for the vivid nightmares, or if I'd experienced a *real* warning from the Wanderer. I would learn the answer to that question a little more than forty-eight hours later, when Madison and I returned to the charred ruins of her uncle's home.

THE ELEMENT

CHAPTER FIVE: THE DISCOVERY

Two Days Later
Inside the Dixie Regional Medical Center
St. George, Utah

With the sunshine outside my window giving me cabin fever, I called for the nurse and told her I was ready to be discharged. She informed me Doc was on his way, and I could start getting ready to leave. Since I'd escaped the fire wearing only my robe, slippers and underwear, Madison ate an early breakfast before departing to go buy some clothes. Her return coincided with Doc's, entering the room holding his cellphone out in front of him.

"Dr. Webster is on the line from Atlanta," he said. "I've got her on speaker."

"Mr. and Mrs. d'Clare," Dr. Webster said, "Doc told me about the fire. How are you doing?"

"I'm all right," Madison replied, "but George is pretty banged up."

"So I heard."

"I'm okay," I said.

"He's got the spirit of a six-month-old unbroken palomino," Doc added.

Dr. Webster laughed. "Good to hear it, and I'm glad you're all together. We have finished the toxicology report on Mr. Dewhurst, and quite frankly my colleagues and I are stumped. We've confirmed his death was caused by Belladonna poisoning, a very rare derivative, and he was indeed suffering from a strain of bubonic plague. We also found strains of cholera and influenza in his tissues. What's puzzling is the strains of these diseases do not match any of the recent ones in our database. They matched much older strains, some dating back centuries."

"Centuries?" Doc asked. "How did you make that determination?"

"From the level of mutation."

"I'm sorry, doctor," I interrupted. "Could you please explain in English?"

She chuckled. "Certainly, Mr. d'Clare. Basically, all diseases mutate over time. That's why last year's flu shot won't prevent you from contracting this year's flu bug. We call these mutations strains. By obtaining tissue samples from Mr. Dewhurst, we compared the strains of diseases in his body to the strains of diseases in cadavers who died from the same illness. This comparison tells us, among other things, if the strain is recent or not. And here at the CDC, we have a vast collection of tissue samples from some very old cadavers.

"The strain of bubonic plague in Mr. Dewhurst matched a strain taken from a woman who died from the plague in the mid-1300's. The strain of cholera matched one taken from a man who died from cholera in the 1830's. Less than an hour ago, my assistant found a match to the influenza strain. It matched the strain taken from a man who died in the worldwide flu pandemic of 1918."

"How can that be?" Doc asked.

"I don't know. Like I said, we're stumped. If I didn't know any better, I'd think Mr. Dewhurst had been immortal. He had contracted every major disease of the last six-hundred years and lived through all of them, before finally succumbing to Belladonna poisoning."

Madison and I stared at each other, not saying a word.

"These developments have prompted my supervisor, Assistant Director Hargrove, to issue a Priority-One Infectious Disease Alert to the World Health Organization. As we speak, he is inviting doctors from around the world to come here and examine Mr. Dewhurst's body. Mrs. d'Clare?"

Madison leaned forward. "Yes?"

"I want you to know I respect your wishes about not performing an autopsy. Unfortunately, when I relayed your request to Mr. Hargrove, he overruled me."

Tears came to Madison's eyes. "Why?"

"He said it's a public health issue, but it can't be. The public would only be at risk if the strains were recent, and there haven't been any reports of new outbreaks of these old strains."

I cleared my throat. "Doctor, this is George again. I thought you were going to freeze Charlie's remains and take cell samples?"

"We did. That's how we determined his cause of death."

"But if you've already taken samples and know what the diseases are, why does your supervisor need to call in a team of doctors?"

"He hopes they can determine where Mr. Dewhurst contracted these old strains."

"Can't these doctors study the samples you've already removed?"

"Yes, but there are other things going on."

"Like what?"

She sighed heavily. "I shouldn't be telling you this, but it's politically motivated. Mr. Hargrove is aspiring to be the next director. By issuing the alert, he's hoping to impress retiring director Ramsey. He's also hoping to impress the doctors, who are all world-renowned specialists. As for Mr. Dewhurst's remains, the team could study the samples we've already removed, but they may need to extract more for further study. If that's the case, an autopsy is less time consuming."

"Please," Madison implored, "could you try to convince them not to cut my uncle apart just to save time?"

"I'm sorry, Mrs. d'Clare. As far as your uncle is concerned, Mr. Hargrove has already relieved me of my duties and assigned himself to the case as the resident medical examiner. Nothing short of a court order can stop the autopsy."

Doc raised the phone up to his mouth. When he spoke, his voice sounded much more serious. "Dr. Webster, could you text me the email addresses of Mr. Hargrove and your retiring director? Ramsey, was it?"

"Mrs. Helen Ramsey. Yes, I can send them to you."

"Good. They'll be receiving a court order within the hour."

Madison's face lit up.

"Are you sure you want to do that?" Dr. Webster asked.

"Yes, I'm sure. With all that's happened, Mrs. d'Clare has enough things to worry about. And if these doctors can extract the needed samples from Mr. Dewhurst's remains without an autopsy, and it's not a public health issue, her decision must stand. She's the next of kin."

"Okay, but just so you know, officially I have to side with the CDC. Unofficially, I'm on your side. And we never had this conversation."

"I understand."

"Also, be forewarned. Mr. Hargrove's ego is as big as his aspirations. He graduated from the school of threats and intimidation. He also has many powerful friends in Washington."

"No worries," Doc replied calmly. "I can hold my own."

After promising to inform us of any further developments, Dr. Webster ended the call. Madison immediately stepped over and gave Doc a hug.

"Thank you," she said, "a million times over."

He patted her on the back. When he replied, his voice changed back to its familiar cowboy drawl. "Never much cared for G-men. The uppity ones tend to forget they work for us taxpayers."

"But Doc," I said, "it sounds like this Hargrove guy could give you some trouble."

"I suppose he could, but I have a friend in Washington too. You probably don't remember the night you were admitted. The emergency room was busier than a one-legged man at a butt-kicking contest, and I was the only sawbones on staff."

I smiled and shook my head. "You're right. I don't remember."

"I do," Madison said. "We waited two hours for George to be taken to surgery."

He took off his cowboy hat, retrieved a business card from under the crown's ribbon, and handed it to me. "This man was the reason you had to wait."

I read it aloud. "T.J. Coleman, Assistant Attorney General, United States of America."

"Seriously?" Madison asked.

He smiled. "Mr. Coleman and his posse were on their way to the Grand Canyon when his appendix decided it didn't like the cut of his jib. He was so grateful I'd fixed him up, he gave me his card and said if I ever needed his services to give him a call. Whatever card this Hargrove has up his sleeve, my ace trumps it, if you know what I mean."

After signing my discharge papers, Doc departed. Turning to Madison, I asked, "What do you think?"

"I think we need to go to Uncle Charlie's home and look in the special place."

* * *

We had originally planned to investigate the coal chute when Doc discharged me from the hospital, but our plans changed when Madison, conducting reconnaissance, observed the activities going on at the burned-down home. Yesterday, she'd driven out to a subdivision adjacent to her uncle's property three times and reported back to me what she'd seen.

The police had barricaded the street near at the outcropping of rocks and posted signs warning trespassers. Each time she'd gone out there, people were gathered at the barricade. With the home being such an attraction, we decided our best chance to get in and out undetected would be in the middle of the night.

After checking out of the hospital, Madison drove straight to the nearest hardware store where we purchased two large flashlights and a package of batteries. We spent the rest of the afternoon in the parking lot of the local high school, watching a little league baseball tournament. Following a late dinner at a nearby restaurant, and still needing to kill some time, Madison drove to where she'd been observing Uncle Charlie's property.

With my eyelids growing heavy, I sat back in the seat and nodded off. The sound of her starting the engine woke me up, and when I looked at the dashboard clock, I couldn't believe the time.

"Is it really two-fifteen in the morning?"

She nodded. "You really zonked out."

"I guess I did. Have you seen anything?"

"Nothing out of the ordinary. Are you okay to go look now?"

"Let's do it."

A short time later, we were making our way into Charlie's subdivision. When we reached the police barricades, she swung the SUV around so it was pointed back the way we came, and parked parallel to the curb.

"Good idea," I said.

She nodded. "Just in case we have to get out of here fast."

We waited a few minutes to make sure no one was around, then got out and proceeded toward what was left of Charlie's home.

Like dark colors running together on a watercolor canvass, the blackened skeletal framework of the collapsed roof rafters blended seamlessly with the moonless sky, making their borders indistinguishable. Three of the four heavily reinforced wood walls, once handcrafted with precision by a skilled craftsman in the pioneer days, now resembled used matchsticks; shrunken and curled. Still standing, the fourth wall sat at an angle, offset by a massive pile of charred debris leaning against it. An unnerving quietness hung in the air, as if the flora and fauna of the surrounding area were pausing to pay respect to a lost companion. The sights and lack of sounds created a haunting memorial to the ferocity of the fire, while at the same time issued a hushed warning for intruders to stay away.

When I had helped Madison move out, I remembered there were only two ways into the basement: the interior stairs and a walkout service entrance in the rear. Since the fire had engulfed the entire structure, the possibility was high the interior stairs no longer existed. When we shined our lights on the place where the stairs used to be, my hypothesis proved correct.

We quickly made our way around to the back and found the stairs leading down to the service entrance mostly clear. The only obstacle was the charred black entry door, hanging crooked by one hinge. Receiving a nod from Madison, I slowly proceeded down. When I stepped off the last stair onto the lower landing, I found myself ankle-deep in black water. After carefully stepping over to the hanging door, I held it open with my uninjured arm and let Madison go in before me.

Once inside, the jaw-dropping devastation literally stopped us in our tracks. There were two uneven holes in the north and south ends of the ceiling, each more than fifteen feet in diameter. On the basement floor beneath each hole, sat a corresponding mound of black debris, roughly eight feet tall by my estimation. Except for several charred pieces of wood still being held in place by framing nails, the previously finished walls were either gone or burned down to the bare cement. The remaining furnishings included a melted ornate light fixture, dangling precariously from a half-burned ceiling joist, and the skeletal remains of the furnace and water heater, standing to the right of where we'd entered.

Madison, who'd been examining what was left of the furnace with her flashlight, stopped and turned to me. "George," she whispered, "look at this."

The gas lines were still connected to the furnace and the water heater. A foot behind the connections, the lines joined together in a "T" coupling and traveled up to the floor above. Shining my light up through the hole in the ceiling, I could see the line connected to another T coupling. The lines, connections, and coupling were intact and unbroken; the two exceptions being where the line had been connected to the stove and fireplace, which were now twisted and sheared off.

"So much for the exploding gas line," I whispered.

She nodded and motioned for me to follow. After squeezing around the edges of the large piles of debris, we came upon the coal chute. Although the chute itself was still in place, the enclosed area beneath it was now burned away. She handed me her flashlight, knelt into the black water, and started feeling around. After producing the remains of a dollhouse and several melted children's toys, she crawled toward the front of the chute and felt the area under the lip.

A moment later, Madison's face took on the same look of stunned surprise she'd had at the hospital.

"George, I think I found it."

She pulled up, and a black portfolio case emerged from the water. Returning to her feet, she made her way around to the front of the chute and set the case down on top of it. Following her over, I handed her back her flashlight.

Scorched black and with one corner burned all the way off, the case had old-fashioned hasps on the front, holding it closed.

Madison looked up at me with tears streaming down her face. "Oh George, why didn't I believe him?"

I wrapped my uninjured arm around her. "It's okay, sweetheart. I thought his story was hard to believe too."

Returning our attention to the case, Madison reached out and unfastened the hasps, and slowly opened the top. Surprisingly, the inside was filled with compact discs, most of which were either burned, warped, or melted together. On the label side of the discs, numbers had been written in black. Pulling a few out to examine them, Madison uncovered what appeared to be the corner of a book. Quickly removing the rest of the discs, we gazed in stunned silence at what we found underneath.

It was easily the oldest, most fragile-looking book I'd ever seen, as if it had been read or referred to since the beginning of time. Much smaller than I imagined, it measured roughly eight inches wide, ten inches long, and two inches thick. Its front cover, made of dark wood, was singed on the same corner as the case. Holding it closed were two weathered leather straps, wrapped around from the back and laced through tarnished buckles on the front. The binding running down the length of the spine on the left side had deteriorated to the point it no longer held the pages, evident from the crooked and uneven way they were stacked. As for the disheveled pages, they were dark manila in color and looked to be unharmed, which coincided with what Charlie had said about Father Vincent's mute assistant transcribing his premonitions onto non-burning silicate paper.

Just as Madison reached in to remove the book, a piece of wood fell through the hole in the ceiling and crashed into the large mound of debris right next to me. I immediately turned off my flashlight and whispered for Madison to do the same. For the next few minutes we stood motionless in the darkness, listening for any sound telling us we'd been discovered. Not hearing anything, I finally turned on my flashlight, as did Madison.

"Let's get out of here," I whispered.

She quickly gathered the compact discs and placed them back in the case, then closed the top and fastened the hasps.

As we turned to leave, a man's voice yelled outside – the same deep and sinister voice I'd heard in my dreams. "Mr. and Mrs. d'Clare? Come out, come out, wherever you are!"

We froze and looked at each other.

"If you bring the book to me now, no one will get hurt. If you force me to come in after you, neither of you will leave here alive!"

I shined my flashlight around, in hopes of finding another way out. Madison, also looking, stopped when her flashlight illuminated the top of the coal chute.

"George, look."

Miraculously, the fire had consumed the piece of wood covering the opening – the way was clear to the outside!

I motioned for her to go ahead of me and helped her step up onto the lip of the chute. After climbing to the top, she threw the case containing the Wordless Book outside. Holding on to the side of the opening with one hand, she reached back to me with her free one. As I took hold and stepped up, the man yelled again.

"All right, have it your way!"

At the top of the chute, I let go of Madison and grabbed the side of the opening. As she rolled out onto the lawn, I heard a splash from the direction of the walkout. With my broken left arm not allowing me to mimic her maneuver, I simply crawled out on my one good hand and knees. Once free of the opening, Madison helped me to my feet. Hurriedly retrieving the case containing the Wordless Book, we took off running.

Although I tried to keep up with her, the combination of a broken arm, cracked ribs, and Parkinson's slowing my right leg reduced my speed to a snail's pace. By the time I made it to the gargoyle-shaped outcropping of rocks, Madison had already reached our vehicle.

As I rounded the rock formation, a shot rang out. The bullet struck the top of a boulder less than a foot in front of me, stinging my face with rock fragments. Dropping to the ground, I continued forward on my hand and knees until I was safely behind the larger boulders in the outcropping. Taking in a few extra breaths, I returned to my feet and hobbled out into the street. Passing the police barricades, I found Madison in our vehicle and ready to go – engine on and passenger door open. When I climbed in, she handed me the case containing the Wordless Book.

"What took you so long?" she asked, smirking.

Before I could think of a clever comeback another shot rang out and the rear and driver's side windows exploded. Madison floored the accelerator, and we took off zig-zagging down the road leading out of the subdivision. Since I hadn't had time to put my seat belt on, her evasion tactics tossed me left-to-right in the seat, aggravating the pain in my injuries.

Approaching St. George Boulevard, the signal light turned red. Madison stopped swerving and slowed down, giving me time to finally fasten my seat belt.

"This is weird," she said. "Who tripped the light?"

Returning my attention to the road ahead, there weren't any vehicles waiting at the light in any direction – the intersection was empty.

"I say run it."

"I agree. Hang on!"

Flooring the accelerator again, our SUV lurched forward. Entering the intersection, she slammed on the brakes, made a hard right turn, and hit the accelerator again. Speeding down the boulevard, we blew through four more intersections before she finally slowed down. For the next few minutes, Madison's eyes alternated back and forth from the road ahead to the rearview mirror.

I grinned. "You know, all these years we've been together, you never told me you used to drive NASCAR."

She smiled for a moment, before the grim look of determination returned to her face. Up ahead, the lights of the freeway were coming into view.

"He knew our name," I said, "so we can't go home."

"I agree," she replied. "We're the only people with the last name of d'Clare in the state of Utah."

She signaled and turned onto the southbound onramp.

* * *

After a short refueling stop in Hurricane, Utah, Madison steered our vehicle south toward Phoenix, Arizona. While she drove, I conducted a more thorough examination of the compact discs inside the portfolio case. There were ten discs in all, but the ones numbered one through five were warped and unplayable.

After ejecting one of Madison's favorite Rod Stewart discs from the audio player, I loaded disc number six and pressed the play button.

When Uncle Charlie's (Aquinas') now-ghost-like voice came out of the car's speakers, Madison and I sat mesmerized, not saying a word.

Since the discs numbered one through five were unplayable, I thought the first half of the story would never be known. Thankfully, at the beginning of the disc, Aquinas included a detailed review of the major events, which enabled Madison and me to piece together what must've happened.

Following the guidance of his father Augustus, Aquinas and his friend Merrick had traveled to Amsterdam, where they found a vein of carmot deep inside a cave near the Amstel River. By ingesting the element, they became impervious to sickness and disease and halted their bodies' aging processes. To hide their ageless appearances from superstitious townspeople, every other decade they moved to a different location. When they felt the carmot wearing off, which occurred every one-to-two-hundred years, they would return to Amsterdam to ingest more of the magical element.

The men toiled at many different jobs to support themselves, while behind the scenes, they secretly worked on deciphering the symbols in the Wordless Book. During idle times, Aquinas taught Merrick things he'd learned from his father, including the arts and sciences, and how to speak and write multiple languages. Other times, Merrick trained Aquinas how to use the weapons of the era, including the sword, the longbow, and several models of evolving firearms.

"At first," Aquinas said, "I planned to hide out with Merrick until we had finished deciphering the entire Wordless Book, and in turn, learn the secret of how to defeat Lucas. As we delved deeper into the book, however, the symbols became more complex, and the math became more convoluted. These developments slowed my plan to a crawl."

Adding to their troubles were numerous encounters with Lucas. No matter where they were or how well they had masked the trail behind them, he eventually discovered their whereabouts. The resulting confrontations had, at times, left both Aquinas and Merrick mortally wounded. If they hadn't ingested the carmot element, they would've died.

Aquinas described one of these encounters, and speculated how Lucas had been able to (time and time again) discover where they were hiding:

"Lucas and his handful of followers found Merrick and me working as longshoremen in Cuxhaven, Germany. The ensuing confrontation was particularly long, lasting through the morning and well into the afternoon. The clash finally ended when we distanced ourselves from them long enough to escape on a clipper ship bound for Edinburgh, Scotland. During the swordplay Merrick suffered a near-fatal wound to his chest. I give thanks to the Almighty for sparing my friend, and to the carmot, for had he not ingested the magical element, Merrick surely would have perished.

"After the battle, I repeatedly examined the steps we'd taken to conceal our identities, and how (once again) our efforts to shroud our location from Lucas had been a failure. I now believe the answer lies in the way the carmot affects the human body. When Lucas poisoned my father and me at Kaffa, he stole a significant amount of carmot – some of which he ingested. With the Punishment of Endlessness already sustaining his life, the carmot instead enhanced Lucas' mental abilities, to include his intuition and his mastery of the *Ways of the*

Wind, or in layman's terms, his ability to control others using the power of suggestion.

"Although this is only my theory, it explains why no matter how far we traveled or how well we disguised ourselves, Lucas eventually found us. For Merrick and me, this made our goal of completing the Great Work much more difficult. Going forward, we had to remain vigilant to the possibility of Lucas appearing at any time."

* * *

The rest of the events described on disc number six picked up the story four-hundred and eighty-six years after the siege at Kaffa. In Aquinas' words:

"Merrick and I had just finished learning Euclidean geometry from an aged college professor. This knowledge enabled us to decipher roughly half of the pages in the Wordless Book and identify three additional locations in the world where we could find the element – the closest being in France. With the vein of carmot in the Amsterdam cave nearly depleted, we set a fire to destroy the rest and proceeded on horseback to Paris.

"The year was 1832, when Merrick and I followed the clues in the rhyming parable to the most spine-tingling place imaginable: deep underground, in the secret crypts beneath the Notre-Dame Cathedral."

PART TWO:
THE CHASE

On the land of the Franks
in a city of light,
where Our Lady's place of worship
stands tall and shines bright.

Beneath lies a pathway
a secret trail of great dread,
which leads to the carmot
at rest with the dead.

Aquinas' and Merrick's interpretation of the second group
of symbols in the first chapter of the Wordless Book

CHAPTER SIX: THE SECRET CATACOMBS

Sunday, 19 February 1832, 07:40hrs
Along the Seine River
Five Miles Northeast of Paris, France

The approaching sounds of two galloping horses disturbed the quiet and serene stillness of the wintry morning, causing the scarce wildlife to run away in fear. Atop the horses sat Aquinas and Merrick, rushing across the French countryside at breakneck speed. When they reached the bank of the river, they proceeded out onto the ice until it cracked under their weight; instantly plunging them into the hip-deep water. Ignoring the freezing temperature, they let out screams of exhilaration as they urged their steeds to keep running. As soon as they'd traversed the waterway and climbed onto the far shore, they turned southwest and bolted on, leaving a cloud of powdery snow in their wake.

Entering Paris, they continued at a fast pace until they reached the center of the city, slowing to a steady trot when the *Notre-Dame de Paris* cathedral came into view; its French-Gothic design and ornate stone figureheads emitting a menacing aura.

"A church so old and regal must have guards," Merrick commented.

Aquinas nodded. "A large contingent no doubt."

"How do you propose we get in?"

"It being Sunday, we'll go to worship."

After finding a post with a watering trough, they tied off their horses and hastened back on foot to the *Rue de la Cité* bridge. Crossing over, they approached the front of the cathedral, its three main doors guarded by soldiers. Unsure of which one to enter, Aquinas approached a man who had just exited.

"Pardon me, my good man," Aquinas said, in French, "we would like to attend…"

The man held up his hand and walked away without answering. Aquinas looked at Merrick and shrugged his shoulders. After asking several more people, who also refused to answer, Aquinas deliberately stepped in front of a man and stopped him in his tracks. He stood roughly four-feet ten-inches tall, looked to be in his mid-thirties, with thick brown hair, dark skin, and a prominent bulbous red nose. He wore a black suit with white cuffs and carried a large book, complete with a collection of quilled pens.

"My friend and I have just arrived, and we would like to attend service. Could you tell me which door to enter?"

"You'll not get in with those longswords and that attire," the man replied.

Aquinas looked down at his shirt and pants. "What is the matter with the way I'm dressed?"

"To enter the cathedral in soaking wet clothes would be quite inappropriate, even for an unsophisticated commoner such as yourself."

When Merrick laughed, the man turned to him.

"You're not much better."

"What do you mean?"

"You smell like dirty feet."

Aquinas laughed. "I think we've been insulted."

Merrick smiled. "I *know* we've been insulted."

"Who are you?" Aquinas asked.

"My name is Davy de la Pailleterie, playwright and man of faith."

"Which makes you an expert on attire for worship?" Merrick asked.

"No, but on the Sabbath I'm the Archbishop's historian and scribe, and therefore know a little bit about clothing and deportment. Now if you would excuse me gentlemen, it's been a particularly trying morning and I have an appointment with a well-aged bottle of wine…"

"Before you leave," Aquinas interrupted, "perhaps you can tell us where we could purchase the proper clothes for worship?"

He looked back and forth at them. "Even an imbecile could tell you two are not interested in worship. What are you up to, or dare I ask?"

Aquinas smiled. "You have a keen eye. What if I were to tell you we are trying to stop a madman from killing everyone?"

"I'd say you're after the Archbishop. He kills me slowly each Sunday morning with his incessant criticism of my prose!"

The men laughed.

"My name is Aquinas and this is my friend Merrick. Where is this well-aged bottle of wine you spoke of?"

"In a tavern not far from here."

"Lead the way. For a man with such humor, we'll buy you a bottle."

Davy smiled. "Perhaps today isn't such a bad day after all. This way gentlemen."

As they followed him, Merrick moved close to Aquinas. Speaking English, he whispered, "It's obvious he's a drunkard, My Captain. Do you think it wise we involve him?"

"He's familiar with the cathedral," Aquinas whispered back, "so he should know the way down to the catacombs."

Merrick nodded. "Which ruse do you wish to employ?"

Aquinas shook his head. "This Davy is a very perceptive man, so I'm not sure we can use one."

When they reached the tavern, Davy held the door open and they proceeded inside. Since it was Sunday and still quite early in the day, the pub was mostly empty. Stepping up to the bar, Davy ordered a bottle of wine and three glasses. Once they were seated, he addressed Aquinas in English.

"Not only am I perceptive, gentlemen, I can speak several languages quite well. Yes, I do like to imbibe in spirits more than most, but I've never allowed my drinking to interfere with my responsibilities. So to gain my trust, before we go any further, I must know the truth. Who are you, and why you want to gain access into the catacombs?"

Aquinas and Merrick looked at each other but didn't answer.

"You're not fortune-seeking grave robbers, are you?"

Aquinas smiled. "We have no interest whatsoever in stealing from the dead."

The waitress arrived and placed the wine and glasses on the table, at which point Merrick retrieved a small gold rock from his vest pocket and handed it to her. The wide-eyed look of astonishment instantly came across the woman's face.

"Thank you, sir," the waitress said. "If there's anything else I can do for you, anything at all, let me know."

After the woman departed, Davy turned to Aquinas. "I see. You have already robbed someone, and you're looking to hide your ill-gotten gains in the catacombs."

Aquinas shook his head. "Let me propose this. If you help us, you'll be handsomely rewarded."

"No, thank you," Davy replied. "Money doesn't interest me. My writing has already earned me more than I'll ever need. Besides, I cannot take your gold knowing full-well no such passage exists."

"It *has* to be there," Merrick said.

Davy shook his head. "As the Archbishop's scribe, many of my duties are in his private library, which happens to be in the basement. There is only one way in and one way out. Besides, the entrance to the catacombs is more than three kilometers from here, over on *Place Denfert-Rochereau*."

Merrick looked at Aquinas. "Could we be mistaken?"

Aquinas held a finger up, silencing Merrick. Addressing Davy, he asked, "Could you excuse us for a moment? We'll be right back."

Davy nodded.

Merrick followed Aquinas to a table on the other side of the room. Retrieving the Wordless Book from under his shirt and some papers from his back pocket, Aquinas made a quick comparison. "*On the land of the Franks* definitely refers to France because the Germanic Franks formed the French Kingdom. As for Paris, the city is commonly known as *La Ville Lumière*, or the city of light."

"And the Notre-Dame Cathedral is often referred to as *Our Lady's Place of Worship*," Merrick added.

"Correct. As for the rest of the parable, it specifically mentions a *secret* trail. Therefore, the entrance must be somewhere in the basement of the cathedral."

Aquinas closed the book, stashed the papers in his pocket, and returned to Davy.

"Will you allow us to see for ourselves?" Aquinas asked.

Davy looked up but didn't answer.

"Allow me appeal to the humanitarian in you. If you help us, you'll be doing great work for your fellow man."

"To what great work do you speak?"

Aquinas looked at Merrick, gave him a slight nod, then returned his attention to Davy.

"Have you ever heard of the Order of the Sentinels?"

Davy took a drink. "A band of elderly clerics searching for the Philosopher's Stone. But those stories are nothing more than folk tales, legends."

"What if I were to tell you the Order is real and there is an element in nature that can transform ordinary rocks into gold?"

"And cure you of disease and prolong your life," Merrick added.

"I'd say you both must've escaped from an asylum."

Aquinas leaned in. "There is much we cannot tell you, but if you help us you'll possibly be saving every man, woman and child in Paris."

"Saving them? From what?" He took another drink.

"Before I tell you, look at this."

Aquinas pulled off his necklace, on the end of which hung a small crystal pendant. Holding it by the chain, he suspended the pendant in front of Davy's face, began twisting it back and forth, and spoke in a relaxed, soothing tone.

"Listen to me very carefully Davy, because the fate of mankind now hangs on the decision you are about to make."

* * *

One hour later, Davy had gained Aquinas and Merrick access into the cathedral. After gathering a torch for each of them, he led the way down a long flight of stone steps to the basement of the cathedral. When they reached the bottom, they proceeded into a large room furnished with desks and chairs. The walls were lined with shelving, each filled with stacks of papers or dusty books of every size.

"Gentlemen," Davy announced, "the Archbishop's private library."

Aquinas made his way down the left side, while Merrick walked down the right, each examining every nook and cranny hoping to find a clue pointing them to a secret passage. They met at a heavy wooden door at the far end.

"What's in here?" Aquinas asked.

"Only the cistern to catch the rainwater," Davy replied.

"Let's have a look."

Davy pulled the door open, knelt, and crossed himself.

"Why do you pay respect?" Merrick asked.

Davy pointed to an elaborate symbol chiseled into the back of the door, a lavish letter "X" superimposed over an equally elaborate letter "P."

"What does it mean?"

"The ancient symbol of *Chi-Rho* is an abbreviation of Christ's name, mostly used in graveyards to..." As his voice trailed off, his eyes grew wide.

"To what?" Aquinas asked.

"To mark where the dead are buried."

"The secret trail must be in here, My Captain." Merrick said.

Proceeding in, they found a room similar in size to the one they'd just passed. The floor was made of cobblestones, with most of the space taken by a large stone reservoir filled with water. The top of the far end of the reservoir was slightly lower than the near end, and had a notch chiseled into it to allow the excess water to run out. When they moved around it to investigate where the water drained, they found the cobblestones stacked to one side, and a large hole in the floor.

Shining his torch over the hole, Davy illuminated a circular staircase leading further down into the darkness below.

"All the times I came in here to fill my jug," he whispered, "I had no idea this was under my feet."

Aquinas and Merrick instantly brandished their swords.

"Lucas is here," Aquinas said. "It appears as though our attempts to destroy the remaining carmot in Amsterdam were not as successful as we had hoped."

Merrick nodded. "His instincts must be as keen as a well-sharpened sword."

"So how do we stop him?" Davy asked.

"He cannot die until the Day of Reckoning," Aquinas replied, "but we can wound his extremities."

"And if we are successful in wounding his extremities?"

"Then we shall contain him," Merrick said.

"With what?" Davy asked.

"These." Merrick pulled open his coat and revealed two pairs of shackles fastened to his belt. "One is for his wrists, and the other for his ankles."

Davy smiled. "Alright then, let us go find this Lucas, wound him and contain him."

He withdrew a small dagger from his belt containing ornate, circular-shaped quillons around the handle. Pulling it from its sheath, he moved toward the opening in the floor.

Aquinas took hold of his arm and stopped him. "Just where do you think you are going?"

"I'm going with you."

"This is not *your* fight, Davy."

"It most certainly is! I do not intend to just sit around hoping you and your friend defeat this madman. I've been praying for an adventure for some time, and now I finally have one. Besides, with the survival of mankind at stake, you'll need all the help you can get."

"You won't be able to do much of anything with that fancy little toad sticker," Merrick said

"I have a sharp tongue, which at the very least, could be a distraction. Now if you please, gentlemen."

Aquinas released his grip, and one-by-one, they descended into the secret catacombs beneath the Notre-Dame Cathedral. As they made their way down the circular stairway, the frigid water seeping in from Seine River cooled the air. By the time they reached the lower landing, they could see each other's breath.

Proceeding through an opening in the wall, they came upon a stone bridge. Shining their torches over the edge revealed a huge chasm, so deep the bottom could not be seen. Unexpectedly, out of the darkness below came a deep, guttural laugh.

Davy's eyes grew wide and he began to tremble. Retrieving a small flask from his vest pocket, he took a drink. With Aquinas and Merrick staring at him, he quickly took another drink and offered them the flask. Both men shook their heads.

"It gives me courage," he whispered.

"Don't listen to him," Aquinas said. "He's only trying to frighten us."

Davy returned the flask to his pocket. "As far as I'm concerned, he has succeeded."

With the echoes of the laugh fading in the distance, Aquinas and Davy proceeded over the bridge side-by-side, while Merrick took a defensive position behind them, walking backwards. Waving their torches back and forth, they entered a corridor made of human remains. Stacked to the ceiling, several of the skeletal heads had fallen out and were laying on the ground along the walkway.

"Man was not meant to be down here," Davy whispered.

"Be brave, my good man," Aquinas said.

After passing through the corpse-laden hallway, they entered a wider tunnel lined with mortared stones. Down each side were sections of tree limbs holding up medieval suits of armor. Next to each set of armor lay a wood casket with an engraved lid.

Davy stepped over and shined his torch on one of the engravings, and his eyes grew wide. "It can't be."

"What is it?" Merrick asked.

Davy quickly moved to the next casket, then the next; his look of astonishment becoming more pronounced with each one he examined. Once he had finished, he knelt and crossed himself. Rising to his feet, he turned to Aquinas and Merrick.

"Do you know who these men are, or rather, were?"

They shook their heads.

As he spoke, Davy pointed to each of the caskets. "Sir Cedric Claxton, Sir Robert Duncan and Sir William Berrett were Knights of the Round Table." He laid his hand on the casket closest to him. "This one proves it. Sir Fredrick Hales was Sir Galahad's right-hand man. If memory serves, these knights never returned from the search for the holy grail."

Aquinas thought for a moment. "They must've found the carmot and died protecting it."

"I wonder why they didn't ingest it to stay alive?" Merrick asked.

"The answer is quite simple," Davy said.

Merrick smiled and replied sarcastically. "Oh? Please enlighten us with your wisdom."

"These were very religious men on a hallowed quest to find the holy grail. Their orders were to return it to King Arthur so he could restore his kingdom. Believing the grail to be sacred, they would've never drank from it. Therefore, when they found the carmot they would've never eaten it."

Aquinas nodded. "Makes sense."

Before they could speculate further, another deep guttural laugh erupted from the darkness, echoing all around them.

"Must he keep doing that?" Davy asked.

"Lucas laughs in this manner when he believes he has the advantage over us," Aquinas explained. "We must hasten our pace."

Proceeding through the tunnel, they emerged in a large square cave. Each side had a tunnel like the one they'd just come out of, with one striking difference: there were clouds of smoke billowing out of the other three.

"Sir, Lucas is destroying the carmot." Merrick said.

"Which means he has finished transforming stones into gold. If he escapes with them, he'll unleash a disease upon the city."

"Which way, My Captain?"

"Three tunnels, three of us."

"Do you think it wise we separate?" Davy asked.

"We have no choice."

Merrick smiled. "You wouldn't want us to deprive you of your adventure, would you?"

Davy gave Merrick a curt smile, retrieved his flask, and took another drink.

"More courage?" Aquinas asked.

Davy replied with a half-hearted grin. "At this point, I need all I can get."

"All right then, Merrick, go left. I'll go right. Davy, you take the one in the middle. If you see anything, cry out."

Davy smiled nervously. "I assure you I will."

The men had only taken a few steps when Lucas emerged from the tunnel in front of them. Dressed in dark leather, he stood roughly six-and-a-half feet tall, with knee-high boots and a long black cloak. In addition to the sword he held in his right hand and the torch he held in his left, there were two bulging saddlebags draped over each of his shoulders.

"You're too late, Aquinas," Lucas said, his deep, sinister-sounding voice echoing throughout the cave. "All I need to do is throw these saddlebags into the streets. The greedy people will do the rest."

Before Aquinas could reply, Davy answered for him.

"Not if we have any say in the matter."

"And who are you little man?"

"Davy de la Pailleterie."

"Davy who?"

"Davy de la Pailleterie. Playwright, man of faith, and protector of my fellow man."

"Aquinas told you of me?"

"He most certainly did. I must say, I am not impressed. I was expecting someone who actually posed a threat, not a charlatan with a satchel full of parlor tricks."

Lucas laughed. "Well, Davy de la Pailleterie, see if I impress you when I remove your head!"

While Davy exchanged words with Lucas, Merrick slowly walked toward the left tunnel and Aquinas advanced toward the right one.

Noticing Merrick heading in the wrong direction, Aquinas yelled, "Where are you going?"

"I'm making my way over to engage Lucas, My Captain."

"He's over here."

"Have you both taken leave of your senses?" Davy interrupted. "He's standing in front of me."

Aquinas immediately realized what was happening.

"He's using the power of suggestion! Regroup!"

While keeping their eyes on the images of Lucas, Aquinas and Merrick hurried back to Davy.

"If we are seeing three of him, which one do we engage?" Davy asked.

"Whichever one attacks first," Merrick replied.

Lucas laughed again. "What's the matter, playwright? Did Aquinas neglect to inform you of my powers?"

Davy took the last swig from his flask, tossed it away, and retrieved his dagger. "Spare me your false concern and your inflated braggadocios. They are beginning to bore me."

Lucas smiled. "I see you have a death wish, little man. I shall therefore oblige you."

The images of Lucas that Aquinas and Merrick were watching abruptly disappeared, while the one in the center dropped the saddlebags and ran straight at Davy. With blinding speed, Merrick leapt forward, stuck his sword out, and deflected Lucas' blade. Following through, he delivered a solid kick to Lucas' midsection, sending him reeling toward Aquinas.

Aquinas crouched and thrust his shoulder upward. The impact knocked Lucas to the ground. Moving over the top of him, Aquinas held his sword with both hands and plunged down. Lucas quickly rolled to the side. Although he avoided his arm being impaled, the glancing blow gashed his right bicep.

Thrusting his leg out, Lucas kicked Aquinas away long enough to return to his feet. Using the flame to keep Merrick away with his left hand, he engaged Aquinas with his sword in his right; his element-enhanced reflexes lightning-fast and cat-like.

After several parries, Lucas thrust his sword toward Aquinas' stomach. The blade glanced off the Wordless Book, knocking the wind out of Aquinas and the book to the ground. Lucas immediately dropped the torch and scooped it up. Backing away from Merrick, he secured it under his belt.

Enraged, Aquinas took a deep breath and rushed straight at Lucas. With the grace of a seasoned matador, Lucas stepped to the side and swung his sword at Aquinas' neck. Merrick's weapon, however, struck first – blocking Lucas' kill-strike by the narrowest of margins. Aquinas flew by, tripped over one of the saddlebags, and fell to the ground.

At the same time, Davy stepped into the fight, plunging his dagger into Lucas' left thigh. The surprise attack drew Lucas' attention momentarily away from Merrick.

With his long blond hair flying, Merrick seized upon his waiver and spun around behind him. When Lucas raised his weapon, the razor-sharp edge of Merrick's blade struck Lucas' left hand, severing the tip of his middle finger.

Screaming in pain, Lucas swung his sword down at Davy, but the playwright raised his dagger and trapped the blade in the quillons. Undaunted, Lucas kicked Davy away and flipped his sword up. When the dagger slid off the end, he caught it in mid-air and reengaged Merrick.

The two exchanged parries at a blinding speed, their sword-on-sword clangs reverberating ever-faster across the walls of the underground catacombs.

Back on his feet, Aquinas rejoined the fight, attacking Lucas' left side. With the dagger being no match for Aquinas' longsword, Lucas sustained multiple wounds to his left arm and leg – each one glowing a pure shade of purple.

"What is this sorcery?" Davy asked, staring wide-eyed at the sight.

"He's ingested the element and it's healing him!" Aquinas yelled. "Keep fighting!"

Kicking Merrick away, Lucas threw the dagger at Aquinas, barely missing him. Turning, he retreated into the tunnel he had emerged from earlier. The blonde archer gave chase, rushing in after him. When Davy made a move to follow, Aquinas took hold of his arm and stopped him.

"You've done enough my friend."

Davy frowned. "But you need my help."

"You can help us by taking his saddlebags and getting out of here."

"Where shall I take them?"

"A kitchen or a pantry. Any place where there is olive oil."

"Olive oil?"

"It will neutralize the toxins and cleanse the stones."

He helped Davy heave the saddlebags onto his shoulders. "Remember, do not touch the stones with your bare hands until *after* they are cleansed."

"I'll remember."

Aquinas ran into the tunnel to help Merrick, emerging in a hollowed-out cavern dripping with moisture. Although the smoke was thick, the walls glowed a bright shade of violet, illuminating the entire cavity. Aquinas momentarily stopped and stared in amazement.

A bigger cache of carmot I've never seen.

Remembering Merrick, he turned his attention to the rest of the cave. A few feet ahead of him on top of a platform, sat another wood casket. The carving on the lid was more elaborate than the ones they'd passed in the corridor. Next to the casket lay pieces of a suit of armor, decorated with the same markings. The supporting tree limbs had been set on fire.

"Merrick!" Aquinas yelled.

No answer.

From behind the casket, Lucas slowly stood up.

"Where is Merrick?"

Lucas smiled.

"Tell me where Merrick is, or I swear I'll…"

Lucas laughed. "You'll do what, Aquinas? Kill me? Please do. Here's my chest, run me through!" He lowered his guard and threw his arms out.

Aquinas stared at him, the rage burning in his eyes.

"All right, I'll tell you what I've done with your precious Merrick, but first I thought you'd want to know you are standing on hallowed ground. It's not every day you bear witness to history."

"What do you mean?"

"Did you not see the other caskets and suits of armor in the passageway?"

Aquinas nodded.

"Do you know who they were?"

"I understand they were Knights of the Round Table who never returned from the quest for the holy grail."

"Exactly! And here lies the most courageous knight of all, Sir Lancelot's son Sir Galahad. Do you have any idea what this means?"

Aquinas shook his head.

"These noble knights, supposedly mankind's epitome of honesty and trustworthiness, having found the most important substance in nature, neglected to share it with the common people."

"I assume since they were men of faith, they believed the element to be sacred."

Lucas scoffed. "So they decided to simply hoard it and die? Why you continue to protect them baffles me. Humans are nothing more than selfish beings."

"You used to be human, Lucas."

"True, but as the years have passed, I have learned from my mistakes."

"Not enough, apparently."

"So tell me, Aquinas, how long must I suffer? A thousand years? Ten thousand?"

"That's not up to me to decide."

"Nor me, which is why I intend to end my existence once and for all."

"You talk of humans being selfish, yet you are willing to kill every man, woman and child to bring about *your* demise."

"Do not judge me, Aquinas! You have no idea what it's like to bear the punishment I have been given. By using the transformed stones in those saddlebags, I shall bring about a plague like the world has never seen. And when mankind falls into chaos, the Day of Reckoning will deliver me from this world!"

"Where is Merrick?"

Lucas pulled open the lid of the casket, revealing Merrick lying unconscious on top of Sir Galahad's skeletal remains. When Aquinas stepped forward, Lucas placed the tip of his sword to Merrick's throat.

"Double jeopardy, Aquinas. Attack me or try to put out the fire, Merrick dies. Do nothing and the rising temperature will destroy the remaining carmot and..." Lucas stopped and looked around. "Wait. Where is the little man?"

"What little man?"

"You know what little man. The playwright. Davy."

Aquinas smiled. "Oh, him. He had business to attend to. He said he'd just come into a fortune of gold stones."

Lucas' scream echoed off the walls.

"It appears you are the one in double jeopardy, Lucas. If you kill Merrick, by the time you get by me you'll be too late to catch Davy before he cleans the stones. Do nothing, then the remaining carmot will melt, leaving you with nothing."

Lucas smiled again. "There is another option. The Wordless Book. Your father said the book foretold *four* locations in the world where the carmot could be found, not just Amsterdam and Paris. Now that I have the book, it shouldn't be too hard to figure them out."

Aquinas laughed. "If I remember right, you were not very good at math, Lucas. Deciphering the symbols will take you decades, perhaps centuries. And even if you do decipher them, you will face the problem of interpreting the rhyming parables."

Out of the smoke behind Lucas, Davy appeared. As he crept slowly closer, the remaining smoke cleared – he still had the saddlebags draped over his shoulders!

Raising his dagger, Davy plunged it toward Lucas' back. The instant before it made contact, the unseen force stopped the blade. Startled, the playwright stood there a moment not knowing what to do.

Lucas turned and delivered a solid left fist to Davy's head, knocking him to the ground. Returning to face Aquinas, he unmercifully plunged the tip of his sword into Merrick's throat.

"No!" Aquinas screamed.

Instantly awake, Merrick began choking and gasping for air. As he tried to climb out, the casket tipped over and fell off the platform sprawling him and the skeleton of Sir Galahad across the floor.

Aquinas lunged his sword at Lucas' leg, but the big man was too fast. Jumping out of the way, Lucas swung his weapon down and knocked the sword from Aquinas' hand. Following up, he stabbed Aquinas in the chest – completely running him through!

Aquinas fell to his knees, then down onto one arm.

Towering over him, Lucas smiled. "You knew this day would eventually come, Aquinas. You and Merrick simply ran out of luck."

Behind him, Merrick crawled over to the wall and spread a handful of carmot on his throat wound.

"I have to hand it to you though," Lucas continued, "you both were tenacious. Not everyone would dedicate their lives to a cause. I shall therefore be merciful and not let you suffer."

He moved over to the side of Aquinas and raised his sword, but the instant he swung it down Merrick's blade blocked it. Lucas turned and was immediately met by follow-on strikes to his right arm and leg. Merrick's lightning-fast blows sent him reeling backwards, where he tripped over Davy and fell to the ground. Moving fast, Merrick dragged Aquinas over to the wall, scooped out a handful of carmot, and spread it on his chest wound.

Returning to his feet, Lucas grabbed the saddlebags and ran out of the chamber. When Merrick turned to follow, the little man stopped him.

"You need not bother," Davy said.

"What do you mean?" Merrick asked, his voice raspy.

"What I mean is, do not trouble yourself."

Still catching his breath, Aquinas lit into Davy. "Have you lost your mind? With those saddlebags of transformed stones, he'll release a disease upon the city!"

Davy smiled. "With four saddlebags full of dirt? I don't think he'll be releasing anything."

"What did you do with the gold?"

"I told you money doesn't interest me. My writing has already earned me more than I'll ever need. I therefore took the saddlebags to the bridge we passed and emptied them into the chasm."

Merrick cleared his throat several times. When he finally spoke, his voice was back to normal. "Good thinking, but with his heightened awareness, I wonder why Lucas didn't notice."

"You're forgetting how unpredictable the carmot is," Aquinas said. "Sometimes it works miracles. A minute later, it can be useless. In any event, we are now left with an even greater problem."

"Greater problem?" Davy asked.

"Yes. Lucas now has the Wordless Book."

"I'm sorry, My Captain," Merrick said.

"No need to be sorry, my friend. Thankfully the carmot was near and you are all right."

"As for the carmot, what shall we do?"

Aquinas thought for a moment. "Let us review the facts. Lucas knows we've deciphered some of the symbols in the Wordless Book, but he *doesn't* know we've identified the two other areas in the world where the carmot can be found. I only wish the rhyming parables were more specific."

"More specific?" Davy asked.

"While some of the phrases are easy to understand, others can be quite vague and open to interpretation," Merrick explained. "Although Aquinas and I have read them so many times we could recite them in our sleep, we only know the *general* areas where the carmot lies, not the *exact* locations."

"If they are as complex as you say, then you have no way of knowing how long it will take this madman to decipher the symbols and glean the information."

"Or which area of the world he will go to first," Merrick added.

Aquinas nodded. "And since we are now living on borrowed time, we are left in quite a predicament."

Davy raised an eyebrow.

"The carmot we've ingested will keep us alive for one, possibly two more centuries." Merrick explained. "If we are unable to obtain more, we will regress back to our original state of being. Therefore, to continue the Great Work, we must find Lucas, contain him, and recover the Wordless Book."

"A tall order, to be sure," Davy said.

"Which is why Merrick and I will split up, and keep watch on both locations," Aquinas said.

"What if he comes back here?"

"If he does, he won't find anything," Merrick said. "Look around you, Davy. The rising temperature from the fire is melting the carmot at a rapid rate. It will soon be gone."

"What can I do to help?"

"First, we must wait here and make sure all the carmot melts," Aquinas replied. "Then we shall go back to the cistern room and conceal the passageway leading down here."

"Why, pray tell?"

"The missing Knights of the Round Table would be a great attraction to scholars and historians. If they came down here, they would undoubtedly explore the rest of these tunnels, find a way down into the chasm, and happen across the transformed stones you cast off the bridge."

"I understand," Davy replied. "Anything else?"

"Just one thing. Merrick, hold the torch close. I want to show Davy something."

Pulling off his necklace, Aquinas held it by the chain, suspended it in front of Davy's face, and began twisting it back and forth.

~ The Wanderer ~

Once Lucas was out of the cathedral, he headed straight for the livery stable and retrieved his horse.

Proceeding over the *Rue de la Cité* bridge, he began yelling, "Gold! I've found gold for everyone!"

Soon a crowd had gathered.

"Where is this gold you speak of?" one man asked.

"Here! Look in my saddlebags. I have gold for everyone!"

He threw the saddlebags into the crowd, at which point the people began fighting to tear them open.

Seeing their greed, Lucas grinned.

"There's nothing here but dirt!" a man yelled.

The smile instantly disappeared from Lucas' face.

"Charlatan!" a woman screamed.

As more and more insults filled the air, some of the people began throwing stones.

Lucas turned his horse and quickly rode away, despising people all-the-more.

When he reached the outskirts of the city, he stopped on the bank of the Seine River and thought about his situation.

All is not lost. I now have the Wordless Book.

Pulling it out from under his belt, he opened the book and examined it. With his intuition telling him it was the *real* Wordless Book, and not a counterfeit like Aquinas' father Augustus had tricked him into taking, his spirits brightened.

After all these years, advantage has finally tipped to my favor! Although I didn't kill Aquinas or Merrick, I took their only means of finding the carmot. And without more of the magical element, they will wither and die.

Remembering the few transformed stones in his pockets, he withdrew a handful. Still covered with the dark-purple residue, he smiled and threw them into the water.

~ Present Day ~

The blinking lights from a bevy of emergency vehicles lit up the approaching highway interchange, coloring the night horizon in rich shades of crimson. As traffic slowed to a crawl, a police cruiser parked in the left lane and facing us came into view. An officer standing in front of the cruiser motioned for all vehicles to move to the right lane. After falling in line, another officer, standing on the dotted lines in the middle of the road, stopped the semi-truck in front of us.

Madison pressed the "Pause" button on the CD player.

"What do we do now, George?"

"Play it cool, sweetheart. We've done nothing wrong."

When the semi moved on, we pulled up.

"What's the trouble, officer?" Madison asked.

His eyes traveled around the driver's side door. "What happened to your window, ma'am?"

"Vandals. We reported it to the St. George police."

He nodded. "We've got an accident ahead involving a chemical spill. This highway is closed until further notice. We're diverting everyone north to Kanab. If you're headed to Flagstaff, you'll have to take 89 east to Page, then south through Bitter Springs."

"Thank you, officer."

"And I advise you to get your window fixed as soon as you can. The weather around Flagstaff can be unpredictable."

"We'll do that. Thanks again."

Madison pulled forward, and we took our place in line behind the semi.

* * *

As soon as we were back up to speed and headed to Kanab, Madison turned to me.

"Are you ready to hear more, George?"

"Are you kidding? I'm chomping at the bit. How about you?"

"I can't believe what I am hearing. I'm just stunned my uncle kept all of this to himself."

She pressed the "Play" button on the CD player.

Aquinas' (Uncle Charlie's) voice came on, giving a summation of the events in the Paris underground.

"Our battle against the Wanderer in the secret catacombs had ended, but not without casualties. In the days that followed, the Seine River, which supplies culinary water to Paris, became contaminated, resulting in a cholera epidemic. More than one-hundred-thousand Parisians ended up losing their lives. I highly suspect Lucas must have cast some transformed gold into the river."

Madison glanced over at me and mouthed the word, "Wow!"

"As for Davy de la Pailleterie, he returned to writing and continued his Sunday duties as the Archbishop's historian and scribe. The talented playwright would eventually garner fame by publishing several books under the pen name, Alexandre Dumas.

"Using the power of suggestion, I made Davy forget what happened beneath the Notre-Dame Cathedral. An exception occurred a little more than ten years later, when I learned Davy had written an adventure novel titled, *The Three Musketeers*. When I obtained a copy and finished reading it, I realized he had fashioned his swashbuckling character "d'Artagnan" after Merrick and me."

Madison and I laughed.

"Splitting up," Aquinas continued, "Merrick and I traveled to different regions of the world where the Wordless Book foretold the carmot could be found. While Merrick kept a watchful eye on the eastern region of the United States, I proceeded to the southern-most tip of South America, and maintained surveillance at Cape Horn's main shipping port.

"Our silent vigil would last more than eighty-six years, until the day finally came when I received a wired message from Merrick, informing me he had spotted Lucas. I immediately booked passage on a steamship heading north and rejoined him.

"At the time, I had no idea we would soon confront the Wanderer at a location even more perilous than the secret underground catacombs. The year was 1918, at the brink of the towering horseshoe waterfall near Niagara, New York."

On the New Frontier
the land's point becomes two.
As the great rivers tumble
the water stays blue.

A maiden stands watch
from ethereal halls,
as the carmot gives life
from a cleft in the falls.

**Aquinas' and Merrick's interpretation of the third group of
symbols in the first chapter of the Wordless Book**

CHAPTER SEVEN: THE NIAGARA ENCOUNTER

Monday, 5 August 1918, 14:35hrs
Along the Niagara River
Thirty-Seven Miles Northwest of Buffalo, New York

The bright morning sun glistened off the water, its tranquil appearance cloaking nature's violence laying a short distance away. As the channel narrowed, the flow accelerated, transforming the slow-moving current into rapids. Reaching the end of the land shelf, the now-raging river separated before plunging more than a hundred and fifty feet into an immense gorge, the cascading water creating three majestic falls. Reaching the bottom, the moisture infused the surrounding air, creating a gigantic cloud dimming the canyon floor.

It was here, amid the picturesque splendor of North America's great natural wonder, where Aquinas and Merrick would again confront the Wanderer.

Aquinas had arrived in Buffalo earlier this morning. He had planned to meet Merrick in a café in the center of town, but when he began walking toward the rendezvous point, his element-enhanced senses detected a man following him. Stopping to look in a store window, he saw Merrick in the reflection. Although he was now sporting a beard and long dark hair, his youthful and fit appearance, emitting a healthy and charismatic glow, were unmistakable.

Merrick moved next to him, pretending to be interested in what the store had to offer.

Aquinas cleared his throat. "According to an article I recently read about North American etiquette, if someone reunites with a friend they haven't seen in over eighty years, it is customary to render a handshake."

Both men laughed and embraced.

"How are you, My Captain?" Merrick asked.

"No worse for wear, my friend. And you?"

"I am well. Tell me, how did you know it was me?"

"Over the years, I've found you to be an excellent swordsman and an unmatched expert with a bow and arrow. Your skills at dying your hair, however, need improvement."

"What do you mean?'

"Your locks are black, but your roots are blonde."

The men laughed again.

Following a lengthy meal filled with reminiscing, they proceeded to the border and crossed over into Canada. Reaching a cliff overlooking the falls, they stopped for a few minutes to take in the sight.

"One of the Almighty's magnificent creations," Aquinas commented.

"It truly is, My Captain. I've been working for a construction company building a new road around the falls, which allows me the privilege of witnessing their grandeur every day. It's still hard for me to believe a woman went over the horseshoe-shaped one in a barrel and survived."

"I remember reading about her. An American schoolteacher, wasn't she?"

Merrick nodded. "Sixty-two years of age, no less. Ever since, people have been trying to eclipse the feat."

"Have any been successful?"

"Only one. With the great height, rocks below the surface, and frigid water, the others have perished."

Aquinas shook his head. "If they only realized life should be cherished, not gambled in a meaningless tempt of fate."

They followed the river upstream until tugboats and a barge came into view. Proceeding into a secluded area of the woods, Merrick removed a tarnished brass spyglass from his pocket, fully extended the lens, and handed it to Aquinas.

"This is what I wanted to show you, sir," he said. "On the other side of the river is Goat Island. Observe the large building."

Aquinas held the spyglass up to his eye.

"Note the barbed wire on top of the fences and the contingent of armed guards," Merrick continued. "Both were put in place less than three months ago."

"What's inside?"

"As far as anyone knows, spare parts for hydroelectrical generators. In the dead of night, however, many trucks have been delivering boxes and piping. Then two weeks ago, this strange activity stopped, which coincided with the day I saw Lucas departing the building. I thought of following him, but with the large number of tourists at the border, I wouldn't have been able to stay with him. That's when I decided to contact you and further investigate this building."

"A wise choice. Do you know who owns it?"

"According to the city office, an American company. There are also two other American companies generating power on the river, which by all accounts were quite lucrative until four months ago."

"What happened?"

"Contrary to the wishes of their stockholders, their presidents agreed to a merger. This new conglomerate is now called the Niagara Consolidated Power Company. They control all the electricity being generated on the American side of the river, to include all dredging operations."

"Forgive my lack of education, my friend, but what exactly is dredging?"

Merrick smiled. "Observe the barge, which the locals here simply refer to as *Old Scow*. It's the vessel being towed."

Aquinas looked through the spyglass. "Why does it need to be towed?"

"It has no propellers. Its engine is being used to operate what is called a *sand sucker*. As the tug pulls it along, it sucks up the rocks from the riverbed and deposits them in the hold."

"For what purpose?"

"So ships won't run aground. As the rocks fill the hold, large hatches on the sides vent out the displaced air."

"Sounds like dangerous work, especially so close to the falls."

Merrick shook his head. "The tugboats aren't allowed any closer than half a mile from the falls, which is considered the *point of no return*."

"And if a ship strays by this point of no return?"

"They would enter the most-treacherous channel in the river, and the swift current would sweep them over the falls."

Aquinas thought for a moment. "But what of the barge? With no propellers, doesn't it run the risk of going by the point of no return?"

"Not really. Once fully laden, another tug joins the first and together they tow *Old Scow* to a landing. The rocks are off-loaded and taken to a landfill. The road, which circles the island, passes the landing and this building."

Aquinas immediately concluded what Merrick was alluding to. "Which means if Lucas has somehow burrowed his way into this company, he now has the means to search for the cleft in the falls, and perhaps a place to store the carmot after he recovers it. Ingenious, but we must be sure."

"I am sure. The day I saw him, he was arm-in-arm with this woman."

Merrick reached into his pocket, withdrew a folded page of a newspaper, and handed it to him. The headline read: "Gwendolyn Phillips Strikes Blow for Women's Suffrage, Becomes Sole Proprietor of Niagara Falls Consolidated Power Company! Millionaire Philanthropist Pledges Sizeable Donation to War Effort."

Aquinas' eyes grew wide. "Just as the Wordless Book foretold."

"Yes, My Captain. Lucas has found the influential woman with the black heart."

"With her money and resources at his fingertips, he's got everything he needs, save the carmot, to bring about the Day of Reckoning. We must hurry. Any ideas on how to breach the building?"

Merrick nodded. "There are two entrances, one on the west end and the large door on the south side facing us. On the east end there is a metal screen at the top of the gable for ventilation. It appears large enough for us to fit through, provided we can pry it off."

"What about the guards?"

"Every evening at ten o'clock there is a change of personnel. The ones who worked during the day go home, and two others arrive, who take turns patrolling throughout the night."

"What do we have for the incursion?"

"In addition to revolvers and knives, I've acquired a grappling hook, rope, ten sticks of dynamite, and a Winchester repeating rifle for you. I'll stand fast with my longbow. If the need arises to eliminate anyone, we may need its silence. I also have a blanket for crossing the fence and two new pairs of handcuffs for confining Lucas."

"You've thought of everything."

Merrick smiled. "What is our plan, sir?"

Aquinas thought for a moment. "If Lucas has already recovered the carmot, we shall ingest some and destroy the rest."

"What if we find nothing?"

"Then we'll make our way to the barge and hide in the hold, which will enable us to be on hand when he does find it."

"One thing still bewilders me, sir. When warmed, the carmot melts. How could it be here, underneath a raging river in the middle of summer?"

"I've given this some thought, so let us review the parable. It first stated, *On the New Frontier, the land's point becomes two.* No great mystery there. Many countries still refer to North America as the New Frontier, and the name Niagara is derived from the Iroquois Indian word meaning, *a point of land cut in two.*"

Merrick nodded. "We were very fortunate to have found the book detailing the history of the region."

"Fortunate? I believe it was divinely provided to us, but that is for another discussion. Let us now examine the next line, which stated, *As the great rivers tumble, the water stays blue.*"

"Self-explanatory," Merrick posited. "The azure water cascading over the falls is a magnificent sight."

"Agreed. And the next line, *A maiden stands watch from ethereal halls,* is referring to the Indian legend."

"Again, from the history book."

Aquinas nodded. "Which now brings us to the most important line of the parable, *as the carmot gives life from a cleft in the falls.* Note how it states the carmot *gives* life, not *gave life,* or *will give life.* The parable is in the present tense, which means the carmot is in a perpetual state of giving. You said the water is frigid. Does it stay frigid all year around?"

"Why yes, now that you mention it."

"Which proves the cleft is open to a vein of carmot, one which remains frozen all year long and cools the water as it flows by. And since the water doesn't melt it, the vein must be quite large."

Merrick smiled. "Superb deduction, sir."

"Thank you. Unfortunately, if we are unable to confine Lucas, we will need to figure out a way to destroy the carmot in the river so he cannot continue to obtain it."

"You need not worry, sir. I pilfered the dynamite from my employer. In addition to building roads, they also perform underwater excavations. The fuses are coated with wax, allowing the charges to go off when submerged. When we locate the cleft, we can significantly enlarge it."

"Excellent. We shall therefore assault the building tonight."

"Tonight it is, My Captain."

* * *

Forty-five minutes after midnight, having made their way onto Goat Island, Aquinas and Merrick arrived at the building owned by the Niagara Falls Consolidated Power Company.

Crouching low in a thicket of bushes, they waited until the guard passed before climbing over the fence. After Merrick's well-placed throw of the grappling hook and another quick climb, they were soon perched on the roof above the gable vent. With Aquinas holding his legs, Merrick bent over the edge and used his knife to pry the vent lose. Two minutes later they were inside, crawling through the roof rafters.

The ceiling was open to the floor below and the lights were on, giving the men a bird's eye view of the interior of the building. Directly beneath them sat tall metal bins full of assorted parts. The far end had been partitioned off and contained a small door and window. Through the window, an office and an exit door could be seen. Between the bins and the partition stood a cube-shaped structure resembling a tool shed, on top of which sat six compressors; each connected to a pipe protruding from one side and emitting a pumping sound. On the side closest to the wall, power cables ran to a fuse box.

"What is it, sir?" Merrick whispered.

"I believe it is called a refrigeration unit," Aquinas whispered back. "It keeps things cold, like an icebox but without the ice. The compressors on top circulate a chemical through the pipes which cool the inside. I've seen pictures of similar ones in trade magazines, but none this large."

"If it does as you say, it would be the perfect place to store the carmot."

Aquinas nodded. "Let's find out."

The office door unexpectedly opened and one of the guards walked out. Remaining motionless, they watched the guard smoke a cigarette, turn, and depart.

Using one of the tall bins as a makeshift ladder, Merrick climbed down to the floor. A moment later, when Aquinas joined him, Merrick pointed to the bottom shelf of a nearby bin.

"Look, My Captain," he said, still whispering. "More evidence."

Among the parts sat several large jugs of olive oil.

"Good work," Aquinas replied. "Now let's see what is in here."

After checking to make sure the guards weren't watching through the small window, they moved around to the front of the refrigeration unit and examined the door. Mounted flush, the door had three large hinges on the left side and a heavy-duty handle on the right. Grasping the handle, Aquinas found it locked.

"How do you propose we get in, sir?" Merrick asked.

Aquinas examined the door for a moment. "Notice the small gap between the striker plate and the edge of the door where the latch is visible?"

Merrick nodded.

"When I first arrived at Cape Horn, I took a job as a night watchman at a shipping warehouse, which gave me time to read many books, magazines and newspapers. Several of the articles were about break-ins which had baffled the local police. When they finally apprehended the burglar, they learned he had been using a clever technique to get through a locked door."

While he was talking, Aquinas retrieved his knife from his belt, slid it between the gap, and pried on the latch; moving it slightly before it sprang back to its previous position.

"When I move the latch back, use your knife to hold it."

In a flash, Merrick had his knife in his hand and slid it into the gap. Working quickly, they soon had the latch fully compressed.

Merrick smiled. "A clever burglar indeed."

When Aquinas pulled the door open, they were met with a blast of cold air. Three racks of shelving lined the interior walls of the refrigeration unit, each holding a wooden box with a hinged lid. Other than a large black "X" marked on the box to the right, and a similar-sized "C" marked on the box on the back shelf, they appeared to be identical. Moving in to investigate, Aquinas opened the box on the right and found it full of gold rocks. Following suit, Merrick opened the box on the left and found it also full of gold but with a strong odor of olive oil permeating from within. When Aquinas opened the box on the back shelf, bright violet light lit up the interior of the refrigeration unit.

"Lucas has apparently found the cleft in the falls," Merrick said.

Aquinas nodded. "And he's been busy."

The men hurriedly scooped out a handful of carmot and began ingesting it. Almost immediately, the magical element went to work, enhancing their instincts and making them feel younger.

Once they were finished, Aquinas smiled. "This should hold us for another century or two."

"What about the rest, sir," Merrick asked. "Shall I prepare the dynamite?"

Aquinas shook his head. "All we need to do is remove the fuses supplying power. The warming temperature will do our work for us."

"Let me guess, you learned how electricity works?"

"You can gain a wealth of knowledge from reading, my friend."

Merrick smiled. "True, but your wealth would be a pittance if I'd have tested your knowledge on dredging a river."

Both men stifled laughs.

"Speaking of wealth, sir, what should we do about the gold?"

Aquinas thought for a moment and retrieved one of the jugs of olive oil. Pulling out the cork, he motioned for Merrick to hold the lid open on the box marked with an "X," and saturated the rocks.

"Fill your pockets," Aquinas said. "They can't hurt anyone now."

Merrick's smile immediately vanished. "My Captain," he whispered, "a guard is coming."

Aquinas quickly retrieved his rifle and moved behind the side of the threshold. Following his lead, Merrick hid behind the opposite side.

"You in there!" the guard yelled. "Come out with your hands up!"

Aquinas removed his necklace, raised his hands, and slowly stepped out. Merrick retrieved an arrow from his quiver and placed it in his longbow.

The guard, a man in his early twenties, had his revolver drawn. When their eyes made contact, Aquinas immediately sensed his nervousness.

"Drop the rifle or I'll shoot," the guard ordered.

Aquinas gently set the rifle down and let the necklace dangle from his free hand.

"Who are you?"

Aquinas answered with a calm and soothing voice. "My name is really unimportant,"

"What do you have in your hand?"

"Oh, this little thing? A crystal pendant I acquired on a recent trip to Calcutta. Quite exquisite, don't you think?" While he was talking, Aquinas slowly moved toward him and began twisting the chain back and forth. "Its beauty is matched by the tranquil effect of the light reflecting off it," Aquinas continued, "making anyone who looks at it sleepy, very sleepy."

The guard's eyelids closed and his mouth dropped open. Relieving him of his gun, Aquinas asked, "What is your name?"

"Johnathan Colby," the guard replied.

"Nice to meet you, Mr. Colby. Now listen to me very carefully. I want you to tell me everything you know about this place and what is going on here."

* * *

After questioning the security guard and removing the fuses supplying power to the refrigeration unit, Aquinas and Merrick exited the building and made their way to the landing where the tugboats and barge lay moored. Boarding the tug *Hassayampa*, they quickly searched the vessel and found no one aboard. Meeting back in the crew's galley, Merrick laid down on a bench, while Aquinas stretched back in a folding deck chair.

"Sir," Merrick said, "from what we learned from Mr. Colby, Lucas is in Kansas delivering two boxes of transformed gold. How will we be able to stop the epidemic?"

Aquinas sighed. "Unfortunately, we won't be able to stop it."

"Do you think it is enough to bring about the Day of Reckoning?"

"My instincts are telling me no. Before my father died, he told me The Wanderer needed a large quantity of carmot to bring about the final day. Although those two boxes will kill many people, I still think he needs to acquire more."

"I'm sorry I didn't take an interest in this building sooner."

"No need to be regretful. You didn't know Lucas had wormed his way into the leadership hierarchy of this power company. We must now focus our efforts on destroying the carmot remaining in the river, and thus deprive him of another source."

"How do you want to proceed?"

Aquinas thought for a moment. "When the tugboat captain reports for duty, we shall use the power of suggestion to persuade him to tow the barge to the cleft in the falls. Before we get underway, we'll transfer to the barge and hide in the hold. When we reach the cleft, we'll drop the dynamite through the hold's ventilation hatch. Hopefully, it will be enough to significantly open the cleft. If all goes as planned, by the time Lucas returns all the carmot in the Niagara River will have melted away."

"You make it sound simple, sir. But there's one thing I don't understand. If Lucas and this Gwendolyn woman discovered the cleft three weeks ago, why did they not wait here until they had mined *all* of the carmot before traveling to Kansas?"

"Good question. The only explanation I can think of is they must've learned of the American Army's embarkation point at Fort Riley. With thousands of troops deploying overseas to fight the war, it is the perfect place to spread a disease around the world. Perhaps by rushing off to Kansas to make the gold donation, they're hoping to clear a path for future donations."

"But sir, he cannot *give* the gold to the troops."

"No, but he can donate the gold to the Army's Quartermaster Corps, who control the currency paid to the troops."

Merrick's eyes grew wide. "And what better way to infect the troops, than by infecting their pay. It's brilliant."

"I agree. Lucas is as cunning as he is brazen. We do, however, have two advantages. When he gained possession of the Wordless Book, he didn't know we had already deciphered the symbols telling of the two remaining locations of the carmot."

"But having discovered the carmot, Lucas and his confederate will surely have ingested it. With their instincts now as sharp as a razor, when they return later today, they'll know we're here."

Aquinas smiled. "I'm counting on it. What better place to contain the Wanderer than in the hold of a dredging barge?"

Merrick smiled. "What is the other advantage?"

"When he comes for us, we will be waiting for him."

~ The Wanderer ~

Lucas and Gwendolyn arrived at the Goat Island building shortly after two o'clock in the afternoon. As they approached in their new Studebaker "Special Six" automobile, Elliot Pierce, the shift supervisor of the guards, and his deputy Steven Byrns met them at the entry gate.

"Ma'am," Pierce said, "we've had a power outage."

Before he could explain, they climbed out of the car and ran into the building. Rushing to the refrigeration unit, Lucas quickly unlocked the latch and threw open the door. Instead of feeling the freezing temperature, the air inside was warm and stale. Hurrying to the wooden box on the rear shelf, he found it empty – the carmot melted and evaporated.

Gwendolyn opened the lid of the unmarked box of gold. Finding it all there, she turned and lit into Mr. Pierce.

"How long has the power been out?"

Pierce checked his clipboard. "It was reported to me at 9:45 this morning, ma'am."

"Did you inform the refrigeration company?"

"Yes ma'am. They sent out a repair man and he found the fuses missing."

"Missing? Who's been in here?"

"No one I am aware of."

"When you swore allegiance to me, I warned you I will not tolerate incompetence!"

Promptly withdrawing a pistol from under her dress, she shot Pierce in the head. As his body fell to the ground, she turned and addressed his second in command. "You are in charge of the guards now, Mr. Byrns. Can you tell me why the repair man hasn't fixed the refrigeration unit?"

Byrns cleared his throat. "He had to return to his company to get some new fuses. He should be back within the hour."

"Very well. See to it Mr. Pierce is taken care of."

Byrns retrieved Pierce's clipboard and motioned to two guards watching from the office window. As they carried the body out, Lucas walked over to Gwendolyn.

"Aquinas is here."

"I sense two men," she replied.

"The second is Merrick."

"But how?"

"Obviously, before I recovered the Wordless Book, they deciphered the symbols telling of this location."

"If they intend to destroy the carmot…"

"Then they are now aboard the barge."

They looked out across the river. The barge was approaching the area of the river where they'd found the cleft.

Gwendolyn motioned to Byrns, who quickly rejoined her.

"Which tug is towing *Old Scow*?" she asked.

Byrns checked the clipboard. "The *Hassayampa*."

"Radio the *Hassayampa* and have Captain Wallace tow it in immediately."

"No, this is my fight!" Lucas snarled. "Radio the *Kinch* to come in and take me out there."

Byrns looked at Gwendolyn then back to Lucas.

"Excuse us for a moment, Mr. Byrns," Gwendolyn said. As soon as the guard was out of earshot, she addressed Lucas in a stern tone. "It's not safe to confront them out there."

"Aquinas and Merrick have meddled in my affairs for the last time, and you're forgetting I am safe no matter where I go."

* * *

Captain John Wallace of the tugboat *Hassayampa* walked toward the stern, where he stopped to check the steel towing cable.

Satisfied the extended tow line was secure, he returned to the bridge. After receiving the "all clear" signal from the other tugs standing by, he eased the throttle forward. As the low rumbling sound of the engines became louder, the eighty-foot-long *Old Scow* tethered behind it slowly moved forward. A moment later, a large pipe began discharging sand, silt, and rocks into the cargo hold.

When the tugboat *Kinch* pulled alongside, Lucas jumped aboard. Entering the bridge, he reached into his pocket and withdrew a large diamond attached to a thin chain. He rocked the jewel back and forth in front of the captain's face. A moment later, the captain was in a trance.

"Why did you return to dredge this area when I told you not to?" Lucas asked.

"Miss Phillips ordered me to, sir," Wallace replied.

"And when did she give you this order?"

"Earlier this morning."

Aquinas' power of suggestion is impressive, but not as strong as mine.

With Captain Wallace still staring out the window, Lucas left the bridge and made his way aft. Taking hold of the tow cable, he swung out over the water and began inching his way toward the barge; his legs dangling merely a foot above the raging river. Less than five minutes later, he boarded *Old Scow*.

Gustave Lofberg, a veteran seafarer of more than forty-two years, and Frank Harris, his young apprentice, met Lucas as he climbed over the railing.

"Are you trying to kill yourself, lad?" Lofberg yelled.

Pretending he couldn't hear over the rumbling noise of the sand sucker, Lucas pointed to his ear and shook his head.

"Follow us to the bridge!"

Walking behind the two men, Lucas retrieved the chain and diamond from his pocket. Soon after, Lofberg and Harris were hypnotized like Captain Wallace.

"Open the firearms locker," Lucas ordered.

Lofberg retrieved a ring of keys from his pocket and opened the compartment.

After tucking two revolvers under his belt, Lucas handed each of the men a rifle. "There are two stowaways onboard who are hiding in the hold. Mr. Lofberg, you shall go aft and cover the rear access hatch. Mr. Harris, you shall cover the forward hatch. When they come out, you are to kill them. Do you understand?"

"I understand," the men replied, in unison.

Once they were gone, Lucas retrieved a rifle for himself and hurried outside to the dredging pipe. As he approached, the rocks and sand spewing into the hold turned violet.

The barge is picking up the carmot. We're over the cleft!

When he reached the hatch and knelt to look in, a massive explosion erupted off the starboard side. The blast hurled rocks, sand, and bits of carmot into the air.

Old Scow instantly tilted hard to starboard, its top deck plunging lower than the water level. The unexpected list and deluge of water knocked Lucas off his feet and carried him to the railing. Reaching out to grab ahold, he lost his grip on the rifle and the water swept it overboard.

Below deck at opposite ends of the barge, Lofberg and Harris were thrown against the port wall, snapping them out of Lucas' spell.

Seconds later, the barge tipped back up, righting itself.

Regaining his footing, Lucas withdrew his revolvers. Returning to the top hatch of the hold, he squeezed by the dredging pipe and dove in.

THE ELEMENT

~ Aboard the Hassayampa ~

Standing motionless, Captain Wallace stared vacantly out the window, unaware the rapid current had changed the heading of his boat, sending him on a collision course with a large sandbar. The instant the tug ran aground the barge listed from the explosion, and the steel towing cable pulled overly taut. The pressure overtaxed the tensile strength of the cable, and like a musician plucking the strings of a harp, the metal strands began snapping one after the other. Seconds later the tow line severed altogether, separating the two vessels and leaving the barge to the mercy of the swift flowing river.

The abrupt grounding of the tug threw Captain Wallace face-first into the front window of the bridge, shattering not only the glass but also his nose and cheekbone. The sharp pain brought him out of Lucas' spell, and when he rose to his feet and looked through the aft window, he shuddered with fright. He immediately pulled the handle of the tug's whistle, signaling an emergency, and activated the *Hassayampa's* disaster beacon.

Grabbing the radio's microphone, he shouted, "Emergency SOS! Repeat, emergency SOS! *Old Scow* is adrift! I say again, *Old Scow* is adrift! Lofberg and Harris are still aboard!"

Receiving the message, the fire departments in Ontario and New York, as well as the US Coast Guard Stations at Fort Niagara and Buffalo, sprang into action. In a matter of minutes, an impromptu taskforce had assembled, its leaders considering all options for an immediate rescue operation. As the news reached the public, thousands of concerned citizens rushed to the banks of the Niagara River to watch the crisis unfold.

Unknown to the agencies coordinating the rescue, or the people watching along the shoreline, there were three other men aboard the barge, two of whom were fighting for the survival of mankind.

As Aquinas' and Merrick's battle to stop The Wanderer raged in the hold below deck, the powerless *Old Scow* floated toward the point of no return, and the fast-approaching rim of Horseshoe Falls.

~ Aboard Old Scow ~

Like rays of sunshine penetrating through pockets of scattered clouds, the light from the carmot pierced the darkness, bathing the inside of the barge's cargo hold in a bright shade of violet. As pieces of the element began transforming the dredged rocks they'd landed on, the rays of light dimmed to a purple glow. A moment later the stones glistened gold, giving the hold the appearance of a treasure trove of unlimited wealth, while at the same time, masking the toxic residue that could unleash a deadly disease.

Crouched behind a bulkhead, Aquinas watched Lucas dive through the open hatch and land in the center of the compartment, brandishing a revolver in each hand. When he moved clear of a mound of gold, Aquinas carefully aimed his rifle and pulled the trigger. The shot struck Lucas' right leg, dropping him into a pile of carmot, but seconds later, having spread the element over the wound, he stood up as if he hadn't been injured. Returning fire, Lucas squeezed off four rounds in succession, whereupon Aquinas ducked back behind the bulkhead, the bullets flashing as they struck the heavy steel.

Merrick, who'd thrown the bundle of dynamite out of the hold's vent hatch, had positioned himself on the other side of the compartment, and when Lucas fired at Aquinas he drew back his longbow, steadied his aim, and released the shot. The arrow sliced through Lucas' right bicep, spinning him around, and he fell to his knees behind another heap of carmot and half-transformed stones. Before Lucas could retrieve another handful of the element, Aquinas fired again. The bullet knocked the revolver from Lucas' left hand.

A second later, another arrow pierced Lucas' right thigh, followed by another hitting his left shoulder. Aquinas followed up by firing three more shots, the salvo striking Lucas' right arm. Barely managing to return to his feet, Lucas attempted to dive into another pile of carmot-rich rocks. Another arrow from Merrick's longbow, however, cut through his left calf and stopped him in his tracks.

The firefight ended in less than a minute, with Lucas on the ground unable to move his extremities. Aquinas stepped out from behind the bulkhead and relieved him of the second gun. Merrick also stepped out, his longbow drawn and ready.

"It's not over," Lucas snarled. "My wounds are already healing."

"It will be," Aquinas replied, "once we have you in a cage."

Aquinas motioned to Merrick. In a flash, the archer brandished a set of shackles. When he attempted to place them on Lucas' wrists, the steel restraints passed *through* them.

Realizing what was happening, Aquinas stepped forward and struck Lucas in the head with the butt of his rifle, sending him face-first to the deck.

"I'm sorry, sir," Merrick said. "I should've been prepared for his hypnotic trickery."

"No apology necessary. We can easily forget his ability to hypnotize his adversaries is just as formidable as his strong physique. As fortune would have it, you have provided us with a way to identify him, even when he's using the power of suggestion."

"What do you mean, sir?"

"When you tried to place the shackles on him, did you notice his left hand?"

Merrick's eyes grew wide. "His middle finger!"

Aquinas smiled. "Precisely. He couldn't hide the missing tip. If he ever escapes us, we must remember that."

After securing Lucas' wrists behind his back, Merrick attached a set of shackles to his ankles. Sitting him up, Aquinas stood guard while Merrick searched him.

"Sir," Merrick said, "he does not have the Wordless Book."

"Most likely in the possession of his confederate," Aquinas replied, "which means before we go any further, we must recover it."

Regaining consciousness, Lucas began laughing.

"What amuses you?" Merrick asked.

"You won't be going any further," Lucas replied.

"What do you mean?"

"You've ingested the carmot. What's your intuition telling you?"

Aquinas and Merrick looked at each other.

Lucas laughed again. "We're about to go over the falls. And when we do, no amount of carmot will be able to save either of you. I, on the other hand, will most-assuredly survive the plunge."

Aquinas motioned to Merrick, who turned and ran to the forward access hatch.

"My new friend Gwendolyn is a very rich businesswoman," Lucas continued. "Perhaps I'll have her company erect a memorial in your honor, but this presents the problem of who will be alive to read it after the disease decimates the population."

Merrick returned out of breath. "Sir, he speaks the truth. The tug is nowhere to be seen, and we are advancing toward the falls."

Lucas smiled. "Double jeopardy again, Aquinas. If you stay here, you'll perish when the barge goes over the falls. If you leave now and save yourselves, I will surely get away."

Aquinas thought for a moment and turned to Merrick. "My friend, I've always known you to keep extra ammunition. Did you save any dynamite?"

Merrick pulled the quiver off his shoulder and turned it upside down. Three sticks fell out.

Aquinas turned to Lucas. "You are forgetting the third option."

"There is no third option," he snarled.

Aquinas smiled. "There is if we sink the barge."

* * *

On the bridge, the young dredger Harris stared wide-eyed and trembling at the course ahead. "What do we do?" he asked, his cracking voice betraying his fear.

The cool-headed and seasoned Lofberg casually walked over and took hold of the wheel. "No worries, lad. We'll beach her. Go aft and drop anchor."

After Harris departed, Lofberg sighted a large sandbar off the starboard bow and spun the wheel. When the rudder turned it struck a submerged boulder, and the aged bolts connecting the steering mechanism sheared off, leaving it inoperable.

Seconds later, Harris reached the anchor. When he pulled the handle, it remained locked in place – its rusty chain jammed against a bulkhead. He ran to a nearby tool locker and met Lofberg coming from the bridge.

"The anchor chain is stuck," Harris said. "I thought you were going to beach her?"

Lofberg calmly handed him a sledgehammer and retrieved a second for himself. "The rudder's unresponsive, so we'd best get moving with that anchor. If we pass the point of no return, no vessel on this river will be able to stop us."

After a bevy of well-placed smacks from both men, the anchor chain still wouldn't budge. Dropping the sledge, Lofberg casually made his way forward and retrieved two long oars. Returning, he handed one to Harris. "Here you go, lad. We'll steer her into a sandbar, and she'll beach herself."

Positioned on the port side aft, the men tried to turn *Old Scow*, but the added tonnage in the cargo hold combined with the swift flowing river made the attempt impossible.

With the mist thickening and the sound of the thunderous waterfall growing louder, Gustave Lofberg, one of the most experienced seamen on the Niagara River, had run out of ideas.

* * *

Below deck, at the forward end of the hold, Merrick twisted the fuses of the dynamite together. Aquinas stood at the opposite end of the compartment, with Lucas shackled at his feet. When Aquinas looked up and signaled for Merrick to light the fuse, Lucas kicked his feet out from under him – the unpredictable element had restored movement to Lucas' extremities!

Like a dexterous contortionist, Lucas slipped his backside and legs through his shackled arms. With his hands back in front of him, he delivered several blows to Aquinas' midsection. Wrestling the rifle away, he aimed the barrel at Aquinas' chest and pulled the trigger.

Trying to ignore the agonizing pain, Aquinas drew his revolver, but Lucas quickly followed up with another shot – the bullet opening another deep chest wound.

As Aquinas' legs crumpled underneath him, Merrick returned from lighting the dynamite. "No!" he screamed.

Lucas whirled around to face him.

In a flash, Merrick retrieved an arrow from his quiver and took aim. The instant he released the bowstring, Lucas fired the rifle. The bullet struck first, hitting Merrick in the right thigh and dropping him to his knees. When the arrow reached Lucas' chest, the unseen force stopped it, and it fell harmlessly to the deck.

Lucas stepped forward to follow up, and Aquinas stuck his foot out and tripped him. Retrieving a revolver from his belt, Merrick sprang back to his feet. As he raised the gun and took aim, an ear-splitting blast erupted from the forward end of the hold.

The explosion sent a molten-hot fireball pluming through the compartment, followed by a bone-rattling shock wave rippling along the scow's keel. The aged rivets attaching the hull plates burst loose, opening a fatal gash in the forward port side. A tidal wave of icy water rushed in through the opening, flooding the compartment.

As *Old Scow's* bow lurched down, its stern rose completely out of the water. The swift current slammed into the superstructure, turning it ninety degrees. Seconds later the bow struck the river bottom and the stern came back down, crashing onto a rocky shoal. The impact dislodged the barge's smokestack, toppling it onto the dredging pipe and sealing the top hatch of the cargo hold. The anchor chain also broke free and began unwinding, plunging the heavy, hook-shaped mooring weight into the water.

Like salt in a shaker, the wild ride threw Merrick and Aquinas into the forward bulkhead then back down onto the deck. Lucas, who'd also been thrown forward, hung on to the bulkhead, but lost his grip when *Old Scow's* stern landed on the shoal. The momentum shot him head-first into the rushing onslaught of water. A moment later, Lucas emerged, aglow from the protective force surrounding him.

Looking at the two men, he laughed. "Double jeopardy again, Merrick! Pursue me and Aquinas dies. Stay here and try to save him, you'll both be killed when the barge goes over the falls. When will you ever learn I cannot be defeated?"

"We've already defeated you," Merrick replied sternly. "With the cleft widened, the carmot is melting as we speak. You're finished."

"Aren't you forgetting something? The Wordless Book tells of another source."

Merrick smiled. "Enjoy the next millennia trying to find it. The book's telling of another source was a ruse Aquinas' father created."

"Spare me, Merrick. Augustus was not as smart as you say."

"He was smart enough to trick you into stealing the wrong book. Now I see he has duped you into believing there is another source of carmot."

"Your bluff is as weak as you are. Now if you will excuse me, I've a dinner engagement with Gwendolyn. She's very astute when it comes to riddles. If all goes as planned, by the end of the week we'll know the location of the final source of carmot."

He dove into the water and disappeared through the gash in the hull.

With the rising water closing in on the top of the compartment, Merrick looked around and caught sight of a violet ray of light emanating from a still-frozen piece of carmot, stuck to a section of driftwood. Reaching out, he recovered the wood and spread some of the element over Aquinas' chest wounds and placed what remained on the bullet wound in his thigh.

As the carmot faded to a dim purple glow, the hold darkened. Coinciding with the lack of light, the water stopped rising and the hold became eerily still.

Grounded on the rocky shoal, with its anchor lodged between two submerged boulders, *Old Scow* had stopped its descent toward Horseshoe Falls – less than ten feet from the point of no return!

* * *

At dusk, with a throng of people watching from the shore, a team of rescuers atop the Toronto Power Building fired a rope over to the barge, which Lofberg and Harris snagged and fastened to a makeshift winch. A cable tied to the rope was pulled over and attached, giving them an avenue to escape. With nighttime approaching, their rescue would be suspended until daybreak. They finally departed *Old Scow* the next morning by sliding along the cable on a breeches buoy.

While the two dredgers abandoned the barge, Merrick remained in the dark and almost-submerged cargo hold, keeping Aquinas' head above water. The wait would last another four hours, until the carmot finally closed his chest wounds and he regained consciousness.

"Where is Lucas?" Aquinas asked.

"Unfortunately, My Captain, he got away." His weary tone betrayed his frustration.

"No worries, my friend. We will have more opportunities."

"How do you feel, sir?"

"Very much alive, thanks to you and the carmot."

"Are you able to support yourself?"

"I believe so."

"There's a pipe right above your head, and another on the bulkhead near your feet."

After a moment, Aquinas replied, "I found them."

"Good. Now stand fast." Merrick disappeared under the water. Almost a minute later, he reemerged. "The forward hatch is open. Do you think you can swim through?"

"I can certainly try."

"After you, sir."

Five minutes later, they stood on the bridge looking out the window at Horseshoe Falls.

Aquinas took a deep breath. "It truly is one of the Almighty's magnificent creations."

"I agree, sir," Merrick replied, "but I must say, I like the view better from the shore."

Aquinas smiled.

Wanting Lucas to believe they'd drowned, they waited until the dead of night before climbing across the rescue cable.

~ Present Day ~

Like a crew of carpenters building a new house, the driving rain hammered against the roof and front windshield of our SUV. As the sounds grew louder, flashes of lightning lit up the night sky, followed by a barrage of thunder reminiscent of a grand finale at a fireworks show.

The CD had ended, and Madison pressed the "Eject" button on the player and handed the disc to me. Just as she started to say something, our vehicle's tires rolled into deep tire tracks in the pavement – tracks filled with rainwater! Almost immediately, an alarm bell clanged, informing us we had lost traction. I placed my hands against the dashboard and braced myself. Madison slowed down and regained control.

"What should we do, George? This storm is getting worse."

I glanced out the window and caught sight of a mile-marker sign, denoting one mile to the next rest stop, five miles to Flagstaff, and a hundred-and-fifty miles to Phoenix. "I say we pull off at the rest stop and wait it out."

She nodded. "Good idea. After listening to that heart-stopping story, I've got to take a restroom break."

"Me too."

Once we were parked, Madison unbuckled her seat belt. "When we get back, maybe we can figure out what to do about this window."

I looked over at her. When I saw her hair, dripping wet and flat against the left side of her head, I stifled a laugh.

"What?" she asked.

"Oh, nothing."

"You were going to say something."

"No, I wasn't."

"George?"

I smiled. "All I was going to say is, you look like a fashion model for bed-head hairdos."

She laughed. "At least I still have hair."

We both cracked up.

After we returned to our vehicle. I retrieved an old jacket I kept in the back seat and made my way to the driver's side. Instructing Madison to open her door, I held the jacket up, and we shut it *in* the door, effectively blocking the rain. By the time I got back inside. I was completely drenched.

Madison leaned over and gave me a kiss. "Thanks, George."

"It's not much, but it should keep you dry for a while."

Just then, the flash of another lightning strike lit up the sky.

"Shall we listen to some more?" I asked.

Madison nodded.

I loaded disc number seven and pushed the "Play" button.

Aquinas' voice came on, summing up the events at Niagara Falls:

"*Old Scow* remains aground in the Niagara River, a short distance upstream from Horseshoe Falls. To the public, its rusty hull represents the valiant efforts put forth to rescue Lofberg and Harris. Behind the scenes, it stands as a testament to the Great Work; the place where Merrick and I stopped the Wanderer before he could gather enough carmot to bring about the Day of Reckoning. Inside the barge's cargo hold, the treasure of gold stones also remains, silently waiting to infect the explorer who discovers them.

"The unclean gold Lucas and Gwendolyn delivered to the U.S. Army at Fort Riley would cause an influenza pandemic lasting three years. American troops deploying to fight in World War I unknowingly carried the virus overseas, where it spread throughout Europe. The sickness would end up killing more than seventy-five million people across the globe. Though devastating, the outbreak was not catastrophic, for soon after scientists developed medications to combat influenza."

Wide-eyed, Madison and I looked at each other, stunned at the revelation.

"Contrary to what Lucas bragged, it would take Gwendolyn and him many years to decipher the symbols in the Wordless Book foretelling the location of the fourth and final source of carmot. Believing they had correctly interpreted the rhyming parable, they flew to Argentina and purchased two multi-purpose cargo vessels for the ensuing search.

"Having previously deciphered the symbols and memorized the parable, Merrick and I would again be waiting to confront them – in the coldest and most inhospitable territory on the face of the earth.

"The year was 1948, at the massive Bitton Glacier in the heart of Antarctica."

At the bottom of the world
the flightless birds roam,
the beakers gather
so far from home.

Where man becomes toasty
and the land points thrice,
the carmot lies frozen
beneath eight lachters of ice.

Aquinas' and Merrick's interpretation of the fourth group of symbols in the first chapter of the Wordless Book

CHAPTER EIGHT: THE FROZEN CONTINENT

Tuesday, 31 August 1948, 11:40hrs
At East Base Research Station, Antarctica

With the south polar winter well underway, the sun completed its daily cycle without climbing above the horizon, leaving only a dim blue glow in the northwestern sky. As it faded into darkness, electrically charged particles in the earth's atmosphere became visible, transforming the skyline into a breathtaking vista of yellow and green luminescence. On the surface below, streams of icy winds blowing inland from the Bellingshausen Sea plummeted the temperature to more than fifty degrees below zero. The colorful lights and freezing wind showcased the contradicting allure of Antarctica: hauntingly beautiful, yet dangerously harsh.

From the edge of the western peninsula, on a gray, rocky atoll aptly named Stonington Island, the now-long-haired and bearded Aquinas watched in awe the spectacle of the aurora lights. Tearing his eyes away, he struck a match and held it to the wick of a lantern, partially revealing a boat landing. After lighting several more, the entire pier came into view, as well as five black wood buildings lying a few yards off the shore. The buildings, constituting the entire American base, had served as his home for the last twenty-nine years.

Aquinas had finally picked up the trail of Lucas and Gwendolyn seven days ago. Working as a longshoreman off-loading a supply ship arriving from the United States, he'd spotted Johnathan Colby, the guard from the Niagara warehouse, approaching on a landing craft.

Hiding behind a stack of cargo, Aquinas overheard Colby tell the dock foreman he was a member of the Phillips Expedition, sent in advance to secure supplies for the upcoming exploration of the Bitton Glacier. The leaders of the expedition, Gwendolyn and Lucas, were scheduled to arrive in ten days.

Making his way to the base's radio room, Aquinas fired off a message to Merrick, who'd been conducting surveillance at Antarctica's other main shipping port on Campbell Island, south of New Zealand. A short time later, Merrick replied. He had booked passage on the *HMAS Brisbane,* an Australian freighter, and would arrive at East Base (weather and ice floe permitting) in a week.

Now, seven days later, and with the *Brisbane* appearing offshore, Aquinas lit the dock lanterns with great anticipation. Although they'd stayed in touch with radio messages and letters, he hadn't actually seen Merrick in more than thirty years.

As the landing craft approached, Aquinas pulled the hood of his coat over his head. When Merrick stepped ashore, Aquinas walked over to him. In the deepest voice he could muster, he asked, "May I carry your bag, sir?"

Merrick stifled a laugh. "According to an article I recently read about south polar etiquette, if someone reunites with a friend in Antarctica that they haven't seen in thirty years, it is customary to render a handshake."

Aquinas smiled. "How did you know it was me?"

"Quite simple, sir. Your hood and facial hair cannot mask your thin physique."

The men embraced.

"How are you, My Captain?"

"I'm doing well. And yourself?"

"Rested and ready to continue the Great Work."

"Excellent. Let's get out of this cold. Follow me to my quarters, we have much to discuss."

Making their way to the smallest of the five buildings, Aquinas lit another lantern and showed him in. Shelves containing a bevy of dry foods and canned goods lined two of the walls, while a multitude of different sized maps of Antarctica blanketed the others, set in place with thumbtacks. On the floor sat two cots and chairs, with a pot-bellied stove radiating heat in the corner.

"As you can see," Aquinas said, "I've spared no expense in providing you all the comforts of home."

Merrick smiled. "It is quite similar to my accommodations on Campbell Island, to include the plethora of Antarctic maps. I've studied them so long, I could sketch the continent blindfolded."

"Let us discuss the maps. But before we begin, can I get you something to eat or drink?"

"Thank you, sir. I dined on the ship, but I'd take a glass of Kaffan ale if you have any."

Aquinas laughed. "Unfortunately, I don't. I do, however, have something I think you'll like."

He retrieved a bottle from a nearby shelf and poured two glasses. Popping the top of a soda can, he added a small amount to each. After handing Merrick one of the glasses, Aquinas raised his. "To the Great Work."

"The Great Work," Merrick echoed.

Merrick took a drink and fell into a coughing fit, prompting Aquinas to slap him on the back.

When he could finally talk, Merrick said, "It kicks like a mule, sir."

"It's my favorite new American drink called a bourbon seven, which contains merely Kentucky bourbon and soda water. I've found the first couple of drinks quite harsh, but the following ones go down rather well."

"If we ever venture to the United States again, remind me to avoid Kentucky."

Aquinas laughed and motioned him to sit down, then took a seat in the other chair.

"You say you've been studying the maps," Aquinas began, "tell me what you've learned."

Merrick cleared his throat. "One of my jobs on Campbell Island entailed procuring new maps for Australian explorers on their way to the Davis Research Station on Princess Elizabeth Land. Many of these maps include detailed topographical illustrations, like the one you have here, but more recent." He pointed to one of the larger maps. "According to the parable, we're looking for a place where the land points three ways. After much study, I found an area where the continental shelf is shaped like a triangle. Do you have a pencil?"

Aquinas retrieved one from his lapel pocket and handed it to him. Merrick stood and plotted the points on the map. When he finished, he connected the dots.

"Now," Merrick continued, "if we plot the center points of the three sides of the triangle and draw a line from these points to the opposite corners, they intersect here, in this area near the southern pole." After drawing the lines, he circled the point where they met. "It is my belief, sir, the carmot lies beneath the Bitton Glacier, near the Crater of Hope."

"Excellent deduction, my friend."

Merrick smiled and sat back down. "Thank you, sir. It also falls in line with the parable telling of where the flightless birds roam and where the beakers gather. I believe it is referring to the penguins making their yearly pilgrimage across the glacier. The last line in the parable is not really important. It's simply referring to the depth of the ice."

"Again, your deductive powers are superlative, and for a time I believed as you do."

Merrick frowned. "Believed? Are you saying my conclusions are incorrect?"

"Not entirely. I believe we will confront Lucas there, but the carmot is in another place. You see, after I arrived, some things became known to me which make me believe the Bitton Glacier is not the place the parable is referring to."

"What things?"

Aquinas took another drink and leaned in. "I've become quite friendly with the commander of this base, an American naval captain named Finn Ronne, who prefers the name Finney. Quite a personable fellow, this Finney, who happens to be one of the older and more experienced explorers of the region. As unbelievable as this may sound, when I first met him, he asked if I was a beaker."

"He asked if *you* were a beaker, sir?"

Aquinas smiled. "I was dumbstruck. He explained a beaker is a common term down here for research scientists."

"I don't understand. Why do they call them beakers?"

"Because of the glass beakers they use in their laboratory experiments. Scientists from all over the world come down here to study the region, and Finney thought I was one of them."

"So if the word *beaker* is referring to scientists, it falls in line with the parable. They would be far from home."

"Yes, which brings us to the next line, *where man becomes toasty*."

"I must admit, My Captain, this one still has me perplexed. From everything I've read, there is no place in Antarctica toasty warm."

Aquinas smiled again. "Once more, Finney provided me the clue. Down here, the word *toasty* doesn't mean anything warm at all. Instead, the word refers to a place where prolonged sunlight can cause snow blindness, and the high altitude can affect a person's mental faculties."

Merrick's eyes grew wide. "Which means the carmot isn't under the Bitton Glacier at all. The glacier sits in the low-lying western peninsula. The Crater of Hope lower still."

Aquinas nodded.

"Then where is it?"

"Let us first examine the last line of the parable which states, *the carmot lies frozen beneath eight lachters of ice*. When I began studying the continent, I happened across this book that had been left behind by a group of scientists." He opened a knapsack from under the shelves of dry goods, pulled the book out, and showed it to him.

Merrick read the title aloud. "Ancient Units of Measurement."

"When we were with the king at Kaffa," Aquinas continued, "a lachter simply meant the length of a man's outstretched arms. According to this book, a lachter can equate to many different lengths of measurement, depending on which area of the world you're in. The average of these multiplied by eight gives us fifteen point four meters, or in American terms, roughly fifty feet.

"Referring to the map, we know the region east of the Transantarctic Mountain Range is at a higher elevation than the west. If we examine this eastern territory a bit more closely, there is only one area where the ice remains fifty feet deep all year around." He stood and pointed to the area on the map.

"The Polar Plateau?" Merrick asked.

"More specifically, here. On the southern edge of the Polar Plateau."

Merrick's eyes grew wide. "The Rae Ice Shelf?"

Aquinas smiled. "Precisely."

Merrick thought for a moment, stood, and traced his finger along the outer boundary of the Rae Ice Shelf. "I fail to see where this area of land points three ways."

"Since most maps are drawn showing what Antarctica looks like nine months out of the year, they fail to show what the continent looks like at the end of the summer."

"Is there a difference?"

Aquinas nodded. "From the end of December through the end of March, the sun shines a great deal longer, warming the wind blowing inland from the Ross Sea. This thaws the ice on the southern edge of the Polar Plateau, partially revealing a natural border under the Rae Ice Shelf. A border whose shape appears to be two sides of a triangle. You can see it here." He pointed to a smaller map.

Merrick examined the area. "But sir, are you sure? Half of the border is indistinguishable."

Aquinas replied confidently. "I am more than sure, my friend. I've seen it for myself."

"Oh? How did you manage that?"

"Several months ago, Finney allowed me to accompany him on an exploration of the region. When we arrived, one of his men fell into a crevasse – a crevasse whose bottom glowed violet."

"Did this man Finney notice it?"

"Did he ever. He wanted to launch a full-scale investigation, but I was able to use the power of suggestion on him and the others.

They now have no recollection of the incident. I have also determined Lucas doesn't know the carmot lies under the Rae Ice Shelf. When I overheard Mr. Colby talking about the Phillips Expedition, he said they would be exploring the Bitton Glacier."

Merrick smiled. "Which means Lucas and his people will be searching in the wrong place!"

"Correct." Aquinas sat back down and took another drink. "So as a ruse, we must proceed to the Bitton Glacier and defend it as if the carmot *is* there."

"But sir, with his heightened awareness, Lucas will know we are there. He will also have his contingent of confederates protecting him."

"I'm counting on it. As for his confederates, we shall eliminate them."

"What are we to do with this Gwendolyn woman?"

I knew he'd ask me about her. I just hope he understands.

"I see no other recourse but to eliminate her too."

Instead of answering, Merrick looked down.

"I know what value you place on women," Aquinas commented, "and at any other time, I would be the first to praise you for your chivalry. But remember what we deciphered in the Wordless Book. *The one who abets the Wanderer, a sorceress black at heart, redemption will be fruitless, for she is seduced by the magical carmot.* She is also more than likely in possession of the Wordless Book. If we are unable to contain Lucas, we will need to decipher the remaining symbols and learn how. Therefore, our first priority is to recover the book."

Merrick remained looking down, not saying a word.

I was afraid of this. He's not listening.

Finally, Merrick raised his head and looked at Aquinas. "My Captain, try to understand. When I lost my beloved Bella during the siege at Kaffa, my world came apart, shattering into a million pieces. From a very young age, I was taught women should always be revered and honored, for they deliver the holy souls into the mortal world."

"I agree with you, but in this instance, we're dealing with a woman who is in league with pure evil. While she is alive, Lucas has a powerful ally with unlimited wealth at his fingertips. To significantly weaken him, we must strip him of both."

"But if we kill her, will we not be just as evil? Could we not simply contain her with Lucas? It would accomplish the same objective."

Aquinas thought for a moment. "Perhaps you're right, but before we confront them, let us be clear on this. If it comes down to a choice between completing the Great Work or eliminating her, we must choose the latter. Do you agree?"

Merrick thought for a moment. "I agree."

"Good. Then let us return to my plan. As a ruse, we will proceed to the Bitton Glacier and defend it as if the carmot is there."

"But sir, won't Lucas sense the carmot is at the Rae Ice Shelf, and not at the glacier?"

"I don't think so."

"Oh? Why not?"

"Tell me, since you arrived, have you sensed the carmot?"

Merrick's eyes grew wide. "Come to think of it, no."

"I have only sensed it one time, when I helped Finney rescue his man from the crevasse. It is my belief the bitterly cold temperatures are shrouding the carmot from perception."

Merrick stood and pointed to the map. "The Bitton Glacier is vast, sir. In all this wilderness, how will we contain Lucas?"

"Since Lucas has reached the same erroneous conclusion as you and I first did, he will search for the carmot under the Bitton Glacier."

"But how does one search *under* a glacier? Does the ice not sit on the ground?"

"According to Finney, thousands of years ago, an enormous land shelf once covered the Crater of Hope. When the ice age came, the Bitton Glacier advanced over it. In time, the shelf collapsed, leaving an immense ice cave underneath. On the glacier's southernmost edge, there is a narrow fissure which leads down to the crater. If many are descending, they must do so in single file. The lowest point of the crater is quite perilous and contains a rather large natural opening in the floor, which Finney refers to as a *bottomless pit*. Knowing Lucas, he will be leading the expedition, with Gwendolyn not far behind. If we can cave in the fissure after they enter…"

"We can separate them from the others," Merrick concluded, "recover the Wordless Book, and contain them."

Aquinas nodded. "And if any of his confederates get through, we shall dispatch them into the pit."

Merrick smiled. "Excellent plan, My Captain, but how will we get out?"

I was hoping he wouldn't ask me that.

"We're not getting out, at least not for a while."

"Sir?"

"After we contain Lucas, we will need to make sure he doesn't escape. Since he cannot die until the Day of Reckoning, we will have to stay with him."

"How will we survive?"

"From what Finney tells me, the north end of the crater is a labyrinth of smaller, interconnected openings, some leading to the surface. While one of us stays with Lucas, the other shall find the way out, return here, and replenish our supplies."

"When do we leave?"

"In the morning. This will give us time to stop at the Rae Ice Shelf and recover some carmot. We'll need it in the event one of us is wounded in the confrontation."

"What of the rest?"

"I first thought of destroying it, but if we are to confine Lucas until the real Day of Reckoning arrives, we will need to keep ingesting it to prolong our lives. I therefore developed something we can use to transport the carmot."

He retrieved a black portfolio case from under the shelf holding the dry goods.

"It looks like an ordinary piece of luggage," Merrick commented.

Aquinas smiled. "Oh, it's anything but ordinary."

He opened the case and turned it around to show him. Inside were eight cylinder-shaped tubes taped together, four on top of four. Each tube measured approximately fourteen inches in length and two inches around. The tubes, brown in color, were connected by a series of wires and small copper pipes.

"They look like sticks of dynamite."

Aquinas laughed. "It's a portable refrigeration unit. The four tubes on the bottom hold the carmot, the three on top hold the batteries, and the one on the right holds the refrigerant. As long as the batteries hold out, it will keep the temperature inside the tubes below freezing."

"But sir, I don't see the need. Doesn't the temperature down here remain below freezing all year long?"

"Yes, but if Lucas escapes, or the need arises where we have to quickly leave Antarctica, we'll be able to take some carmot with us."

"You've thought of everything."

Aquinas shrugged. "Hopefully, we'll never have to use it."

"Amen to that, sir."

"I've procured dogs, sleds, and enough food and supplies to last both of us roughly four weeks." Aquinas walked over to the larger map and pointed to East Base. "Weather permitting, and taking in account rest periods for the dogs, it will take us eight days to reach the Rae Ice Shelf and recover the carmot, two days to traverse back across the Transantarctic Mountains to the Bitton Glacier, and an additional day to descend the crevasse to the Crater of Hope." As he spoke, his finger slid across the map to each location.

"What about weapons?"

"Good news there. Finney is so pleased with my work, he has placed me in charge of base security, which means I have the key to the weapons locker. We have handguns, rifles, a few sticks of dynamite, and some detonators at our disposal. I also have something very special for you."

He moved over to the wall containing the shelves of canned goods and retrieved a shiny new longbow and quiver full of arrows from the top shelf.

Merrick's eyes grew wide. "Magnificent," he whispered. "Absolutely magnificent."

"I had it specially made and shipped here from one of the leading bowyers in London. It's made of hickory, purpleheart, and lemonwood. And those state-of-the-art, swallow-tailed arrows can bring down an elephant seal if need be."

Merrick pulled one from the quiver to examine it.

"It's so light."

"That's because the arrows are fashioned from aluminum."

Merrick looked up, his eyes watery with tears. "A glorious gift, My Captain."

"What's the matter? Is there a flaw in the weapon?"

Merrick shook his head. "You've gifted me handsomely, sir, but I have nothing to give you in return."

"The fact you are here helping me with this undertaking is gift enough."

"I shall therefore reiterate the promise I made to you before we escaped Kaffa, and hereby pledge my life to the Great Work."

Aquinas smiled. "Thank you, my friend. To spend an eternity with Lucas and me in an ice cave is a lot to ask."

"Sir, I deem the task of saving our fellow man a privilege. Whatever you ask lays no burden upon me."

This time tears welled up in Aquinas' eyes.

* * *

After recovering some carmot at the Rae Ice Shelf, Aquinas and Merrick doubled back across the transantarctic mountain range. Two days later, amid the piercing cold wind of a swirling ice storm, they arrived at the southern edge of the Bitton Glacier.

While constructing a temporary shelter for the sled dogs, Merrick paused to rub his hands. "This place should have been named the Crater of Cold!"

"Do you not know how the name came about, my friend?"

Merrick shook his head.

"When Sir Jason Bitton and his party discovered the glacier, one of his men, an unfortunate fellow named Hope, dreamt of a paradise beneath the ice."

"Why was he unfortunate?"

"He'd suffered a head injury from a fall and had gone mad. When the men descended into the crevasse and found the pit, Hope threw himself into it. Sir Bitton subsequently named the crater after him."

"I sense no paradise, My Captain. In my opinion, neither man nor beast were meant to be here."

"I agree, which is why it is the perfect place to contain Lucas once and for all."

Clicking on their flashlights, the men began the long climb down.

~ The Wanderer ~

Back at East Base Research Station, Lucas stepped ashore. With his senses on alert, he stopped to look around before turning to help Gwendolyn off the landing craft.

"What is it?" she asked.

"My intuition is telling me Aquinas and Merrick are here, but I'm not sensing the carmot."

She looked around. "Me neither. Do you think our calculations are incorrect?"

Lucas looked around again. "If Aquinas and Merrick are here, the carmot must also be here."

"When we embark for the glacier, I'll give the men orders to kill anyone who approaches our party or tries to interfere with our expedition."

Lucas nodded.

"No one is going to deprive us of the riches the carmot will bring," she continued, "nor from the disease that will be unleashed when we transform the stones. And when society crumbles, you and I will be delivered from our mortal existence, and we will be left as the immortal rulers of the underworld."

Eleven days later, the Phillips Expedition arrived at the southern tip of the Bitton Glacier. Taking point, Lucas led them down into the fissure toward the Crater of Hope.

* * *

Hearing voices approaching, Merrick gingerly stepped across the ice-covered rim of the bottomless pit and rejoined Aquinas. "They draw near, My Captain," he whispered.

"Very well," Aquinas replied, also whispering. "Ready your longbow."

While Merrick withdrew an arrow from his quiver, Aquinas eased the detonator's handle up, and rechecked his rifle and handgun. Clicking off their flashlights, they crouched behind a tilted boulder and waited. A moment later, a light from the cave entrance pierced the darkness and they heard Gwendolyn's voice.

"If that idiot Finney is to be believed," she said, "we must be getting close to the cave."

Lucas entered first, followed by Gwendolyn, Jonathan Colby, and another man.

"He is to be believed," Lucas said. "Here's the pit he spoke of."

While the others pointed their flashlights at the circular opening in the cave's floor, Lucas walked up to the edge and peered down.

"See anything?" Gwendolyn asked.

Lucas shook his head and proceeded around the rim. When he reached the other side, he stopped and held up his hand.

Gwendolyn snatched a revolver from her coat pocket. Following suit, Jonathan Colby and the other man brandished handguns. Colby turned back toward the cave entrance and yelled for the others in their party to stop. After shining their lights around and not hearing anything, Gwendolyn moved by the rim of the pit and joined Lucas.

"Do you sense them?" she asked.

Lucas kept his eyes on the way ahead. "I'm not sure."

Gwendolyn turned back to Colby. "Get the rest of the men in here! Have them search up ahead. Remember to shoot to kill!"

"Yes ma'am," Colby replied.

As he turned to carry out the order, Aquinas pushed down on the handle.

The deafening explosion engulfed the upper half of the cave in a gigantic fireball, and sent an avalanche of ice chunks raining down, burying the cave entrance and the man behind Colby.

The concussion wave knocked Lucas and Gwendolyn to the ground, as it did Colby, who'd been standing nearest to the explosion and closest to the edge of the pit. To stop himself from being swept over the side, he wrapped his arms around an outward-slanting stalagmite, but the life-saving maneuver left him hanging over the precipice.

As the fireball dissipated across the icy ceiling, Lucas and Gwendolyn returned to their feet. At the same time, Merrick drew back on his longbow and released the shot. The arrow passed through Lucas' left bicep, spinning him around, and he crashed into Gwendolyn. The collision coincided with Aquinas firing his rifle, throwing his aim off, and the bullet narrowly missed Gwendolyn's head before disappearing into the newly formed wall of ice behind her.

Recovering, Lucas dove for his weapon. The instant he had it in his hands, the cave plunged back into darkness. Undaunted, Lucas fired in front of him in a sweeping motion until his gun clicked.

Hearing the empty chamber, Aquinas turned on his flashlight and pointed the beam at Lucas. Merrick released two arrows in rapid succession. The first arrow sliced into Lucas' right elbow, followed by a second passing through his right thigh.

Lucas fell to one knee. A moment later, he appeared to gather himself and began yelling.

"You cannot defeat me, Aquinas! Do you hear? You cannot defeat me!"

Two more arrows from Merrick slashed into Lucas' forearms, while a third appeared to stop after penetrating his thick coat. Unable to use his arms to catch himself, Lucas fell face-first to the ground.

Aquinas shined his flashlight on Gwendolyn and nodded to Merrick. The archer delivered two quick arrows, the first hitting her right shoulder and the second passing through her right forearm.

Screaming, Gwendolyn dropped her revolver and fell to the ground. Writhing in pain, she raised her left hand.

"She has surrendered, sir," Merrick said. "Do we really need to kill her?"

Aquinas thought for a moment. "Stand fast for now."

"What about Mr. Colby?"

Aquinas pointed his flashlight at the slanted stalagmite over the bottomless pit, and found Colby gone.

"It appears nature has done our work for us, as far as Mr. Colby is concerned."

"Shall I retrieve the book, sir?"

"Yes. But remain alert."

Merrick hurried to Gwendolyn and raised his longbow. "Madam, I believe you have something belonging to us."

"I don't know what you're talking about," she snarled.

Merrick smiled. "Very well, you give me no recourse." He pulled back on the bowstring and steadied his aim.

Using her left hand, she slowly unfastened her coat and withdrew the Wordless Book. Merrick snatched it out of her hand and tossed it back to Aquinas.

After unfastening the leather straps and thumbing through it, Aquinas re-secured the book and placed it in the black portfolio case. "Good work, my friend. Now let's get those shackles on Lucas."

Aquinas held his rifle on them, while Merrick hastened back to the slanted boulder. Setting his bow and quiver down, he retrieved the shackles. Watching Merrick return to Lucas, Aquinas felt an icy chill crawl down his spine.

"Wait!" he yelled.

Merrick stopped in his tracks. "What is it, sir?"

Aquinas slowly looked around. After a moment, the feeling passed. "Nothing. You may proceed."

Merrick turned back to Lucas. "Hands behind your back."

Slumped over, Lucas didn't move.

"I said put your hands behind your back."

Lucas remained still.

Merrick dropped the shackles and retrieved his revolver. When he was within three feet of Lucas, he kicked his legs. The big man fell to one side, revealing the point of a bloody arrow sticking out of his back. As Aquinas moved the beam of his flashlight up, Lucas' face *transformed* into the face of Jonathan Colby.

"Sir, Lucas must be…"

"He's using the power of suggestion!" Aquinas yelled. "Fall back!"

Just as Merrick turned and took a step, a shot rang out. The bullet grazed the side of his head, dropping him to his knees.

Aquinas sprang to help, but the instant he moved out into the open another shot rang out. The bullet shattered the stock of his rifle and tore it from his hands. Landing on top of the tilted boulder, the weapon slid out of his reach. Ducking back behind the boulder, Aquinas retrieved his revolver. When he stood to fire, two more shots hit him; the first knocking the revolver from his hand, and the second piercing his abdomen, sending him to the ground.

Waiting a moment to catch his breath, Aquinas crawled to the far end of the boulder and leaned out.

The beams of two flashlights were trained on Merrick, one held by Gwendolyn and the other coming from somewhere behind her. Merrick had returned to his feet but still looked confused.

"Merrick, take cover!" Aquinas screamed.

Oblivious to the peril he was in, Merrick looked around and slowly placed his hand on his head where the bullet had grazed him. Before Aquinas could yell another warning, two more shots rang out. The bullets struck Merrick in the chest, and he staggered toward the edge of the bottomless pit. Gwendolyn ran over and delivered a solid kick to his midsection, sending him over the side.

"No!" Aquinas screamed, his pain echoing off the icy walls as much as his voice.

Lucas' deep laugh replaced the echo, followed by a salvo of shots peppering Aquinas' position.

When the gunfire finally ended, Lucas spoke. "You cannot defeat me, Aquinas. Now your foolish endeavor has cost Merrick his life."

Dazed and heartbroken, Aquinas collapsed behind the slanted boulder. Ever since he could remember, Merrick had been by his side. They'd grown up together in Kaffa and had faced personal tragedies side-by-side. When he'd originally called upon Merrick to help him with the Great Work, the blonde archer pledged his life to the cause without hesitation. In the centuries since swearing his loyalty, Merrick had become the brother he never had. Even though the possibility of losing him had always been present, Aquinas never believed the day would come. In the blink of an eye, Merrick, the man who had saved his life more times than he could remember, was gone.

With tears streaming down his face, Aquinas felt a sense of déjà vu. The Great Work had cost him the life of his father and now his best friend, the two people in his life he respected and admired above all others. Thinking of his father, he silently spoke to him.

You told me I needed faith, father, but how can I continue? If I'd only recognized Lucas was using the power of suggestion to disguise himself as Colby, Merrick would still be alive. I have failed you again.

Through the pain of his wounds and the anguish in his heart, he unexpectedly heard the voice of his father, emanating from behind the cave's wall.

"You will only fail me if you do not continue, my son. Now hasten your escape."

"How, father?"

"Use the tools in front of you!"

Feeling around, Aquinas located the flashlight and clicked it on. Examining the wall more closely, he found an opening at the base he hadn't noticed before – just big enough for him to crawl through. Remembering Merrick's penchant for saving ammunition, he retrieved his quiver and dumped out its contents. Among the extra arrows and bullets were two sticks of dynamite. Twisting the fuses together, he again heard his father's voice.

"After you make your escape, you *must* decipher the remaining symbols in the book. Only then you will find the answer."

Aquinas took a deep, painful breath, and retrieved the portfolio case containing the carmot and the book. Striking a match, he lit the fuse of the dynamite, and quickly crawled through the small opening.

Six days later, in excruciating pain, Aquinas emerged from a crevasse and stepped onto the icy outer surface of the Bitton Glacier. Having used his entire supply of carmot, his senses remained alert, but the unpredictable element had failed to work its magic on the gunshot wound in his abdomen. He realized his only chance of survival depended on him obtaining more carmot.

Finding the sled dogs dead, he cinched up his coat and staggered out into the frozen wilderness.

~ The Wanderer ~

Gwendolyn aimed her flashlight at the newly formed wall of ice chunks covering the cave entrance, then toward the similarly filled-in area on the opposite wall, blocking the way ahead.

"So, what do we do now?"

"Nothing, until your people dig us out," Lucas replied calmly.

"But Aquinas has recovered the Wordless Book!"

"He recovered the book because of *your* insistence on bringing it along."

She shined her flashlight on his face. His intense stare sent a shiver down her spine. "I thought we might need it if our interpretation of the parable turned out to be wrong."

"Which apparently it is. If our interpretation had been correct, Aquinas would still be here, fighting to his last breath to keep us from the carmot."

"Could he have already found it and destroyed it?"

Lucas smiled confidently. "He wouldn't dare."

She raised an eyebrow. "What makes you so sure?"

"Think about his predicament. He's trying to stop us from obtaining the carmot and bringing about a global epidemic. He knows I cannot be fatally wounded. Therefore, if he wishes to continue his foolish quest to interfere with our plans, he will need to save some carmot for himself to stay alive."

Gwendolyn thought for a moment. "But if he hasn't destroyed the carmot, he must've discovered it in another place."

"Precisely. This entire confrontation was a ruse to make us believe the carmot is here."

"Assuming that is true, there must be another area of land pointing three ways."

Lucas nodded. "It also means the carmot could be anywhere on the continent."

She walked over and placed her arms around him. "I'm sorry I insisted on bringing along the Wordless Book."

"Don't worry, darling. It will soon be back in our possession."

Her eyes grew wide. "What makes you so confident?"

"Because I look at the situation in practical terms. Aquinas is wounded and without hope. Even if he has ingested the carmot, without the sled dogs he can only go so far in this freezing environment. Merrick's demise will also factor into the equation, for it will surely eat at his soul. When we get out of here, we shouldn't have too much trouble tracking him down."

"When we finally capture him, what will you do?"

The intense stare returned to Lucas' face. "I shall torture him until he divulges the location of the carmot, dismember his body, and feed it to the orca whales."

Gwendolyn smiled and embraced him. "I like your plan."

~ Present Day ~

When Aquinas described, in agonizing detail, how he had lost his best friend Merrick, Madison started to cry. Not long after, I noticed a multitude of used facial tissues on the floor at her feet. I reached out and pressed the "Pause" button on the CD player.

"What are you doing, George?"

"I thought you might need to take a break."

"No, I'm alright."

"Are you sure? This is a lot to take in."

"I'm sure."

"Alright, but if it gets to be too much, let me know."

I pressed the "Play" button.

We soon learned Aquinas' escape across Antarctica eventually fell short. Lost in a storm, out of food, and with hypothermia setting in, he finally collapsed approximately seventy-five kilometers from the Rae Ice Shelf.

"As the bitter cold slowly drained the life from my body," he said, "I recalled a page of symbols in the Wordless Book. When I had deciphered them all those years ago with Merrick, the rhyming parable hadn't made sense. Now, I understood its meaning with crystal clarity – the parable is talking about me!

"Looking for the sun, my eyes darted in all directions, but the overcast sky and swirling snow prevented me from seeing anything beyond a few meters. Surrendering to the fatigue, I laid my head down and fell asleep."

The crusade to stop the Wanderer had taken Madison's uncle to many perilous locations in the world, but none so dangerous as this.

Aquinas, the last protector of mankind, had arrived at death's door.

When his brave knight falls
the great soldier shall flee.
Approaching life's veil
a red sunrise he'll see.

Although his way lost
and his grand faith in falter,
his life shall be saved
by a nobleman's daughter.

Aquinas' and Merrick's interpretation of the first group of symbols in the second chapter of the Wordless Book

CHAPTER NINE: THE TANAKA EXPEDITION

Tuesday, 5 October 1948, 10:35hrs
On the Polar Plateau, Antarctica

A changing weather pattern in the Southern Ocean shifted the trajectory of a violent, easterly gale blowing inland from the Weddell Sea. Turning south, the wind traveled along the slope of the transantarctic mountain range, before dissipating over the heart of the frozen continent. The low-lying storm clouds hovering over the polar plateau immediately began to disburse, allowing scattered rays of sunlight to break through and illuminate the white crystalline terrain.

On a ridge overlooking the plateau stood Japanese businessman and explorer Yuuto Tanaka, and his son Toshiro. As they watched over the seven scientists on the expedition, the voice of Yuuto's daughter Sara blared from the speaker of a two-way radio.

"Father, come in," she said. "This is urgent!"

"Yes," Yuuto replied. "What is it?"

"There's a man out here who has been shot."

Yuuto and Toshiro looked toward the rock formation she'd been exploring and saw Sara waving at them in the distance.

"You mean you have found a man's body who apparently died from a gunshot wound?" Yuuto asked.

"No, father. He's alive."

"Is there anyone else nearby? Another expedition, perhaps?"

She looked around. "I'm not seeing anyone."

"Stand by. We're on our way."

Yuuto handed the radio to Toshiro and put his goggles back on.

Toshiro clipped the radio in his belt. "How could anyone survive alone out here with a gunshot wound?"

Ever the Shinto philosopher, Yuuto replied, "The ways of the gods are too deep for us to comprehend. For whatever reason, this man has fallen across our path. It is our duty as fellow human beings to help him."

"I advise caution, father."

"Duly noted. Inform the others."

As Toshiro sped off, Yuuto climbed aboard his dog sled. A short time later, he'd traversed the distance to the rock formation. Sara, who'd been kneeling next to the wounded man, rose to her feet.

"His pulse is so weak," she said, "I almost missed it."

Yuuto looked around, seeing nothing but the desolate frozen tundra in all directions. "I wonder how he came to be out here?"

"I don't know, but he had this clutched in his hands." She held up a portfolio case.

Quickly climbing off the sled, Yuuto took the case from her and began examining its contents. When he opened the Wordless Book, his eyes grew wide and his hands began to tremble. With care, he reverently closed the book and placed it back in the case.

Turning to Sara, he said, "Listen to me very carefully. You are not to mention this book to anyone."

"But…"

"Not to anyone! Do you understand?"

"Yes, father."

"I'll explain later, but right now you must call upon all of your nursing skills to save this man's life."

She nodded and returned to tending to the wounded man.

Just then, Toshiro arrived with the seven scientists. With all members of the Tanaka Expedition accounted for, Yuuto began coordinating the rescue, barking out orders like a drill sergeant.

As Yuuto watched Toshiro and the others fashion a lean-to from tent poles and attach it to his sled, his thoughts returned to a time when he was much, much younger. As sure as the sun rose in the morning sky, he knew finding the man with the Wordless Book was no coincidence.

* * *

Yuuto Tanaka was born February 29th, 1904, the only child of wealthy parents. As he grew to manhood, his father was overly strict, confining him to his studies rather than allowing him to play with his friends. This, in turn, drove him closer to his loving mother, who leant a sympathetic ear. When he got older, these restrictions led to arguments, the majority of which young Yuuto lost to his stringent father.

One such quarrel occurred just after he turned seventeen when his father forbade him from attending a school function, insisting instead he stay home and work through some math problems he'd been having trouble with. Normally dutiful and submissive, his mother took Yuuto's side in the argument. Finding himself outnumbered, his father relented on the condition they first listen to a story about their ancestor.

"Your grandfather instructed me to wait until you turned twenty years of age before telling you this," his father began, "but since you and your mother have decided to go against my wishes, I will reveal it to you now. There are two reasons why I have been so stern with you. First, I love you with all my heart and I do not what you to fall into the graces of unscrupulous people."

"But father, I won't…"

"Please listen!" he yelled. His outburst instantly quieted the young man.

"The second reason is because your education will help prepare you for the Great Work, should it come to you."

"What great work?"

His father retrieved a rolled-up manuscript of many pages from a nearby cupboard and laid them out on the kitchen table. "You know what this is?"

"It is our family's Kojiki," Yuuto replied.

"Which is?"

"The Record of Ancient Affairs."

"Correct. It was handed down by the Tanaka fathers, generation after generation, until it finally came into my possession when your grandfather gave it to me. Our Kojiki is different than all the others, even the one belonging to the Imperial family."

Yuuto looked down at the manuscript. "What makes it different?"

"Our Kojiki contains sections of a diary written more than six-hundred years ago, shortly before our ancestor embarked on the Great Work."

He pulled a few of the papers off the top until he found the right page and pointed to the writing. "Read this aloud."

Yuuto cleared his throat. "Having witnessed man's inhumanity to man more times than I care to remember, I believe evil spirits exist in the world, and that they exude their power and influence in many ways. One such spirit has manifested itself in the form of a man who cannot die, whose sole purpose is to kill. This came to me not in dream, but rather from a blind sage who talks in rhymes, and whose visions of the future resonate the truth. I have joined his followers, who call themselves the Order of the Sentinels, and have pledged my life to stopping this evil spirit, known to us only as the Wanderer."

Yuuto paused and looked up. "What does this have to do with me?"

His father pointed to the manuscript. "Read the next two passages."

"The blind man is fearful the Wanderer may be near, prompting him to employ secrecy. He now whispers his visions to a learned man who cannot speak. The mute writes down what he hears in the form of symbols we cannot understand. We have bound these pages together into a book – a book without words. I am hopeful the mute will soon reveal to us the method of how to read the symbols so we can be ready to confront the Wanderer."

"Now the last passage," Yuuto's father interrupted. "It is the most important one."

"There is much fear and sorrow in our ranks," Yuuto read. "The blind sage has died, as has his mute assistant, leaving us not knowing how to interpret the symbols in the Wordless Book. Before his spirit left his body, the wise sage said there was a way to use the sacred substance carmot to defeat the Wanderer. Some among us believe carmot to be a myth and have abandoned us, while those of us with faith have decided to go out into the world and find the sacred substance. We set sail on the *Conviction* at dawn."

Yuuto again paused. "The sacred substance carmot? What does he mean?"

"Keep reading," his father replied.

"I have not told the others about a meeting I had with the blind sage before he died, where he foretold the voyage of the *Conviction* and that only one will return. He also proclaimed many years from now, one of my heirs will be born on the rarest of days in the year of the sheep, who will be of great assistance to the Great Work.

"Of my descendants, I ask only two things. First, become educated and lead a spiritual life, for both will prepare you for the work ahead. Second, if you are born in the year of the sheep and you happen to cross paths with someone bearing a book without words, they are to be revered. Offer your allegiance and assistance, for this person carries with them the heaviest of burdens."

When Yuuto looked up this time, he found his father's eyes burning into him.

"*You* were born in the year of the sheep, Yuuto."

"You believe I will be called upon for this Great Work?"

"I do. The diary was written in the same hand as the rest of the Kojiki, therefore it is to be believed."

"Just because the Kojiki is written in the same hand," his mother interjected, "doesn't mean our Yuuto will be called upon."

His father turned to her. "You're forgetting the blind sage said the heir will be born on the rarest of days. Yuuto's birthday falls on February twenty-ninth, a day that comes only once every four years." Addressing Yuuto, he said, "Everything I've done, the decisions I've made for you, were to prepare you for this undertaking. If you'd rather waste your time at a meaningless social event, go ahead. But remember, the more you study, the more educated you will become. And having an education will make you better prepared for the Great Work."

Against his mother's wishes, Yuuto decided to heed his father's advice and stay home and study. He didn't know why, but something about the story sounded true.

* * *

Stopping every eight hours to rest the sled dogs, the Tanaka Expedition sped back to their ship, *Emperor's Pride*. Although the eight-day journey across the polar plateau had exhausted the men, Yuuto ordered them to immediately pull anchor and get underway. Two days later, after maneuvering through the treacherous ice floe surrounding the Antarctic continent, they were headed northward toward the Japanese mainland.

Early in the morning, Yuuto heard a knock on his cabin door.

"Father," Sara said, "the man has wakened."

Yuuto sprang from his bed and opened the door. "Good work!"

"But I didn't do anything."

"What do you mean?"

"I know this will sound impossible, but when Toshiro and I removed the bullet, his insides began to glow purple. As the glow dimmed, the wound closed."

Yuuto's eyes grew wide. "So he *is* who I suspected. Who saw this happen?"

"Only Toshiro and me."

"Good. Do not mention this to anyone. From now on, no one is allowed into the sick bay or to speak with this man without my permission."

"Why? Who is he?"

"I believe he is the revered one our ancestor spoke of in the Kojiki."

This time, Sara's eyes grew wide.

* * *

Aquinas could see his father Augustus standing at the threshold of an open door. When he tried to crawl toward him, the doorway moved farther away.

"Go back, Aquinas. It is not yet time for you to cross over."

"I have failed you, father."

"No, my son, you still have time."

"But without Merrick, how can I go on alone?"

"You are not alone, nor will you ever be alone, for I will always be with you. Now return to your mortal existence. Remember, the key to defeating the Wanderer lies in the Wordless Book."

Augustus faded from his sight.

Awakening, Aquinas felt the waves of the choppy sea and realized he was in the cabin of a ship. Looking out the window, a flag waving from the mast drew his attention. From its slanted red stripes and circle, symbolizing the rising sun, he knew it to be Japanese.

Could the parable be true?

Turning his attention back to the cabin, he realized he wasn't alone. An Asian man stood across the room, young, in his early twenties, and wearing a white shirt and black pants.

"Where am I?" Aquinas asked, his raspy voice barely audible.

The man walked over to him, but before he could answer the door opened and two more people, an older man and a young woman, wearing the same attire entered the room. The older man appeared to be roughly fifty years old, while the woman looked to be near the same age as the young man. As the three conversed with each other in Japanese, Aquinas quickly glanced at their left hands.

Good. None of them are missing the outer segment of their middle finger.

When their conversation ended, the older man slowly walked up to the side of his bed, got down on his knees, and bowed his head.

"You need not bow to me," Aquinas said.

The man replied in English. "Forgive me, venerable one. I meant no disrespect."

Aquinas smiled. "There is nothing to forgive. Please stand."

The man returned to his feet. "Can we bring you nourishment?"

Aquinas rose to a sitting position. "Water and something to eat, if it's not too much trouble."

The older man relayed his instructions to the others. The young man nodded and exited the cabin. The young woman retrieved a glass of water from a nearby table and handed it to him.

Aquinas took a drink and set the glass down. "Where am I?"

"You are aboard the Japanese research vessel *Emperor's Pride*," the older man replied, "currently heading north through the Southern Ocean. I am Yuuto Tanaka, at your service."

"Pleased to meet you, Mr. Tanaka. My name is Aquinas."

As Yuuto bowed again, the young man returned with a bowl of steaming rice and a wooden spoon. He handed them to Aquinas.

"This is my son Toshiro and my daughter Sara."

They bowed like their father. When Sara rose to her feet, her penetrating green eyes captivated Aquinas.

"Sara has informed me your wound has healed itself. Was it the sacred substance carmot?"

"You know of the carmot?"

Yuuto nodded.

Aquinas looked around.

"You needn't worry about the Wordless Book. It is still in the case, locked away in my safe."

"How do you know of the Wordless Book?"

As Yuuto began reciting the pages from his family's Kojiki, Aquinas felt his eyelids getting heavy. Laying back down, he fell asleep.

* * *

Opening his eyes, Aquinas found himself back at the Crater of Hope, crouched behind the slanted boulder. The sound of Merrick's voice echoed off the icy walls.

"Help me, My Captain!"

Looking around the side of the boulder, he saw Merrick standing in the same place where Gwendolyn had kicked him, near the icy rim of the bottomless pit.

"Help me, My Captain!"

As Aquinas rose to his feet and stepped out, Merrick's face began to change. Not believing what he was seeing, Aquinas stood motionless, entranced by the macabre sight. When his features sharpened, Lucas' face had replaced Merrick's!

"Help me, My Captain!" he said again, then laughed.

An instant later the chilling sight vanished.

"Your power of suggestion doesn't scare me!" Aquinas yelled. "Show yourself!"

Lucas' deep, guttural laugh grew louder as it reverberated off the cave's icy walls.

"Show yourself!" Aquinas bellowed again.

When Lucas spoke, his voice emanated from all around. "Keep looking over your shoulder, Aquinas. No matter how far you go, I will find you."

"Save your threats. They no longer frighten me."

"Mark my words. When I find you, I will kill you and take the Wordless Book. Once I recover the remaining carmot from Antarctica, I will bring about a disease so deadly it will plunge mankind into chaos!"

"You possessed the book for almost thirty years. You and your confederate must be complete imbeciles in mathematics and geometry."

"Keep looking over your shoulder," Lucas replied, ignoring the insult. "Remember what I told you. When I find you, I will kill you!"

* * *

With Lucas' warning still ringing in his ears, Aquinas woke to find Yuuto, Toshiro, and Sara standing over him.

"You gave us quite a scare," Yuuto said.

"What happened?"

"I was reciting our family's Kojiki when you lost consciousness. We could not wake you."

"How long was I out?"

"A few minutes."

"How do you feel?" Sara asked.

Aquinas slowly sat up. "I think I'm all right."

After taking his pulse and checking his heart, Sara nodded to her father.

"Whatever it was, it appears to have passed," Yuuto said. "May I continue reading our family's Kojiki?"

"Certainly."

As Yuuto recited the passages, Aquinas was overcome by emotion. Embarrassed, he put his hands over his eyes.

Noticing, Yuuto stopped reading. "Does something sadden you?"

"My father was the one who returned from the voyage of the *Conviction*. Until now, I was unaware anyone else had knowledge of the Great Work."

Yuuto nodded and continued reading. Once he had finished, he looked up. "When my daughter found you on the plateau and showed me the Wordless Book, I knew you were the revered one my ancestor wrote about."

"Your daughter found me?"

Yuuto nodded. "She saved your life."

Aquinas looked at Sara.

His life shall be saved by a nobleman's daughter, just as the Wordless Book foretold!

"I concluded the Wanderer had shot you," Yuuto continued, "so we hastened your escape."

"Can you tell us what happened?" Toshiro asked. "How did you come to be on the Polar Plateau?"

Thinking of Merrick, tears welled up in Aquinas' eyes again.

"It's alright," Sara said, in a calm, soothing tone. "You are safe now."

Aquinas stared at her, momentarily speechless. Her soft voice was as hypnotic as her captivating eyes. Realizing they were still awaiting an answer, Aquinas cleared his throat.

"I don't know where to begin."

"Tell us about how you came to be involved in the Great Work," Yuuto suggested.

For the next two hours, Aquinas told them the story. After recounting how he'd lost Merrick at the Crater of Hope, he hung his head and wept.

Yuuto, Toshiro, and Sara immediately got down on their knees and bowed again.

"You honor us with your presence, Aquinas," Yuuto said.

"I am not worthy of your honor."

Yuuto shook his head. "I respectfully disagree. You recovered the Wordless Book. Therefore, the Great Work can continue."

"A wise man once told me losing one battle does not necessarily mean the entire war is lost," Toshiro commented.

"I have lost my father and a man I considered a brother. If that's not losing a war, I don't know what is."

Sara put her hand on his shoulder. "You've been through a very trying ordeal and your heart is heavy. From what you've told us, your father and Merrick were warriors of great distinction. Such warriors can never be replaced, only succeeded."

"Succeeded?"

Yuuto smiled. "What my daughter means is we wish to help you with the Great Work."

"I can't ask you to do that. Lucas' power of suggestion is strong. He can fool you with his lies and disguises. By rescuing me, you've probably already placed your lives in danger."

"If our lives are already in danger," Toshiro said, "the point is moot."

"What about your families?"

"You are looking at our family," Yuuto replied. "I lost my wife in the war, and my son and daughter have yet to find worthy spouses."

Aquinas started to protest again, but Sara's gentle voice stopped him. "From what you've said, this evil man Lucas is intent on creating a sickness that kills every man, woman, and child. The burden of trying to stop him is far too great for one man to bear alone. So we humbly ask, what can we do to help you?"

As she was talking, Aquinas looked into her eyes and his heart melted. Her poised and gentle demeanor, coupled with her angelic voice cast a spell on him. It felt as if every word she spoke connected with him on a deep, spiritual level. She reawakened feelings he hadn't experienced in a long time.

Throughout the centuries, Aquinas had met many women worthy of falling in love with. Knowing he would outlive them, he had suppressed those feelings and spurned their advances. Sara was different, and her beauty rekindled his longing for a female companion.

"According to my father, the answer to defeating Lucas lies in the Wordless Book. Perhaps you could help me decipher the remaining symbols?"

Yuuto thought for a moment. "If you wish us to help you decipher the symbols, we should start from the beginning."

"Why start from the beginning? Merrick and I have already deciphered roughly half of the pages?"

"We are not familiar with your methods or the disciplines of math you used to reach your conclusions. If we are to be successful, we must establish a fundamental understanding of the book from its beginning. As for how long it takes, it does not matter. We are at your disposal until this undertaking is completed."

"We'll need a secluded place for a very long time to work on the calculations."

"How about this ship? We can stay at sea and work in seclusion."

Aquinas looked around. "Okay, but just so you know, deciphering the symbols is a long, laborious task. You first must correctly measure the symbol all way down to the millimeter, which is a challenge all its own. The measurements are plugged into every conceivable mathematical equation. By *every* equation, I mean algebra, calculus, geometry, combinatorics, number theory, dynamical systems, and differential equations. That's the short list. I haven't even mentioned the physics-related equations or the probability theorems."

Toshiro's eyes grew wide. "How will you know when you've found the correct equation?"

"The answers will equal numbers ranging from one to twenty-six. These answers correspond with the letters in the English alphabet. Merrick and I spent decades working on some of the more advanced pages, and we never finished."

"Decades? I cannot believe it would take so long."

Aquinas locked his eyes on Toshiro. "Believe it. As the book progresses, the symbols become more complicated and the equations more complex. Once the letters are known, placing them in the proper order is another challenge. If you haven't made a mistake, then comes the task of correctly interpreting the rhyming parable. Although some parables are elementary and rather easy to understand, others are obscure and incomprehensible."

Toshiro started to say something, but Aquinas held up his hand.

"One more thing. When you immerse yourself in deciphering the symbols, it can become an obsession. If you allow them to take over your every waking thought, you can easily miscalculate simple deductions. Case in point, Lucas and Gwendolyn had the Wordless Book in their possession for nearly thirty years, and they still went to the wrong place in Antarctica."

"My apologies, I did not mean to offend," Toshiro said. "From what you've described, deciphering the Wordless Book sounds like fun."

"What did you say?"

Toshiro smiled. "I said it sounds like fun."

Aquinas looked at Sara. "Am I missing something?"

She laughed and shook her head. "My brother has always enjoyed the challenge of mathematics. Five of the last six years he attended school, he was the all-around champion of the Tokyo Invitational."

"The Tokyo Invitational?"

"The Tokyo Educator's Invitational Mathematics Tournament."

Toshiro leaned forward. "It should have been six, but my senior year the deciding judge was a relation to my closest competitor."

Aquinas smiled. "Perhaps it is I who should apologize."

"No need," Yuuto said. "My son's youthful exuberance frequently masks his mature intellect. But back to the matter at hand, do you believe the sacred substance will be safe in Antarctica?"

"My instincts are telling me yes, but circumstances could change if Lucas discovers the land under the Rae Ice Shelf points three ways."

"Are there any other places where he could obtain the sacred substance?"

Aquinas shook his head. "The book tells of only Amsterdam, Paris, Niagara Falls, and Antarctica. Merrick and I destroyed the first three."

"Since you did not decipher all of the symbols, is it possible there could be other places?"

"It's possible, but I don't think so. The book is structured like any other, meaning it has chapters. The chapter telling the locations of the carmot mentioned only those four areas of the world."

"We shall therefore employ some of our resources to watch over Antarctica."

Aquinas raised an eyebrow. "Some of your resources?"

"Let's just say I know some people who will help us."

Toshiro chuckled. "My father is much too modest. Our family's business survived the war relatively intact. In the three years since, the Tanaka Corporation has become a powerful international shipping conglomerate. That is one of the reasons we were in Antarctica, to see if it would be viable for us to open our shipping lanes through the Southern Ocean."

"I'm curious. What are the other reasons?"

"Ever since I was young," Yuuto said, "I've had a desire to explore. After losing my wife, I decided to fulfill this desire. When the war ended, I purchased this ship from a member of the Emperor's family and began exploring the world. Now, it will serve the Great

Work." He turned to Toshiro. "Send a message to our stockholders. Tell them we intend to expand our routes in the Southern Ocean, to include ports of call on Antarctica."

Toshiro retrieved a pad of paper and pen from a nearby counter and began writing.

"Along with being a skilled engineer, my son helps me manage the day-to-day affairs of my shipping business."

"What about your daughter?"

"Sara also wears two hats. Not only is she a skilled nurse, she is also my company representative. Combined, Sara and Toshiro have trusted contacts at nearly all the major seaports in the world."

"And since Gwendolyn Phillips is very well known in the business community," Sara added, "my brother and I can call upon our contacts to shadow her movements."

Aquinas nodded. "Sounds like a good plan, but remember Lucas is as arrogant as he is clever. His power of suggestion is strong, and he uses this power to its fullest advantage. He can trick people into seeing things, or divulging information they would otherwise keep secret."

"A wise man once told me an opponent who is overly-sure of himself will ultimately be defeated," Toshiro said. "Their ego will be their undoing."

"But if one of your contacts happens to fall under Lucas' spell, how can we be sure they won't disclose your name?

"We cannot be sure," Yuuto said, "but I have faith we can evade him by erasing all evidence of our south polar expedition, and by becoming like swift water."

"Swift water?"

"A wise man once taught me no one is ever outmatched by an opponent," Sara said. "They only lack the knowledge of how to defeat them. To gain this knowledge, become like swift water and keep moving. Your opponent will eventually tire and show their weakness."

"Can I guess the name of this wise man you and your brother keep mentioning?"

Sara and Toshiro smiled and looked at their father.

Yuuto walked over to a cabinet and removed a bottle of Junmai-shu sake. After filling four small glasses, he handed one to each of them. Clearing his throat, he raised his glass.

"Aquinas, from this point forward we stand with you in the Great Work."

When he drank the smooth and tasty rice wine, tears came to Aquinas' eyes. Losing Merrick had left him without hope of ever stopping Lucas. Now, with Yuuto, Toshiro, and Sara, his chances had increased by a factor of three.

~ The Wanderer ~

Back on the South Polar Plateau, Lucas looked off into the distance, studying the snowy terrain. After several minutes, he turned and walked back to Gwendolyn. "Someone has intervened on Aquinas' behalf. My intuition is telling me he is no longer on the continent."

"I agree. So what do we do? We need the book to recover the carmot."

"We shall call upon people you know."

"People I know?"

"Yes. We will need to investigate all recent expeditions to Antarctica, and what better way than through your business connections?"

"Even with my business connections, it won't be easy."

"Nothing is ever easy, as far as Aquinas is concerned. In this instance, however, it shouldn't be too much trouble. Instruct them to report only Japanese expeditions."

"Why only Japanese?"

"Because of the parable in the Wordless Book. Don't you remember?"

Gwendolyn shook her head. "I've better things to do than try to remember those idiotic rhymes."

Lucas smiled. "My pet, you are much too impatient. One of the parables spoke about the great knight's leader seeing a red sunrise, which is the symbol on the Japanese flag."

"Oh, all right. When we get back to East Base, I'll send out some messages to my contacts in Japan."

"If the rest of the parable is to be believed, we will find Aquinas with a woman."

"A woman?"

Lucas nodded. "A nobleman's daughter who will supposedly save his life. Perhaps the daughter of the man who rescued him."

"And if we find Aquinas with this nobleman's daughter?"

"I shall play the part of a Samurai executioner and behead her in front of his eyes! Mark my words, Aquinas will rue the day he interfered in my affairs."

Gwendolyn smiled and embraced him. "I love it when you talk like that."

* * *

Returning to Tokyo, Yuuto Tanaka ordered the seven scientists onboard the *Emperor's Pride* to never divulge they found a wounded man on the polar plateau. To ensure their secrecy, he promised each of them a large sum of money. Once they had departed, he destroyed all evidence of his ship's journey, going as far as setting fire to the official logbooks. A week later, after delegating control of his corporation to a hastily assembled board of trustees, Yuuto dropped out of sight of the Japanese business community.

Contacting the explorer Finn Ronne at East Base, Toshiro learned Gwendolyn Phillips and the big, dark-haired man accompanying her had returned to the United States. Calling one of his trusted contacts in America who owned a private investigation firm, he had them placed under surveillance. A few days later, the contact reported Gwendolyn and her escort, who was using the name "Lucas Carter," were at her company's headquarters in Chicago.

While Yuuto and Toshiro worked on destroying the trail behind them and shadowing the Wanderer, Sara and Aquinas took on the not-so-easy task of renaming the ship and scheduling resupply runs. Inventing a new name for the ship, Sara thought of her family's Kojiki and Aquinas' story of his father. Two days of re-painting later, she called everyone together and rechristened the ship, "*Renewed Conviction.*" As for resupplying the ship, Sara and Aquinas set up a random schedule at different seaports along the Japanese mainland.

With the unpredictable carmot restoring his health, Aquinas spent more and more of his time with Sara. Throughout the next two years, his love for her blossomed, as did her feelings toward him. On one occasion, they were strolling in the gardens outside of the Kin Kaku-ji Temple in Kyoto.

"Like you, this majestic temple and its grounds are a natural wonder all their own," Aquinas said.

"It is exquisite," Sara replied. "My father comes here often to pay tribute to our ancestors."

"Are they buried here?"

She shook her head. "They helped build the temple. The undertaking began in the late fourteenth century, shortly after you were born."

"Does my age bother you?"

She laughed. "Not in the least. It's not every day a girl gets to be courted by a handsome man who happens to be over six-hundred years old. Lucky for you, my father is old fashioned. When I turned fourteen, he made me promise to choose a suitor who is older and well-established. He makes me repeat this promise every year on my birthday."

Aquinas stopped and pulled her close. "Will he give me permission to marry you?"

"Not until you have courted me for three years."

"Must it be so long?"

She nodded. "He believes three years is the minimum time needed for a man and woman to get to know each other."

Aquinas leaned in and kissed her. After the long, extended embrace, he looked into her eyes. "I'm in love with you, Sara Tanaka, and want you to be my wife."

"I'm in love with you, Aquinas, and I want you to be my husband. But it will fulfill my father's wishes if we wait. In the scheme of things, another year is not long."

Aquinas could see the conviction in her eyes. "Very well. I respect your father too much to go against his wishes."

One year later, Aquinas asked Yuuto Tanaka for permission to marry Sara.

Yuuto offered his blessings.

* * *

In the garden of an ancient shrine, amid a colorful array of cherry blossoms, Aquinas took Sara's hand. As he knelt to recite his wedding vows, the moon moved in front of the sun, darkening the sky. The eclipse triggered his memory of a page of symbols he'd partially deciphered with Merrick many years earlier. Although they hadn't deciphered the entire parable, they did figure out the first two sentences – sentences more ominous than the others in the Wordless Book.

"What's the matter, my love?" Sara whispered.

"Nothing. Nothing at all."

Dismissing the sentences as a misinterpretation, he repeated his vows and slipped the ring on Sara's finger.

Early the next morning, Toshiro received word from his contact in America. Gwendolyn and Lucas were still in Chicago. Thinking it would be safe, Aquinas surprised Sara by taking her on a honeymoon trip to Tokyo. The absence of any confrontations with the Wanderer brightened Aquinas' spirits, making him happier and more optimistic than he'd been in a long time. He believed a divine mentor had guided Sara and her family to him, and together they could complete the Great Work.

Rejoining Yuuto and Toshiro, the four immediately went back to work deciphering the Wordless Book. As the symbols increased in complexity, so did the errors in their calculations. At times, even the gifted Toshiro found himself making mistakes.

When they became mentally exhausted from working on the symbols, Sara and Toshiro taught Aquinas how to speak their language, and karate, the Japanese martial art of self-defense. Aquinas' element-enhanced learning abilities absorbed the training like a sponge.

To stay connected to the outside world, when the four pulled into port to resupply, they participated in recreational activities.

Taking turns to decide what activity to take part in, Sara normally chose hiking or swimming, while Toshiro favored more-thrilling activities, such as water-skiing and hang gliding. Yuuto and Aquinas enjoyed going to plays, or if they were near a large city, taking in the latest American movie, preferably a western.

The four also became familiar with the latest firearms, and discussed strategies of how to confront the Wanderer, should he discover their whereabouts. One of these discussions took place on the bridge of *Renewed Conviction*. After providing a lengthy description of Lucas and his abilities, Aquinas asked if anyone had a question.

"I do," Toshiro said. "His power of suggestion gives him a distinct advantage. Do we possess an advantage over him?"

Aquinas thought for a moment. "Two things come to mind. First, he doesn't know you, Sara, or Yuuto, and therefore doesn't know the skills you possess in battle. Second, you have the advantage of being able to identify him. Regardless of the strength of his power of suggestion, he cannot mask the missing tip of his left middle finger. Above all else, remember you cannot inflict a fatal blow, but you can injure his extremities."

"So our strategy is to injure his arms and legs?" Yuuto asked.

Aquinas nodded. "In any way possible. And just so we are clear on this, we must be ruthless in our attack, because if we fail, he will be merciless dealing with us. If we cannot injure his extremities, we must administer a blow to his head and render him unconscious. When he is asleep, he will not be able to fool us with his power of suggestion, and we'll be able to shackle him."

"Say we are able to shackle him," Sara interjected, "what are we to do with him? I mean, what do we do with a man who cannot die, who is obsessed with genocide?"

"Merrick and I pondered that question. Our plan was to capture Lucas and keep him chained in an ice cave beneath the Bitton Glacier.

If we had been successful, we would've used the carmot to stay alive and watch over him until the Day of Reckoning. After losing Merrick, I remembered something my father told me just before he died. He had partially deciphered one of the more-complex symbols, which foretold a weakened man will play a part in defeating the Wanderer. It is therefore imperative we learn who this weakened man is."

"And while we are doing that, we must continue to evade Lucas and his people," Toshiro said.

"Correct. We must also develop a contingency plan in the event our evasive tactics are unsuccessful, or in case Lucas kills one of us. Aside from that, there is one other thing we can do, but it will require your utmost trust in me."

"Name it," Yuuto said.

"Using hypnosis, I can try to condition your minds to resist Lucas' power of suggestion. I don't know if it will work."

Yuuto, Toshiro, and Sara looked at each other and nodded.

"You have our permission," Toshiro said. "And if your method fails, we have something we could use as a last resort."

Aquinas raised an eyebrow. "Oh?"

"When I purchased this ship from the emperor's family," Yuuto explained, "I found it had been wired for self-destruction with explosives. Hidden in the bridge, the galley, and in every cabin, is a tiny switch. If the switch is pressed, it allows five minutes to abandon ship before it goes off. When I took possession of the vessel, the explosives were removed, but I know someone who can re-supply us."

Aquinas' eyes grew wide, and he reached out and took Sara's hand. "You would actually choose suicide?"

"We are traditionalists by nature." Sara said. "If given the choice, we would choose death before dishonor. To be captured would be shameful."

Before Aquinas could reply, Yuuto held up his hand. "The destruction of the ship could possibly injure the Wanderer's arms and legs to the point he is rendered harmless. Do you not agree?"

Aquinas thought for a moment. "Perhaps you're right, but I shall pray our confrontation doesn't go that far."

~ Present Day ~

When disc seven ended, I pushed the "Eject" button on the CD player.

"The storm is letting up," Madison said. "Are you okay if we go?"

"Sure, but to where?"

"I don't know."

"According to the sign we passed, Phoenix is a hundred-and-fifty miles away."

"It will take us a little more than two hours to get there."

"I'm okay with that. And I know just the thing to help pass the time."

I loaded disc number eight into the CD player, and Aquinas' voice, once again, came through the speakers.

"By staying at sea, and randomly selecting ports to replenish our supplies, the four of us eluded the Wanderer for the next nineteen years. As the time passed, we inched closer to deciphering the remaining symbols in the Wordless Book. The secret of how to defeat the Wanderer now seemed within my reach, and I dreamt of the day when I could put all of this behind me and devote myself to my beloved wife. Unfortunately, my dream would end abruptly, on the day coinciding with Sara deciphering four pages of symbols – the first parable being the same one I remembered on my wedding day.

"Unfortunately, I would learn a harsh lesson, one whose meaning wasn't shrouded in a symbol or confusing parable: warnings in the Wordless Book should be heeded."

If the sun falls dark
on the day of tomorrow,
the omen will signal
a union of sorrow.

Then passed the ides of autumn,
one-fourth and a score,
the great soldier's heart
will be broken once more.

Sara's interpretation of the second group of symbols in the second chapter of the Wordless Book

CHAPTER TEN: THE STORM

Friday, 15 October 1971, 05:25hrs
Aboard *Renewed Conviction*
Sixty-Seven Kilometers Southeast of Yokohama, Japan

Like a switch had been turned on under the water, an array of multi-colored lights appeared on the distant seascape. As the ship drew closer, the lights grew brighter, outlining the thriving metropolis of Japan's second-largest city. Under the backdrop of the starry night, the Pacific Ocean reflected the scene, the mirror image of the buildings appearing three times their actual size. The rich hues of color brightened the panorama to a near-daytime intensity, before fading away into an endless refraction beneath the surface.

As Aquinas stared out the cabin window marveling at the view, he reached behind him and found Sara gone.

Strange. Sara never gets up before me.

Immediately alert, he rose out of bed and looked down the hall. Checking the lower deck, he saw the light on in the room where they worked on deciphering the Wordless Book. Proceeding down the stairs, he found Sara curled up on the sofa. Her puffy red eyes told him she'd been crying.

Sitting down, he pulled her into his arms.

"My love," he said gently, "what on earth has upset you?"

"I couldn't sleep, so I came down here and reviewed our work again."

"You've been up all night?"

She took a deep breath and pointed to six poster-sized papers taped to the wall. "I've deciphered pages thirty-five through thirty-eight."

Aquinas' eyes grew wide. "*Four* pages?"

She nodded. "I found an error in Toshiro's calculations."

Aquinas glanced over at the papers. "This is unbelievable. No, this is incredible! I can't wait to tell your father!"

When she didn't respond, he looked at her and saw tears welling up in her eyes.

"I don't understand. Why are you crying?"

"I believe the parables are referring to you again, but the one I deciphered from page thirty-five is different than the others."

"In what way?"

"It describes *if* something happens, *then* something else will happen."

"I cannot believe it is so dour. Here, let me have a look."

He kissed her on the forehead, stood, and walked over to examine the six papers. The page on the left side contained the same complex sets of math problems they'd been working on for eighteen months. Three-quarters of the problems now had a large red X written over them. Underneath them, in Sara's tiny handwriting, were different sets of equations.

The second page had the new solutions listed left to right. Underneath each solution were corresponding letters of the alphabet. The third page, numbered 2-2, contained numerous sentences, all but four had been crossed out. The three papers on the far right, numbered 2-3, 2-4, and 2-5 respectively, were similar to the paper numbered 2-2, but with different sentences.

As Aquinas began reading the first parable, a knot formed in the pit of his stomach. The first two sentences matched the ones he'd partially deciphered with Merrick many years earlier. When he read the next two sentences, the knot tightened. After quickly reading the parables on the other pages, he went back to page 2-2 and read it again. Retrieving a small notebook and pen, he quickly transcribed all of them.

"In the Shinto religion," Sara said, "a wedding day is considered a day of tomorrow, celebrating a couple's new future together."

Aquinas smiled. "It doesn't necessarily mean the parable is referring to *our* wedding day."

"But it specifically describes the eclipse. How can you ignore that?"

"I'm not ignoring it." He finished writing and looked up. "Tell me, in the years we've been together, have I made you happy?"

"Yes."

"And you have made me happier than you will ever know. Therefore, it cannot possibly be referring to our wedding day. Our union is one of joy, not sorrow."

"Perhaps the sorrow has not yet happened?"

"We cannot worry about something that may or may not happen."

Just then, Yuuto and Toshiro walked in.

Rising to his feet, Aquinas announced, "Sara has deciphered four entire pages of symbols!"

Yuuto's eyes grew wide. "Four?"

Aquinas nodded proudly. "She found an error in our calculations. See for yourselves."

They moved over to examine the papers.

After reading the parables, Toshiro returned to the math problems and shook his head. "I cannot believe I made such a foolish error."

"We all missed it," Aquinas said. "I should've reminded everyone, including myself, that if deciphering the symbols becomes an obsession, it's easy to miss simple deductions."

When Yuuto finished reading, he turned to Aquinas. "Could the parable be referring to you again?"

"We were discussing the parable when you came in, father. Aquinas thinks they are not about him because we are happy. I'm concerned the sorrow has not yet happened."

"What we need is a point of reference," Aquinas stated. "Unfortunately, it doesn't give us one."

"Perhaps we need to look at it a different way," Yuuto said. "Let us concentrate on what we *do* know."

"Okay," Toshiro said, "I'm willing to give it a try." He retrieved a marker. "Let's assume the union in question is referring to Sara and Aquinas' wedding day."

He turned and wrote "August 1, 1951" below the parable.

"We know *ides* means the middle day of a month," Yuuto said, "normally the fifteenth." Toshiro turned and wrote "15" below the date.

"But it doesn't make sense," Sara said, "Autumn is a season, not a month."

"True," Aquinas replied, "but in this instance, I believe the parable is referring to the middle day of the middle month of autumn. Since autumn is comprised of September, October, and November…"

Yuuto smiled. "The month *must* be October."

Toshiro wrote "Oct" before the number "15" and checked his watch. "Wait. Today is October fifteenth!"

"Patience," Yuuto replied, "We still must identify the year."

"We know a score of years equals twenty," Aquinas said. "A fourth of which would be five."

Toshiro turned and wrote "1976."

Sara turned to Aquinas. "So if the parable is referring to our wedding day, whatever happens to make our union sorrowful won't happen for another five years?"

Aquinas smiled. "Which means we have time to mitigate this sorrow, whatever it may be."

"What about the other three parables?" Toshiro asked.

Aquinas silently reread them. "I see no cause for concern. They do not read as a warning."

"I agree," Yuuto said. "And since we have time, I believe a celebration is in order."

"A celebration?" Toshiro asked.

"Yes. Your sister has deciphered four entire pages of symbols in one night."

"Father," Sara said sternly, "even though Toshiro made a mistake in the calculations, I wouldn't have found it if he hadn't taught me the math."

"We shall therefore celebrate *both* of your abilities. We are now only two chapters away from learning all the secrets in the Wordless Book."

"I'd say that's cause for a celebration," Aquinas said.

Toshiro smiled. "May I suggest lunch at the Arashiyama? It's not tourist season, so there shouldn't be too many people, and our old dock at the marina should still be vacant. We can take the commuter train from there, just like the old days."

"An excellent choice," Yuuto said. "Contact the harbormaster at Osaka Bay, and tell him *Renewed Conviction* is coming in, and our destination is the Kaiyukan Marina."

"But father," Sara interjected, "shouldn't we stay on board and tend to the ship? Last night's weather report said the approaching typhoon is the largest ever recorded."

"This morning's report said it was turning out to sea," Toshiro countered.

Yuuto smiled. "It's settled. We will celebrate at the Arashiyama Restaurant. It will be nice to see Cousin Leo again."

"Cousin Leo?" Aquinas asked.

"Leonard Ngura. He owns the restaurant."

"He's not really a cousin," Sara explained, "it's just the name he goes by. When my father attended Hokkaido University, they roomed together."

"We both had the same ambition," Yuuto said, "to open our own businesses. He made out rather well, despite his compulsion for cleanliness."

Aquinas raised an eyebrow. "His what?"

"He obsessed over keeping himself clean. It was a phobia he grew up with. Some days, he would wash his hands more than fifty times. He eventually sought counseling, which helped him channel his obsession to his business."

Toshiro laughed. "You'll see when we get there. His restaurant is so clean you could eat off the floor."

Aquinas smiled. "So where is this Arashiyama restaurant?"

"Not far from the famous bamboo forest and mountain range of the same name."

"Their soba is delicious," Sara added, "and the view is quite magnificent."

~ The Wanderer ~

On the uppermost floor of Hotel Okura, inside the posh executive suite, Lucas and Gwendolyn sat at a long, ornate table eating brunch. Behind them, corner windows, running floor to ceiling, afforded a spectacular view of the city of Kobe. Everything in the room appeared clean and immaculate, the lone exception being the small, unpainted shipping crate and its pried off lid sitting on the far end of the table.

When the phone started to ring, Gwendolyn leisurely took a sip of water, wiped her mouth with a napkin, and picked up the receiver.

"Yes, this is Miss Phillips." After listening for a moment, she screamed, "Your job is to find them! Do not contact me again until you do!" She slammed the receiver down.

"Another false alarm?" Lucas asked.

She nodded.

"I told you not to offer such a high reward to our contacts. Now they have employed underlings to the search, who are seeing Aquinas and the Tanakas on every street corner. Yesterday they were hiding in a fish market in Tokyo. Last night they were barricaded in a room above a restaurant in Yamaguchi. This morning they were seen on a pier in Sapporo."

She stood and walked over to a mirror hanging inside the suite's entry door. "What am I supposed to do, just sit here and wait?" She primped up her silver wig and checked her makeup. "It's been fifty-three years since I last ate any carmot, and I don't want to start growing old again."

He laughed. "Really? When you put on the disguise, you make such a beautiful, aged businesswoman."

"I only wear this insufferable disguise to fool people into thinking I'm growing older."

Lucas walked over and put his arm around her. "Relax, my pet. We shall soon get rid of your senior citizen persona. When you assume control of Phillips Industries as your only living heir, you'll not have to wear a disguise for the foreseeable future. As for the carmot, it should last well into the next century, if not longer. We'll recover the book and decipher the symbols well before you start to age again."

"But how can you be so confident? It's been almost twenty years, and we are still no closer to finding Aquinas."

He smiled. "Oh, but we are. Remember when we first arrived? We both sensed Aquinas and the book, but we couldn't pinpoint the exact location. Thanks to our people talking to the seafarers and longshoremen, we now know why: they are onboard Tanaka's ship. The only time Aquinas sets foot on the mainland is when they resupply, which explains why, from time to time, we sense he is here."

Gwendolyn walked over to the table and took another drink. "But what makes you so sure we will find him here in Kobe? I see nothing distinctive about this city."

"No? What about the Nakamura triplets? We found them in Kobe, and they are quite distinctive."

"We can easily recruit murderers for hire in any large city."

Lucas nodded. "But these three are not merely murderers for hire. They are identical in appearance and equal in their ruthlessness, which fits perfectly into our plans. Coaxing them away from the underboss of Japan's most powerful crime organization was no small feat."

"Don't break your arm patting yourself on the back. They cost me a lot of money, and two of them can't even speak."

"I wasn't looking for accolades," Lucas replied, irritated. "We needed people who are unscrupulous and know this country. The triplets were born and raised here, and they have the reputation as the best assassins money can buy. The fact two of them are mute doesn't matter. Using the power of suggestion, I have complete control over Hiroshi, the one who can speak. He's the leader. Whatever he orders them to do, they'll do. Therefore, whatever I order him to do, they'll do."

"True, but why must we stay here in Kobe? There are much nicer hotels in Tokyo."

"We're in Kobe, because it sits in the center of the continent, which gives us a distinct advantage. When our search teams find Aquinas and the Tanakas, we can be there in minutes from this location."

"I hope you're right. The helicopter and pilot we have standing by on the roof are also costing me a small fortune."

"A mere pittance compared to what the carmot will bring."

She thought for a moment. "When we recover the book, we will still have to decipher those insufferable symbols and determine where we made the error in the math. Couldn't we hire someone to decipher them for us? Someone expendable we could eliminate later?"

Lucas shook his head. "When we capture Aquinas, we won't need to. I intend to have the triplets kill the Tanakas, one at a time, in front of him until he divulges the location of the carmot."

"What if he still refuses to answer?"

"I shall simply kill him, recover the Wordless Book, and seize his papers. We'll be able to use them to discover where we made the mistake in our own calculations."

The phone rang again, and she snatched the receiver. "Yes, this is Gwendolyn Phillips." As she listened, her face lit up. "We'll be right there." She slammed the receiver down. "That was our mole in the harbormaster's office at Osaka Bay. They just cleared a ship named *Renewed Conviction* to dock at the Kaiyukan Marina. It matches the description of the *Emperor's Pride*. They reported three men and one woman aboard."

"Excellent. I'll inform the triplets and the other search teams to meet us there."

After making the calls, Lucas retrieved the shipping crate from the table and followed Gwendolyn to the roof.

* * *

Ten minutes later, the helicopter carrying Lucas and Gwendolyn landed in the grassy outfield of a baseball diamond, two blocks from the Kaiyukan Marina. The instant he stepped off the helicopter, Lucas sensed Aquinas.

"Is he here?" Gwendolyn asked.

"You tell me."

She stepped down next to him and closed her eyes. "He's close but moving away from us."

"Very good. Now open your eyes. What is the first thing you are drawn to?"

She opened her eyes. "The train tracks. He's on a train!"

"Precisely."

Just then, a long, black limousine turned in from the street and parked a short distance away. A chauffeur got out and opened the rear door, and the Nakamura triplets emerged. They stood just under six feet tall, with dark hair combed straight and cut off at the eyebrows. Their black pants and white shirts looked to be tailored to perfection. Instead of suit coats, each sported a black bullet-proof vest. As for weaponry, they wore the same: a holstered gun on the right side and a sheathed kukri knife on the left.

Taking the lead, Hiroshi Nakamura proceeded over to the helicopter, with the other two following close.

"Sir," Hiroshi said, "the four on the boat boarded a train. Their next stop is the Arashiyama station."

Lucas smiled. "Get in. I've got something for you."

As they climbed aboard, he reached into the shipping crate and handed each of them a new Uzi submachine gun and three full magazines of ammunition.

Less than a minute later, the helicopter passed the slow-moving commuter train and landed on the hill a short distance from the train depot. Using binoculars, Lucas observed the train pulling into the station. Three men and one woman disembarked and proceeded to the restaurant across the street.

"That's them," Lucas said.

"Finally, after all these years," Gwendolyn said, shaking with excitement.

Addressing the triplets, Lucas asked, "Are you ready?"

Each of them nodded.

When Gwendolyn moved to follow, Lucas held up his hand. "Stay here."

She frowned. "But I want to kill one of them."

Lucas retrieved an Uzi for himself and loaded a magazine. "It's too dangerous. Besides, you have a more important job to do. When the other search teams arrive, set up a perimeter around the restaurant. If anyone tries to leave, kill them."

"Oh, alright."

He turned to the triplets. "Let's go."

Lucas led them down the hill toward the Arashiyama Restaurant. When they reached the side entrance leading into the kitchen, he held the door open.

"After you, gentlemen."

* * *

Wave after wave of hurricane-force winds slammed into Kyoto's northern coastline, destroying hundreds of beachfront homes and buildings. The severe rain swelled Lake Biwa beyond its capacity, and as the surge increased the natural embankments gave way. Unleashed, the rumbling floods rushed to the surrounding lowlands, sweeping away an untold number of lives. As the power lines toppled, the warning blasts of the civil defense sirens slowly faded, leaving only the sounds of the driving wind and rain. In seconds, the one-hundred-thirty-kilometer stretch of land between Kyotango to Tsuruga lay in ruins.

Like a real-life Godzilla monster wreaking havoc on the Japanese mainland, Typhoon Fujin made landfall!

One-hundred kilometers to the south and unaware of the impending storm, Aquinas, Sara, Yuuto and Toshiro made their way from the train depot to the Arashiyama restaurant. Once inside, a waitress led them down a dimly lit hallway to a red velvet curtain. When she pulled the curtain aside, revealing the dining room, Aquinas' mouth dropped open.

Twelve steel tables, their tops polished to a mirror finish, sat evenly spaced against the rear wall of the immaculate restaurant, their far ends positioned in front of twelve, similarly set-apart windows. Each seat afforded a spectacular view of the Arashiyama mountain range. At the other end of the tables sat a glass case on a pedestal, each containing a jade statuette of one of the twelve animals in the Japanese calendar. Suspended over each of the tables hung a large, lighted mirror, reflecting the view outside and the statuette down onto the polished tabletop. On the far right, a door opened to an outside observation deck running the length of the building.

When the waitress seated them at the far-left "Year of the Horse" table, Aquinas looked on in wonder at the view outside. In the foreground, the sun highlighted the tall, grassy embankments of the Hozugawa River, transforming their normally drab fall colors into rich hues of yellow and orange. In contrast, the distant mountains stood dark and cloud-covered, periodically illuminating from flashes of scattered lightning. Aside from the occasional clinking of utensils, the only sounds were gusting winds and the rumbling of distant thunder.

A minute later, Cousin Leo, cleaning rag in hand, entered the dining room and came over to their table. After introducing Aquinas, Yuuto began reminiscing with him. As they talked, Leo cleaned the glass case containing the "Year of the Snake" statue at the table next to them. After taking their order, he checked on the other patrons, which included a family of four and an elderly couple, before departing through a swinging door into the kitchen.

Festive at first, Aquinas soon began to worry. Removing the small notebook from his pocket, he opened it to the page where he'd written down the warning parable, immediately quieting the others.

"What's the matter?" Sara asked.

"I'm not sure," he replied. "Give me a moment?"

"Certainly."

After silently rereading the parable, he focused his thoughts on the third sentence – the one describing the date.

Then passed the ides of autumn, one-fourth and a score.

Rereading it again, he realized it could be interpreted a different way.

One-fourth could be referring to one-fourth of a year, not one-fourth of a score of years!

He hurriedly did the math.

Toshiro could be right. The parable could be referring to today.

He suddenly had the feeling they were in imminent danger. Looking around, the family and the elderly couple were leaving.

Something isn't right.

Just then, Cousin Leo returned to the dining room. When he walked by one of the suspended mirrors, Aquinas caught sight of his reflection.

It can't be!

His eyes darted to Cousin Leo and back to the mirror.

Lucas!

Quickly looking away, he continued watching out of the corner of his eye. Lucas picked up a tray of dishes and proceeded back into the kitchen. When the swinging door reached full-travel, Aquinas caught sight of a body lying on the floor – unmistakably the real Cousin Leo.

Before he could warn the others, he experienced another feeling more powerful than the previous one. This new sensation was so strong, it momentarily rendered him speechless. A violent gust of wind slammed into the building, knocking several wall decorations to the floor. With the lightening over the mountain range increasing in frequency, and the cannon-like claps of thunder growing louder, Aquinas knew what his element-enhanced senses were telling him.

The typhoon!

Returning the small notebook to his pocket, he reached under his jacket and retrieved his gun. "Arm yourselves," he said, speaking low. "Lucas has found us."

Yuuto, Sara, and Toshiro immediately brandished their weapons.

"Where?" Sara asked.

"He's using the power of suggestion to masquerade as Cousin Leo."

Yuuto's eyes grew wide. "How? He knew things from our younger days."

"That *was* the real Cousin Leo. When he took our order to the kitchen, Lucas murdered him and took his place."

"Are you certain?"

"When he passed by a mirror, I saw Lucas' face in the reflection."

Yuuto thought for a moment. "Uncle Leo was a good friend, whom we shall mourn at another time. His unfortunate death, however, has uncovered another weakness of our adversary."

Aquinas nodded. "Lucas' power of suggestion cannot shroud his mirror image."

"If he has taken the place of Cousin Leo," Toshiro interjected, "why is he not attacking us?"

"First determine your enemy's strength," Yuuto said. "If I were in his position, that is what I would do."

"As for Lucas' strength," Aquinas said, "I'm sensing several heavily-armed men with him, with many more arriving soon."

"What shall we do?" Sara asked.

"Normally, I'd suggest we run, but we have a more pressing problem." He pointed to the flashing lightning outside the window. "What we've been watching is the leading edge of the typhoon."

Sara's eyes grew wide. "It didn't return to the sea?"

"No, which leaves us with two possible courses of action. We can either stay here and fight, or we can escape out the back and take our chances in the typhoon."

Just then, the kitchen door swung open and two men entered the room. Wearing aprons, each carried a large round serving tray. They looked identical, even in the way they carried the trays – vertically, as if they were hiding something.

"Everyone down!" Aquinas yelled.

He'd barely gotten the words out, when the men dropped the trays, revealing their submachine guns, and opened fire.

Yuuto and Toshiro dove to the floor, crawled to the end of the table, and took cover behind the "Year of the Snake" pedestal. Just as fast, Aquinas tipped over the table where they'd been sitting, grabbed Sara's hand, and pulled her down behind it.

The bullets peppered the tabletop and shattered the mirror hanging overhead. As the spray of hot lead moved left to right, the glass case holding the jade horse exploded.

When the look-alikes stopped to reload, Yuuto and Toshiro returned fire. The salvo of bullets struck the men, staggering them for only a moment. Aquinas realized why.

"They're wearing bullet-proof vests! Aim for their heads or legs!"

The kitchen door burst open and Lucas stormed in, dressed like the first two men but no longer disguised as Cousin Leo. Machine gun in hand, he took his place between the two look-alikes. Before he could fire, however, another wave of violent wind struck the restaurant bringing down several ceiling mirrors and the remainder of the wall decorations. The lights went out, plunging the already-dim dining room into darkness. A loud snapping sound followed, emanating from somewhere outside the building.

Just then, the power pole from in front of the restaurant crashed through the ceiling! The jagged, broken-off end impaled the man standing to Lucas' right, killing him instantly. As the top of the pole fell, its fiery transformer glanced off a ceiling rafter, sending it spinning down toward the henchman standing to Lucas' left. The pole's crossarm swatted him to the floor and pinned him under the burning transformer. As the flames engulfed him, the man shrieked and thrashed around. A moment later, the man stopped moving and his last breath gurgled from his lungs.

Lucas looked back and forth at the two men for a moment and let out a bellowing scream. Raising his weapon, he opened fire. The bullets glanced off the tipped-over table Aquinas and Sara were kneeling behind and struck Toshiro. Dropping his gun, he reached out to retrieve it. Lucas leveled the Uzi on him and squeezed the trigger. The hail of bullets struck Toshiro's chest and abdomen, dropping him to the floor – his eyes staring and vacant.

The shooting finally stopped when Aquinas heard a click.

Lucas is out of ammunition.

He leaned out, but before he could fire, Sara's loud gasp drew his attention. Quickly surveying the room, he saw Toshiro lying motionless in a growing pool of blood.

"No!" he screamed.

Like a man possessed, Aquinas squeezed off one round after another. Three of the bullets struck Lucas' left leg, sending him to his knees. Yuuto placed his gun in his belt and sprang into action. Jumping out from behind the pedestal, he ran up and delivered a series of punches to Lucas' head and stomach. When the big man fell to the floor, Yuuto pounced on top of him and continued the assault. Retrieving his gun, Yuuto flipped it around and used the butt end to strike a tooth-rattling blow to the side of Lucas' head.

As Yuuto rolled off the prone body, Lucas' face *transformed* into the face of the two look-alikes. Coinciding with the change, a deep, guttural laugh drowned out the sounds of the raging wind and thunder.

"He's not Lucas!" Aquinas yelled. "He's using the power of suggestion! Take cover!"

In a swift defensive move, Yuuto pulled the unconscious man over the top of him. A spray of gunfire erupted from the behind the hall curtains, striking the third look-alike multiple times in the back and head. When the room fell silent, Yuuto shoved the fatally wounded man off him and crawled over to join Aquinas and Sara.

"Are you injured?" Aquinas asked.

Yuuto shook his head.

"Why did it have to be Toshiro?" She asked, sobbing.

"We must believe the gods had their reasons," Yuuto replied, his voice cracking.

"We've got to get out of here," Aquinas whispered. "I'm sensing more heavily armed men approaching."

Sara looked up, teary-eyed and shaking. "But Lucas is blocking the way we came in, and the power pole is preventing us from reaching the door to the observation deck. We're trapped."

Aquinas pointed to the large window. "Are we?"

"Where will we go?"

"I know of a place just north of here," Yuuto interjected.

"Are you thinking of the bomb shelter, father?"

Yuuto nodded. "It served us well during the war, it can serve us again now."

"How far is it?" Aquinas asked.

"Less than a kilometer."

"Sounds like our best option. Are you ready, my love?"

Nodding, Sara wiped her eyes and slapped a new clip of ammunition into her handgun.

Following suit, Yuuto reloaded his weapon.

"Draw his fire," Aquinas said. "Once he's expended his ammo, I'll make my move."

When Sara and Yuuto leaned out, more gunfire erupted from the behind the curtains and they quickly moved back. When the barrage ended, Sara and Yuuto leaned out again and sent a volley of return fire into the hallway.

In a flash, Aquinas picked up a chair and threw it at the window. When the pane shattered, the driving wind transformed the once-immaculate dining room into a maelstrom of flying glass shards and swirling debris.

Quickly climbing through, Aquinas, Sara, and Yuuto took off running toward the Hozugawa River. Seconds later, a multitude of shots rang out behind them. Though barely audible above the sounds of the violent storm, Aquinas' element-enhanced perception enabled him to hear them.

"He's firing at us again! Take cover!"

Diving into the tall grass lining the embankment, Aquinas spun around and saw Lucas standing outside on the observation deck, reloading his machine gun. When he raised his weapon, a ferocious blast of wind uprooted a nearby tree and crashed down on top of him. Although the invisible force surrounding Lucas prevented him from being killed, the tree was so large it trapped him underneath it.

Another sign the Almighty is on our side.

Turning around, Aquinas found Sara crawling toward him. "Are you alright?"

"I'm okay."

"Where's your father?"

"I don't know."

"Yuuto!" Aquinas yelled.

Nothing.

Searching the surrounding area, they found Yuuto face down and unresponsive. When Aquinas rolled him over, his hand came away bloody – trickling out of a bullet hole behind his right ear.

"Father!" Sara screamed.

Aquinas checked Yuuto's pulse. "He's still alive, but we can't stay here."

As if by magic, the ferocious wind tapered off, and everything became calm and quiet.

Looking around, Aquinas sensed what was happening. "The eye of the storm is passing over us. We don't have much time. Do you know the way to the bomb shelter?"

Sara stared at Yuuto, not responding.

Aquinas took hold of her arm. "My love?"

"It's been a few years, but I think I can find it."

"Help me get him up."

With Yuuto draped over his shoulder, Aquinas followed Sara north along the shoreline of the Hozugawa River.

* * *

Aquinas readjusted the throttle and pulled the handle of the antiquated gas generator. After several more attempts, it sputtered to life.

"We've got power, but I don't know how long it will last."

Returning to the room where he had set Yuuto down, he tried the light switch. The bulb flickered and came on, illuminating the interior of the World War II-era bomb shelter.

Sara knelt and began examining Yuuto.

"How is he?"

"The bullet entered the parietal bone and did not exit. I have no way of knowing how much brain tissue is damaged."

Tears came to Aquinas' eyes. "I'm sorry. This is all my fault. I should've insisted we not leave the ship."

"I disagree. You had no idea Lucas had discovered our whereabouts."

"It was too risky. Now Toshiro is dead, and your father is critically wounded."

"We knew the risks when we decided to help you decipher the Wordless Book."

Remembering the book, Aquinas checked his belt and made sure it was still there. Suddenly, an idea came to him.

The carmot can save Yuuto!

"What is it?" Sara asked.

232

"When the storm abates, I propose we return to the ship, proceed back to Antarctica, and recover some carmot."

Sara shook her head. "My father is in no condition to travel."

"We should be able to find a vehicle to carry him."

"And if we don't? It's almost sixty miles from here to the marina."

"I don't need to tell you how valuable your father has been to the Great Work. I cannot simply stand around and wait for him to die. If need be, I would carry him to the ends of the earth to save his life."

"But it will require many medical supplies. If his condition deteriorates, we will need a respirator."

"I shall therefore raid the nearest hospital and get them, to include a respirator."

"After a storm like this? The hospitals will be overwhelmed. You'll be lucky if they give you an adhesive bandage."

"Which makes it the perfect time to conduct a raid. When we get back to the ship, prepare a list of everything you think we'll need. Before departing, we'll stop at the Izou Hospital in Osaka. It's right off the river."

"And if the ship is not seaworthy?"

Aquinas smiled. "I have faith it will be."

* * *

Two days later, having commandeered a civil defense truck, Aquinas, Sara, and the wounded Yuuto arrived at the Kaiyukan Marina. Amid the utter devastation of wrecked vessels and debris, one ship remained afloat: *Renewed Conviction*. After a quick inspection, which miraculously found only the radio smashed, Aquinas powered up the engines and unhooked the mooring lines.

Stopping at the Izou Hospital, Aquinas used the power of suggestion to pilfer a respirator and the needed medical supplies. They were soon making their way out of Osaka Bay.

Later in the evening, Sara stepped into the bridge and moved in close to Aquinas. He placed his arm around her.

"How is your father doing?"

"Right now, he's stable. Quite frankly, I don't know what is keeping him alive."

"It must be a sign from the Almighty. His work here is not yet done."

Reaching the Philippine Sea, Aquinas steered a course south, back to Antarctica.

CHAPTER ELEVEN: THE REACQUAINTANCE

Present Day
Southbound on Highway 85
Sixty Miles South of Phoenix, Arizona

The swirling winds whipped the tan dirt off the desert floor, creating a multitude of twisting dust devils. Weaving their way across the scarce vegetation, the spinning cones shook the outstretched arms of saguaro cacti and sent an untold number of circular sagebrush branches scurrying along the desolate landscape. Although still early in the morning, the temperature had climbed above one-hundred degrees, signaling the beginning of another hot, rainless day. The winds and triple-digit heat were normal for this part of the country: the parched, arid state of Arizona.

Madison and I had traveled non-stop from Flagstaff, riveted to her uncle's voice emitting from our vehicle's audio speakers. His passionate telling, coupled with his vivid descriptions, had a hypnotic effect on me, transporting me back in time to his confrontations with Lucas. Madison had also been completely captivated, evident by the wide-eyed looks of wonder and tears she shed throughout.

When compact disc number eight ended, I removed it from the player. "How about we stop at the next town? I could use a break."

"Good idea, George. We need to get some gas anyway."

Eight miles later, we exited the highway and proceeded down the main street of Gila Bend. Steering our SUV to the nearest gas station, Madison drove up to the nearest pump and stopped. I looked over at her, and she broke down crying. Leaning over, I patted her hand, and she buried her face in my shoulder.

What am I going to say if she asks me what we should do?

After a few minutes, she finally spoke.

"I wish he would've trusted me and hadn't kept all of this to himself."

"I don't think it was a matter of trust, sweetheart. He was just trying to protect you."

"But if he'd have told me sooner, I would've helped him." Retrieving a facial tissue, she sat up, dabbed her eyes, and looked around. "So what are we going to do? It's only a matter of time before this S.O.B. catches up to us."

"Hopefully, we'll know what to do after we listen to the last two CDs."

"But how are we going to stop him, George? We barely made it out of St. George alive. I don't have the skills to fight, let alone fight someone like him. And with Parkinson's slowing you down, you wouldn't stand a chance either. No offense."

"None taken."

She was right. I'd been in only two fistfights my entire life and had lost them both, and that was *before* I'd been diagnosed with the disease.

"It's just, I'm scared, George. And with the Wanderer being able to disguise himself with the power of hypnosis, we can't trust anyone."

"I agree. That's why I think our best option, for now, is to have as little contact with people as possible and keep moving."

"To where, exactly?"

"How about we decide after I visit the restroom?"

"Oh, sure. Go ahead. I'll get the gas."

I made my way inside and followed the signs. Located on the east side of the building, I first had to pass through a long hallway, one side of which had large windows with the bright morning sun blazing in. When I pulled open the men's room door, another man exiting pushed from inside, knocking me backward. With my left arm immobile and my right leg weak from the disease, I fell to the floor.

The man coming out immediately knelt to help me, but with the sun shining in through the window behind him, I couldn't see his face.

"My apologies," he said, with a familiar-sounding baritone voice. "Can I give you a hand?"

"Thanks."

When he pulled me to my feet, I recognized him. "Deputy Alvarez?"

"Call me Bob, but I'm afraid you have me at a disadvantage."

"I'm George d'Clare. We met a few years ago at the senior center."

He took a step back and looked me over. Sneaking a peek at his left hand, his middle finger had all its segments.

"Oh, yes. Now I remember. You were with the Parkinson's support group. Are you okay?"

"I think so."

"Glad to hear it. Again, sorry about the door." He turned to leave.

"Um, Deputy?"

He stopped and turned around.

"Do you think I could have a moment of your time?"

He hesitated.

"Please? It's very important."

"Okay. I'll be in the coffee shop."

"Thanks. I appreciate it."

Talk about lucky! Running into the big, muscular Sherriff's deputy could not have happened at a better time.

Following my visit to the restroom, I returned to the front of the store and glanced over to the coffee shop. Sitting with Bob was another familiar face: Deputy Crystal Rivers.

Barely able to contain my excitement, I rushed outside. Madison, who'd finished refueling, had pulled our SUV up to the front of the building.

"You won't believe who's here. Bob Alvarez and Crystal Rivers."

"Who?"

"You remember. The two deputies who came to the senior center with Captain Hank and the Washington family."

Her eyes widened. "What are they doing here?"

"I don't know. I didn't get a chance to ask." I gave her a quick account of how Bob had accidentally knocked me over, and that they were waiting for us in the coffee shop.

Madison retrieved the portfolio case containing the Wordless Book, placed it in a reusable grocery bag, and followed me inside. Making our way through the growing number of patrons, we soon reached the corner booth and joined the deputies.

Dressed in shorts and a blue polo shirt, Bob could have easily been mistaken for a professional weightlifter; his pronounced muscles stretched the fabric to the limit. The lean and thin Crystal, dressed in sweatpants and a t-shirt, looked ready to run a marathon. Although I couldn't put my finger on it, something about her appearance appeared to be missing.

"Deputies," I said, "you remember Madison."

"And I believe you know my wife Crystal," Bob replied.

"You're married now?"

He nodded. "We tied the knot just over a year ago."

"Congratulations," Madison and I said, in unison.

"Please, have a seat."

Madison set the grocery bag on the table and slid into the booth next to Crystal. I settled in next to her.

"We're sorry about interrupting your day," Madison said.

"You didn't," Crystal replied. "We were just deciding on whether to stay another night, or head home to Ogden."

Bob got right to business. "What brings you to Gila Bend?"

As Madison started to reply, tears came to her eyes. Unable to get the words out, she looked down and began crying. Crystal immediately pulled a napkin out of the table dispenser, handed it to her, and put her arm around her. I took note: Crystal's left middle finger had all its segments.

"There, there, honey," Crystal said, "Things can't be that bad."

"Oh yes they can. We're in a lot of trouble, and we don't know what to do."

"What kind of trouble?" Bob asked.

I cleared my throat. "There's a murderer after us."

Crystal raised her head and looked at me. "What?"

"I said, there's a murderer after us."

Although Bob said nothing, I found myself locked in the crosshairs of his penetrating stare.

"The name he's going by is Lucas Carter." I continued. "He's an associate of Gwendolyn Phillips."

"And who is Gwendolyn Phillips?"

"She's one of the richest women in the world."

"Wait," Crystal interjected, "Are you talking about *the* Gwendolyn Phillips, the CEO of Phillips Industries?"

"One and the same."

"I know who she is. I saw her speak once at a conference about women in business."

"Who did this man Lucas supposedly murder?" Bob asked, getting the conversation back on track.

"My Uncle Charlie," Madison said, "or I mean, Charles Dewhurst."

"Did you see this murder take place?"

"No, but before he died, Charlie told us Lucas poisoned him and his father."

Bob nodded to Crystal, and she retrieved a pen and a small notebook from her purse and began writing.

"When and where did this take place?"

Madison wiped her eyes. "He didn't tell us the exact day he was poisoned, but he said it happened overseas in a city called Kaffa."

"Did he say why this man poisoned him?"

"Yes. Uncle Charlie came into possession of a very old and rare book, written by a clairvoyant in the Middle Ages. He said Lucas will stop at nothing to get his hands on it."

She gave them a short summation of the events in St. George, and how we'd barely survived the fire that destroyed her uncle's home.

"When we went back to Charlie's house and found the book," Madison concluded, "we were shot at. Take a look at our SUV." She pointed to it outside the window.

Bob looked for a moment. "Did you report this to the St. George police?"

We shook our heads.

"Why not?"

Overcome with emotions again, Madison buried her face in her hands. I reached out and took hold of her arm. I noticed the crowd waiting for coffee had grown significantly in the last few minutes, and that she'd attracted the attention of some of the patrons standing nearby.

I leaned in. "We couldn't go to the police," I whispered, "because Lucas is controlling them."

"Controlling them? How?"

"As hard as it is to believe, with hypnosis."

Bob and Crystal looked at each other. From their raised-eyebrows and wide-eyed expressions, I could tell they didn't believe me.

"Seriously, George," Crystal said. "Hypnosis?"

"I know it sounds crazy, and I was skeptical too. But Madison's uncle said Lucas is an expert in the *Ways of the Wind,* which is an ancient art of how to control others using the power of suggestion." I went into detail about what happened after the two break-ins at Charlie's home, and how the St. George deputies had tried to persuade us to stay at a hotel.

"What are the names of these two officers?" Bob asked.

"Jim Davis and Steve Hansen."

"I'll admit it sounds a little strange, but couldn't they have just been concerned for your safety?"

"No!" Madison exclaimed. "Those deputies were more concerned about getting us away from my uncle's house than they were about solving the break-ins."

"All right, for the sake of argument, let's say it's true. Why would a rich businesswoman associate herself with a murderer?"

"Because of the book."

"And what, exactly, is in this book?"

As she spoke, Madison dabbed her eyes with another napkin. "The book tells where to find a rare element in nature called *carmot.*"

"And what's so special about this carmot element?"

"According to my uncle, carmot can do many things, like cure diseases and prolong life."

Intrigued, Bob leaned in. "Is that why Lucas wants to get his hands on this book? Because he has a disease?"

"No, that's not the reason," I replied.

"Then what is?"

Wait till he hears this!

"As scary as it sounds," I whispered, "Lucas wants to use the element to start a global pandemic in hopes of killing every man, woman, and child."

"Oh please, George," Crystal said, "save the drama for the theater."

"We're not making this up!" Madison said.

"These are some very serious allegations you're throwing out," Bob said.

I met his piercing stare with my own. "I wouldn't have asked for a minute of your time if I wasn't serious."

Bob thought for a moment. "Could we see the book?"

"Yes, but not here," Madison said.

Bob turned to Crystal. "How about we go back to your parent's house?"

She scoffed. "You're not saying you believe this crazy story, are you?"

Bob patted her arm. "Not entirely, but I would like to look into it."

"Why?"

"Because I happen to know Jim Davis. Before he moved to St. George, we worked together. The officer they described doesn't sound like the Jim Davis I know."

"But Bob, do you really think someone could hypnotize him?"

"My gut instinct is telling me no, but to be fair to George and Madison, I'll reserve judgement until after I talk to Jim. I'll give him a call when we head over to the reservation."

"Seems like a waste of time," Crystal commented.

He smiled. "Look at it this way. *Someone* shot up their vehicle, and I'd like to find out who."

Crystal exhaled loudly. "All right." She turned to Madison and me. "Have either of you ever been to the Gila River Indian Reservation?"

Madison and I shook our heads.

"It's not very far. Follow us."

* * *

A myriad of ancient adobe dwellings lined the sides of the dirt road, etching a lonely, indelible mark into the desert terrain. In between some of these structures sat a new, rambler-style home, complete with a modern vehicle parked under an open carport.

We followed Bob and Crystal to one of these new homes and parked our SUV along the road. Madison retrieved the grocery bag containing the Wordless Book, and we followed them inside. The interior of the home was hot and dark. So much so, it felt as if I'd stepped into a sauna. Just as my eyes adjusted, Crystal opened a curtain, brightening the room to a blinding intensity. When my eyes adjusted again, I noticed Bob setting the thermostat. Soon after, cold air began circulating.

The furnishings looked like any other modern home, to include a fireplace with a built-in circulating fan, a big screen TV, and a large sectional sofa. Three sections of the sofa surrounded a matching ottoman, upon which sat several magazines and a remoat control for the TV. Other than a framed photo of an elderly Native American couple, sitting on the mantle above the fireplace, the room was devoid of any decorative wall hangings.

Bob motioned us to the sofa. Madison set the grocery bag on the floor next to the ottoman, and we sat down.

Wow! This has got to be the most comfortable couch I'd ever sat on.

"This sectional is nice and comfy," Madison commented, reading my mind. "Is it new?"

Crystal nodded. "We just got it last week."

"Forgive me," I said. "I may fall asleep."

Bob chuckled. "You won't be the first."

Addressing Crystal, I asked, "Do your parents always keep their home this hot?"

"My parents died last November."

Completely embarrassed, I didn't know what to say.

"It's okay, George," Bob said. "You didn't know."

Madison took hold of my hand. "We're sorry for your loss."

"No need to be," Crystal replied. "They lived long and happy lives."

"They passed only one day apart," Bob added, "which was fitting, considering they'd been married for seventy-two years."

"Geez," I exclaimed. "If I could be so lucky."

Crystal smiled. "We put their house on the market for a while, but when it didn't sell we decided to keep it. We use it now as our private getaway, or most-recently, to recover."

I looked at Bob. "To recover?"

When he didn't answer, Crystal explained. "Earlier this year, Bob interrupted a robbery at the City Credit Union. One of the thieves was an ex-con who recognized him from the jail. The scumbag pulled a gun and took a shot at him."

"Oh, my goodness," Madison said. "It's a miracle you weren't killed."

"Miracle is right," Crystal replied. "A fragment of the bullet hit him in the head. Luckily, it missed his vital brain tissue, and hardly did any damage at all. The doctor said the chances of that happening are astronomical."

"I don't see any scars where they operated on you," I commented.

He smiled. "That's because they didn't. The fragment is in so deep, the doctors can't remove it."

"You look like you're doing well, considering."

"I get a few headaches from time to time, but other than that, I'm alright."

"Don't let him fool you," Crystal interrupted. "The county forced him to retire. Ever since, his blood pressure has been high. So, we decided to come down here and get away for a while."

"All right, enough about me," Bob said. "Let's have a look at the book."

While he cleared off the top of the ottoman, Madison retrieved the portfolio case from the grocery bag and set it on her lap. Pulling out the compact discs, she handed them to me.

"What's on the discs?" Bob asked.

"My uncle telling his story," Madison replied. "Unfortunately, the fire destroyed half of them."

Removing the Wordless Book, Madison laid it down on top of the ottoman.

"Wow!" Crystal exclaimed. "That *is* old."

After examining several pages, Bob looked up. "There aren't any words, just drawings of symbols."

"When the symbols are deciphered," Madison explained, "they contain messages of what the clairvoyant saw in his visions."

"How do you decipher them?"

"You measure them, down to the millimeter, and plug the numbers into mathematical and geometric formulas."

"Which formulas?" Crystal asked.

"According to Charlie, all of them."

"*All* of them?"

Madison nodded. "When you find the formula where the answers fall between one and twenty-six, you've found the right formula. The answers, in turn, correspond to letters in the English alphabet. Placed in the correct order, the letters spell out a rhyming parable."

"The parable contains the message," I added.

"And you say these messages tell where to find this carmot element?" Bob asked.

"Yes," Madison replied, "among other things."

Crystal looked up from examining the book. "Bob, look at this." She pointed to a symbol with a faded equation written in pencil below it. "That's the *parallel postulate* formula."

"The what?" Madison and I asked, in unison.

"The parallel postulate. It's Euclidean geometry. I had to write a thesis on it for my master's degree."

I realized what was missing about Crystal: her bookbag. When we had first met her, she'd been studying calculus and always carried around a bookbag with a laptop computer in it.

"You've got a master's degree in math?"

"No, George," Bob interrupted. "She's got a doctorate in math."

"Now dear," Crystal said, "you know it's not official until I hear back on my dissertation."

Bob smiled. "She's got it in the bag."

"I'm curious," I said. "How did you go from being a sheriff's deputy to having a doctorate in math?"

She laughed. "When I was working on my criminal justice degree, I had to take math to fulfill a general ed requirement. I found I had a knack for it."

With her knowledge, she could help us decipher the remaining pages in the Wordless Book!

"Congratulations," Madison said, "even if it is a bit premature."

"Yes, congrats," I added. "What an awesome accomplishment."

"Thanks," Crystal replied. "When I retire at the end of the year, I'm hoping to land a teaching position at the new high school they're building down the street. Then Bob and I will move down here permanently."

"She's got it," Bob said. "Signed, sealed, and soon to be delivered."

"Bob," she said sternly, but with a smile, "there's going to be a lot of qualified people applying."

"But how many of them are full-blooded Pima Indian with a doctorate degree in math?"

From her dark skin and facial features, I already knew Crystal was a Native American, but up until now, I didn't know which tribe she belonged to.

Bob picked up the stack of compact discs and examined them. "Do you mind if we listen?"

"Only if you promise to reserve judgement until after you've heard the entire story," Madison replied

"Fair enough." He looked at Crystal. "Honey?"

"Okay. I'll try to keep an open mind. But first, would anyone like a cold bottle of water?"

Madison and I nodded.

"Bring three," Bob said. "I'll see if I can find the old boombox."

As soon as we were alone, Madison leaned close to me. "George," she whispered, "they'll never believe the element can transform rocks into gold."

"Unfortunately, I don't see any way around not telling them about it. Wait. Remember when we first met Crystal?"

Madison shook her head.

"She always carried around a laptop computer. If she still has it, and can access the Internet, we could have her look things up as the story goes along. Once they realize Charlie was telling the truth, they'll *have* to believe us."

"I hope so, George, because if they don't, I don't know what we'll do."

Just then, Bob returned to the room carrying a portable CD player and set it on the floor in front of the ottoman. A moment later, Crystal came in and passed out the bottles of water, then Bob and her sat down on the section of the sofa facing us.

"Before you hear my uncle's incredible story," Madison began, "we need to tell you what he told us before he died. And fair warning, you're going to find it hard to believe."

"I already find it hard to believe an element in nature can cure diseases and prolong life," Crystal said.

"I'm so glad you said that," I interjected. "Do you still have your laptop computer?"

She nodded.

"Do you have internet access out here?"

"Believe it or not, George, the Indian reservation has a better internet service provider than most major cities."

"Good. We'd like you to be our fact checker."

"Fact what?"

"My uncle's story spans many years and intersects with historical events," Madison explained. "As it goes along, you can look things up and check his accuracy."

"All right. I'll go get it."

A few minutes later, she was sitting on the sofa with her laptop in front of her. "Okay, I'm ready."

Madison looked at me. "Where should I begin?"

"You could start by answering one question," Bob said. "If, as you say, Lucas wants to kill everyone, why does he want to get his hands on an element that cures diseases?"

"Because carmot can do many things, not just cure diseases."

"Give us an example."

Madison glanced over at me, and I nodded.

"If you place carmot on a rock, it can transform the rock into pure gold."

"Oh, come on!" Crystal said.

Bob remained staring, his cold, penetrating eyes boring a hole into Madison.

"Let me finish," Madison implored. "If you use the element to transform rocks into gold, it leaves a toxic residue – a residue that could infect a person with a deadly disease."

"You've heard of the plague striking Europe in the 1300's called the Black Death?" I asked. "Madison's uncle said that plague began when someone near Kaffa changed rocks into gold and got infected."

Crystal quickly typed a search into her laptop computer. When the results displayed on the screen, her eyes grew wide. "Bob, listen to this. It is believed the plague known as the Black Death entered Europe through Kaffa in 1347. Following a prolonged siege, the Mongol army commander Khan ordered his men to catapult the infected dead bodies of his soldiers over the city walls. This was the first documented use of biological warfare in battle. Although the soldiers protecting Kaffa eventually repelled the Mongols, the city's inhabitants unknowingly carried the disease onboard ships bound for Europe. Fortress Kaffa still stands today but is now called Feodosia."

"Interesting," Bob said, "but what does this have to do with Lucas?"

Madison looked at me and took a deep breath. "Using the power of suggestion, Lucas ordered the Khan to catapult the infected corpses into Kaffa."

"But that's preposterous," Crystal said. "How could Lucas still be alive today? No one can live that long. Next you'll be telling us he found the fountain of youth."

"And if he did find the fountain of youth, what's his motive?" Bob asked. "*Why* does Lucas want to kill everyone?"

"Go ahead, sweetheart," I said. "Tell them."

"Because Lucas was punished by Jesus Christ to remain living until the Day of Reckoning. To end his existence, he wants to use the element to destroy the world."

With wide-eyed looks of stunned surprise, they remained staring. So much so, you could've heard a pin drop.

* * *

Due to the multitude of questions Bob and Crystal asked us throughout, it took Madison and me close to an hour to recount what her uncle had told us before he died. To impress upon them the grave threat Lucas posed, I suggested they listen to the first three discs (CD's numbered six, seven, and eight) and proceed from there. Since Madison and I had already listened to them on the drive down from St.

George, we sat back in their comfortable sofa and listened again. Not long after, I fell sound asleep. When I woke, Madison was talking.

"That's as far as we got," she said. "We haven't listened to the last two discs yet."

"What do you think, honey?" Bob asked, addressing Crystal.

"Honestly, I'm not sure. He *sounded* believable, and from what I've found on the Internet, his story checks out."

When I yawned and sat up, Madison turned to me. "George, you're finally awake."

"Yeah, I really dropped off. What's going on?"

"Crystal was just saying Charlie's story checks out, but she's not sure she believes it."

"What does Bob think about it?"

"Good question."

My eyes traveled over to Bob.

He took a deep breath. "At first, I thought someone might be playing an elaborate joke on you two. But after listening to the voice on those discs, I'm beginning to wonder."

"Let me play devil's advocate for a moment," Crystal said. "What are we talking about here? An element that magically stops the aging process, changes ordinary rocks into gold, and can also cause a deadly disease?"

"I know it sounds impossible, honey," Bob replied, "but I'd like to reserve judgement until after I hear the whole story."

He removed disc number eight from the CD player and loaded disc number nine.

* * *

For the next hour, we listened to Uncle Charlie (Aquinas) tell what happened when he returned to Antarctica and attempted to recover some carmot and save Yuuto Tanaka's life. To summarize these events as being catastrophic would be an understatement.

With the loss too great
for the soldier to bear,
he'll lay down his arms,
praying death finds him there.

But six days before harvest
in an icy fjord,
he'll regain his faith,
and pick up his sword.

Sara's interpretation of the third group of symbols in the second chapter of the Wordless Book

CHAPTER TWELVE: THE RETRIEVAL

Monday, 1 November 1971, 02:13hrs
Approaching Coats Land, Antarctica

A rare, out-of-season squall in the Weddell Sea sent a mammoth windstorm toward Antarctica. Moving east, the gusts picked up speed before slamming into the ice-encrusted coastline. As the swirling gales traveled over new-fallen snow, the powdery flakes became airborne, creating a maelstrom of ice tornados; each cutting a swath in the terrain like a sculptor's chisel. Then as quickly as it had blown in, the wind abated leaving a bright, full moon in the crisp, clear sky.

While the storm raged, Aquinas successfully navigated *Renewed Conviction* through the dangerous ice floe surrounding the south polar continent. When the skies finally cleared, he sighted a small coastal inlet. Steering through the thin, rocky opening, he brought the ship to a stop a short distance from the shore.

Making his way below deck, he found Sara asleep in Yuuto's room, curled up in a chair next to his bed. The only sounds were the long, rhythmic breathing of her father, and the pumping sound of the respirator.

Aquinas knelt, took hold of Sara's hand, and kissed it. "We have arrived," he whispered.

She stirred and opened her eyes. "We are in Antarctica?"

He nodded. "I found a secluded cove to disembark. The Halley Research Station is within walking distance."

She leaned up, yawned, and rubbed her eyes. "What time is it?"

"Two fifteen."

"I must check on my father."

She moved over to the bed and began taking Yuuto's vital signs. With watery eyes, she said, "His pulse is weak, and his blood pressure is extremely low."

"I shall leave immediately."

"You said it might take as long as two weeks to recover the carmot?"

"Yes, depending on what our English friends have in the way of transportation. When I worked at East Base, Finney told me the Halley station was one of the most frequented on the continent. If that's still true, I should be able to commandeer a Snowcat and significantly reduce the time. Now remember, after I leave, take the ship out a few kilometers and drop anchor."

Sara looked up with tears in her eyes. "What shall I do if the Wanderer finds me and my father while you are gone. With the radio inoperative, I'll have no way of warning you."

Aquinas wrapped his arms around her. "I've given that some thought, and I believe I've found a solution; one involving the horseshoe hanging on the door to the bridge."

Sara tilted her head. "I don't understand. My father told me he found it on the grounds of the Royal Palace the day he purchased the ship from the Emperor's family. Believing it was a sign of good fortune, he hung it on the door."

Aquinas smiled. "Over the years, I've encountered many people who consider horseshoes to be symbols of good fortune. Some European clerics even went as far as hanging them in places of worship to ward off evil spirits. Like your father, they displayed them with the heel up, so it resembles the letter U."

"Why?"

"Because they believed displaying it in this manner kept the good luck from running out. For our purposes, if the situation becomes dire, turn it upside down. That will tell me Lucas has discovered us, and he or his confederates are onboard."

"As a last resort, I could always push the button."

She pointed to the self-destruct switch attached to the underside of the built-in table.

Aquinas shook his head. "I have faith it won't come to that."

"And if it does? I'd rather die by my own hand than…"

He placed a finger over her lips, quieting her. "What you are suggesting is out of the question. Suicide is not an option. If Lucas captures you, I shall use the book as a bargaining chip to set you free." He pulled her close and used his thumbs to wipe the tears from her cheeks. "I'll take a walkie-talkie with me, so leave the other one on. I'll contact you when I am back within range. Whatever happens, remember I love you with all my heart."

Tears streamed down her cheeks. "I love you, too."

Aquinas kissed Sara goodbye and made his way to the top deck. Lowering a life raft, he began rowing ashore. Stepping onto the icy beach, he removed his necklace from around his neck and hurried to the Halley Research Station. When he reached the main entrance, he knocked until a bank of floodlights came on, which lit up the building and surrounding area. A moment later, a man's voice answered, high-pitchcd with a British acccnt.

"State your name and your business," the man said.

Thinking of a name to use, Aquinas remembered a war movie he'd watched with Yuuto. "Hello there, my good man." he said, with a pronounced British accent. "My name is Gary Cooper, Captain of the *HMS York*. To whom do I have the pleasure of speaking with?"

The door slowly opened, and a man stepped out with a gun in his hand. He looked to be roughly forty years old, stood six feet tall, with thinning brown hair and a full red beard.

"I'm Kenneth Smyth, maintenance supervisor of the Halley Research Station."

Aquinas stuck out his hand. "Pleased to meet you, Mr. Smyth."

Smyth didn't move, and kept his gun pointed at Aquinas.

"I say, is the firearm really necessary?"

"We've been robbed a half-dozen times this year," Smyth replied coldly. "Now here you are, knocking on our door at two thirty in the morning. What do you want?"

"I lost my ship in the ice floe and was hoping to find some shelter."

Smyth looked him over. "If that's true, where's your crew?"

"I lost them with the ship."

"Isn't a captain supposed to go down with the ship?"

Aquinas nodded. "Normally, but unfortunately my crew mutinied and cast me adrift."

"Mutinied? Why?"

"They were obsessed with becoming rich. You know, they actually believed my little crystal pendant could guide them to a treasure of gold in Antarctica. Fortunately. I was able to pass them a fake…"

"What crystal pendant?" Smyth interrupted

Aquinas suspended the pendant in front of Smyth's face and began twisting it back and forth. "Beautiful, don't you think?" he asked, in a calm, soothing tone.

After a moment, Smyth's eyes went into a stare and his mouth dropped open. Aquinas reached out and took his gun. "Now tell me, Mr. Smyth, how many people are inside the station?"

"Two."

Aquinas' eyes grew large. "Why so few?"

"The others are with the Americans, conducting research at the Bitton Glacier."

Aquinas nodded. "What are the names of those here with you, and what do they do?"

"Meadows assists me with maintenance. Ingram is the station cook."

"I would very much like to meet them."

"They're asleep."

"Then we shall wake them."

* * *

Ninety minutes after hypnotizing Meadows and Ingram, Aquinas had everything he needed for the eighteen-hundred-kilometer trek to the Rae Ice Shelf, including a supply of food and climbing gear to descend the crevasse. Much to his surprise (and delight) the British possessed the United States' Antarctic Snow Cruiser, with an extra one-thousand-gallon fuel tank attached to its roof.

Aquinas remembered what he'd read about the large, all-terrain vehicle. "I thought the Americans had abandoned the Snow Cruiser. How did it end up here?"

"A few years ago," Smyth explained, "one of our expeditions happened across it on the polar plateau and towed it in. Following a lengthy overhaul, and the addition of new studded snow tires, it can now go virtually anywhere on the continent."

"What's its range?"

"With full tanks of petrol, a little over two-thousand kilometers."

Aquinas thought for a moment. "Why didn't the scientists conducting research at the Bitton Glacier take it with them?"

"The Americans don't know we have it," Meadows said.

"Who among you knows how to operate it?"

"Meadows and I know how," Smyth replied.

"You two shall therefore accompany me on a top-secret mission for the Queen."

Smyth's and Meadows' eyes grew large.

"As for our destination, head in the direction of the polar plateau."

"Yes sir," the men replied, in unison.

After watching Aquinas, Smyth, and Meadows depart, Ingram, the station cook, made his way to the radio room.

* * *

Running the Snow Cruiser at full throttle, and with Smyth and Meadows driving in shifts, it took Aquinas only six days to traverse the polar plateau, recover the carmot from the Rae Ice Shelf, and return to the Halley Research Station. To keep his senses razor-sharp, while down in the crevasse collecting the element, he ingested several handfuls.

The morning of the sixth day, Aquinas arrived back at the station in a panic. Since returning within radio range of the ship, he'd been calling Sara continuously on his walkie-talkie, but she hadn't answered. Wasting no time, he quickly planted another suggestion in the minds of Smyth and Meadows, making them believe they'd completed the mission for the Queen.

"What are we to do now?" Smyth asked.

Aquinas replied with a question of his own. "What do you normally do?"

"Refuel and inspect the Snow Cruiser, stow it in the garage, and write a report telling what we accomplished."

"Then report you explored the polar plateau, but do not mention me. Under no circumstances are you to divulge where we went. To do so would mean certain death. Do I make myself clear?"

"Yes sir," Smyth and Meadows replied, in unison.

After releasing them from the hypnotic trance, Aquinas retrieved the portfolio case and sprinted back to the inlet where *Renewed Conviction* lay anchored offshore. Retrieving his binoculars, he examined the ship. Although still dark, the dim, pre-dawn light outlined the horseshoe on the door of the bridge, still hanging upright.

I'm not sensing Lucas, but something is terribly wrong!

He concealed the case behind some ice chunks on the shore and took the raft out to the ship. Armed with a handgun, he climbed over the railing and silently crept to the bridge. Finding nothing out of the ordinary, he made his way to the stairs and proceeded down to the lower deck.

Except for Yuuto's cabin, all the doors were open. Checking the first compartment, he found the drawers and closets open, the contents dumped on the floor. Finding the other compartments ransacked, he moved down the hall to Yuuto's cabin. Standing off to the side of the door, he reached out and grasped the handle. When he opened the door a crack, the hair on the back of his neck stood up.

It's too quiet...I'm not hearing Yuuto's respirator!

"Sara?" he whispered.

"Yes, my love?"

Aquinas pushed the door all the way open, leaned over, and looked inside. Sara sat motionless in a deck chair, her wrists and ankles bound. From the way her unblinking eyes stared straight ahead,

Aquinas could tell she'd been hypnotized. In the bed a few feet away, lay the lifeless body of Yuuto Tanaka.

Aquinas' heart sank, and his hands began to tremble.

I know Lucas is here, but I'm still not sensing him!

Just then, Lucas' deep laugh filled the compartment, sending a chill down Aquinas' spine. Like a spectral apparition, Lucas emerged from the shadows behind Yuuto's bed, revolver in hand. Moving close to Sara, he pointed the gun at her head.

"Double jeopardy again, Aquinas. If you attack me, I shall kill her. If you try to get away, I'll have Gwendolyn torture her. And believe me, Gwendolyn's methods are quite draconian. Now drop your weapon, surrender the Wordless Book, and tell me where the carmot is."

Aquinas hesitated.

Lucas placed the barrel of his gun against Sara's head. "Do not test my patience."

Begrudgingly, Aquinas lowered his gun and let it fall to the floor. "How did you find me?"

Lucas laughed. "You surprise me, Aquinas. After all this time, I thought you knew how strong my power of suggestion is. While searching for you, I visited almost every research station on shores of this continent and conditioned the minds of several of the occupants. When you arrived at the Halley Station and absconded with the Snow Cruiser, Mr. Ingram contacted me. I must say, you have a very formidable wife who knows how to take care of herself. So formidable, I wasn't sure we'd found the right ship."

"What makes you say that?"

"She killed two of my men, with her bare hands no less. I thought to myself: a fierce warrior like her couldn't possibly be your wife."

"So what convinced you?"

"When I chased her down, she did the strangest thing. She proceeded to the bridge and turned the horseshoe hanging on the door upside down. Of course, knowing how well you plan your actions against me, I knew she was attempting to send you a signal. Very clever.

"You also did an excellent job conditioning her mind. When I hypnotized her, she wouldn't disclose where you had gone to recover the carmot. Even when I turned off the respirator and killed her father, she remained silent. You also provided me the means to remain hidden from you."

Aquinas' eyebrows raised. "How?"

"While searching for you on the polar plateau, I happened to find a small vein of carmot. I gave some to the scientists in Gwendolyn's company, and they have since made some interesting discoveries. Did you know cold temperatures shroud the carmot from detection? If I place cold compresses around my upper body, it prevents someone like you, who has ingested the carmot, from sensing me."

Lucas unzipped his parka, revealing a vest with pockets full of ice packs.

So that's why I couldn't sense he was here.

"The scientists also found the carmot to be highly volatile," Lucas continued. "If attached to an explosive device, it increases the blast yield exponentially. The more carmot, the more destructive the detonation. Do you have any idea what this means?"

Aquinas shook his head.

"I now have a method to unleash a worldwide epidemic, one that will surely plunge the world's governments into chaos. All I'm lacking is a significant amount of carmot. Which now brings me to you. Are you going to surrender the Wordless Book and tell me where I can find the carmot on Antarctica?"

Aquinas motioned to Sara. "Only if you let her go."

"You are in no position to bargain!"

Aquinas crossed his arms confidently.

"Very well, Aquinas, you leave me no recourse."

Lucas pulled the hammer back on his revolver and squeezed the trigger.

"No! Wait!" Aquinas screamed, but it was too late.

The booming shot struck Sara's left temple, killing her instantly.

Shattered, Aquinas' knees buckled and he collapsed to the floor. As his mind tried to comprehend what he'd just witnessed, his vision became blurry and tunnel-like.

Lucas stepped around Sara and retrieved Aquinas' gun. "Did you not think I was serious?"

Aquinas could hear him talking, but couldn't understand what he was saying.

Lucas knelt next to him and smiled. "Now tell me, are you going to answer my questions, or must I have Gwendolyn torture you?"

When Aquinas didn't answer, Lucas pistol-whipped him across the face.

Aquinas remained silent.

"Alright," Lucas snarled, "we'll see if your tongue will loosen when Gwendolyn starts cutting off your toes. Before this day is over, you will beg me to kill you."

He kicked Aquinas to the floor, where he landed next to the cabin table – within arms-reach of the hidden self-destruct button.

Lucas retrieved the walkie-talkie clipped to his belt. "*Phillips One*, come in."

"This is *Phillips One*. Go ahead," Gwendolyn replied.

"I've captured Aquinas."

"Excellent!"

"He's not talking, so bring your tools."

"Understood. I'm on my way."

Hearing Gwendolyn's voice momentarily cleared Aquinas' vision.

Lucas clipped the walkie-talkie back onto his belt. "Let's go. On your feet."

As Aquinas slowly rose from the floor, he reached under the table and pressed the button.

In five minutes, it will all be over.

Lucas nudged Aquinas with his gun, and they made their way down the hallway and ascended the stairs to the main deck. When they stepped outside, the ship *Phillips One* pulled alongside. On her deck stood Gwendolyn, holding a metal case. On each side of her, a deckhand stood ready with a rope. When the two ships were close enough, the deckhands lashed their railings together and helped Gwendolyn cross over.

"My pet," Lucas said, "allow me to properly introduce you to the man we've been pursuing, the mighty Aquinas."

Gwendolyn laughed. "Up close, he doesn't look mighty to me. In fact, just the opposite."

"Don't let his appearance fool you. Aquinas is quite formidable. Would you believe, after I killed his wife and father-in-law, he still wouldn't surrender the Wordless Book or tell me where the carmot is?"

Gwendolyn smiled. "I shall remedy that."

She set the case down on the deck, opened the top, and pulled out a ball peen hammer and a carpenter's chisel. "I can't decide. Should I start with his fingers or toes?"

Lucas grinned. "Start with his toes so he won't be able to run away."

She ordered the two deckhands to hold Aquinas steady. Instead of struggling or thrashing about, Aquinas remained calm, staring off into the distance.

"Would you mind removing his boots, dear? I just did my nails."

An ear-splitting explosion suddenly blew out the windows of the cabins below deck, shaking the ship with the force of a nine-point earthquake. A plume of fire and smoke followed, engulfing not only *Renewed Conviction,* but also the port side of *Phillips One.*

The sights and sounds of the blast fully awakened Aquinas from his shocked state and aroused his survival instincts. Using martial arts moves he'd learned from Sara and Toshiro, he broke free from the men holding him and delivered a vicious chop to the throat of the man to his left, crushing his windpipe. When the man fell, he knocked over Lucas and Gwendolyn. Spinning around, Aquinas connected a solid roundhouse kick to the man on his right, breaking his neck.

Quickly recovering, Lucas rose to his knees and raised his gun. Before he could get a shot off, a second explosion, more powerful than the first, split the hull of *Renewed Conviction* lengthwise amidships. The port side began to slide away, while the starboard side, still tied to the now-burning *Phillips One,* stayed upright.

The blast launched Aquinas onto the descending port side, where he rode it down to the water and jumped clear of the fiery wreckage. Although the pinpricks of a thousand needles of freezing water took his breath away, the carmot in his system kept his mind thinking and his muscles fueled, and he began swimming toward the shore.

Thrown the other way, Lucas and Gwendolyn landed on the burning deck of *Phillips One.* With the unseen force protecting him, Lucas rushed into the fiery maelstrom, where he pulled a lever releasing the ship's only lifeboat. Returning to Gwendolyn, he whisked her up in his arms and jumped over the side.

Less than a minute later, the starboard side of *Renewed Conviction* disappeared under the water, leaving only the fatally damaged *Phillips One* burning on the surface.

Once on shore, Aquinas quickly retrieved the portfolio case and took off running toward the Halley Research Station. When he reached the station, he found Smyth and Meadows refueling the Snow Cruiser. "Nice to see you again, gentlemen," he said. "There's been a change of plan."

"Who are you?" Smyth asked.

Aquinas suspended his necklace in front of them and began twisting the chain. A moment later, the men were under his control again.

"We must leave at once," Aquinas said. "Queen's orders."

"To where?" Meadows asked, staring and with a blank look on his face.

"To Belgrano, the Argentine base. Do we have enough petrol for the trip?"

"Yes." Smyth replied, also staring. "Belgrano is only three-hundred-and-fifty kilometers away."

Aquinas smiled. "Good. Let us be on our way, gentlemen."

Six hours later, the Snow Cruiser arrived at the Belgrano Station. Comprised of nine buildings, the installation sat atop the ice overlooking Piedrabuena Bay. The ice tapered down to a pier at the water's edge, where a ship, the *Rising Sun*, lay docked. Aquinas remembered the ship's name from a list of Tanaka freighters Toshiro had shown him. The *Rising Sun* served primarily as an Antarctic resupply ship.

After thanking Smyth and Meadows for their service to the Queen, Aquinas released them from the hypnotic trance. Grabbing the portfolio case, he hurried to the *Rising Sun* and found the ship preparing to disembark; the engines were revving with power, and the dock workers were removing the mooring lines. Just as the deckhands began to disconnect the gangway, Aquinas jumped aboard.

He was immediately met by two men, a younger deckhand armed with a pistol, and an older man, wearing a hat of the Japanese Navy.

"What is the meaning of this?" the older man asked. "Who are you?"

"I beg your pardon," Aquinas replied. "My name is Gary Cooper. I'm a friend of Yuuto Tanaka. He said I could gain passage on your ship."

The officer looked at him for a moment. "I'm Captain Matsuki, commander of the *Rising Sun*. I haven't seen Yuuto in a very long time. Is he well?"

"He's doing very well," Aquinas lied.

"What about his son Hirohito, and his daughter Kiki?"

"His son's name is Toshiro, and I am married to his daughter Sara. Do you have any more trick questions?"

Captain Matsuki dismissed the deckhand, turned to Aquinas, and offered his hand. "My apologies, Mr. Cooper. A ship's commander must always be careful of who he allows on board."

Aquinas smiled and shook his hand. "No need to apologize, captain. Can you tell me where you are headed?"

"To our Australian base of operations at Sydney, if we can navigate through the ice floe."

"Is it bad?"

Matsuki nodded. "Recent weather has left the Weddell Sea littered with icebergs. I detest crossing under these conditions, but the ship is scheduled for maintenance and the men want to be home for the holidays."

"Do you have room for one more?"

"For the son-in-law of Yuuto Tanaka, we shall make accommodations."

~ The Wanderer ~

Two days later, aboard the ship *Phillips Two*, Lucas and Gwendolyn watched the Halley Research Station disappear in the distance behind them.

"I've never been so cold in all my life," Gwendolyn said, irritated. "We were lucky our second ship was nearby."

"Luck had nothing to do with it," Lucas said curtly. "I was the one who ordered the captain to remain close."

"Oh, excuse me," she snapped, "I forgot to thank you for preplanning this contingency."

Lucas exhaled loudly. "I told you Aquinas was a formidable opponent. Who would have thought he had rigged Tanaka's ship with explosives?"

"All I know is we almost died out there."

"Correction, my pet. *You* almost died out there."

Gwendolyn locked her eyes on Lucas. "And if the bombs had blown off your arms and legs, where would we be now?"

Lucas chuckled. "The punishment I live with would've prevented that from happening."

"But aren't you the least bit upset?"

"Yes. With myself for underestimating Aquinas' power of suggestion. The way he conditioned the minds of the two maintenance men, Smyth and Meadows, was amazing, to say the least. When I hypnotized them, they wouldn't tell me where they had gone with Aquinas in the Snow Cruiser. When I pressed, Smyth's brain ruptured."

"Do you think it was a mistake to eliminate Meadows too?"

Lucas shook his head. "We learned the range limit of the Snow Cruiser, so we know the carmot is within eighteen-hundred kilometers of the Halley Research Station. This significantly narrows our search area, but we still need the Wordless Book to check our calculations and pinpoint the exact location. But not to worry, my pet. We'll capture Aquinas soon enough."

"Where do you think he'll go?"

Lucas thought for a moment. "Since I have killed all his loved ones, he really has no place to go. My instincts are telling me he'll become desperate, and desperate people tend to make foolish mistakes. When Aquinas makes his mistake, we shall be there waiting for him."

"So what do we do?"

"Call your business associates and find out which Tanaka freighter resupplied the Belgrano research station."

* * *

Ten hours later, a bevy of mountainous icebergs floated into the path of the *Rising Sun*. Already traveling slow, Captain Matsuki ordered the ship to stop. When the course ahead finally cleared and he gave the order to proceed, the ship remained frozen in place. Drifting with the floe, *Rising Sun* entered a long, narrow fjord surrounded by towering columns of ice.

Alone in his quarters, Aquinas' thoughts returned to the devastating events on board the *Renewed Conviction,* and the full weight of losing Sara, Yuuto, and Toshiro came crashing down on him. He replayed the events in his mind, repeatedly, until he began to second guess the decisions he had made.

How could I have been so wrong? To leave Sara alone on the ship with her critically injured father was unconscionable. I should've never involved her and her family. Now they are all dead because of me!

Tears flowed down his cheeks, and he buried his face in his hands. With his thoughts turning dark, he began thinking of how he could end his life.

All at once, the sounds of the ship quieted, as if time itself had come to a standstill. Out of the deafening silence, he heard his father's voice, emanating all around him.

"My son."

Aquinas raised his head and looked around, but no one was there.

Augustus spoke again. "Your heart is heavy."

It can't be!

"Father?" Aquinas asked, his voice trembling. "Where are you? I cannot see you."

"You must move on."

"Move on? How can I move on? I have failed you again."

"You have never failed me, nor will you ever fail me."

"But three more people are dead because of me, including my beloved Sara. She was my world! I no longer have a reason to live."

"Yes, you do! You *must* continue the Great Work!"

"How can I continue knowing I caused the death of innocent people?"

"No matter how much it hurts, you must put these events behind you. At this very moment, mankind hangs by a thread over a deep abyss. The actions you take or fail to take will decide the fate of every man, woman, and child."

Aquinas didn't answer.

"Turn to your faith, my son."

"Faith? Will faith bring Sara back? Will it bring back Yuuto and Toshiro?"

"You must understand, everyone has a purpose in life, and like nature, a season. When their purpose is fulfilled, the season comes to an end and the soul is called home. Those you loved are gone because they had served their purpose. If you give up now, the help they gave you will be for naught, and their deaths will be rendered meaningless."

"But father, Lucas cannot be defeated."

"Yes, he can!"

"How?"

"The answer lies in the final chapters of the Wordless Book."

Aquinas shook his head. "I have tried to decipher the chapters, but they contain so many convoluted symbols, it is impossible to measure them accurately."

"Be patient. In the coming years, technology will enable you to accurately measure the symbols."

Aquinas slumped. "In the coming *years*? How long must I continue?"

"You have traveled far, but you still have a long journey ahead. I must leave you now, so you may hasten to your rendezvous."

"What rendezvous?"

"You will soon meet someone who will play a significant role in the Great Work. Think of the last parable your wife deciphered. Above all else, do not let the Wanderer regain possession of the Wordless Book. The answers you seek are in there. Goodbye, my son."

"Goodbye, father."

When the sounds of the ship returned, Aquinas' mood brightened. Like a magician waving a wand, his father's words took away his feelings of guilt and self-recrimination. Retrieving his small notebook, he turned to the page where he had jotted down the parables.

After rereading them several times, he closed the notebook and looked out the window of his cabin. The ship had broken free of the ice floe. Aft, the icebergs were disappearing in the distance. Ahead, the course appeared clear.

Had the Wordless Book foretold my future again?

~ Present Day ~

When disc nine ended, Bob ejected it from the CD player.

"Before I start the last one," Bob said, "does anybody need anything?"

"I'll take another water," I said.

"Me, too," Madison said. "And if it's not too much trouble, could I get some tissues?"

"Are you alright, sweetheart?" I asked.

She nodded. "I'm okay. This is just a lot to take in."

"What about you, honey?" Bob asked.

Crystal shook her head. "I'm good."

After retrieving the bottles of water and the tissues, Bob loaded disc ten into the CD player and pressed the "Play" button.

We soon learned the Wanderer's relentless pursuit of Aquinas had crossed the shores of the United States a second time. Unlike the encounter at Niagara Falls in 1918, this time the chase would occur on the west coast, in a state bordering the Pacific Ocean.

Unfortunately for Aquinas, he would again find himself trapped, and as Lucas predicted, he would become desperate. To escape, he chose a dangerous course of action – one resulting in him becoming the focus of the longest, most extensive manhunt in the history of American law enforcement.

The year was 1971, the day before the Thanksgiving holiday, onboard a commercial airliner, approximately fifty miles north of Portland, Oregon.

When the soldier returns
to the land of the states,
he'll find his path blocked
all closed are the gates.

But when he takes flight
like an eagle he'll soar,
and his escape from the Wanderer,
will become one of lore.

Sara's interpretation of the fourth group of symbols in the second chapter of the Wordless Book

CHAPTER THIRTEEN: THE DRASTIC MEASURE

Wednesday, 24 November 1971, 13:35hrs
Inside Portland International Airport, Oregon

The busiest travel day of the year had started out slow, but by mid-morning a horde of passengers had converged on the terminal, filling the concourses to capacity. As half of the people, who had arrived on inbound flights, inched their way to the baggage claim area, the other half moved in the opposite direction, toward the departure gates. Almost all the travelers were in route to join family and friends for tomorrow's Thanksgiving holiday. Aquinas, however, had arrived for an entirely different reason: to escape the Wanderer.

Yesterday, when the ship *Rising Sun* docked in Sydney, Australia, Aquinas hastily disembarked and caught a taxi to the airport. Entering the terminal, the hair on the back of his neck bristled, signaling danger. Ignoring his enhanced senses, he proceeded to the nearest ticket counter and purchased a ticket on the first available flight out; nonstop to San Francisco.

When the plane landed fifteen hours later, he sensed danger again. Looking out the cabin window, he saw a multitude of police cars and a similar number of black, full-sized vans, with "Phillips Security" logos emblazoned on their side panels, parked outside the terminal. No less than forty armed men, comprised of policemen and Phillips security personnel, were checking people as they came out.

I've got to get out of here! Gwendolyn has gained favor with the local police. Combined with her people, they have sealed off all the exits around the San Francisco airport!

Since the flight he was on offered follow-on service to Portland, Aquinas remained on board.

Ninety minutes later, when his plane touched down in Oregon, Aquinas experienced the same unsettling feelings he'd had in Sydney and San Francisco. With the portfolio case in hand, he made his way off the plane and proceeded to customs where he used his crystal pendant to hypnotize an agent into believing he had seen his passport. Returning to the crowded concourse, his eyes darted back and forth across the throng of holiday travelers, but he couldn't see anything out of the ordinary.

Strange! Everything appears normal.

Wading through the sea of humanity, he emerged at the far end of the lengthy concourse. When he walked by the conveyer belts in baggage claim, and the airport exit doors were within sight, he saw a contingent of Phillips security and police checking the identifications of people as they exited. Turning around, he made his way over to the other side of the terminal and found the airport's front doors also sealed off.

Returning to the concourse, he ducked into the nearest men's room. Standing at a sink, he waited until a man entered who appeared to be the same height and build as himself. The man wore a black suit, complete with a white shirt and thin, clip-on tie. He also sported a full beard, with close to the same hair color as his.

After waiting a moment for two other men to leave, Aquinas approached the bearded man. Withdrawing the crystal pendant from his pocket, he held it by the chain and began twisting it one way, then the other. "Pardon me, sir," he said, "Could I interest you in a necklace for your loved one?"

"No, thank you."

"Are you sure? Take a closer look. It's quite unique."

When the man looked directly at the pendant, his eyes went into a vacant stare.

"What is your name?"

"Dan Morgan."

"And what do you do for a living, Mr. Morgan?"

"I'm an aircraft production supervisor at Boeing."

"Sounds like challenging work."

"It can be, at times."

"I need to exchange clothes with you and relieve you of your wallet."

Dan's eyebrows wrinkled, and his face took on a questioning look. "My clothes and wallet?"

Aquinas smiled. "Don't worry. I'll reimburse you at my earliest convenience. Now, if you would, please follow me to the handicap stall."

Ten minutes later, Aquinas emerged from the restroom wearing Dan's suit. Following a shave and haircut at the airport barber shop, he proceeded to the front of the terminal, toward the airline ticket counters. Stepping up to one, he rang the desk bell. A dark-haired woman in her mid-thirties came out of the back room. She wore a salmon-red, long-sleeve sweater, which matched the airlines' colors, and a nametag with "Judy" printed on it.

"Welcome to Northwest Orient Airlines," she said. "How can I help you?"

"When does your next plane leave?" Aquinas asked.

She checked the schedule. "Flight 305, with service to Seattle-Tacoma, departs at 2:50p.m."

"I'd like a ticket."

"One way or round trip?"

"One way."

Judy quickly checked the flight manifest. "You're in luck, sir. There are plenty of seats available. Could I get your name?"

Before Aquinas could answer, a commotion broke out near the exit doors behind baggage claim. He saw Dan, dressed in his clothes and looking disoriented, surrounded by five Phillips security men. When he couldn't produce his identification, the security men threw Dan to the floor and handcuffed him.

"I'm sorry, Dan."

"And your last name?" Judy asked.

Aquinas' eyes returned to Judy. "I beg your pardon?"

Judy explained, "I'll need your last name for the ticket."

Aquinas realized he'd spoken out loud. Not wanting to raise her suspicions, he decided to just go with Dan as his first name and use the same last name of the movie star he had used before.

After typing in the name, Judy said, "Alright, that'll be twenty dollars."

"Only twenty?"

Judy smiled. "Northwest Orient is running a holiday special today."

Aquinas withdrew Dan's wallet from his pocket, retrieved a twenty-dollar bill, and handed it to her.

Judy handed him his ticket. "You're all set. Boarding will begin at 2:30, Gate Five, in the B concourse."

"Thank you."

"You're welcome. Have a good flight, Mr. Cooper."

~ The Wanderer ~

Five minutes after Aquinas' plane departed for Seattle, a sleek, high-speed Learjet, painted black with the Phillips Industries logo on the tail, landed in Portland. After parking at an arrival gate reserved for wealthy corporate executives, Lucas and Gwendolyn disembarked the aircraft. Her company's lead security man, Trevor Warner, met them at the bottom of the boarding ladder. Trevor, a tall, muscular man with a deep baritone voice, smiled as they descended the stairs.

"How goes the search?" Gwendolyn asked.

"We got him," Trevor replied.

"Are you sure it's him?"

Trevor nodded. "He's got a beard, mustache, and is dressed just as you said."

"Where is he?" Lucas asked.

"He's being held in the airport security office. This way."

When they began to follow Trevor, Gwendolyn moved close to Lucas. "I'm not sensing Aquinas," she whispered.

"Neither am I. But the carmot can be unpredictable."

Trevor led them down the side of the busy concourse, through a side door, and down a short hallway to the security office. Ten Phillips security men were crowded in the doorway. When they saw Gwendolyn and Lucas, they snapped to attention.

"Make a hole," Trevor said, his booming voice reverberating off the walls.

When the men moved aside, Lucas and Gwendolyn followed the big man in.

Inside the security office, two airport policemen sat at a desk, one talking on the phone and the other writing a report. The man in custody sat in a corner with his head down, his wrists handcuffed behind his back and his ankles shackled.

Lucas squeezed in to get a closer look. "Aquinas?"

The man raised his head.

279

"That's not him!" Gwendolyn screamed.

Trevor's eyes widened. "What? He *has* to be the one. He fit the description, blue parka, jeans, and white sweatshirt."

Lucas turned to Trevor. "You've arrested the wrong man, Mr. Warner. You know what we do to incompetent people."

The big man broke out in a sweat.

Lucas smiled. "But since I'm feeling a bit generous today, I'm going to give you another chance. Redeploy your men to the airline ticket counters. I want a list of everyone who has purchased a one-way ticket in the last hour."

"Yes, sir," Trevor replied. "What about him?" He motioned to the man in custody.

"Get rid of him."

Trevor turned and addressed the other men. "You heard the boss. Grab him and let's go!"

Once the men had gone, Lucas and Gwendolyn stepped out into the hallway, away from the police officers.

"If Aquinas caught a plane, what do we do?" Gwendolyn asked.

"No worries, my pet. When Mr. Warner returns with the list and we identify the flight, we'll simply order the pilot to return here."

"And how, exactly, will we do that?"

Lucas smiled "By you making a few phone calls to some very important people."

~ Northwest Orient Flight 305 ~

As the aircraft climbed to cruising altitude, Aquinas closed his eyes.

This plane-hopping can't go on forever. With Lucas, Gwendolyn, and her people working with the airport police, it's only a matter of time before they capture me.

He opened his eyes and looked around the cabin. The stewardesses were explaining what to do in the event of an emergency and pointing where the oxygen masks drop down from the ceiling. When Aquinas closed his eyes again, a thought occurred to him.

I need to come up with a unique and elaborate plan, one that creates an emergency. Something so big federal officials will have to get involved. And while Lucas is dealing with them, I'll be able to slip away.

He opened the portfolio case and checked the contents again. The Wordless Book was still there, along with the tubes containing the carmot, the batteries and the refrigerant. Looking at the components, he stifled a laugh.

I have to agree with Merrick. The tubes do resemble sticks of dynamite. Thank goodness airport security didn't search my carry-on case.

He remembered reading a story in the newspaper about a man who'd recently been arrested for attempting to extort money by hijacking an airplane.

Wait...that's it! Extortion would surely cause federal officials to become involved.

With his mind now racing, Aquinas retrieved a pen, a piece of paper, and an envelope from the portfolio case. Scribbling a note on the paper, he placed the note in the envelope and waited for the stewardesses to make their way down the aisle with the drink cart. When they reached his row, a stewardess with the nametag "Flo" asked, "Can I get you something, sir?"

"Bourbon and soda, please."

When she handed him the drink, he gave her a twenty-dollar bill and the envelope.

"I'll have to get you some change."

"Miss, I think you'd better look at my note."

After opening the envelope and reading the paper inside, Flo looked up and smiled nervously. "Is this a joke?"

Aquinas shook his head. "This is anything but a joke. Now if you please."

He motioned for her to take a seat. When she sat down, Aquinas opened the portfolio case and showed her the contents. Her eyes grew wide, and he quickly closed it.

"As you can see, I am deadly serious."

Now in a cold sweat, Flo stared at the case for a moment, before finally looking up. "Do you have a grudge against Northwest?"

Aquinas smiled. "No, miss. I just have a grudge. Now tell me, what is the pilot's name?"

"Scotty," she replied nervously. "Or, I mean, Captain Bill Scott."

"Please inform Captain Scott from this point forward, I am in command of this aircraft. When we reach Seattle airspace, he is to fly in a holding pattern until my demands are met."

Flo took a deep breath. "What are your demands?"

Aquinas handed her the pen. "Take this down. I want two-hundred-thousand dollars in a knapsack by 5:00pm."

Flo scribbled his instructions on the back of the note.

"I would also like four parachutes, two primary and two reserve, and a fuel truck standing by when we land."

She looked up. "Anything else?"

Aquinas smiled. "Yes. In the knapsack with the money, I want one bottle of Kentucky bourbon."

"Okay, I'll let the captain know."

When she stood to leave, Aquinas stopped her.

"Before you go," he said, "I'd like to show you something."

He reached in his pocket and retrieved his necklace. With the crystal pendant suspended in front of her eyes, he began twisting the chain.

~ *The Wanderer* ~

Trever Warner blasted through the door leading to the airport security office, almost tearing it off its hinges.

"Got him!" he yelled.

Lucas and Gwendolyn, sitting in the office, jumped to their feet and met him at the door.

"What have you learned, Mr. Warner?" Gwendolyn asked.

"In the last hour, only three people have bought a one-way ticket. Two of them were women. The man who bought the ticket gave his name as Dan Cooper. He's on Northwest Orient 305 to Seattle."

"Excellent," Lucas said. "We know Mr. Nyrop, the President of Northwest Orient."

Gwendolyn smiled. "I'll make a phone call." She turned and rushed to the phone in the security office.

Addressing Trevor, Lucas said, "Excellent work Mr. Warner. You are forgiven for what happened earlier. Tell your men to stand by. When the aircraft returns, we shall make our move."

"Yes, sir." Trevor hurried back down the corridor to his men.

Lucas rejoined Gwendolyn just as the call connected to her company's Chicago headquarters. After obtaining the information from her secretary, she dialed the number.

"Don Nyrop? This is Gwendolyn Phillips of Phillips Industries. We met a few years ago at the Business Executives Conference. I was wondering if I could have a moment of your time…"

Don interrupted her, and the look of stunned surprise came across her face. She placed her hand over the mouthpiece, and whispered, "Don was just informed one of his planes has been hijacked. Flight 305 from Portland to Seattle. The hijacker's name is Dan Cooper."

Lucas thought for a moment. "Very clever, Aquinas," he whispered. "Very clever indeed." Addressing Gwendolyn, he said, "This could work to our advantage. Tell him we know Mr. Tolson at the FBI. When the plane lands, we could arrange to have their field agents storm the plane and shoot the hijacker."

She took her hand off the mouthpiece. "Allow me to help you, Don. I happen to know Clyde Tolson, who is J. Edgar Hoover's top deputy. After the plane lands, I'm sure I could persuade him to send in his agents…"

When Don interrupted her again, she rolled her eyes and waited for him to finish. "But surely you're not thinking of paying? It could set a bad precedent…"

After the third interruption, Gwendolyn slammed the receiver down and screamed.

"Idiot!"

~ *Northwest Orient Flight 305* ~

While the plane circled in a holding pattern above the Seattle airport, Aquinas, with his crystal pendant in hand, made his way through the cabin, hypnotizing each of the thirty-six passengers into believing they were seeing a different person.

I simply hate using the power of suggestion to commit such a crime, but it's the only option I can think of to escape Lucas.

When he finished planting the suggestion in the minds of the other two stewardesses, Flo called him over to the cabin phone.

284

"Captain Scott wants to talk to you," she said, handing him the receiver.

"Yes, captain?"

"Northwest Orient has met your demands," Scott said.

"Very well, you have my permission to land. Once we're on the ground, I'll give you further instructions."

When Flight 305's wheels touched down, Aquinas rose to his feet. Addressing Flo, he said, "While I talk to Captain Scott, I need you and the other two stewardesses to close all the window shades."

Eyes staring, she nodded and turned to carry out the order.

Aquinas walked over to the cabin phone and picked up the receiver.

"Captain Scott?"

"This is Captain Scott."

"Do not taxi to the terminal. Stay on the ramp apron."

"How far do you want me to go?"

Aquinas crouched and looked out the window in the cabin door. "Stop under those bright lights ahead on the right. Once we're parked, call for the fuel truck and inform the police they can deliver the ransom."

"What about the passengers?"

He's a good man. One I could have a drink with if the situation were different.

"When the aircraft is refueled and the ransom is in my hands, I'll release the passengers. After you relay my instructions, I'll outline a flight plan to our next destination."

"I'll let them know."

~ *The Wanderer* ~

On the Portland airport tarmac two hours later, a bevy of ground crew personnel prepared the Phillips Industries Learjet for takeoff. Inside the aircraft, Lucas, Gwendolyn, and Trevor sat around a polished oak table in the main cabin, listening to the radio. In front of the radio sat a large map of the western United States.

Just then, Captain Derrick Hull, Lucas and Gwendolyn's personal pilot, entered the cabin. Derrick, a thin, balding ex-Air Force pilot with more than twenty years of flying experience, was familiar with both military transports and civilian aircraft.

"I just talked to a friend of mine in Seattle," Derrick said. "Northwest Orient paid the ransom. Flight 305 is taking off as we speak."

"We heard," Trevor said.

"Fools," Gwendolyn grumbled.

"Does your friend know where the plane is headed, Captain?" Lucas asked.

"305's pilot filed a flight plan to Mexico City, but they won't make it that far. The 727's range is twenty-two hundred miles, tops. If he intends to go anywhere south of the border, they'll have to land and refuel."

"Any ideas where?" Gwendolyn asked.

Derrick pointed to the map. "Just guessing, I'd say Reno. It's not as busy as the major airports and it sits roughly in the center of the flightpaths heading south. But there are many other small, out-of-the-way airports along the way where they could land."

Gwendolyn turned to Trevor. "Contact your people and have them converge on the Reno airport. It'll be faster if you use the radio. Captain, show him how."

"Yes, ma'am."

Derrick turned and exited to the cockpit. Trevor followed close behind.

Deep in thought, Lucas rose from his chair and began pacing back and forth.

"What is it?" Gwendolyn asked.

"We're forgetting Aquinas' intelligence. He didn't demand four parachutes for nothing."

Gwendolyn's eyes grew wide. "Do you really believe he plans on jumping?"

"At this juncture, anything is possible. Yesterday, I would've never thought Aquinas capable of carrying out an extortion plot against a major airline, all in hopes of escaping us. I will not underestimate him again." Lucas walked over to the cockpit. "Captain, one more question."

Trevor stepped aside.

"Can someone successfully parachute from the 727? I'm talking about a clever, well-educated man who is desperate."

Derrick thought for a moment. "If he has knowledge of how airplanes work, he could order the pilot not to pressurize the cabin, and to fly at the minimum speed required to keep the plane in the air. With the aft stairs to jump from, it's entirely possible."

"Thank you, captain. If there are any further developments from your friend, I want to know immediately."

"Yes, sir."

Lucas walked over and sat in the chair next to Gwendolyn.

"If Aquinas does jump, where do you think it will be?" she asked.

Lucas' finger moved down the map. "If he jumps in Washington, Oregon, or Northern California, he runs the risk of landing in a forest and injuring himself. But with the element coursing through his veins, he shouldn't be scared of the terrain."

"What about Nevada?"

"Possibly. But if I were him, I'd want to get off the aircraft as soon as possible and slip away while the authorities are still mobilizing to find me."

"So where should we go?"

Lucas thought for a moment. "We stay put for now."

"Here? What on earth for?"

"If he lands anywhere near here, we'll sense him and the book."

"But what makes you think it will be near here?"

Lucas smiled. "Call it intuition."

~ Northwest Orient Flight 305 ~

The dim lights running along the sides of the center aisle faintly illuminated the abandoned coach section of the aircraft. A variety of magazines and newspapers strewn around in the empty seats were all the possessions remaining of the travelers who'd hastily disembarked the plane a short time ago. Adding to the haunting ambiance were the intermittent sounds of the fuselage shaking as the airframe passed through pockets of turbulence, and the distant rumble of the aircraft's engines.

Other than the flight crew, only Aquinas and the stewardess Tina remained onboard. While she stood in a trance, he removed his tie tack and tie and tossed them into his seat. Picking up one of the primary parachutes, he placed it on. After fastening the straps, he retrieved one of the reserve parachutes. Satisfied both chutes were secure, he looked around.

What can I use to tie the case and the bag of money to myself?

When his eyes fell on the other chutes, he got an idea. Placing his foot on one of them he pulled the rip cord. When the chute popped open, he turned to Tina.

"Do you have a knife? Something stronger than an eating utensil?"

"We have a razor knife for opening boxes," she replied.

"Perfect."

He followed her to a stewardess station, where she opened a compartment, pulled out the knife, and handed it to him. Returning to the open chute, he cut off two cords connecting the backpack to the canopy.

When he finished, he turned to the still-hypnotized stewardess. "One other thing. I need a can of soda."

She opened one of the drawers of a nearby drink cart and handed it to him.

"Now join the flight crew in the cockpit."

When she turned to leave, Aquinas opened the portfolio case and placed the bottle of bourbon on one side of the tubes, and the can of soda on the other. Using one of the cords he'd removed from the open parachute, he tied the case to the right side of his belt. Using the remaining cord, he tied the knapsack of ransom money to his left side. Quickly making his way to the rear of the aircraft, he lowered the aft stairs.

As he climbed down, the cold rain began to pelt his face, but he didn't feel it. Instead, he felt extremely fortunate. His impromptu idea of hijacking the airplane had gone off without a hitch. While the plane was on the ground in Seattle, the police or Gwendolyn's people could've easily assaulted the plane, overpowered him, or killed him.

It's a sign. The Almighty wants me to continue the Great Work.

Taking a deep breath, Aquinas let go of the handrail and jumped into infamy.

~ Present Day ~

Bob, who had started taking notes, reached over and pressed the "Pause" button on the CD player.

"Sorry. I need a minute to catch up. I'm not the fast writer I used to be."

"It's okay, Bob," Crystal said. "I need to take a break and stretch for minute. Does anyone else need anything? More water?"

"Yes," Madison and I said, in unison.

A short time later, we were hovered around the CD player. Bob pressed the "Play" button, and Aquinas' voice came back on.

"Unknown to me at the time of the hijacking, Gwendolyn's tentacles had grown significantly in the political landscape. With her powerful voice influencing Clyde Tolson, the deputy director of the FBI, a four-state manhunt began the next morning, encompassing Oregon, Washington, California, and Nevada.

"While an army of agents scoured the possible drop zones within the plane's flightpath, a bevy of investigators worked with local police to chase down leads in nearby towns, and question suspects who fit my description. No stone was left unturned in trying to identify me.

"From all outward indications, the notorious skyjacker who the public came to know as D. B. Cooper had committed the perfect crime and disappeared into the vast wilderness of the pacific northwest. With no body, parachute, or ransom money returning to circulation, many came to believe I had plummeted to my death, and a hunter or hiker would someday discover my remains.

"Behind the scenes, I had survived the daring jump. Although injured, I believed my luck had changed for the better, and I would be able to elude Lucas long enough to decipher the remaining symbols in the Wordless Book.

"My feelings of good fortune would be short-lived, however, when I called upon another innocent family to help me. Like the

Tanakas, this family included only three people: Bud King, his wife Starr, and their six-year-old daughter Maddie."

From a bird made of steel
whose wake rumbles like thunder,
his escape in the sky
will leave masses in wonder.

Though hurt from the plunge
he will find his direction,
and a daughter of kings
will spur his redemption.

Sara's interpretation of the fifth group of symbols in the second chapter of the Wordless Book

CHAPTER FOURTEEN: THE KINGS

Thursday, 25 November 1971, 06:45hrs
On the Western Shore of Lake Merwin, Washington

As the predawn light slowly brightened the cloudy sky, the motionless, half-frozen lake emerged from the darkness. Surrounding the still water, a landscape of white, snowy trees and foliage also appeared. The driving wind and freezing rain of the night before had moved eastward, leaving a surreal, post-storm silence in their wakes. Together, the dreary backdrop and lack of sounds created a peaceful ambiance, while at the same time, served as a warning that a harsh winter would soon arrive.

In the slushy, ice-cold water, Aquinas tried again to free himself. When he moved, a new shockwave of pain jolted his brain, forcing him to stop until the surge passed.

During the jump, when he had pulled the rip cord, the abrupt jerk of the deployed parachute broke his belt, and he lost the knapsack containing the ransom money. Although he'd hung on to the portfolio case containing the carmot, it flew from his hand when he landed, and his ankle snapped. To make matters worse, the parachute landed on top of him and he became tangled in the lines. As he tried to crawl ashore, the chute snagged on some jagged rocks, trapping him in the shallow water just off the beach.

Unbearably cold, Aquinas again tried to move, but when the wave of pain followed this time, he became dizzy.

* * *

Bud King saturated the charcoal briquettes with starter fluid and retrieved a match from the front pocket of his plaid coat. A moment later, the fire roared to life. Satisfied the campground's built-in grill would stay lit, he proceeded to the water's edge, baited his fishing hook, and cast the line into the water. A hundred feet behind the grill sat Bud's white pickup truck with a full-sized camper. On the roof of the camper, a thin trail of smoke climbed skyward from a heating pipe.

Just then, the door of the camper flew open and a young girl jumped out. She had thick, shoulder-length brown hair, which covered the hood of her bright blue parka. The legs of her black pants were tucked inside an oversized pair of rubber boots. The boots, bright pink in color, had a gaudy, flowery design printed on them. From inside the camper, her mother yelled.

"Wait! You forgot to zip up your coat."

"I don't need to zip up my coat!"

"Yes, you do, young lady. I won't have you traipsing around in the cold. You'll get sick."

"No, I won't. Daddy has the fire going."

"Maddie Emily King!"

Her mother's use of her full name in a loud, stern tone stopped her in her tracks.

Bud's wife Emily Starr King (Starr to her family and close friends) stepped out of the camper. She sported the same hair color and style as her daughter and wore a similar blue parka. The only difference being the leg bottoms of her denim pants were tucked inside tan hiking boots. Kneeling, she helped Maddie line up the front sides of her coat and pull the zipper up.

"There you go," Starr said.

The little girl ran toward her father. "Daddy, are we really going to have fish for breakfast?"

Bud smiled. "I'm hoping so, sweetheart."

When Maddie reached his side, she looked around. "How many have you caught?"

"I haven't caught any yet. I just got started."

Starr walked up next to them. "Don't worry, Maddie. If your father gets skunked, we'll go look for a restaurant."

Maddie tilted her head. "I thought a skunk was a stinky cat."

"It also means when you don't catch any fish."

All three laughed.

Starr kissed Bud on the cheek. "You know, we really could go look for a restaurant."

"Give me an hour? If I haven't caught any by then, we'll leave."

"Can I go look for rocks?" Maddie asked.

Starr looked down the shoreline. The beach curved before disappearing behind a high piece of ground. "Sure, but stay on the beach where we can see you."

When her daughter walked away, Starr turned to Bud. "How are you doing?"

"I'm okay."

"But you didn't sleep."

When he cast his fishing line again, his eyes watered. "I was thinking about dad. I can't believe he's gone."

"I understand. I remember losing sleep when my dad passed."

He placed his arm around her. "I know this isn't how you wanted to spend Thanksgiving, but I just wanted to visit dad's favorite fishing hole one last time before we go home. What I'm trying to say is, thanks for being okay to stop and spend the night here."

"You don't have to thank me. I enjoyed it."

Suddenly, they heard Maddie yelling. "Daddy! Mommy!"

They looked down the beach and saw her running frantically toward them. When she was within arm's reach, her mother knelt and picked her up.

"What on earth is the matter, sweetheart?"

"There's a sea monster down there," Maddie replied, panting heavily.

"Where?"

She pointed to the bend at the end of the beach.

"What does it look like?" Bud asked.

"It's big and puffy like a marshmallow, and it has a man tied to it."

Starr smiled. "Are you sure it's a man?"

Maddie nodded. "He asked me for help."

Bud reeled in the fishing line and set his pole on the ground. "I'll go have a look."

He proceeded down the shoreline and disappeared around the bend. A moment later, they heard him yell.

"Starr, it's a skydiver! He's hurt! Bring me my hunting knife and the first aid kit!"

Starr and Maddie rushed to the camper. After retrieving the two items, they took off running down the beach. Rounding the bend, they found Bud standing next to the injured skydiver. Behind them, a partially submerged parachute floated on the water.

"He said he landed last night and broke his ankle," Bud said, "and got tangled in the parachute lines."

"Why is he wearing a suit?" Starr asked.

"I haven't had a chance to ask. He keeps passing out. Hand me the knife and I'll cut him loose."

While Bud went to work on the parachute cords, Starr knelt beside the injured man.

Aquinas opened his eyes.

"Can you hear me?" Starr asked.

He nodded.

"You're going to be alright. My name is Starr King. This is my husband, Bud."

Aquinas acknowledged with a nod.

When Starr moved to the side, Maddie scurried to stay behind her.

"And this is our daughter. Maddie, say hello."

She poked her head out. "Hi."

Grimacing from the pain, Aquinas forced a smile. "Hello, Maddie. How old are you?"

"Six."

"My name is Aquinas."

The little girl looked up at her mother. "I've never heard that name before."

"I'm from…eastern Europe. Where are you from?"

"Ogden, Utah."

As a force of habit, Aquinas glanced at Bud and Starr's left hands. Both parents had all segments of their middle fingers.

"We're on our way home from a funeral," Starr explained. "Bud's father passed away, and he wanted to visit his dad's favorite fishing hole."

"My condolences, Mr. King."

"It was a blessing. He was old and sick."

"We'll get you to a hospital as soon as we can, Mr. Aquinas," Starr said.

Aquinas shook his head. "No…No hospital."

"Why not?"

"There's someone after me…I've got to…get away."

"But you need a doctor," Bud said. "Your ankle needs to be set."

Aquinas shook his head. "I can't let him…find…me." His voice trailed off and he lost consciousness again.

"Mr. Aquinas?" Starr asked.

He didn't respond.

Starr looked at Bud and asked, "What do you think he meant by that?"

"He must be delirious from being out in this freezing water all night," Bud replied. "Let's get him on the beach."

Starr turned to Maddie. "Stand back, sweetheart."

The little girl didn't move.

"It's okay. There's nothing to be afraid of."

Maddie pointed to the water. "What about that?"

"That's not a sea monster, it's a parachute. This man is what we call a skydiver. He jumped out of an airplane and landed here."

Maddie's eyes grew wide. "He jumped out of an airplane?"

Starr nodded.

When they began moving him, Aquinas woke up and began writhing in pain.

"Sorry," Starr said. "We need to get you out of the water so we can immobilize your ankle."

Aquinas motioned Bud for the knife and cut the shoulder straps of the parachute. With all his might, he pushed himself up to a sitting position.

"I had a black case," Aquinas said, panting heavily. "If you can locate it, I'll be able to address my ankle."

Bud and Starr looked around.

Maddie pointed farther down the shoreline. "Is that it?"

The portfolio case lay on the water's edge.

"That's it."

Maddie ran and retrieved the case and hurried back and handed it to Aquinas.

Opening the case, Aquinas quickly removed the lid from one of the tubes of carmot. Using two fingers, he scooped out a small amount and spread it on his ankle. The carmot slowly went to work, transforming from a light violet color to dark purple. A wave of intense pain bolted through Aquinas when the bone straightened. A moment later, he rose to his feet and gingerly took a few steps.

Bud stared wide-eyed, while Starr and Maddie gasped.

"I don't believe what I just saw," Bud said.

"Are you a magician?" Maddie asked.

Aquinas smiled. "Why yes. Yes, I am. Would you like to see more tricks?"

Maddie nodded.

Screwing the lid back on the tube, Aquinas placed it in the case. Reaching into his pocket, he withdrew the necklace with the crystal pendant. A few minutes later, Bud, Starr, and Maddie were hypnotized.

"First and foremost," Aquinas said, "you are never to reveal to anyone you found me. Your lives may depend on it. Do I make myself clear?"

They nodded in unison.

"I assume you have a vehicle?"

"A truck," Bud replied.

"Is the bed empty?"

"No. Our camper is on the back."

Aquinas thought for a moment. "Mrs. King, I'd like you and Maddie to return to your truck and fill the floor of the camper with as much snow as possible. Time is of the essence, so you must hurry."

Starr took hold of Maddie's hand and they rushed off.

Aquinas carefully slid Bud's hunting knife into an empty belt loop and took a few more steps.

Miraculous! No pain at all!

Aquinas sniffed the air. "Is that a fire I'm smelling?"

Bud nodded.

"Help me gather the parachute. We need to erase all evidence I landed here."

~ *The Wanderer* ~

In the aft compartment of the posh Phillips Industries' Learjet, Gwendolyn wakened. Jumping out of bed, she rushed to the forward cabin, and found Lucas seated at the table studying a map.

Lucas looked up. "I see you've become aware Aquinas is back on the ground."

Gwendolyn nodded. "Do we know where he is?"

"My intuition is telling me he's close, approximately fifty miles from our present position,"

"How come we didn't sense him last night when he landed?"

Lucas shrugged his shoulders. "Who knows? He may have come down in heavy snow or icy water. Or it might simply be the unpredictable carmot. Regardless, he has let his guard down again."

"Which direction?"

"You tell me. Remember what I taught you."

She closed her eyes and took a few deep breaths. Opened her eyes, she pointed at the map. "Here. In the vicinity of Lake Merwin."

Lucas smiled. "Precisely, my pet. I've ordered Mr. Warner to mobilize our security detachment. He'll be back momentarily to pick us up."

"Do you think we'll be able to finish this business today?"

"I don't know. Aquinas is like a cat with nine lives. He is clever, elusive, and very resourceful. Therefore, to mitigate the chance of him escaping again, I have decided to kill him on sight when we catch up with him."

Gwendolyn's eyes grew wide. "But what about the book? We need it to find the carmot in Antarctica."

"We know he has the book," he replied, "and we know every move he has made since landing in San Francisco. If he *doesn't* have the book on him, we'll retrace his steps to find it."

"But what if he hides it in the snow, or somewhere out in the forest?"

"The snow will eventually thaw, and our enhanced senses will detect it. So you see, any way you look at it, Aquinas is expendable."

Gwendolyn embraced him. "I love your deductive reasoning."

* * *

With Maddie and Starr buckled in, Bud walked to the back of his truck. Aquinas stood waiting at the open door of the camper.

"How much fuel do we have?" he asked.

"A little over a quarter of a tank," Bud replied.

"How far can we go?"

"Roughly fifty miles. If you want to go any farther, we'll have to gas up in Woodland."

"Is Woodland a small town?"

Bud nodded. "A few gas stations and restaurants. The interstate highway ties in there."

"Sounds like it has everything we need. Proceed to Woodland."

Aquinas removed the partially used tube of carmot from the portfolio case, unscrewed the lid, and threw it toward the shore. It rolled to the water's edge.

Hopefully, it will divert Lucas.

Stepping up into the camper, he shut the door and climbed onto the mound of snow Starr and Maddie had gathered. The forward wall of the camper had a small window opened into the rear window of the truck's cab, with a cut-out piece of foam insulating the opening.

This should give me a perfect vantage point.

With the authorities looking for a man wearing business attire, Aquinas thought it would be a good idea to change out of the suit. Since he was roughly the same height and build as Bud, he looked through several drawers and found an extra set of Bud's clothes. Soon after, he had changed into denim pants and a plaid flannel shirt. With Bud's sneakers fitting loose, he put on extra socks until they fit. Wrapping his old shoes up in the suit, he placed the bundle next to the door.

Quickly clearing the snow from a section of the floor, he sat down and pulled a blanket over himself and the portfolio case. Working fast, he scooped the surrounding snow up around him.

As they made their way along the winding Lewis River Road, Aquinas conversed with Bud, Starr, and Maddie.

"So what do you do for a living, Mr. King?"

"I'm a carrier for the Post Office."

"A noble profession. And you?"

"I stay at home and take care of Maddie," Starr said.

Aquinas smiled. "An equally challenging occupation, no doubt."

"She can be a handful at times, but all in all, raising her has been quite easy."

"How so?"

"Maddie was born with a very high I.Q. She reasons things out faster than most children her age. Doctors think she'll someday become a doctor or a scientist."

"I want to be a princess, Mommy."

Could she be the one my father foretold?

Aquinas smiled. "My dear, sweet child, I think you already are a princess."

Maddie's face beamed. "Will you sing with me?"

"Certainly."

For the next half-hour, they filled the truck with renditions of children's songs.

Following a brief stop in Woodland, where they refueled and bought some breakfast sandwiches at a fast-food restaurant, Bud drove to the end of the main road and entered the on-ramp of the interstate highway. Just then, coming from the opposite direction, a bevy of Phillips Security vans exited the highway and turned up the road toward Woodland.

When he sighted the vans, the ceaseless threat of Lucas hit Aquinas like a sledgehammer, and he became afraid – not for himself, but for the King family.

What am I thinking? I should have never involved more innocents in the Great Work! The pain from my broken ankle must have affected my judgement. At my earliest opportunity, I must get away from them!

"Mr. King, please exit at the next rest stop."

"Yes, sir."

Forty miles later, they pulled into a rest stop overlooking a valley of thick trees. The stop consisted of an old, run-down visitor's center, with a faded sign hanging on the side of the building proclaiming, "Restrooms Inside."

When Bud parked the truck, Aquinas climbed out of the camper and threw the suit bundle into a nearby garbage can. Retrieving the portfolio case, he walked up the driver's door and motioned for Bud to roll down the window.

"Thank you for your assistance, Mr. King. Remember, never reveal to anyone you found me. Do you understand?"

Bud, Starr, and Maddie nodded in unison.

"Once I am gone, you will be free to do as you wish. Goodbye."

Aquinas ran to the edge of the parking lot and vanished into the forest.

Released from the hypnotic suggestion, Maddie spoke first.

"I have to go potty, Mommy."

"Zip up your coat."

"Lock your door," Bud added. "I've got to go, too."

As Bud, Starr, and Maddie entered the shabby-looking visitor's center, a white Phillips Industries van exited the highway and pulled into the rest stop.

~ *The Wanderer* ~

Thirty-five minutes earlier, the van carrying Lucas, Gwendolyn, and Trevor made its way along the Lewis River Road; its speed hampered by the multitude of hairpin curves. When Trevor, who was driving, slowed to a crawl around a particularly sharp bend, Gwendolyn lost her patience.

"How much longer, Mr. Warner?"

Trevor's eyes met hers in the rear-view mirror. "The last sign said forty-one miles to Lake Merwin, ma'am."

"Can't you drive any faster?"

"If I go any faster, we'll end up in the river."

Gwendolyn sighed loudly. "This is insufferable!" She turned to Lucas and found him with his eyes closed. "How can you sleep at a time like this?"

Lucas opened his eyes. "I wasn't sleeping. I was trying to get a fix on...Aquinas'...position." His voice trailed off and his eyes went into a stare.

"What is it?"

"My intuition is telling me Aquinas is behind us and moving away quickly."

"Are you sure?" Gwendolyn asked. "I'm sensing he's still ahead of us."

Lucas shook his head. "Now I'm getting mixed signals."

"So what do we do?"

Lucas thought for a moment. "We divide and conquer."

"What?"

"We split our forces." He leaned forward. "Mr. Warner, radio the others and tell them Miss Phillips and I are taking this vehicle. Then pull off to the side of the road and join them. If you find Aquinas at Lake Merwin, you are to kill him immediately. Do you understand?"

"Yes, sir." Trevor picked up the receiver and made the call.

After rounding another sharp turn, Trevor slowed to a stop and climbed out. The van directly behind them pulled up alongside and Trevor climbed in. As they drove away, Lucas slid into the driver's seat, turned the van around, and sped off in the opposite direction.

Thirty minutes later, with his intuition guiding him, Lucas exited the highway, pulled into the rest stop, and parked next to the only other vehicle: a white pickup truck with a full-sized camper.

* * *

As Aquinas hurried through the forest, the hair in the back of his neck unexpectedly bristled. Stopping to look back, he instantly sensed danger. Closing his eyes to concentrate, images of death flashed in his mind, and he heard Lucas' deep laugh travel across the countryside.

"No!" he screamed.

Opening his eyes, he heard the familiar voice of his father.

"Aquinas, you must go back. The Wanderer has murdered those who helped you."

With his intuition telling him his father was right, Aquinas dropped the portfolio case and fell to his knees. Tears began streaming down his face.

"I'm sorry, my son."

Aquinas gulped in a breath of air. "More innocent blood on my hands."

"You are not to blame. Lucas is the one who took their lives."

"But Father, I *involved* them! If I hadn't asked them to help me, they would still be alive."

"As with your wife, they served their purpose and have been called home. But you must go back."

"Go back? If Lucas has murdered them, shouldn't I hasten my escape? I cannot change things if I go back."

"The young girl is still alive."

Aquinas' eyes grew wide. "Maddie lives?"

"Yes. You must rescue her at all costs. In the coming years, she'll play a significant role in the Great Work."

"How can I rescue her? Lucas will surely detect me."

"You must shroud yourself."

"How? By packing my clothes with snow?"

"Use the snow to shroud the carmot. As for you, there is a better way. Remember how the doctors tried to cure those infected with the Black Death?"

"Bloodletting?"

"Yes. It will thin the carmot in your body and prevent the Wanderer from sensing you."

Aquinas stood and wiped the tears from his face.

"I must leave you now, my son. Remember, the girl will play a significant part in defeating the Wanderer. To learn the secret, you must finish deciphering the Wordless Book."

As Augustus' voice faded into silence, Aquinas opened the case and began scooping in handfuls of snow. Once he was finished, he closed the case, pulled Bud King's hunting knife from his beltloop, and rolled up his sleeve.

* * *

Staying behind the trees, Aquinas slowly approached the run-down visitor's center. Bud King's truck was now flanked by two vehicles: on the far side, a white Phillips Security van, on the near side, closest to Aquinas, a Washington Highway Patrol car.

The doors of the patrol car opened, and two troopers climbed out. As they walked toward the front door of the visitor's center, Lucas and Gwendolyn came out to meet them. Aquinas ducked behind a large pine tree and dropped to his knees. After a moment, Gwendolyn proceeded to the van, while Lucas remained talking to the troopers.

He doesn't know I'm here!

Just then, two more patrol cars pulled into the rest stop, and the troopers climbed out.

Aquinas set the case on the ground and shoved it under the pine tree's low hanging branches. Staying on his hands and knees, he crawled around to the rear of the building. There were two doors, one in the center and the other on the left side. Finding the center door locked, he moved to the door on the left and tried the handle.

The door opened.

Slipping inside, he flipped on the light switch and found he was in a utility closet. He now faced two doors on each side of the inner wall, opposite from where he had come in, separated by a rusted-out water heater and a dusty, antiquated gas furnace.

Proceeding to the door on the left, he slowly turned the handle and pushed the door open, revealing the men's room. To his left were three dirt-encrusted sinks, one of which was hanging, half-ripped from the wall. To his right were two urinals and a toilet stall, its door closed. Entering, he slowly crept to the stall and peered through the crack between the wall and the door. On the toilet sat the body of Bud King, blood dripping from his nose, and his lifeless eyes staring into nothingness. Shuddering at the sight, Aquinas quietly returned to the utility closet and closed the door.

Opening the second door, he entered the women's restroom. There were three stalls, all with their doors closed. Making his way to the first stall, he peered through the crack and found Starr's lifeless body much like Bud's, nose bloody and eyes staring. Hurrying back to the utility closet, he slowly closed the door.

Standing there for a moment, wondering what to do, he heard a faint whimper.

"Maddie?" he whispered. "Are you in here?"

"Yes," she replied, also whispering.

Aquinas' eyes traveled back and forth, but he couldn't tell where her voice was coming from.

"Come out, sweetheart."

"Are the bad people gone?"

"No, they are still here."

"The bad people hurt my daddy. My mommy told me to hide in here and not come out until she gets me."

Tears came to Aquinas' eyes. "Your mommy told me to come get you. If you come out, I'll take you to her."

Dusty and dirty, Maddie emerged from a tiny crawlspace behind the furnace.

Removing the necklace from his pocket, he held the crystal pendant in front of her eyes and began twisting the chain. A moment later, he had her hypnotized again.

"When we leave this place, you must remain silent. Do you understand?"

She nodded.

"Take my hand. We must hurry."

He opened the outside door, and they took off running. When they reached the trees, he motioned her to get down and they crawled to where he had left the portfolio case.

Leaning out from behind the tree, Aquinas found the scene much the same as before. Gwendolyn was still in the van, and Lucas was still talking to the troopers.

Just then, another Washington Highway Patrol car pulled in and parked next to the others, which happened to be the last space in the row, and only a few feet from the tree line. This car carried only one trooper, who opened his door but remained in the vehicle, talking on the radio.

Aquinas reached under the tree, retrieved the portfolio case, and handed it to Maddie.

"Wait here. When I signal you, bring me the case."

He took the necklace out of his pocket and slowly crawled out of the trees. When he reached the patrol car, he rose to a kneeling position.

His voice low and soft, Aquinas called out to the officer. "Help. Please help me."

When the trooper stopped talking and turned his head, Aquinas dangled the crystal pendant in front of his face and twisted the chain. A moment later, his eyes went into a stare and his mouth dropped open.

Aquinas motioned to Maddie. When she was within an arm's reach, he took the case from her and opened the rear door.

"Get in."

Returning his attention to the trooper, Aquinas noticed the rank insignia on his collar and the name on the front of his uniform.

Still speaking softly, Aquinas said, "I need you to listen to me very carefully, Lieutenant Adams. This is what I want you to do."

A moment later, Adams backed out of the parking space. As he drove by Lucas and the other troopers, he rolled his window down. "I'm needed at the station. Carry on with the search. If something breaks, let me know."

He proceeded to the southbound onramp of the interstate highway. Twenty-five minutes later, he pulled up to the front of the Portland Bus Terminal, and Aquinas and Maddie climbed out.

When they disappeared into the terminal, Lieutenant Adams drove away, completely unaware he had aided in the escape of the most wanted man in America.

* * *

By thinning his blood of the element, Aquinas successfully eluded Lucas and Gwendolyn for the next five decades. Using the power of suggestion, he made Maddie forget the horrible events at the rest stop, and instead, made her believe her parents had died in an airplane accident. To keep their identities a secret, he introduced

310

another suggestion, convincing her that her name was Madison Alexandra Dewhurst, and he was her uncle Charlie; formalizing her first name and randomly choosing her middle and last name from a book he once read.

As the years passed, Aquinas poured his heart into the role of Madison's surrogate parent. Watching her mature from the shy little girl into a strong, responsible adult made him feel proud, and gave him a sense of atonement for involving her family.

Using half of the carmot he'd recovered in Antarctica to transform rocks into gold, Aquinas bought himself a car and the secluded Victorian-era house in St. George, Utah. As a cover, he began working for the U. S. Forest Service as a Mining and Metallurgy Specialist; a position requiring him to work alone in remoat locations, and out of the mainstream public.

As for the Wordless Book, the breakthrough came when Aquinas finally finished deciphering the lengthy second-to-the-last chapter of symbols. Studying the rhyming parables, he realized they were describing Madison's husband George! After re-checking his calculations several times, he hurriedly made plans to go visit them and tell them about the Great Work.

Sadly, fate would intervene less than twenty-four hours later, when a lightning storm in the middle of the night caused a power outage, and the remaining carmot in his freezer melted. Coinciding with the loss of the element, he began experiencing abdominal pains reminiscent of the aches he'd experienced when he contracted the Black Death and when Lucas had poisoned him with Belladonna. The remaining carmot in his system was wearing off, and his body had started degenerating back to its original state.

Since taking over the Great Work from his father seven-hundred years earlier, Aquinas had evaded the Wanderer countless times, but now, without more of the magical element, he faced an enemy he couldn't escape from – his own mortality.

CHAPTER FIFTEEN: THE ABDUCTION

Present Day
Inside the Rivers' Home
Gila River Indian Reservation, Arizona

Madison's loud sobs echoed off the living room walls, and I squeezed her tight. For the last hour, as we learned the secrets of her uncle's hidden life, she had been weeping on-and-off. Hearing the fate of her parents, however, sent her into an outburst of inconsolable crying. Finally regaining control of her emotions, she looked up at me, her watery blue eyes puffy and bloodshot.

The haunting recording of her uncle had stopped, and Bob reached over to turn the CD player off. Just as his finger reached the button, however, Aquinas resumed his recitation.

"When I felt the pain return to my body, I knew my time was short. I made these recordings so you, Maddie, would be prepared to take over the Great Work and finish what my father and I had started. I never wanted to involve you in this business, but from what I've uncovered in the second-to-last chapter of the Wordless Book, the point has been rendered moot. The parables read:

The first year of great change,
as the calendar leaps,
the people will choose

THE ELEMENT

a young leader of kings.

And on the fifth of Sextilis,
near a great lake of salt,
a boy born sinistro,
near the land's great fault.

The Wanderer will come,
in a merchant's guise,
seeking man's end,
aspiring to die.

But no fearless warrior,
nor soldier, nor king,
will defeat the immortal
and powerful being.

The secret instead
lies in the right hand,
of the boy who matures
a weakened man.

"I'm positive the parables are referring to George. The 1960s were years of great change. 1960 was a leap year and was the same year America elected John Kennedy to be President, the youngest president at the time. The old word for August is Sextilis, and sinistro means left-handed. The added mentioning of the Great Salt Lake and the Wasatch fault line, and his description of Parkinson's disease, makes it a positive match. George is the one Father Vincent foretold."

I must admit, it did sound like the parables were describing me. Bob, Crystal, and Madison must have been thinking the same thing, because when I looked up, they were staring at me.

"There is still one chapter remaining that I haven't been able to decipher," Aquinas continued, "which contains the secret of how George can use the carmot to defeat the Wanderer. Like the previous chapter, the symbols are many and some are faded, which makes it nearly impossible to measure them accurately. But with your ingenuity, Maddie, I know you'll either find a way, or find someone who can help you decipher them."

The sound crackled for a moment, before Aquinas' voice resumed.

"One final word on the Wanderer. From research I conducted on the Internet, and from reports I've received, I can tie Lucas to every major outbreak of sicknesses plaguing mankind over the last seven centuries! Most recently, three years ago, he and Gwendolyn traveled to Wuhan Provence, China, where the Coronavirus began. In 2013, they were on holiday in West Africa when the Ebola Virus broke out. And in 1981, they were in Cameroon, South Africa, where the HIV/AIDS virus is believed to have started." He sighed heavily. "The list goes on.

"When Lucas told me the scientists in Gwendolyn's company had studied the carmot, I asked myself why. Why would he disclose the secret of the element to anyone? After much thought, I believe he is trying to synthesize it, and these recent outbreaks are simply trial runs of a much broader plan to create a virus that will decimate the world's population. If Lucas is successful in recreating the element, he won't need the carmot in Antarctica or the Wordless Book. He'll be able to unleash a deadly disease on his own. Therefore, it is imperative you decipher the last chapter of symbols in the book and learn how to defeat him."

"Maddie," he concluded, his voice cracking, "I know I should have told you about this when you came of age, but I just couldn't bring myself to admit to you I was responsible for involving you and your family, and am therefore to blame for your parents' deaths. I hope and pray you will find it in your heart to forgive me. I love you."

The CD abruptly ended, and Bob reached over and turned the player off.

The four of us sat there for a minute, not saying a word.

Finally ending the prolonged silence, Bob cleared his throat. "Do you remember any of this, Mrs. d'Clare?"

Wiping her eyes, Madison shook her head.

He turned to Crystal. "What do you think, honey?"

Crystal looked up from her laptop. "As far as the viruses are concerned, Aquinas was dead-on. The Coronavirus began in Wuhan Provence, China, and Ebola and HIV started in the areas of Africa he mentioned."

She set her laptop down, moved over to the ottoman, and began looking through the Wordless Book.

Bob's eyes returned to Madison. "With your permission, Mrs. d'Clare, I'd like to call an old friend of mine in the FBI. He knows all about the D. B. Cooper skyjacking."

Madison nodded.

"Who's that?" Crystal asked.

"Tim McCurdy."

"Do I know him?"

"You've met him once, but you probably don't remember. He showed up at our wedding reception with the blonde woman who was twice his size."

"That skinny little black man is an FBI agent?"

Bob nodded. "He's also a pilot in the Air Force Reserve. Many moons ago, we shared a room at the police academy. His dad was one of the investigators on the D. B. Cooper case."

He retrieved his cell phone and began going through his contacts.

"Here he is." A moment later, he had Agent McCurdy on the line. After exchanging greetings, Bob placed his phone on "speaker mode" so we could all hear.

"Tim," Bob began, "I'd like to ask you some questions about the D. B. Cooper case."

"Sure, but my dad was the real expert. God rest his soul."

"Oh, I'm sorry to hear that."

"Yeah, a heart attack got him a little over six months ago. He went to his grave regretting never being able to identify Cooper."

"Did he ever discuss the case with you?"

"Every time we got together. What do you want to know?"

Bob looked through his notes. "When Cooper demanded the ransom, did he ask for a bottle of Kentucky bourbon?"

Agent McCurdy didn't reply.

"Tim? Are you still with me?"

"Yes, but how do you know that?"

"For now, let's just say I might have a lead." Bob turned to another page of notes. "Did Cooper leave a clip-on tie onboard the aircraft?"

"Yes."

"Did he also leave a tie tack?"

"Now you're blowing me away. Yes, he left a tie tack, but the bourbon and the tie tack were never made public. Dad and his team of investigators kept a tight lid on them."

"Okay, let me ask you this. Is there anything your dad said about the Cooper case that sounded odd?"

Tim hesitated for a moment, before replying. "You know, now that you mention it, there was one thing. Every passenger gave a different description of Cooper. Some said he was tall, others said he was short. Wavy hair, straight hair. Young, old. What he was wearing. Dad said if he didn't know any better, he'd swear Cooper had hypnotized them."

Bob's eyes grew wide, as did Crystal's.

"One last question, Tim. If the skyjacker purchased his ticket and signed the note demanding the ransom as Dan Cooper, where did the letter B come from?"

Tim laughed. "That's easy. The press misreported his name as D. B. Cooper, and the name stuck. Simple as that. Can you tell me about this lead you found?"

"If my hunch checks out, you'll be the first to know. But first, I need you to check the bureau's files and see if they have any information on three people who went missing right around the time of the skyjacking. The first is Dan Morgan who worked at Boeing in Portland. The other two are Bud and Starr King, husband and wife, from Ogden, Utah."

"Anything else?"

"Yes," Bob replied, "run a check on Lucas Carter and Gwendolyn Phillips of Chicago."

"Gwendolyn Phillips?"

"Yes. She's the CEO of Phillips Industries."

"What do you want to know?"

"Mostly background information. Anything you can find. And keep this on the down low."

"Got it. How soon do you need it."

"Yesterday."

"Alright, I'll see what I can find, but I can't promise anything. I'm leaving for reserve duty tonight, and I still have to go home and pack."

"I thought you were going to retire?"

"I was, but they gave me an offer I couldn't refuse. I'm now a test pilot on experimental aircraft."

Bob chuckled. "Sounds like something right up your alley."

"I love it. But let me let you go. If I find anything, I'll call you back."

When the call ended, I looked over at Crystal. Her wide-eyed stare was transfixed on a page of the Wordless Book. I nudged Madison and motioned for her to look.

Noticing, Bob placed his hand on hers. "What is it, honey?"

Crystal's eyes broke away from the book and traveled to each of us, before settling on Bob.

"I know how we can decipher it!"

~ The Wanderer ~

Two Utah Highway Patrol cars, their sirens blaring and red lights flashing, sped south down the Arizona freeway towards Phoenix. Close behind, two Phillips Security vans, black with dark-tinted windows, kept pace.

Aboard the trailing van, behind the driver, sat Lucas. In his hand, he held a cell phone, linked via satellite to Gwendolyn's office computer in Chicago. On the screen, Gwendolyn's face beamed with an ear-to-ear grin.

"I just sent you the FBI report," she said. "You won't believe it."

Lucas switched the phone's display to show his email. A moment later, her message, titled "d'Clare Info," appeared in his inbox. As he began pouring over the report, his eyes grew wide with astonishment.

Has the pendulum finally swung in my favor?

"And the news gets better," Gwendolyn continued. "Did you notice the name of d'Clare's former commander on his performance reports?"

Lucas switched the phone's display to show the electronic documents and checked the signature blocks. "General Richard Joseph. Why is that important?"

"He's a civil servant now, who's present duty assignment happens to be supervisor of the Pegasus Airfield at McMurdo Station."

Lucas switched the phone's display back to her. "Have you confirmed this?"

"Yes. I checked with our contact in the Air Force Secretary's office."

"This will work perfectly in our plans."

Gwendolyn smiled. "It's like they were gift wrapped and given to us. All we need now is the book."

"Pardon me, sir," the driver interrupted, "We've got company."

Lucas turned around. An Arizona Highway Patrol car, with its lights on and siren wailing, was now behind their vehicle. Unlike the Utah patrol cars ahead of them, this car only had one officer.

"We don't have time for this!" Lucas snarled. "I'll call you back."

"What do you want me to do?" the driver asked.

Just then, the van passed a road sign, indicating one mile to the Gila Bend exit.

The book is close. I can feel it!

"Call the others and tell them to take the next exit," Lucas ordered, "then pull off to the side of the road. I'll deal with the Arizona policeman myself."

After making the calls, the driver followed the three other vehicles down the off-ramp, where they slowed to a stop. Lucas checked his gun and stepped out of the van.

When the Arizona trooper climbed out of his patrol car, Lucas rushed up to him – catching the officer completely by surprise. Touching the side of the man's head, the trooper's eyes went into a stare and his mouth dropped open.

"What is your name?" Lucas asked.

"William Pullman," the trooper replied.

"Very well, Officer Pullman. I need you to return to your vehicle and contact your superiors. Tell them you are assisting the FBI and Utah Highway Patrol chase down a dangerous criminal."

Pullman immediately climbed back in his patrol car and made the call. A moment later, he leaned his head out the window. "My chief wants to talk to whoever is in charge."

Lucas took the microphone from him. "This is Agent Carter of the FBI. To whom am I speaking?"

"Captain Martin Reynolds," the man replied. "Arizona Highway Patrol."

"Your Officer Pullman has interrupted our high-speed pursuit of a murder suspect."

"We weren't informed of any high-speed pursuit."

"That's not my problem, Captain. What *is* a problem is the longer we are delayed, the more likely the suspect will get away. I'll have the field office contact you. Are we free to go?"

"Certainly, Agent Carter. Are you at liberty to tell me who the suspect allegedly murdered?"

"A fellow agent."

After ending the call with Officer Reynolds, Lucas quickly planted a suggestion in Officer Pullman's mind. A minute later, Lucas stepped back into the van. Addressing the driver, he said, "We shouldn't have any more trouble. Inform the others to follow us. We're taking the lead now."

Back inside the Arizona Highway Patrol Car, Officer Pullman withdrew his gun from his holster, pointed the barrel at himself, and pulled the trigger.

* * *

When Crystal said she knew how we could decipher the symbols, I envisioned years of late nights working on countless, convoluted math problems. Upon telling us her plan, it didn't sound as difficult as I first imagined.

"I can scan the final chapter of the book into a computer file and enhance the faded lines," she explained. "Once the lines are legible, I can plot the end points of each line of the symbols."

"But with some of those symbols written over each other, how will you be able to separate them?" I asked.

"For my doctoral dissertation, I used a computer program to convert two-dimensional images into three-dimensional objects. I can import the scan into the same 3D program and separate the symbols by layers; like peeling an onion. Once they are separated, we'll be able to measure them."

Madison leaned in. "Say you are able to separate and measure them, how will we find the right math formula?"

Crystal smiled. "By using an app on my phone."

"Are you serious?"

She nodded. "All I have to do is plug in the numbers, set the parameters to check all the math equations, filter the answers to numbers less than or equal to twenty-six, and match them to letters in the alphabet. The app can also work with geometric and calculous equations."

"But won't it give us just a bunch of letters?" I asked. "I mean, with as many symbols as there are, there must be more than one parable. When we build the words with the letters, how do we tell which words go with which parable?"

"By keeping the layers separate. As for building the words, have you ever played a computer game called Jumble?"

Madison and I shook our heads.

"All you do is type in a bunch of random letters, and the computer figures out the words or phrases you could spell from the letters you entered. I've got the app for it too. May I scan the pages, Mrs. d'Clare?"

Madison nodded.

Crystal picked up the Wordless Book. "The scanner is in the other room. You can come with me if you'd like."

Madison followed Crystal out of the room. Bob and I sat on the couch, and talked more about Lucas, Aquinas, and the Wordless Book.

Roughly ten minutes later, Bob stood and stretched. "Can I get you another bottle of water, George?"

"Yes, thanks."

When he departed for the kitchen, I heard a faint knock at the front door. Rising to my feet, I crept over and looked through the peephole. A cold chill instantly traveled down my spine!

The mannequin!

I looked away and blinked several times before returning to the peephole. The emotionless, plastic eye was still staring at me! A deep, guttural laugh followed, emanating from all around me. At the same time, I heard a voice in my head.

"Open the door, Mr. d'Clare."

The eye moved away from the door, revealing eight more mannequins.

The voice persisted. "Open the door!"

I tried to resist, but the voice was too powerful. Reaching down, I unlocked the door, and turned the handle.

Just then, Bob came back into the room.

"George, what are you doing?"

Paralyzed with fear, I couldn't answer, nor could I move.

Hurrying over, Bob pushed me away. When he reached for the handle, the front door burst open, knocking him to the floor. With their guns drawn, the four St. George policemen, Davis, Hansen, Blair, and Greyson rushed in. Four Phillips Security men followed, each armed with an assault rifle.

While the officers kept their weapons pointed at Bob and me, three of the security men began searching the rest of the house. The one remaining began examining the charred portfolio case with the CDs.

Suddenly, I heard a scuffle and yelling in the other room. A moment later, the three security men returned with Crystal and Madison. Clutched in the hand of one of the men, was the all-important Wordless Book.

Then a big man walked in. He stood roughly six-and-a-half feet tall, with a broad, muscular physique. His jet-black hair was cut short (over the ears and blocked in back) military-style. He wore a tight polo shirt, slacks, and dress shoes, all black, fitting him to perfection. His most striking feature, however, wasn't his imposing physique, but rather the unsettling feeling surrounding him – like an aura of danger.

The security man walked over and handed him the book.

"Good work," the big man said.

"And look at this, boss."

"Interesting."

He looked back and forth at the portfolio case and the book, lined up the burnt edge, and placed the book inside. When he picked up one of the CDs, I noticed the tip of his left middle finger was missing.

Lucas!

He examined the CD for a moment and smiled. With his free hand, he retrieved a cell phone from his pocket and pressed a number.

"The book is ours."

I could hear a woman's voice reply, who I took to be Gwendolyn Phillips. "I'll assemble the research team."

Lucas looked over at Madison and me. "You may not need to. Aquinas has left us a present."

"A present?"

"Yes. Not only the book, but an oral history of his exploits on compact discs. I'll listen to them and call you when I learn something." He pocketed his phone and set the CD back in the portfolio case.

He handed the case back to the security man. "Put it in my van."

Lucas walked over to Madison. "Madison d'Clare. Or may I simply call you Maddie?"

"Lucas," Madison replied mockingly, "or may I simply call you mass murderer, or how about psychopath?"

"Oh, please, Maddie, I've been looking for you for some time. You really should be more friendly."

"Friendly? You murder my parents and you expect me to be friendly?"

The smile left Lucas' face and his eyes narrowed. "How did you learn of this?"

"Find out for yourself, you piece of trash!"

"Very well." He motioned to two of the security men. "Hold her."

Kicking and scratching like a wildcat, Madison fought the two men, but they were too powerful.

I stepped toward her to try to help, but Lucas *transformed* into the mannequin again, stopping me in my tracks. Bob and Crystal also moved to intervene but were immediately met with guns pointed at their faces, held by the four St. George policemen.

As Lucas moved close to Madison, his face returned to normal. Reaching out, he touched the side of her head. Her eyes instantly went into a stare.

He moved over to Crystal and Bob.

"Mr. and Mrs. Alvarez, I want to personally thank you for helping us capture these dangerous criminals. If not for your call to Officer Davis, they would still be at large."

When Officer Davis spoke, his staring, unblinking eyes betrayed his deep hypnotic state. "You did the right thing by calling me, Bob. I'll see to it you get the reward."

Bob remained silent.

"You don't really think we're buying this, do you?" Crystal asked.

Lucas smiled. "You will, Mrs. Alvarez. Believe me, you will."

In a blink, Lucas reached out and touched Crystal and Bob, much like he had Madison. When their eyes went into a stare, he turned and addressed the four policemen.

"Your work here is done. Return to your regular duties."

The St. George officers holstered their weapons and quietly filed out the front door. As soon as they were gone, Lucas returned his attention to Bob and Crystal.

"Do you have firearms in this house?"

They both nodded.

"When my men and I leave with the prisoners, you, Bob, will retrieve your weapon and shoot your wife. Once you realize what you've done, you will become so distraught you will kill yourself."

After making Bob repeat the order, Lucas turned to me. As he approached, his face transformed back into the mannequin!

I stepped back, tripped over the ottoman, and fell to the floor. Looming over me, Lucas laughed hysterically. I closed my eyes and prayed the scary apparition would go away.

"Mr. d'Clare?"

I slowly opened my eyes.

He had changed back into Lucas.

Unbelievable!

"Do not worry, Mr. d'Clare. I'm not going to kill you or your wife, at least not yet. You're both much too valuable to me."

He gestured to the security men, who ushered us out to the two unmarked vans. We were then separated. I was placed in the lead van with Lucas, and Madison in the other with the four security men.

A short time later, we were on the interstate, heading north toward Phoenix.

* * *

Once the vans had driven off, Bob relaxed. Crystal, however, remained motionless, staring off into the distance.

"Honey, are you alright?"

Crystal didn't answer.

"Believe me, this is going to hurt me a lot more than it will you."

He delivered a hard slap across Crystal's face.

"Are you back with me?"

She placed her hand on her cheek. "I'm with you, but why did you slap me?"

"Lucas hypnotized you."

Her eyebrows raised. "He did?"

Bob nodded.

"How come he didn't hypnotize you?"

"He tried to, but it didn't work. So I faked it."

"I wonder if it has something to do with the bullet fragment in your head."

"Who knows?"

Crystal looked around. "Where are the d'Clares?"

"Lucas took them and the book."

"To where?"

"I wish I knew."

"Oh Bob, what are we going to do?"

"I don't know. This ability Lucas has to hypnotize people is incredible. I would have never believed it if I hadn't seen it with my own eyes. I just wish I hadn't called Jim Davis."

Just then, Bob's phone rang. The caller identification displayed the name "Tim McCurdy."

Bob placed his phone on speaker mode. "Hi Tim."

"Bob, I've got some news. Portland resident Dan Morgan, age thirty-five, worked in the Aircraft Production Division at Boeing from 1965 to 1971. He was reported missing by his wife on Thanksgiving Day. According to the report, he was returning home from a conference in Charlestown, South Carolina, and disappeared after his plane landed in Portland.

"Also, I found out something interesting about the hijacking. In June of 2000, the FBI conducted a Spectro-analysis of the tie tack Cooper left on the aircraft, and found titanium residue, which is commonly used in aircraft production. Are you thinking Morgan was D. B. Cooper?"

"No, I don't think so."

"But Bob, it all fits."

"I know it does, but for now, let's just say I think he was collateral damage. What about Bud King?"

Tim shuffled some papers. "Ogden residents Bud King, age thirty-two, and his wife Emily, also thirty-two, were found dead in the restroom of a rest stop, off Highway 5, forty miles south of Woodland, Washington."

"How did they die?"

"As strange as it sounds, they both suffered fatal brain aneurysms."

Bob thought for a moment. "What about their daughter Maddie?"

"She remains missing. No one has ever come forward with information on her."

"Did you find out anything on Gwendolyn Phillips?"

"Yes, and you're not going to believe it." Tim shuffled more papers. "Gwendolyn Phillips, age forty, born and raised in Northern Illinois. Resides in the Phillips Tower, downtown Chicago. She was named Chief Executive Officer of Phillips Industries in 2001, making her the third-in-a-row to be appointed to the position, dating back to the turn of the twentieth century."

"What do you mean by third-in-a-row?"

"The current Gwendolyn Phillips inherited the company from her mother, who was also named Gwendolyn, who had inherited it from *her* mother, again named Gwendolyn."

"What's so hard to believe about that?"

"I found a photo of the grandmother in a vintage newspaper article, and several photos of the mother in a trade magazine. When I compared those pictures to a photo of the current Gwendolyn Phillips posted on the company's web site, I couldn't believe how much they looked alike. So much so, I scanned the photos into the bureau's new Facial Activity Recognition and Monitoring program. Guess what I found?"

"All three are the same woman?".

"Yes! But Bob, how could it be? The program is state-of-the-art and can distinguish between identical twins. What's going on?"

"Before I tell you, I'd like to get a few more facts straight. What about her company?"

"Up until 2008, Phillips Industries was one of the largest corporations in the world. Gwendolyn Phillips had a personal net worth in excess of ten-billion dollars before the bottom fell out."

"What happened?"

"The financial crisis. If not for a government bailout, she would have gone bankrupt. Phillips took another hit in the Flash Crash of 2010. To remain solvent, she sold the company's aircraft division to Boeing. She still maintains a corporate office in Chicago, and still runs the Phillips Research and Development Branch, but all-in-all, the company is a fraction of what it used to be."

"What about Lucas Carter? Did you find out anything on him?"

"He's been a constant companion of Miss Phillips for as long as anyone can remember. So what does all this have to do with the D. B. Cooper case?"

"Once I connect the dots, I promise I'll let you know."

Bob ended the call and pocketed his phone.

"What do you think?" Crystal asked.

"I don't know what to think. Regardless, without the last chapter of the Wordless Book, we're at a dead end."

"Oh, we've got the last chapter. I managed to scan it before those goons busted in on us."

Bob hugged her. "Baby, you're beautiful!"

"So what do we do?"

Bob thought for a moment. "Why don't you work on deciphering the symbols. I'll call some people I know. I've got a pretty good idea where Lucas is heading, but I don't know how he's going to pull it off."

"Sounds like a plan."

* * *

Sitting in the back seat of the van, handcuffed to the arm rest, I felt utterly helpless. To make matters worse, my Parkinson's symptoms had returned, making my right arm and leg quake with tremors. Before leaving home, I had placed a week's worth of medication in our SUV. Now, miles from where we'd left our vehicle on the Indian reservation, my dopamine-starved brain was sending sputtering signals to my muscles.

Unknown to me at the time, I would soon learn Lucas' plan to annihilate mankind, and how it (surprisingly) involved me being healthy. To assure its success, he would give me a different type of medication – the legendary carmot element!

PART THREE:
THE GREAT WORK

CHAPTER SIXTEEN: THE REACTIVATION

Two Days Later
Inside the Commander's Main Briefing Room, 446th Airlift Wing
Joint Airbase Lewis-McChord, Washington

The morning sun shining in through the windows struck an elaborate display case, illuminating a plethora of trophies and plaques, silently telling the history of the Air Force Reserve organization. On the left side of the case stood an American flag, and on the right, a banner with the acronym "446 AW" embroidered on it. A row of eight picture frames, containing official photographs of the President down to the wing commander, placed in "chain-of-command" order, adorned the wall between them. To my left, a floor-to-ceiling mural spanned the length of the room, depicting the unit's cargo aircraft lineage, ranging from the C-45 Expeditor to the C-17 Globemaster III. In the center of the painting, written above a faithful illustration of a C-130 Hercules, the proud title read, "The Rainier Wing – *In Omnia Paratus*," Latin for "In All Things Ready."

What am I doing here?

I remembered waking up in the 446th Logistics Readiness Squadron. I knew I'd been hypnotized, but I couldn't snap myself out of it; the powerful suggestions Lucas had planted in my mind were too strong. I felt lethargic, and my mental processes had slowed to a snail's pace, a sobering reminder that I hadn't taken any Parkinson's medications. Along with feeling sluggish, everything appeared cloudy and out of focus.

I must be dreaming of rejoining the Air Force Reserve.

After being issued a full ensemble of uniforms, I found myself in the base alterations shop, where they added nametapes and captain's bars to my uniform shirts, field jacket, and hat. The next thing I knew, I was in the 446th's headquarters building, entering the briefing room.

Now in my new Air Force uniform, I stood at the end of a long, dark-oak table, its polished woodgrain top worn at the edges. Ten modern office chairs surrounded the table. The largest, undoubtedly the commander's, sat at the opposite end facing me.

The sight of the briefing room evoked memories of my time in the service, when I had first met Madison. As for Madison, I was worried sick. I hadn't seen her since we were captured by Lucas and his henchmen at the Indian reservation.

Please God, don't let any harm come to her!

The door behind me opened and a middle-aged colonel walked in. In his right hand he carried a black briefcase with the Air Force symbol emblazoned on the side. A strap around his left shoulder held a small, expensive-looking portable ice cooler. He walked over and set the case and the cooler on the table next to me. I glanced over and noticed he was missing the tip of his left middle finger.

Lucas!

After popping open the cooler, he reached in and pulled out a large hypodermic needle, its plunger pulled back and the barrel full of violet-colored liquid. Turning to me, his face contorted. When his features sharpened, he had transformed into the mannequin!

It's only a trick. An apparition just to scare me.

My attempt to self-rationalize failed dismally, and as he drew closer my heart began to race. I tried to back away, but he moved too fast. In one swift motion, he stabbed the needle into my arm and injected the fluid. After fully compressing the plunger, he tossed the hypodermic back in the cooler and closed the lid. Turning back to me, his face contorted again and he appeared as Lucas.

Feeling dizzy, I staggered backward and fell to the floor. I closed my eyes, but instead of helping, the dizziness grew more severe. My stomach rolled and I became nauseous. As my mouth began to over-salivate, the dizziness abated. At the same time, I *felt* the carmot – rumbling up my arm like a diesel locomotive!

In seconds, the element penetrated the blood-brain barrier in my neck, and the dying Parkinson's-affected cells began to reenergize and multiply. Damaged neuro networks, which had been sending sputtering signals from my brain to my muscles, started bridging the sensory gaps, restoring the movement and strength I'd lost from living over a decade with the disease. The pain in my broken arm and ribs also abated, withering to a dull ache before disappearing all together.

Touching my mind, the element flooded my consciousness with visions from my past. I unexpectedly remembered conversations I'd had with friends long forgotten and could recall the words in every book I'd ever read. Feelings of being useless also evaporated, invigorating me with a renewed love of life. Overwhelmed, my eyes filled with tears.

An instant later, I could see and hear the world around me with crystal clarity. As my senses improved, so did my intuition, supercharging my ability to detect non-verbal signals. These expanded cognitive abilities shattered Lucas' hypnotic spell, and I no longer feared him or the mannequin.

Lucas set the cooler on the floor, opened his briefcase, and pulled out a 9mm handgun. Motioning me to get up, I slowly returned to my feet.

"I know what you are thinking and feeling, Mr. d'Clare. It happens to everyone who partakes of the carmot. But your newfound strength and courage will not last long. I only gave you a derivative. You'll be back under my control soon enough."

"So why give it to me at all?"

"Because part of my plan calls for you to be physically fit, at least for a short time, until I recover the remaining carmot in Antarctica."

"I thought Gwendolyn's scientists would have synthesized it by now."

His eyes grew wide. "How do you know this?"

"Madison's uncle had his suspicions."

"I see. Aquinas always was a smart, albeit foolish man. To answer your question, we've come close, but have not yet been able to replicate it. By the way, thank you for recovering the Wordless Book. It's a shame it is now worthless."

"Worthless?"

Lucas nodded. "Aquinas' pitiful recordings told me everything I needed to know. The final source of carmot is at the Rae Ice Shelf."

"Where is Madison?"

He smiled. "She is safe. Miss Phillips is looking after her."

"I want to see her."

"You will, *after* we recover the carmot."

From the way he quickly looked away and avoided eye contact told me he was lying.

"Rest assured, Mr. d'Clare," he continued, "I wouldn't think of harming a hair on your wife's head. Like you, she is too important to my plan."

"So what, exactly, is your plan?"

Lucas checked his watch. "Very well. I don't mind talking. We have time before the briefing." He sat down in a chair at the end of the table. Motioning me with his gun, I took the seat next to him.

"Let me preface, Mr. d'Clare, by saying Aquinas was quite clever in concealing his whereabouts. It took me quite some time to find him."

"So how did you find him?"

"We have an operative at the CDC. When he informed us a man had died in southern Utah of bubonic plague and Belladonna poisoning, and that he had a niece named Madison, I knew it was Aquinas. To be one-hundred-percent sure, I ordered an investigation, which revealed your wife's history began shortly after Maddie King disappeared."

"When you murdered her parents," I added sarcastically.

Unfazed by my remark, he simply nodded. "Their deaths were unfortunate. In any event, I also learned you and your wife, at one time, were members of the Air Force Reserve. After reviewing your records, I realized how valuable you both could be to my plan."

"In what way?"

"You and the Air Force Reserve are going to help me recover the carmot."

"Why do you need the Reserve's help? Doesn't Gwendolyn have a fleet of airplanes and an army of personnel at her disposal?"

He frowned. "Unfortunately, not anymore. Bad investments have had a detrimental effect on her business."

"I still don't see how I can help you. I've never been to Antarctica."

"True. But General Richard Joseph has."

The name evoked fond memories of my former commander who recommended me for a commission. "What does he have to do with this? He's retired."

"From the Reserve, yes. But Joseph is still associated with the military in a civil servant capacity. He's the current supervisor of the Pegasus Airfield at McMurdo Station."

"I don't understand. Why don't you just use your power of suggestion on him?"

"Because several years ago he nearly lost his life in an automobile accident. He suffered a severe concussion. Although my power of suggestion is strong, I have trouble with people who have suffered brain injuries. You are my insurance policy."

"How so?"

"After reading his glittering reviews of your performance, Joseph will trust you."

"So where does Madison fit in?"

"Think about her career, Mr. d'Clare."

"She became a First Sergeant, then later the Command Chief…"

"*Not* her reserve career."

Remembering what Madison used to do at her civilian job, developing random sets of numbers for the Intercontinental Ballistic Missile launch codes, sent a cold chill down my spine.

He laughed. "Once I recover the carmot, I will unleash a plague and decimate mankind. And this time, there will be no Aquinas standing in my way."

The door behind us opened and a lieutenant carrying a small cardboard box entered the room. Lucas immediately lowered his gun and transformed his face back into the middle-aged man.

"The wing commander is on his way," the lieutenant said. "Are you ready, Colonel?"

Lucas stood. "We're ready."

When the lieutenant returned to the door, Lucas quickly placed his gun back in the briefcase and closed the lid.

"Stand up, Captain d'Clare," he whispered.

I remained sitting.

"Let me remind you, we have your wife. Any attempt to disrupt my plans will result in her immediate execution. Now stand up."

Begrudgingly, I rose to my feet.

"Room, ten-hut!" the lieutenant yelled.

A brigadier general, whose uniform nametape read "Nelson," entered the room, walked around the table, and stood in front of the commander's chair. Four colonels, two women and two men, followed him in. The lieutenant, still carrying the box, followed the officers to the table.

"Take your seats," General Nelson said. "I know it's a busy drill weekend, so thank you all for being here on such short notice. This meeting is hereby deemed top-secret. Lieutenant Smith will collect your cellphones."

The lieutenant hurried around the table, placed all the phones in the box, and quickly exited the room.

"For those of you who don't know them," the general continued, "this is Colonel Carter and Captain d'Clare from the IG (Inspector General) office." Starting with the two female officers to his right, he introduced his staff. "These are my group commanders, Colonel Perkins, ops, Colonel Hunter, maintenance, Colonel Bird, mission support, and Colonel Reynolds, meds. Colonel Carter, give them the run down."

There was something strange about the way General Nelson's eyes stared when he paused between the introductions, then it dawned on me.

He's been hypnotized!

Like a seasoned military man with superlative briefing skills, Lucas stood and confidently addressed the officers.

"The Captain and I were slated to conduct a surprise inspection of your Maintenance Group today, but one hour ago I received a call from General Knudson at Headquarters cancelling it. A situation has developed at the south pole. We've lost contact with the Amundsen-Scott Research Station. Our satellites picked up a flash, which may or may not have been an explosion. If it was an explosion, we could have mass casualties. General Knudson wants your wing to support an out-of-cycle *Operation Deep Freeze* to investigate. Captain d'Clare and I will accompany as observers. Your performance will determine your inspection rating."

"Begging the colonel's pardon," Colonel Hunter said, "but aren't there other units closer?"

Lucas shook his head. "Under normal circumstances, this tasking would be assigned to an active-duty C-5 or C-17 unit. Although the C-5 can land at McMurdo, it's too big to land at the research station; the adjacent land we use as a runway is too short. As for the C-17, on Friday, Boeing's engineers found a problem with the flight control computer. A critical, urgent-action tech order will be sent out tomorrow, grounding the fleet, leaving the remainder of the Air Force's inventory of cargo planes to carry the load. With most of them tied up with *Operation Inherent Resolve*, the 446th has the only C-130 available, tail number 272."

"272 is scheduled for a structural inspection," Colonel Hunter said. "We towed her to the phase dock an hour ago."

Lucas ignored her. "General Knudson wants 272 because it has made the Deep Freeze run before, and can easily be configured with skids, an auxiliary fuel tank, and JATO (Jet-Assisted Take-Off) rockets. It's also one of the few C-130s with in-flight refuel capability."

Wow! Lucas did his homework and he knows the lingo.

"But the crew chief has already stripped the cargo bay to bare bones," Hunter countered.

Lucas replied condescendingly. "I suggest you tell him to put it back together."

From the way Colonel Hunter's jaw stiffened, I could tell she couldn't stand him.

"I haven't seen any requests come down for refuel support," Colonel Perkins said.

"General Knudson is coordinating refuelers with the 151st Air Refueling Wing out of Salt Lake. They are flying training missions out of Hickam this month."

"What about flight crews? We normally take three."

"Two should be sufficient. They can spell each other every twelve hours."

"I'm assuming you'll need Meds support?" Colonel Reynolds asked.

Lucas shook his head. "We already have a critical care air transport team from the 15th Medical Group standing by at Hickam. We'll pick them up on the way." Addressing Colonel Bird, Lucas asked, "Do you have B-bags?"

I remembered B-bags contained cold weather clothes and winter survival gear.

"Sure," Bird replied. "I'll need a list of who is going, and their uniform and shoe sizes."

"Is the colonel aware winter has begun in Antarctica?" Colonel Hunter asked disdainfully. "We're talking perpetual night and hurricane-force winds."

"Are you aware we can land on instruments?" Lucas asked, matching her tone.

"At McMurdo, but how are you going to land at the research station? The approach vector is so small, it's hazardous to land there even in the summer."

"By airdropping these."

Lucas reached into his briefcase and withdrew a round metal object, not much bigger than a softball, with "TM-21" stenciled on it. "It's a terrain mapper, the latest innovation from Phillips Industries. All we need to do is drop several of these within proximity of the station, and they will scan a digital map of the area. Once uplinked to a navigation controller onboard the aircraft, we'll have the coordinates to land."

"Even on instruments," Hunter countered, "if 272 gets caught in an ice storm, you could lose one C-130 and a lot of reservists."

"Weather shows a lull in the storms for the next seventy-two hours. Now if you'd like to take this up with General Knudson, I can get him on the phone."

"No, that's not…"

"It may interest you to know, the general selected the 446th because your pilots have the most experience flying in and out of Antarctica, and you have an aircraft that can do the job."

After another uncomfortable pause, Hunter replied, "Okay, fair enough. How soon do you want to leave?"

"As soon as your maintainers can get it ready. Hopefully before noon."

Hunter bristled. "Before noon? That's impossible!"

Out of the corner of my eye, I saw Lucas make a small gesture toward General Nelson with his left hand.

"That's enough, Colonel," Nelson said.

"But sir…"

"I said that's enough! When we lost the airlift competition last month, you said it wasn't a true test of our capabilities, and you wished command would give us a real challenge. Well here it is! It's time we show everyone what the Rainier Wing can do. Get 272 ready to fly as soon as possible. That's an order! Put every maintainer on it if you have to. If you are unable or unwilling to do the job, I'll fire you and get someone who can. Do I make myself clear?"

Colonel Hunter slunk down in her seat. "Perfectly clear, sir."

"Very well. Captain d'Clare, could you come up here a moment?"

Unexpectedly the center of attention, I rose to my feet. As I approached, General Nelson stood.

"Colonel Carter tells me this is your first assignment since you came out of retirement."

"Yes, sir," I replied, nervously.

He smiled. "Let me be one of the first to say, welcome back to the United States Air Force."

As I shook his outstretched hand, I looked across the table at Lucas, grinning ear-to-ear.

Quick and to the point, the briefing was over. In less than ten minutes, Lucas had done what I once thought impossible: hypnotize an Air Force general into giving him a cargo aircraft, along with two crews to fly it.

* * *

Ten hours later, I was sitting in the dark, drafty cargo bay of Aircraft 272, trying to think of a way to stop Lucas. In front of me, taking up roughly a third of the compartment, sat the gigantic auxiliary fuel tank; its curved pipes extending outward like the tentacles of an octopus.

To my left were two empty seats and a large roll-away toolbox used by the crew chief. To my right, the backup aircrew, five in number, lay sleeping on make-shift hammocks fashioned from cargo netting. Behind them, a tube-shaped privacy curtain hung open from the ceiling revealing a portable toilet. Aft of the curtain, the main cargo door spanned the width of the compartment, its upward slant matching the contour of the aircraft. Two huge, piston-powered hydraulic actuators, one on each side, held the door closed.

The only sounds were the loud, monotonous, throbbing of the engines and the fuel sloshing in the auxiliary tank.

During the flight, Lucas had met with each crew member and hypnotized them. Once he had finished, he sat down next to me and touched the temple area of my head.

I pretended to fall asleep.

"Captain d'Clare?"

I didn't reply.

"Captain d'Clare!" he said again, more forcefully.

I slowly raised my head and found myself face-to-face with the mannequin! This time, however, it didn't scare me. Wanting him to *think* I was still afraid, I purposely bulged my eyes and shivered.

When his face changed back to normal, he waved his hands in front of my face several times. Unflinching, I kept staring.

"That's better, but just to be sure…"

In a flash, he retrieved a knife from his belt and stabbed me in the stomach.

Don't react! Don't react!

Miraculously, I remained stone-faced and unmoving.

He smiled. "Good. Now that you are back under my control, I can proceed with my plan."

I waited for him to turn away before looking down. The wound, glowing purple, had already started to close.

The carmot truly is magic!

Just then, the pilot's voice boomed over the cargo bay's speakers. "We're on final approach. Everybody buckle in."

* * *

When we landed at Hickam Air Force Base, Hawaii, six men boarded the plane. Four wore blue Phillips Security uniforms and were armed with AK-47 assault rifles.

The fifth man, who Lucas referred to as 'Mr. Ash,' was almost as big as him, tall and muscular. Armed with a 9mm pistol, he wore the same style uniform as the first four, but white in color, and had several wrenches and a flashlight clipped to the front of his belt. What made him stand out was his incessant giggle, as if he found humor in everything.

The sixth man, armed with a revolver, was much older than the others – in his late seventies, I estimated. He wore an antiquated flight suit, complete with a faded, out-of-date Air Force pilot's jacket with the name "Hull" on the nametape. I remembered the name from Aquinas' recitation, and concluded he must be Derrick Hull, Gwendolyn's personal pilot.

After refueling, and loading four large chest freezers, a hi-powered electrical generator, and a pallet of meals, we were back in the air. Using the power of suggestion, Lucas' plan to steal an Air Force plane to recover the carmot had (so far) gone off without a hitch.

From Lucas' non-verbal signals, I knew he had no intention of letting me see Madison, and as soon as he was done using me to get what he wanted from General Joseph, I would be expendable. More importantly, if he succeeded in recovering the carmot, and he uses it to change rocks into gold, there would be no stopping him from using the toxic residue to release a deadly disease upon the world.

Although my situation appeared hopeless, I did have a few advantages, the first being my health. The carmot had cured me of Parkinson's disease and healed my broken arm and ribs. Even if only temporary, I hadn't felt this good in years. In addition, Lucas had underestimated the power of the diluted element he had injected into me, and in doing so, had failed in his attempt to hypnotize me again.

Another advantage I had was my experience on the aircraft. During my civilian career, I had been temporarily assigned to work on the C-130s as a fuel mechanic. My tenure was so short, the base's personnel office had neglected to include it in my official employee record.

Lucas didn't know that!

With the carmot enabling me to remember everything I had ever read, I thought back to my fuel training. My eyes followed the largest pipe from the auxiliary tank, across the ceiling of the cargo bay, down the wall on the other side, and to a valve just aft of the privacy curtain. Stenciled on the wall next to the valve were the letters "MFSV," which stood for "Main Fuel Shutoff Valve." Used by maintenance personnel to check the distribution system of the tanks, the MFSV, when closed, cuts off the fuel supply to the engines.

Sitting in the cargo bay of 272, pretending to be hypnotized, I silently worked on my plan to bring down the aircraft.

CHAPTER SEVENTEEN: THE CRASH

Twenty Hours Later
Approaching Pegasus Airfield
McMurdo Station, Antarctica

From out of the darkness, an array of lights appeared on the horizon. As we drew closer, the lights grew brighter revealing a cluster of buildings. Long, arc-shaped snow drifts lay against the north sides of the structures, giving them an igloo-like appearance. On their roofs, protruding pipes released steam and smoke immediately turning them ninety-degrees before dissipating into the wind. Clenched in the jaws of the polar winter, this desolate place seemed a fitting setting for me to continue Aquinas' Great Work.

Sleep had evaded me throughout the seven-thousand-mile flight from Hawaii, but I wasn't tired; another benefit, I concluded, from the carmot. Instead, my mind had been combing through the schematic diagrams I had read many years earlier about the C-130 fuel system.

I knew the course of action I had been contemplating would result in the death of me and the other Air Force members, but I couldn't think of any other alternative. I wasn't trained in hand-to-hand combat. Even if I managed to fight my way through his heavily armed men, Lucas possessed superlative hand-to-hand combat skills.

In addition, the invisible shield protecting his body, as Aquinas described, made him virtually invulnerable.

Since I stood no chance of defeating Lucas physically, I resolved to defeat his plan, but it all depended on me staying alive until *after* he retrieved the carmot at the Rae Ice Shelf. Then when I disable the aircraft's fuel valve, the element will hopefully be incinerated in the crash.

I found it ironic: for most of my early adult life, I had performed maintenance on Air Force planes to keep them flying. Now, I wanted nothing more than to sabotage one.

Although I would never see Madison again, it gave me peace knowing if I succeeded, everyone would be safe from another deadly pandemic. As for dying, I had already resigned myself to a slow, debilitating death from complications related to Parkinson's disease. Now, knowing I would go out fighting, I felt exhilarated.

Despite a stiff crosswind, we touched down at the Pegasus Airfield without incident. Lucas ordered me, Ash, and the Air Force flight crews to follow him, and told the pilot Hull and the four Phillips Security men to remain onboard.

Even though I had donned my cold weather gear, including thermal underwear, mukluks, parka, and gloves, nothing could have prepared me for the freezing temperature rushing in when the big cargo door opened. As if swatted by a cactus, every inch of my exposed skin felt pin pricks of sub-zero air.

Outside the aircraft, we were greeted by two men. One of them, dressed in uniform, stepped forward and saluted. As he spoke, the steam from his breath puffed from his full-face ski mask.

"Welcome to McMurdo Station. I'm Major Dave Miller, the Air Force Liaison, and this is Robert Graham, Services Division."

Lucas returned his salute. "I'm Colonel Carter. I've got two tired aircrews needing a place to bed down."

Miller turned to Graham. "Take them to the lodging office and get them some rooms."

As the aircrews walked away, Lucas motioned for me and the giggling Ash to stay with him. Knowing the Air Force members had disembarked the aircraft, and that they wouldn't be onboard the last leg of the journey, somewhat eased the burden of my decision to sabotage the fuel valve.

"Has the refuel truck been called?" Lucas asked.

"You'll have to get authorization from the airfield supervisor first, sir," Miller replied. "Follow me."

He led us to a three-story building just off the flight line, whose ice-encrusted sign above the door read "Transit Alert." Once inside, we climbed a flight of stairs to the second floor and proceeded down a hallway, passed several cubicles, and into General Joseph's office.

The minimally decorated room was much like the one he'd had at the reserve unit. Two photographs adorned the desk, one of him and his wife Tracy, and the other a group photo of a multitude of their children and grandchildren. An award plaque shaped like the state of South Carolina, centered on the wall behind the desk, constituted the office's sole wall decoration.

"Mr. Joseph will be with you in just a moment, sir," Miller said. "If there's anything you need, my cube is the first on the right as we came in."

When Miller stepped out, Lucas leaned over and whispered in my ear. "You are good at following orders, Mr. d'Clare. When Mr. Joseph gets here, you will act like his long-lost friend. If you do as you are told, your wife will remain alive." He motioned to Ash, and the laughing henchman took a position next to the door.

A few minutes later, Richard Joseph came in, talking on a cell phone. He looked mostly the same as I remembered him, thin and in good shape, with only a few minor differences: his hair had gone completely gray, and his black, horn-rimmed glasses had been replaced by modern-looking wire-framed spectacles. Ending his phone call, his eyes traveled by Lucas before locking onto me.

He smiled. "George d'Clare?"

"Yes, sir."

"Well, I'll be." He brushed away my outstretched hand and gave me a friendly hug. "It's been…how long has it been?"

"I think the last time was at Colonel Mac's funeral."

"That long? Time does fly, doesn't it? How have you been? How is Madison?"

I glanced over at the smiling Lucas, then back to him. "She's doing well."

"Feisty as ever, I'll bet."

"Yes, sir. How is your family doing?"

"The kids are doing well, popping out grandbabies like rabbits."

"What about Tracy?"

He frowned. "I lost Tracy two years ago to breast cancer."

"Oh, I'm sorry to hear that."

"No need to be sorry. We'll be together again someday."

"I admire your faith, sir."

He slapped me on the arm and smiled. "You can drop the formality, George. I'm not your commanding officer anymore. Around here they call me Joe, which is better than Richard or Dick. What about you? I remember you saying you'd been diagnosed with Parkinson's disease."

I answered carefully. "It's…in remission."

"Remission? I've never heard of Parkinson's going into remission. That's fantastic. So what made you decide to put on the uniform again?"

"Perhaps I can answer that," Lucas interrupted. "I'm Colonel Carter. I coaxed Captain d'Clare to come out of retirement and join my inspection team. May I say, it's a pleasure to meet you."

"Inspection team?" Joe asked.

Lucas nodded. "After reading your reports on how well Captain d'Clare performed during your Operational Readiness Inspection (ORI) I had to have him on my team."

"I can't fault you there. As my Project Officer for the ORI, there was no one better. Please."

He motioned for us to sit down.

"You're lucky your aircraft made it here in one piece," Joe said. "The weather front moving in from the north is turning into a big one. Possible Category 3 winds."

"We're aware of the storm," Lucas replied, "which is why we must depart as soon as possible to stay ahead of it."

Joe shook his head. "I'm sorry Colonel. I can't authorize any flights in these conditions."

"We have orders to proceed to the Amundsen-Scott Research Station. There may be mass casualties."

"Who's going to fly you? Major Miller informed me your aircrews checked into lodging."

"We have a third crew, rested and ready to go."

"I'm sorry, Colonel. For the time being, you're staying put."

While Joe was talking, Lucas reached into his pocket and retrieved a gold necklace, upon which hung a shiny diamond.

"There's another reason why it is imperative we get to the station. What do you make of this?"

Lucas began rocking the chain back and forth.

"Take a close look at the diamond," Lucas said, in a slow, soothing tone.

Joe examined it a moment. "What's to look at? A diamond's a diamond."

His power of suggestion isn't working! Joe can't be hypnotized!

Lucas nodded to Ash, who unzipped his coat and retrieved his gun from his belt. Laughing, he pointed it at my head.

Joe sprang to his feet. "Now just a damn minute."

"Take your seat, Mr. Joseph," Lucas said coldly, "unless you'd like to see our jovial Mr. Ash decorate your office with Captain d'Clare's brains."

Ash laughed louder.

Joe slowly sat back down. "What's this all about?"

"What it's about is you providing us with fuel, certain pieces of equipment, and authorizing our flight."

Joe looked at me. "George?"

Still pretending to be hypnotized, I remained silent.

"I'm afraid he cannot answer you," Lucas said. "I have complete control over him. Tell him, Captain d'Clare."

"His people have taken Madison," I said stoically. "If I don't follow his orders, they'll kill her."

Joe fixed his attention back to Lucas. "What is it you want?"

"Aside from refueling our aircraft, these items." Lucas pulled a piece of paper from his pocket and handed it to him.

Joe read it aloud. "One Sno-Cat rigged with a winch, rope and climbing equipment, short-range walkie-talkies, portable floodlights, and a box of signal flares." Joe looked up at him. "Anything else?"

"Yes. I want you to accompany us."

"What for?"

"Because you are now a liability, and I'm not one to leave a liability behind. Now order your maintenance crew to refuel our aircraft and load the equipment. I'd also like to speak with Major Miller again."

While Joe made the calls, Lucas addressed Ash. "Take Captain d'Clare back to the aircraft. His business here is over."

Ash giggled. "Yes, Mr. Carter."

As I rose to leave, Major Miller entered the room.

Lucas shook his hand. "Have a seat, Major. We have much to discuss."

* * *

Ninety minutes later we were back in the air, headed for the Rae Ice Shelf. To restrain Joe and me, Lucas' men ran the handcuffs through a cross section of a bulkhead in the cargo bay, and secured our wrists together – essentially pinning us in place. I hadn't seen Lucas since I was brought back to the aircraft, but I could hear him conferring with the pilot, Hull in the cockpit.

An hour went by, and as the aircraft lumbered on, Joe kept asking me questions. I refrained from answering, however, to keep up the appearance of still being hypnotized. When the last Phillips Security man finally fell asleep, I leaned over.

"I'm sorry, sir," I whispered, "I want them to think I'm still hypnotized."

"Who is he?" Joe whispered back, "and what does he want?"

"His name is Lucas. He's a murderer who is obsessed with recovering a substance called carmot from the Rae Ice Shelf. If he's successful, he'll use it to start a deadly pandemic."

"Why? Is he a mental case?"

"You're not going to believe what I'm about to tell you."

"Spit it out."

"Lucas was punished by Jesus Christ to remain living until the final day. By starting a pandemic and killing as many people as he can, he hopes to bring about the Day of Reckoning and end his existence."

Joe's eyes grew wide.

For the next half-hour, I relayed to Joe the how Madison's uncle had been involved in a seven-hundred year struggle to stop Lucas. When I had finished, Joe sat without saying a word.

"So what do we do?" he finally asked.

Something about the way he asked the question made me turn and look at him directly. Out of the corner of my eye, I caught sight of his left hand resting on his lap. The middle finger of his glove was bent awkwardly to the side.

Lucas!

"I don't know what to do," I replied.

"Don't you have any ideas?"

I shook my head.

"None at all?"

When I looked at him again, his face *transformed* into Lucas' face.

"You almost had me fooled into thinking you were still under my spell, Mr. d'Clare. I can see in your eyes what you are thinking, but do not judge me. You don't know what it's like to live day after day, century after century, with no end in sight. In any event, I'm glad you don't know what to do, because there is nothing you *can* do."

He retrieved a key from his pocket. After unlocking himself, he motioned me to raise my right arm and attached the cuff to my wrist.

"Nothing to say, Mr. d'Clare?"

"But I heard you talking to the pilot in the cockpit. How did you manage to sit here next to me and do that?"

He smiled. "You still haven't grasped the magnitude of my power of suggestion, have you? Perhaps this will enlighten you. Did you know your former commander met with a tragic end after authorizing our flight?"

I shook my head.

"Yes, I'm afraid Major Miller had a mental breakdown and shot Mr. Joseph in his office, before taking his own life."

Tears came to my eyes.

Laughing, Lucas turned, made his way forward, and climbed the stairs to the cockpit.

* * *

An hour and thirty-five minutes later, after circling the area and dropping a bevy of the sophisticated TM-21 terrain mappers, we landed a short distance from the Rae Ice Shelf. As soon as the aircraft slid to a stop, Lucas returned to the cargo bay.

Addressing Ash, he asked, "Did you inspect the climbing equipment?"

Ash laughed. "Yes, sir. It's all loaded in the Sno-Cat."

"Excellent! Issue three flares to each man."

"What about him?" He pointed to me and giggled. "Do you want me to ice him?"

Lucas walked over to me. "Did you hear that, Mr. d'Clare? Mr. Ash finally laughed at something funny. He wants me to give him the order to *ice* you. Considering the Antarctic environment, very funny, don't you think?"

I didn't answer.

"Don't harm him," Lucas said, addressing Ash again. "If his wife cannot be persuaded to give me the launch codes, we can use him as leverage. Mr. Hull is staying behind to keep the engines running, so I'll have him watch over Mr. d'Clare."

Lucas made his way to the stairs leading up to the cockpit. "Mr. Hull!" he yelled. "Could I see you back here for a minute? And bring your firearm."

A moment later, Hull came down the stairs, gun in hand.

"What is it, boss?"

"I'm leaving Mr. d'Clare here with you. Keep an eye on him."

Lucas handed him the key to the handcuffs.

"Will do."

"How long do we have before the weather turns bad?"

Hull checked his watch. "An hour-and-a-half. If we wait too long, we risk icing up."

"Very well. Be prepared to take off the minute we get back."

As the cargo bay opened, another brain-numbing blast of cold air filled the compartment. Lucas climbed into the passenger seat of the Sno-Cat next to Ash. A moment later, they disappeared into the wintery darkness.

Hull walked back to the cargo door controls, and after pushing a few buttons, the two huge hydraulic actuators pulled the door closed. When he walked by me, I stopped him.

"Could you unlock me? I have to use the toilet."

He raised his gun. "Don't try anything."

Cautiously, he reached over and released my cuffs. Staying a safe distance behind me, he followed me to the rear of the bay.

"Can I use the toilet without you watching?"

"Okay, but hurry up," Hull replied, irritated. "I've got to get back to monitoring the engines."

I pulled the privacy curtain closed and waited a moment, before opening it just a crack so I could see him. He walked back to the stairs leading to the cockpit. After climbing up just far enough to afford himself an elevated view of the cargo bay, he sat down.

Opening the back of the privacy curtain, I leaned out and examined the main fuel shutoff valve. Like I remembered, it had a flat metal lever on one side, somewhat resembling a steel ruler, and an electrical plug with a screw-on locking ring on the other. If I were to pull the lever down and close the valve, Hull would receive a warning signal and cycle the switch in the cockpit. If it failed to work, the standard procedure would be to send the crew chief to check the valve, and if needed, manually re-open it. For my plan to work, I needed to disconnect the wires and disable the valve so it *couldn't* be reopened, which would starve the engines and cause a flameout.

Back inside the curtain, I peeked out. Hull was still sitting on the stair overlooking the cargo bay. Opening the curtain, I noticed the half-empty box of signal flares sitting next to the pallet of Meals Ready to Eat (MREs) just aft of the auxiliary fuel tank and out of Hull's view.

If my plan to close the valve fails, I can start a fire!

"Can I have an MRE? I'm hungry."

"Go ahead," Hull replied, "and bring me one too."

Using the fuel tank as cover, I bent down and quickly stuffed my coat pocket full of flares. Slipping on my gloves, I grabbed two MREs and walked back to my seat.

Hull raised his gun. "Set the MREs down and cuff yourself to the bulkhead."

"How can I eat if both my hands are cuffed?"

He thought a moment. "Which hand do you use to eat with?"

"My left."

"Okay then, cuff your right hand."

I placed one end of the cuffs around a thin area of the bulkhead and the other end loose around the bottom of my right glove. Luckily, Hull was too preoccupied reading the labels of the MREs to notice.

"Which one do you want," he asked. "Meatloaf or lemon pepper chicken?"

I remembered several Airmen (including myself) getting sick after eating the meatloaf MREs. My intuition, however, told me Hull was going to give me the opposite of whichever one I chose.

"I'll take the meatloaf," I replied.

He tossed me the chicken, turned, and made his way to the cockpit.

* * *

Roughly an hour and fifteen minutes later, a horn blasted outside the aircraft.

Lucas and his men had returned.

Hull hurried down the stairs from the cockpit and made his way to the cargo door controls. When he lowered the door, the Sno-Cat backed in. An assortment of large ice chunks were now strapped to its bed and roof. Encased in each of the chunks, was the all-important carmot element. Strangely compelling, I couldn't tear my eyes away from the violet-glowing substance. So pure and natural, as if the ice held the *essence* of a great power not of this world. It also seemed truly frightening, as if the carmot wasn't meant to be found by mortal man.

Lucas climbed out of the vehicle. "Let's get these loaded ASAP!"

Two of his men went to work cutting off the cargo straps and pushing the chunks off, while the others began loading them into the freezers. The laughing Ash, brandishing a mountaineer's pick, broke up the larger chunks so they could fit.

Lucas walked over to Hull. "Did you have any trouble with Mr. d'Clare?"

He handed him the key to my handcuffs. "No, sir. He's been as quiet as a church mouse."

"Very well. Return to the cockpit and prepare for takeoff."

Hull hesitated and pointed to the chunks of ice containing the carmot. "How much does all of that weigh?"

Lucas shrugged. "A couple of thousand pounds, more or less. What does it matter?"

"Keeping the engines running used more fuel than I estimated. Our destination is at the extreme range limit of this aircraft. To conserve fuel, we'll need to lighten the load."

"Will it be enough if we leave the Sno-Cat here?"

"I can't be sure until we're in the air."

"When we take off," Lucas replied, "climb to five-thousand feet and do not pressurize the cabin."

As Hull disappeared up the stairs, Lucas walked back and assisted the men loading the carmot. Once the freezers were full, he motioned to Ash.

"We need to get rid of excess weight, so we're leaving the Sno-Cat."

"I'll take care of it," Ash replied.

While Ash drove the Sno-Cat out of the cargo bay, Lucas walked over to me.

"I saw you staring at the carmot, Mr. d'Clare. Beautiful, don't you think? I now have more than enough to complete my plan, and there's nothing you or anyone else can do to stop me."

"Aren't you forgetting something? By now, the Air Force Reserve will know there is no Colonel Carter and that there is no emergency at the research station."

"Perhaps."

"But how are you going to explain it when we land back at McMurdo?"

He smiled. "Who said anything about landing back at McMurdo?"

"So where are we going?"

"Oh, did I forget to mention it? How absent-minded of me. Our new destination is Easter Island."

"Why there?"

"Because the last ship in the Phillips Industries fleet is there, waiting for us. By the time the Air Force Reserve locates this aircraft, we shall be long gone."

Ten minutes later, laden with the most-precious cargo in the world, Aircraft 272 lifted off from the Rae Ice Shelf.

* * *

While the aircraft was still climbing, Lucas came down from the cockpit and walked back to where his men were sitting. They immediately unbuckled their seat belts and stood at attention.

He smiled. "I wanted to personally thank each of you for our successful endeavor in Antarctica."

Except for Ash, he shook their hands one at a time and gave them a friendly embrace. There was something strange about his overly-friendliness which made me do a double-take.

He's whispering something to them.

If not for my element-enhanced senses, I would have missed his lip movements altogether. At the same time, Ash stood by, clicking his flashlight on and off, and laughing to himself.

After embracing the four men, Lucas walked over to the cargo door controls. A moment later, the huge door opened, filling the bay with another dose of icy air. Once the door was all the way down, he turned and nodded.

Like mindless zombies, the men removed their firearms, and calmly walked single file out of the back of the aircraft! Even though they were his henchmen, witnessing the murder of four men made my stomach roll over.

Lucas closed the cargo door, while Ash, still laughing, gathered the assault rifles.

Walking up to me, Lucas smiled. "What's the matter, Mr. d'Clare? You look like you are in shock."

"How can you take lives so indiscriminately?"

"They had served their purpose."

His callousness made me shiver more than the cold temperature.

Pull it together! If I don't stop him, millions of people will die.

Lucas turned and addressed Ash. "Bring the weapons to the cockpit and stow them in the crew's locker."

"What about him?" Ash pointed at me. "Can I ice him now, Mr. Carter?"

"I'll check with Mr. Hull. If we need to get rid of any more weight, I'll let you have some fun with him."

As they climbed up the stairs to the cockpit, I removed my gloves, placed them in my coat pocket, and began working my hand out of the handcuff. After few pulls and a painful scrape on my thumb knuckle, I was free.

Creeping over to the toolbox, I opened the lid and found several different sized open-end wrenches. Selecting the longest and heaviest one, I tucked it up under my left coat sleeve and closed the lid. After hurrying back to my seat, I sat down and took hold of the handcuff, carefully concealing my freed wrist.

A few minutes passed, before Ash came back down the stairs. Behind him, I could see Hull sitting in the captain's chair, while Lucas, in the co-pilot's seat, stared intently at the instrument panel.

As he approached, Ash moved back and forth, purposely blocking my view. Giggling, he drew his handgun and pistol-whipped me across the face. The teeth-rattling blow split my lower lip open, and almost made me lose my grip on the handcuff.

Ash laughed. "I bet you'd like to know what they are talking about, wouldn't you?"

I didn't answer.

"After we eat dinner, Mr. Carter said I get to have some fun with you."

When Ash turned and walked away, I slid the wrench out from under my coat sleeve. Rising to my feet, I took a step toward him and swung the wrench as hard as I could into his head. He crumpled to the deck.

Retrieving his gun, I moved to the back of the auxiliary fuel tank and kicked the bottom pipe several times until the connector began to leak a steady stream. Hurrying to the fuel valve, I unscrewed the locking ring and popped off the electrical plug. Grabbing hold of the plug with both hands, I pulled with all my might, and the aged wires snapped like dried twigs. Tossing the plug away, I turned the switch off and began bending the lever, first away from the valve then back towards it. After a succession of bends, the steel weakened, and the lever broke off in my hand.

With the valve disabled, I made my way to the rear of the cargo bay. No sooner had I ducked down behind the far-aft freezer, the plane shook and the loud throbbing of the engines somewhat quieted. Coinciding with the shake, warning bells clamored from the cockpit, and I could hear Lucas and the pilot.

"What is it, Mr. Hull?"

"We're in trouble. Our left and right outboard engines just flamed out."

"What do you mean they flamed out?"

"They turned themselves off."

"Turn them back on."

"I can't! The master fuel valve won't reset."

The plane shook again, followed by more warning bells.

"Now we've lost our left inboard engine," Hull said, his voice cracking.

When the plane shook a third time, the silence of the engines drowned out the clamoring alarm bells.

"Where is the master fuel valve?" Lucas shouted.

Hull didn't reply.

"Get ahold of yourself, Mr. Hull! Where is the master fuel valve!"

"It's...it's in the cargo bay. Aft of the toilet."

"Mr. Ash!" Lucas yelled.

Silence answered him.

"I'm smelling fuel!" Hull screamed.

"Mr. d'Clare must have done something. How long do we have?"

"I...I don't know!"

"Think, Mr. Hull! How long do we have?"

"If I launch the JATO pods and keep the nose up, maybe two minutes."

"Launch the pods. I'll take care of Mr. d'Clare."

As the aircraft lurched up from the rockets, Lucas jumped down the cockpit stairs, gun in hand.

Remembering what Aquinas said about targeting his extremities, I took aim at his legs and squeezed the trigger – the gun clicked!

Lucas moved around the unconscious Ash and stepped out into the open.

He smiled. "You really didn't think I'd trust a muscle-bound imbecile like Ash with a loaded gun, did you Mr. d'Clare? Stand up."

I tossed the gun to the deck and rose to my feet, but remained behind the freezer so he couldn't see my hands. Reaching into my coat pocket, I slowly withdrew a flare.

"Repair the fuel valve at once, or I will kill you where you stand!"

I pointed to the electrical plug and the broken lever. "That might take some time."

His eyes grew large. "Do you really want to destroy yourself?"

"No, but it's better than you wiping out mankind with another global pandemic."

"Surely you must know I will live through the crash."

I smiled. "Without the carmot, you'll be powerless."

"You'll see how powerless I am when I put a bullet in your head."

I struck the flare.

The flash made Lucas flinch, and when he fired his gun, the bullet whizzed by my right ear. I threw the flare toward the auxiliary fuel tank. It landed in the puddle of fuel below the dripping connector, instantly igniting the tank.

From the cockpit, Hull shrieked, "We're going in!"

Then the aircraft hit something.

The impact was so violent, it drove the freezer into me, which knocked me back on top of the cargo door. For a moment, the plane righted itself, giving me a few precious seconds to wrap my arms around one of the big hydraulic door actuators.

I glanced back to see what had happened to Lucas, and a second impact cracked the airframe open like an eggshell. At the same time, the piercing shriek of tearing metal filled the air. A split-second later, the entire tail section tore away from the main fuselage, sending me spinning off into the freezing black oblivion.

Like a thousand roman candles going off at once, a massive explosion lit up the darkness – undoubtedly from what was left of the aircraft impacting the icy terrain.

I braced myself, closed my eyes, and prayed for a painless death. The collision came, but not as I had envisioned it. Instead of my body splattering on impact, the tail section landed on a downward-slanting ice formation! Keeping my arms locked around the big actuator, I rode the wreckage down like a toboggan, until the ice finally leveled off and the tail section slid to a stop.

Trembling, I laid there for a few minutes, not believing I was still alive. With my hands becoming numb from the freezing cold, I retrieved my gloves from my pocket. Slipping them on, I slowly crawled out of the wreckage.

When I stepped onto the frozen surface, something cracked. Not a faint, knee-bending pop, but a loud sound of ice breaking all around me. Before I could react, the ice beneath me gave way! Freefalling, I bounced back and forth, each collision creating a new shock wave of pain in a different part of my body. Seconds later, I crashed through a thin layer of ice, and another and another. When I finally landed on a solid surface, my head hit the ice.

Feeling tired, I laid my head down and fell asleep.

~ The Wanderer ~

Lucas nervously paced in front of the fiery remains of Aircraft 272. Once the flames died down, he retrieved the flashlight from Ash's dead body and began searching around the smoldering wreckage. After following the skid marks made by the tail section, and finding the hole in the ice, he returned to the main crash site and searched the fuselage.

The four chest freezers had been completely destroyed on impact, their precious loads of carmot now melted. Moving further into the debris, he retrieved a metal box resembling a suitcase.

Opening the box, he pushed the power button and a computer screen came to life. After establishing a link with the "Conquest," a Phillips Industries orbital satellite, Gwendolyn's face appeared on the screen.

"Where are you?" she asked. "I've been trying to reach you."

"We've had a setback. Mr. d'Clare decided to be a hero and crash the plane."

"What? You've crashed? Where?"

"Somewhere on the Transantarctic Mountain Range."

"How?"

"Apparently, sometime during his tenure working for the Air Force he gained knowledge of the C-130."

"What about the carmot?"

"All is lost."

"No!" Gwendolyn screamed.

"I'm sorry, my pet."

After taking a moment to compose herself, she took a deep breath. "What about d'Clare?"

"Mr. d'Clare is now a permanent resident of Antarctica."

"What about Derrick?"

"Mr. Hull, Mr. Ash, and the rest of the men are dead."

Gwendolyn sighed. "So what do you want me to do?"

"There's nothing you can do. I'll return to the Rae Ice Shelf. We left a Sno-Cat there and I can use it for shelter. Then I'll make my way back to McMurdo Station and wait for the first flight out."

"You realize it could take months."

"Unfortunately, I agree," Lucas replied calmly.

"How can you be so composed?"

"Because this time I blame myself for the setback. I should have looked further into Mr. d'Clare's work history. Since we left enough carmot at the Rae Ice Shelf to complete our objective, we'll have to plan another operation to come back…"

"We won't have to," Gwendolyn interrupted.

"What do you mean?"

"That's why I was trying to contact you. Two hours ago, I received a call from our research lab. Professor Davenport and his team believe they have successfully synthesized the element."

Lucas' mouth dropped open.

"Although it is an agonizingly slow process," Gwendolyn continued, "I have ordered them to start full production immediately,"

"Excellent news! What about Mrs. d'Clare?"

"I'm having her moved to Site Few this afternoon. By the time you get here, we should have more than enough carmot to proceed with the plan."

Lucas smiled. "Don't hurry. After what her husband did, I shall take my time with Madison d'Clare."

His menacing tone sent an exciting shiver down Gwendolyn's spine.

* * *

I opened my eyes. The icy temperature and complete darkness made me think I had died. When I moved, my throbbing head and body aches told me otherwise.

Trying to ignore the pain, I struck a flare.

My heart sank.

Two towering walls of ice, one to my left and one to my right, traveled up as far as I could see. The walls came together behind me, while in front, the opening disappeared into shadows.

THE ELEMENT

It didn't seem fair. I had miraculously survived the crash, only to fall into a crevasse!

To make matters worse, while examining my surroundings, I unexpectedly felt my Parkinson's symptoms return.

The element had worn off!

When the weakened man thwarts
the Wanderer's plan,
he'll become trapped
in the ice-covered land.

But deep in the darkness,
he'll follow the course,
that leads to the knight
and the heavenly Source.

Crystal Alvarez's interpretation of the first group of symbols in the last chapter of the Wordless Book

CHAPTER EIGHTEEN: THE CREVASSE

On the Transantarctic Mountain Range
Antarctica

A ferocious stream of freezing wind blew into the chasm, causing a multitude of moaning sounds to echo off the lofty, icy walls. The complete absence of light, combined with the persistent noise and unyielding cold, made it seem as if I'd fallen into a ravine haunted by bodiless spirits.

I had remained in the same spot for hours (perhaps days?) until a stinging blast of cold wind struck my face. I tried to stand, but my legs gave out under me. I reached down and felt my feet – they were numb.

I suddenly had a stark realization: *If I stay here, I'm going to die.*

Gritting my teeth, I pushed myself up to a sitting position and instantly became dizzy. With my head pounding and ears ringing, I waited a moment for the unsteadiness to pass. Striking a flare, I checked myself for injuries. Although my body ached from the bumps and scrapes I'd received in the fall, nothing was broken.

Checking my supplies, I found four flares remaining in my coat pocket, and a freeze-dried chocolate brownie left over from the MRE.

Feeling weak from the Parkinson's, and too dizzy to stand, I began to crawl. When the flare finally burned out and the darkness returned, I used the wall as a guide. I had only moved a short distance, when the ice beneath me began to slant downward and soon steepened to the point I began to slide. Several anxious minutes later, the surface leveled and I came to a stop.

I struck another flare, and my mouth dropped open.

What is this?

I had slid into a gigantic underground cavern, stretching into the distance as far as I could see. Towering ice walls, with huge elaborate sculptures (biblical in nature) had been chiseled into them, rising more than a hundred feet off the ground. The tops of the walls were curved over, forming a domed ceiling. In the center of the cavern floor, water trickled along a half-frozen stream.

Crawling to the shore, I tasted the water.

It's not salty!

Cupping my hands together, I gulped the refreshing water until my stomach ached. With the flare burned out and everything black again, I followed the stream for more than an hour, until I passed over a rise and caught sight of a light in the distance.

Are my eyes playing tricks on me?

I blinked several times.

The light is still there!

Moving toward it, I soon closed the distance enough to tell the light had a violet color.

Carmot!

With my hopes skyrocketing, I crawled ever faster, until my burning shoulders felt like they were going to fall off. Drawing closer, the light was shining out of a tunnel in the base of the wall, ahead and to the left of me. A gigantic sculpture of the sun had been chiseled into the icy wall above the tunnel, its lower rays elongated and pointing toward the entrance. A few feet from the opening, I passed over a strange piece of ice protruding from the ground. With my mind focused on the carmot, however, I ignored it and kept crawling.

A short distance beyond the strange ice, the tunnel widened into a large, circular chamber. My mouth dropped open again. Thick ice, as smooth as a newly surfaced skating rink, lined the walls, floor, and ceiling. Embedded in the ice, a treasure trove of carmot glowed a pure shade of violet. A blinding white beam of light, with rays brighter than the sun, shined from the center of the chamber. The beam moved slowly around the chamber in a circular pattern like a lighthouse. The light emanated from a small round stone, roughly the size of a ping-pong ball, sitting atop a stalagmite of ice.

Moving toward the stone, I unexpectedly began to feel better. My thoughts cleared and the ringing in my ears and dizziness went away. The bumps and bruises from the fall dulled to minor aches before dissipating altogether. My ankles stopped hurting and feeling returned to my feet. The weakness and tremors from Parkinson's disease also abated. When I was within arm's reach of the stone, a newfound strength energized my muscles, and I rose to my feet.

Unbelievable!

I reached out and picked up the shining stone, and a feeling of warmth came over me. More than heat, it felt like a loving, nurturing force had wrapped its comforting arms around me. All my cares and worries felt meaningless, as if I were being silently assured everything was going to be alright. The feeling was so powerful, it brought tears to my eyes.

Using the stone as my guiding light, I made my way back through the tunnel to the large, sculpted cavern. When I reached the opening, the strange piece of ice I had crawled over drew my attention. Casting the beam of light on it, I could see it wasn't a piece of ice at all, but instead the forearm of a man frozen *in* the ice! His face appeared young, mid-to-late twenties by my estimation. His thick blonde hair hung down to his shoulders, and the tight antiquated snow suit he had on accentuated his broad, muscular physique.

Could it be?

With an unseen force guiding my actions, I set the stone on the ground next to the man, pointed the beam of light at him, and stepped back. Out of nowhere a mist appeared, thickening to the point I couldn't see my hands in front of me.

A few minutes passed.

When the mist dissipated, the ice surrounding the man had melted away. Looking closer, I noticed his chest rising and falling. The realization sent a bone numbing chill down my spine.

He's breathing!

I'd never believed in miracles before, but I couldn't deny what had just happened.

Aquinas' best friend Merrick had returned to life!

* * *

I moved the shining stone behind me, walked up, and knelt next to him. Roughly five minutes later, when he finally sat up, he looked even younger than he did when the ice had first melted around him.

I smiled. "Welcome back to the land of the living, Mr. Merrick."

"How long?" he asked, his voice just above a whisper.

"Have you been unconscious?"

He nodded.

"Seventy years, give or take."

Alarmed, his eyes grew wide and he looked around.

In a flash, he grabbed me by the collar, brandished a knife he had hidden under his coat, and placed it against my throat. His lightning-fast move took me completely by surprise.

"Very slowly," he said, with rage burning in his eyes, "remove your left glove, lest my blade opens your carotid artery."

I slid my glove off, and his eyes darted to my hand.

"Who are you?"

"My name is George d'Clare," I squeaked.

"How do you know my name, Mr. d'Clare?"

"Charlie, er, I mean Aquinas told me of you."

The fury in his eyes immediately vanished, and he lowered the knife. "Where is My Captain? I wish to speak to him."

I hesitated before answering. "I'm sorry. He died."

"No!" Tears welled up in his eyes.

"It happened a little more than a week ago. The carmot in his body finally wore off."

"Aquinas told you of the carmot?"

I nodded.

"And how did you come to know him?"

"It's a long story…"

Merrick held up his hand, stopping me in mid-sentence. Reaching up, he felt the side of his head and looked down at his chest. "I had been shot. Where did you find me?"

"Right here. You were frozen in the ice."

"If I was frozen, how were you able to wake me from the dead?"

"I didn't wake you. The stone did."

He looked around. "What stone?"

I moved aside.

Squinting, he slowly rose to his feet, walked over, and took a closer look.

"I found it in a cave full of carmot," I explained.

"*You* found this stone?"

I nodded.

He thought for a moment. "By any chance, do you have a malady that weakens you?"

"I have Parkinson's disease."

Merrick's eyes grew wide. "By everything holy, the prophecy was true." He dropped to one knee and bowed his head. "Forgive me, My Lord."

"Forgive you? For what?"

"For treating you harshly. I thought you to be Lucas in disguise. I will accept any punishment you see fit."

"No need for that. Please." I motioned for him to stand.

"As you wish, My Lord."

He rose to his feet, but kept his head bowed.

"Call me George."

"Very well, My Lord George."

"No, just George."

He raised his head. "But you are the weakened man the Wordless Book foretold. You are to be protected, revered, and treated with the utmost respect."

"Times have changed. You're not disrespecting me by calling me by my first name."

He smiled. "Very well, George. Please call me Merrick."

I offered my hand, and he shook it.

"It is an honor to meet you, Merrick."

"The honor is mine. To finally meet the weakened man who holds the key to defeating the Wanderer."

"You must be mistaken. I have no key."

"Oh, but you do. You have found the Sacred Stone."

"The what?"

378

"The Sacred Stone. Do you not know the tale?"

I shook my head.

"When the Almighty created the world, He touched the Earth with a spark of life. Legend tells the spark first struck a stone – a Sacred Stone emitting His divine, life-giving force."

No longer squinting, his eyes were now locked on the stone.

"Many clerics spent their entire lives searching for it," he continued. "When we were together, Aquinas studied ancient texts in hopes of pinpointing the stone's location but was never successful."

"I don't understand. I thought you two were trying to find the carmot to keep it out of Lucas' hands?"

"We were. You see, ice captures some of the magical properties of the light emanating from the stone. Observe." He pointed to the far wall of ice. The area where the light struck the wall now glowed violet. "The transformation has already begun."

"So the Sacred Stone is the *source* of the carmot?"

"Correct."

"But how does that explain carmot being found all over the world? From Aquinas' account, you traveled to Amsterdam, Paris, Niagara Falls, and here to Antarctica."

He smiled. "Legend further tells the Earth's continents were once islands, connected in the south polar region. At the center lay the Isle of Atlantis. An ancient race of people who lived there found the Sacred Stone. Recognizing its importance, they carved this massive cathedral out of the ice for which to worship it. The people lived in paradise for more than a thousand years, until, by Plato's account, one terrible day and night, when it all came to an end on *their* Day of Reckoning."

Fully engrossed in the story, I leaned in. "What happened?"

"The people had fallen into decadence, eventually going to war over control of the stone. The Almighty, disgusted with the pettiness of man, hurled a heavenly body at the Earth. The impact was so powerful, it knocked the Earth off its axis and separated the south polar land mass. The only people to survive the destruction lived on the outer-most peripheries."

I read about this in college.

"Which explains why the Earth's magnetic north isn't true north, and why the continents are still drifting apart today."

"Precisely. You are quite educated, George."

"Not really. I took a class in geology once. But enough about me, tell me what happened to the carmot."

He smiled. "Almost all of the carmot was lost in the cataclysm, the exceptions being the places mentioned in the Wordless Book. The stone was also thought to be destroyed, but as we can see..."

"Wow! That's the most incredible story I've ever heard."

"No, George. What's incredible is the Almighty thought me worthy enough to bring me back to life, and that He chose a weakened man to find the Sacred Stone of Atlantis."

* * *

Sitting on the frozen ground, huddled around the stone, Merrick and I talked for more than an hour. I told him how Aquinas had left recordings of their exploits, and how Madison and I became involved in their undertaking to stop the Wanderer. Throughout the telling, I observed the extent of his emotions.

When he learned Aquinas had been rescued by the Tanaka Expedition and taken to Japan, had married Sara, and subsequently lost his wife, tears flowed from his piercing blue eyes. When I told how Aquinas had hijacked a passenger jet and became the focus of the largest manhunt in American history, his laughter echoed off the ice cave's towering walls.

Conversely, the look of rage returned to Merrick's eyes when I explained how Lucas had murdered Bud and Starr King, but brightened again when I relayed how Aquinas had rescued Madison. I finished by telling him how I had stopped Lucas' latest plan by sabotaging the Air Force plane.

"After the crash, I fell into a crevasse," I concluded. "That's how I found you."

"To risk your life for your fellow man is the epitome of bravery, George. You should be honored."

"It is you and Aquinas who should be honored."

He shook his head. "We never achieved our goal of containing Lucas. But now, when you confront Lucas with the Sacred Stone, we shall imprison him once and for all."

He thinks I can defeat Lucas.

"But Merrick, if I confront Lucas with the stone, I won't know what to do."

He smiled. "Have faith. The Almighty will guide your actions."

I could see the conviction in his eyes. He truly believed what he was saying.

"Very well then, I think the first order of business is us getting out of here."

"And finding some food," he added.

I reached into my coat pocket and retrieved the MRE packet.

"What do you have there?"

"What's left of my MRE. A chocolate brownie."

"What is an MRE?"

"A military acronym for Meal Ready to Eat."

He smiled. "Surely you jest."

I shook my head. "It's not very much, but we can share."

I opened the pack, broke off half of the brownie, and offered it to him. "Go ahead."

He tasted it. "Magical!"

"If you need a drink to wash it down, there's water." I pointed to the stream.

After finishing off the brownie, and getting a few handfuls of the refreshing water, Merrick asked me more about Aquinas.

"George, was he comfortable when he died?"

How can I put this delicately?

"His body was decimated from the Black Plague, Belladonna poison, and about a half-dozen other major diseases."

Tears came to his eyes again. "And where did this happen?"

"In a hospital in southern Utah."

"After we contain the Wanderer, could you take me to where he is buried? I'd like to honor his memory and decorate his grave."

"I'm sorry, I completely forgot. Aquinas isn't buried, at least not yet."

"Oh? Where is he?"

"The CDC took his body to Atlanta."

"What is the CDC?"

"The United States' Center for Disease Control. When the doctor at the hospital couldn't figure out why Aquinas had all those diseases and poisons in his body, he called in the CDC."

"Why Atlanta?"

"The CDC's headquarters is in Atlanta."

"But if My Captain is dead, what do they hope to accomplish?"

"They want to conduct a thorough autopsy in hopes of averting an outbreak of a disease. I understand their headquarters is a state-of-the-art facility, where they can conduct the examination and study his body in a sterile, controlled laboratory."

He nodded. "Prudent."

"Madison tried to stop them with a court order."

"Why?"

"She doesn't believe in autopsies. Quite frankly, she didn't want her uncle's remains cut into pieces."

"Was your wife successful?"

"I don't know. We were abducted by Lucas before we could find out."

He thought for a moment. "Help me to understand something, George. Doesn't taking Aquinas' body across the country pose a risk for an outbreak?"

I shook my head. "I don't think so. The CDC takes every precaution. They froze his body before they took it."

Merrick's eyes grew wide. "What did you say?"

"They froze his body…" As the revelation dawned on me, my voice tapered off.

"So, if the Sacred Stone revived me…"

I finished his thought. "It might be able to revive Aquinas."

Merrick sprang to his feet. "We must leave here at once!"

"Shouldn't we gather some carmot?"

He shook his head. "The Sacred Stone will supply us with all the carmot we will ever need. Let us be off!"

* * *

In choosing which direction to go, Merrick and I ruled out the way I had entered the cave. Even if we were to make it back to the place where I had crashed through the ice layers, without ropes and pitons, the steep, slick walls of the crevasse would've made climbing impossible. With Merrick insisting I carry the Sacred Stone, we proceeded deeper into the immense cavern.

Despite having Parkinson's disease for the last eleven years, and Merrick having been frozen in the ice for so long, the magical stone had rejuvenated our bodies with an endless supply of energy. So much so, we were soon running!

Reaching the end of the gigantic chamber, we found three dark tunnels, with an elaborate sculpture of the moon carved in the wall above them. When I shined the light of the stone onto the tunnel to the right, the edges glowed, but when I shined it onto the other two, they remained dark.

"Apparently, we are to go right."

"Let us make haste, George. My Captain awaits."

Proceeding into the opening, the passageway began to slant upward. A short time later, we reached the surface and stepped out into the stormy, bitterly cold Antarctic night. Taking a moment to warm our hands in the light of the stone, the driving wind abruptly abated. An unnatural, eerie silence fell over the land, as if time had come to a standstill.

"What is happening?" I asked.

"I do not know, George, but it is best not to question the ways of the Almighty."

"So what do we do now? I mean, the stone will protect us from the cold, but how do we get out of here?"

When Merrick answered, his voice had a calm surety, making me feel safe. "Our first priority is food, so I suggest we make our way to the crashed airship and recover some of those meals you spoke of."

"Then?"

"Then we leave this continent, go to Atlanta, and awaken Aquinas."

"Okay, but how do we find the crash site?"

He thought for a moment. "Use the stone."

I held the stone out in front of me and panned the light around us. A glowing path illuminated in the ice.

Incredible!

"You are a man of faith, Merrick."

He smiled. "Indeed I am."

In the cold, endless night
three heroes arrive,
on a swift bird of prey
that descends from the sky.

To wake the great soldier
from his unending sleep,
they'll race to the north,
to the Land of the Creek.

**Crystal Alvarez's interpretation of the second group of symbols in
the last chapter of the Wordless Book**

CHAPTER NINETEEN: THE RESCUES

Two Hours Later
Approaching Aircraft 272 Crash Site
On the Transantarctic Mountain Range, Antarctica

A breathtaking kaleidoscope of aurora lights colored the night sky, painting the atmosphere in rich hues of green, yellow, and red. The pure-white beam of light emanating from the Sacred Stone outshined all of them, illuminating our path through the icy terrain like a laser beam. The combination of lights and the strange stillness made me feel like an astronaut traversing the surface of another world.

With the stone providing us an endless supply of energy, Merrick and I trudged across the slippery, uneven ground. The beam of light eventually guided us toward a dark blemish on the land. As we drew closer, the blemish became a debris field. At the far end lay what was left of Aircraft 272. Shining the light on the wreckage, the violence of the crash sent shivers down my spine.

The impact had completely pulverized the forward section of the airframe, the cockpit (including the pilot, Derrick Hull) pulverized into pieces no larger than a tennis racket. Like the tail section, the right wing had sheared off, leaving only twisted metal, broken pipes, and severed wire bundles. The left wing, blackened from the fire but still attached, jutted out from the main fuselage at a forty-five-degree angle. Inside the fire-ravaged cargo bay lay the charred remains of the four chest freezers and the burned body of Lucas' henchman Ash, his constant grin now skeletal.

I couldn't believe I had survived.

"It appears your plan succeeded," Merrick said.

I shined the light around and noticed sooty footprints leading away from the crash site. "Unfortunately, Lucas lived through it."

Merrick nodded. "As he always does. But do not fret, George. At the very least, you have disrupted his plan and bought us time to escape this continent, revive Aquinas, and plan a new strategy."

I admired his positive attitude.

"It may take some time for us to find our way to the nearest research station," he continued, "so I suggest we keep looking for the food."

We began scouring the outer fringes of the debris field, and soon came across the smashed crate containing the MREs. Luckily, four were still inside, unopened in their plastic brown wrappers.

Reading the labels, I asked Merrick, "Which do you prefer, beef stroganoff, chicken cordon bleu, pork tenderloin, or halibut?"

Before he could answer, the thunderclap of a sonic boom, followed by the unmistakable rumble of jet engines, disturbed the calm serenity. As the sound of the engines grew louder, blinking lights of an aircraft appeared in the multi-colored sky – heading directly toward us!

"What is it?" Merrick asked.

"We've got company."

"Who?"

"I don't know. It could be Lucas' people looking for him."

"We must hide. Conceal the Sacred Stone and follow me."

I tucked the stone in my coat pocket, and after gathering the MREs, Merrick and I ran back to the wreckage. Ducking underneath the outstretched left wing, we crouched down behind the smashed freezers.

No sooner had we concealed ourselves, the aircraft, the likes of which I'd never seen before, roared by. With its running lights outlining its shape, it looked like the combination of a SR-71 Blackbird spy plane and a CH-47 Chinook helicopter. Passing overhead, it circled back around and its propellers *tilted*, bringing the aircraft to an abrupt stop in mid-air. The propellers tilted again, stirring a cauldron of snow, and it slowly landed like a spaceship directly in front of us.

Oh great, just what we don't need: to be abducted by a UFO.

As the deafening roar of its engines died down, a door on the side of the strange aircraft opened. A big man jumped out, wearing a full ensemble of cold weather gear and holding a handgun. On his chest, he had the rank insignia of Colonel.

"George d'Clare!" he yelled.

I don't believe it! I recognize his voice!

In a flash, Merrick's knife was in his hand. "Stay behind me, George. I will protect you."

"No need. He's a friend."

"A friend?"

"He's the deputy sheriff who helped Madison and me."

When I made a move to step out, Merrick stopped me.

"Let us be sure," he whispered. "Shine the light of the stone on him."

I retrieved the stone and pointed the beam at Bob. His eyes went into a stare and he lowered his gun.

"Please remove your left glove!" Merrick yelled.

Bob showed us his hand. Once we saw his middle finger had all its segments, Merrick and I walked over to him.

"Are you alright, George?" Bob asked, still somewhat dazed.

"I'm okay," I said, shaking his hand. "Boy, are we glad to see you."

"Whew!" he exclaimed. "That's some flashlight."

I shined the beam away from us and showed him the light emanating from the stone.

Bob examined it for a moment. "How is it possible?"

"The Sacred Stone's powers have no bounds," Merrick said.

"Who are you?"

"Allow me to introduce you," I said. "Bob Alvarez, meet Merrick."

Bob's eyes widened.

"Pleased to meet you, constable," Merrick said.

Bob slowly shook Merrick's outstretched hand. "Call me Bob. But how…"

"Any news of Madison?" I asked.

He shook his head. "We've been too busy trying to get down here and find you."

"Tell me," Merrick interrupted, "is there room on your airship for both of us?"

Bob nodded.

"Time is of the essence. It is imperative we leave for the States immediately."

"Why?"

"We'll fill you in on the way," I said.

"Alright, get in. And watch your head."

I pocketed the Sacred Stone and we climbed aboard. Sleek and polished inside, the strange aircraft had only eight seats, two for the pilot and co-pilot, and six behind them in the cargo bay, three on each side, facing inward. Directly behind the six aft seats, four aluminum-framed stretchers hung from the ceiling by straps, stacked over each other in pairs like bunk beds. Surrounding the stretchers were a bevy of compartments, with labels denoting medical supplies. Pilot helmets, complete with full-face oxygen masks, also hung on hooks attached to the walls.

Bob secured the door and introduced Merrick and me to the two pilots, Colonel Oliver Cheng and Major Timothy McCurdy.

"Welcome aboard," Colonel Cheng said.

"Thank you, Colonel," I replied, shaking his hand.

"No need for formalities out here. Call me Ollie."

Major McCurdy offered his hand. "And I go by Tim."

Following suit, Merrick shook their hands. "I've never seen such an airship."

"That's because the military has never publicly acknowledged the DART's existence," Bob commented.

"The DART?" Merrick and I asked, in unison.

"Deep Arctic Rescue Transport, but on this mission, I guess you could call it an *Antarctic* transport."

"It's a modified V-22 Osprey," Ollie explained, "retrofitted for medical rescue. It's the latest Army-Air Force collaboration, a product of one of our dark programs at Groom Lake."

From my time in the military, I knew "dark program" was a term used for a classified military defense project, and "Groom Lake" referred to Area-51, the secret air base in Nevada.

Seeing the confused look on Merrick's face, I whispered, "He means top-secret."

Merrick nodded. "How fast can it go?"

"Top speed, Mach-five."

"But we've flown it faster," Tim added.

"And by Mach-five, you mean?"

"Five times the speed of sound."

Merrick's eyes grew wide. "How fast can it take us to North America?"

"Where in North America?" Ollie asked.

"Atlanta."

Ollie and Tim turned to face the instrument panel and began pressing buttons.

"Taking in account delays from inflight refueling, at top speed, four hours," Ollie said.

"It is imperative we leave immediately," Merrick said.

"Why Atlanta?" Bob asked.

"We need to stop the CDC from performing an autopsy on Aquinas' body."

"Why?"

Merrick turned to me. "Show them, George."

I retrieved the Sacred Stone from my pocket, which instantly lit up the interior of the aircraft in pure-white light. Aiming the beam aft, the five of us stared at the stone, completely captivated.

"It is a marvel, is it not?" Merrick said. "A stone touched by the hand of the Almighty."

"I found it in the crevasse," I explained. "Merrick was frozen in the ice, and it brought him back to life."

After a moment, Bob cleared his throat. "And you think it will bring your wife's uncle back to life?"

"Yes. Dr. Webster told Madison and me the CDC froze his body before they took it to their headquarters."

"If we have any hope of defeating Lucas," Merrick interjected, "we must proceed at all possible speed to save My Captain."

"What do you guys think?" Bob asked.

Without taking his eyes off the stone. Ollie replied, "We're under strict orders to investigate the crash site and return to Groom Lake."

"We'd be crazy to jeopardize our careers for one man…" Tim added, also spellbound.

In a flash, Merrick snatched the stone from my hand and pointed the beam directly at Ollie, then at Tim. Their eyes widened further and their mouths dropped open.

"Aquinas is not merely *one man*," Merrick said, speaking slowly. "Without him, mankind would not have survived the fourteenth century. Do you understand?"

Ollie and Tim nodded.

Merrick handed the stone back to me. "Now tell me, what time is it in Atlanta right now?"

Tim turned and checked the instrument panel. "Three-thirty in the morning."

"So if we leave now, we can be there just after dawn, can we not?"

"Yes," Ollie replied. "But how do we explain…"

"You won't need to explain anything," Bob interrupted, "Just get us to the CDC." Bob turned to Merrick and me. "I'm coming with you."

Merrick grinned. "Bob Alvarez, you are welcome to come help us save My Captain. Now, gentlemen, shall we get underway?"

"Alright," Ollie said, "everyone buckle in, put a helmet on, and snap up your oxygen masks."

Merrick's smile vanished and his eyebrows wrinkled. "What for? I've never worn a helmet. Not even in battle. They are too cumbersome."

"We'll be cruising at an altitude of eighty-five-thousand feet," Tim explained. "The air gets a little thin up there."

"It's okay," Bob reassured. "It's necessary on an aircraft like this. And look, it's got a headset and microphone so we can talk to each other."

While Bob helped Merrick, I retrieved a helmet hanging next to the stretcher. Soon after, we were streaking across the sky at supersonic speed.

"Tell me Bob," Merrick said, "in all this frozen wilderness, how did you find us?"

"Tim, would you care to explain?"

"Sure. The DART is equipped with the latest heat sensing technology. When we entered Antarctic airspace, we picked up your heat signatures. Your position corresponded with the signal we've been receiving from Aircraft 272's black box."

"Black box?" Merrick asked.

"The aircraft's flight data recorder," I explained. "In the event of a mishap, the black box emits a signal so rescue personnel can find it. Most aircraft are equipped with them these days."

"Ingenious!"

"The DART's specialized reconnaissance system also has long-range facial recognition capability," Tim continued, "linked via satellite to the FBI's computers at Quantico. That's how we knew one of you was George."

"I don't know if you remember," Bob said, "but just before Lucas kidnapped you and your wife, I contacted Tim to run check on Gwendolyn Phillips."

I thought Tim's name sounded familiar.

"But you said Tim worked for the FBI."

"I do," Tim said. "I'm also a weekend warrior."

"What do you mean by that?" Merrick asked.

"I'm an FBI agent during the week, but one weekend a month and two weeks out of the year I serve in the military."

"Merrick, do you remember when I told you I was in the Air Force Reserve for twenty-two years?" I asked.

He nodded.

"That's what I did. During the week I worked for the Air Force as an aircraft mechanic."

"Are all of you weekend warriors?" Merrick asked.

"Nineteen years next month," Ollie said. "On the civilian side, I'm an airline pilot."

"And you, Bob?"

"Fifteen years active duty in the Army," he replied, "and going on ten in the Army Reserve while serving as deputy sheriff."

Merrick smiled. "What a pleasure it is to meet men with not one, but two noble professions."

From everyone's upturned cheeks, I could tell they were smiling under their oxygen masks.

"Bob, did you tell them Aquinas' story?" I asked.

"Most of it. They understand the threat Lucas poses to the world."

"If I may ask," Merrick said, "you said you picked up our heat signatures when you entered Antarctic airspace. We must be thousands of kilometers inland. How did you get here so fast?"

"Do you want to explain, Ollie?"

"Sure. The DART is powered by eight engines, four J-62 turbojets and four V-25 Rolls Royce tilt rotors. The turbojets are the most powerful, fuel-efficient engines ever produced, and the tilt-rotors allow us to take off and land vertically."

"Bob," Tim said, "there's a call coming in. It's your wife."

"Can you patch her through to the intercom?"

"Sure. Just give me a sec."

A moment later, we heard Crystal's voice.

"Hello? Bob, are you there?"

"Hi honey."

"Bob! I've been worried sick."

"Don't be. We found George d'Clare. He's on the line with us now."

"Hi Crystal," I said.

"George, I'm so glad to hear you're alright."

"Thanks."

"I'm kind of in a hurry, so I've got to make this fast. Bob, yesterday after you left, I found Madison's cell phone between the cushions of the sofa. It kept ringing so I answered it. It was Susan Webster, the doctor from the CDC. She said Assistant Director Hargrove is proceeding with her uncle's autopsy tomorrow…"

"No!" Merrick yelled.

"Who's that?" Crystal asked.

Bob raised a finger, quieting Merrick. "Never mind. It is imperative we stop the autopsy. Our lives may depend on it."

"I'm one step ahead of you. I'm on my way to Atlanta now. Dr. Webster is picking me up at the airport."

Bob's eyebrows raised. "What? How?"

"I finished deciphering the last chapter of the Wordless Book."

"Magnificent!" Merrick said.

"Bob, who is that?"

"I'll tell you when we get there. But go on, you were saying you deciphered the last chapter?"

"Yes. I don't understand a lot of the parables, but one said, '*To wake the great soldier from his unending sleep, they'll race to the north, to the Land of the Creek.*' I searched the Internet, and found Atlanta used to be inhabited by the Creek Indian tribe. I figured it must be referring to Madison's uncle, so I booked a seat on the redeye. Oh, we're boarding now."

"Baby, you're amazing. By the time you get there, we'll probably still be an hour behind you."

"What? Where are you?"

"I'll tell you when we get there."

"Do you want us to wait at the airport?"

"No, we won't be landing at the airport."

"But Bob, even if Dr. Webster lets me in to the CDC building, how can I stop the autopsy?"

"I don't care what you have to do, just don't let them touch his body!"

* * *

During the rest of the flight north, Bob, Tim, and Ollie filled us in on the events after Madison and I were abducted.

"After Lucas kidnapped you and your wife," Bob began, "Tim called me back and confirmed some things Aquinas said about the skyjacking, facts never made public."

"Who'd have thought, after all these years, to find out D. B. Cooper was really a hero," Tim commented.

Merrick laughed. "If anything, My Captain is a master of improvisation. But please continue, Bob."

"Since Lucas now has the recordings and the Wordless Book, I figured it would be only a matter of time before he made his move to return to Antarctica. I thought he'd wait until spring when the weather clears. Two days later Tim called me. Tell them, Tim."

"Word came down about an accident at an Antarctic research station. Since Ollie and I were test flying the DART, we thought we'd be tasked for a rescue operation. After all, this aircraft was designed for just such a mission. Then our commander informed us the 446th Airlift Wing was heading the rescue, and that a C-130 out of McChord had been scrambled."

"Turns out there was no emergency," Ollie added, "and no one had ever heard of the mission commander, Colonel Carter. As you can imagine, an imposter stealing an Air Force plane upset a lot of brass in the Pentagon."

"Brass?" Merrick asked.

"High-ranking military officers." I explained,

"One of our satellites tracked 272's flight path to the crash site," Tim said, "and we were sent in."

"When Tim called and told me the stolen aircraft had been found," Bob added, "and he and Ollie were being sent to Antarctica to investigate, I called a few people I know. I managed to get a copy of 272's operational orders. When I saw George's name on the list of mission personnel, I asked Tim if I could come along."

"Simple as that?" I asked.

From his upturned cheeks, I could tell he was smiling under the oxygen mask. "I have a top-secret security clearance, and a few connections of my own at the Pentagon."

"Since the DART is a joint Army-Air Force project," Tim said, "our commander was, shall we say, *persuaded* to let Bob come with us."

"It does help to know the right people, does it not?" Merrick commented.

Bob chuckled. "It has its advantages. As for Lucas, we picked up his heat signature too, bearing north toward the Rae Ice Shelf."

"I'd give a king's ransom to find out what he plans to do now."

"Oh, we know what he plans to do. At least a part of it."

"We do?" Merrick and I asked, in unison.

"Twenty hours ago, one of our satellites intercepted a communication between him and Gwendolyn Phillips. Tim, play it for them."

Listening to the conversation, and hearing Lucas' ominous voice say, "After what her husband did, I shall take my time with Madison d'Clare," tears came to my eyes.

Merrick reached out and grasped my arm. "I know the pain you are feeling, George. But you can take solace in knowing Lucas is trapped in Antarctica for the next few months, which hopefully should give us enough time to find your beloved wife."

"But she could be anywhere."

"Gwendolyn mentioned they were moving her to *Site Few*," Bob said.

"That's not much to go on."

"Agreed," Merrick said, "but when we awaken My Captain, he'll know where to look."

* * *

The DART slowed to sub-sonic speed, and Ollie's voice came over the headset.

"CDC headquarters dead ahead. We're in luck. They've got a heliport."

"That's a pretty big building," I commented. "What floor do you think their laboratory is on?"

"I just found the building plans on the G-Net," Tim said.

"G-Net?" Merrick and I asked, in unison.

"Government Internet. It's a data retrieval system for federal employees. Here it is. The forensic lab is underground, basement level two."

"Keep the engines running," Bob said, "we may need a quick getaway."

"Okay, but when this is all over, you'll owe us a beer."

"If we can pull this off, you'll each get a case."

The tilt rotor engines came whining to life, drowning out the rumbling sounds of the turbojets. As the aircraft slowed, the forward momentum almost threw me off the stretcher.

"Oh, no!" Tim exclaimed. "Listen to this."

The voice of a female reporter came over the headset. "...what we know so far. Early this morning, an unidentified Native American woman, armed with a handgun, took hostages at the headquarters of the CDC. SWAT is on the scene, but there is no telling how long this standoff will continue. Wait. Another report is coming in."

When the reporter paused, Merrick asked, "What does she mean by SWAT?"

"Special weapons and tactics," I replied. "An elite arm of the police."

The reporter's voice came on again. "Police have confirmed shots have been fired, but it is not known whether anyone is injured."

Bob unbuckled his safety belt, tore off his facemask and helmet, and shed his parka. Merrick and I did the same. Before taking off my coat, I retrieved the Sacred Stone and placed it in my pants pocket.

"There's a lot of police down there," Ollie said.

Bob squeezed by Merrick and looked out the window.

Hoping to calm Bob's fears, I said, "Just because shots were fired, doesn't mean..."

"Come on, Ollie!" he screamed. "Set this thing down!"

Seconds later, the DART landed on the helipad. Bob slid the door open and jumped out, with Merrick and me following close behind. We sprinted to a set of double doors. Once inside, we blew by several deserted offices and rushed to the stairs.

When we reached basement floor number two, a contingent of Atlanta policemen and CDC security personnel stopped us. One of the policemen, a heavy-set man with bushy gray hair and a matching mustache, was speaking into a walkie-talkie.

"SWAT One, this is Cap," he said. "Take her out."

He turned to us, and I could see bars on his shoulders, denoting his rank of captain. The nametag on the front of his uniform read "Fredrickson."

"Where did you come from?" he asked. Not waiting for us to answer, he raised his walkie-talkie and said, "Sergeant Pierce, I thought you said you cleared the building."

A voice on the walkie-talkie replied. "I did, sir. I combed the floors myself."

Bob flashed his Army identification. "I'm Colonel Bob Alvarez. I can defuse this situation."

Unfazed by Bob's credentials, Captain Fredrickson replied in a condescending tone. "You have no jurisdiction here, Colonel. SWAT is running the show now."

"This is a matter of national security," Bob persisted. "Now order your men to stand down."

"Who do you think you are, barging in here and telling me what to do? This is an active crime scene!"

"Look, Captain, the woman in there is my wife!"

"Well, your wife has shot someone, so we'll leave it to SWAT!" He motioned to several of the other officers. "Get them out of here."

Merrick smiled. "George, if you please."

I pulled the Sacred Stone from my pocket, which instantly lit up the hallway in a blinding sea of light. As the beam struck Captain Fredrickson and the other officers, they stopped talking and moving, as if they'd been frozen in place!

Incredible!

Bob plucked the walkie-talkie from Fredrickson's hand, and we took off running down a long hallway. I kept the beam of light shining ahead of us, freezing the police and security officers along the way. Bob, sprinting to the left of me, radioed the SWAT team.

"SWAT One, this is Cap. Stand down."

A voice on the walkie-talkie replied, "Say again, Cap. You're breaking up."

"I said stand down!"

At the end of the hallway, a side door opened. Dr. Webster flanked by two uniformed policemen, came out. When I shined the beam of light on them, the officers froze in their tracks. Dr. Webster, however, appeared only slightly stunned; still able to move, but with her eyes fixated on the light.

I lowered the stone. "Dr. Webster."

Her eyes met mine. "Mr. d'Clare? What's up with the light?"

Bob stepped in front of me. "I'm Crystal's husband. Where is she?"

She pointed behind her. "In the lab, just around the corner."

We turned the corner and found three SWAT officers, two crouched in shooting positions. The third stood to the right of a stainless-steel door, its window panel shot out. From inside the lab, I could hear someone banging on a door.

The instant I shined the beam of light on the officers, they fired their weapons. When the bullets emerged from their rifle barrels, they stopped in mid-air and fell to the floor!

Unbelievable!

I looked at Bob. From his wide-eyed expression, I could tell he didn't believe it either. When my eyes traveled to Merrick, I found him smiling.

"The power of the Sacred Stone is limitless," he said.

Bob stepped around the now-frozen officers and approached the door from the side.

"Honey?" he yelled. "Don't shoot!"

"Bob?"

"Yes, it's me."

"Show me your left hand!"

Bob raised his left hand, spread his fingers, and stepped out into the open.

"Okay, come on in."

I cupped my hand over the stone and we followed Bob in.

The lab consisted of two rooms, the first used for scientists to change into personal protective equipment, evident by the five changing stations and benches on the left side. The wall to the right contained observation widows and an access door, its windowpane shattered.

Entering the second room, polished steel cabinets lined the walls and a circular-shaped lighting panel hung from the ceiling. A large, stainless-steel examination table sat in the center of the room, directly below the lights. On top of the table lay the body of Aquinas.

The banging emanated from a door on the opposite side of the room from where we came in. A wheeled cart, used to move medical supplies, had been rolled in front of the door. A blood pool, roughly the shape of a small watermelon, stained the floor between the cart and the table. In the center of the pool sat a surgeon's scalpel, a bone saw, and several other medical instruments.

Holding a handgun, Crystal rose from behind the table. Bob rushed to embrace her.

"Are you alright?" he asked, tears rolling down his cheeks.

She laid her head on his shoulder. "I am now."

"It looks like someone gave you some trouble."

"I'll say. A piece of work by the name of Hargrove. We showed him a copy of the court order to stop the autopsy, and he tore it to pieces. Then, when Dr. Webster went to get the director, Hargrove led the science team in here and they started to cut into Aquinas' body. I shot the glass out, but he didn't stop, so I shot him."

"Is he dead?"

She shook her head. "He'll live, but he won't be walking for a while."

"Lucas told me he had an operative at the CDC," I commented. "It must be Hargrove."

"Makes sense," Bob said, "but where is Hargrove? And the other scientists?"

"In the supply closet," Crystal replied, pointing to the door with the cart in front of it.

"You are to be commended, Madam," Merrick said.

Crystal looked at him. "Who are you?"

"My name is Merrick, at your service."

Crystal's eyes grew wide. "Merrick?" She looked at Bob. "How?"

"You're about to find out."

As we surrounded the examination table, Dr. Webster, still wobbly from the beam of light, joined us. Up close, the sight of Aquinas' grotesque remains sent shivers down my spine.

"My Captain," Merrick said, his voice trembling, "Lucas is not yet contained, so we must awaken you."

With tears streaming down his face, Merrick motioned to me. I set the Sacred Stone on the table and pointed the beam of light directly at Aquinas. As if we were all given a silent command, the five of us stepped back.

Like in the Antarctic crevasse, a mist appeared out of nowhere, and soon grew so thick it obscured the entire laboratory. The banging on the supply closet door abruptly stopped, plunging the room into a deafening silence.

Captivated, we stood there for several minutes, until the mist began to dissipate. When it cleared enough for me to see Aquinas, the open sores on his face had healed! His tight, healthy skin made him appear young, like he did when Madison first introduced me to him all those years ago. A moment later, his chest began to rise and fall!

Crystal and Dr. Webster gasped, but Bob, Merrick, and me remained silent, not taking our eyes off the miraculous sight.

Merrick leaned over and spoke softly into Aquinas' ear. "I once read a book about spiritual etiquette, that stated when a friend summons a friend back from the afterlife, it is customary to render a handshake."

Aquinas smiled and opened his eyes. "Merrick?"

"Yes, My Captain. I am here."

"That's funny. I was having a conversation with my father. He said you had something you wanted to show me."

Merrick grinned. "I do indeed, sir. Behold the Sacred Stone of Atlantis."

"The Sacred Stone? Surely you jest."

"No, My Captain. The weakened man found it."

"George d'Clare?"

"One and the same," I said.

He raised his head and looked at me. Taking hold of Merrick's hand, he rose to a sitting position. I slid the stone over to him.

Aquinas' eyes locked on the stone. "By all that is holy, the legend was true. The source of the life-giving carmot."

"Yes, sir," Merrick said.

Tearing his eyes away from the stone, Aquinas looked around. "And who are these people?"

I introduced Bob, Crystal, and Dr. Webster.

"Where is Maddie?"

"We don't know. She is being held captive by Gwendolyn Phillips."

"And what of Lucas?"

"He's a prisoner of Antarctica for the next few months." Merrick replied.

"And the Wordless Book?"

"It is in Lucas' possession, My Captain, but it doesn't matter."

"Oh?"

"Mrs. Alvarez has finished deciphering the final chapter."

Aquinas' eyes darted to Crystal. "*All* of them?"

She nodded. "I had a good scanner and the right apps."

"You used technology?"

She nodded.

Aquinas smiled. "I'd very much like you to explain to me how you did it."

"Not right now," Bob interrupted. "We've got to get out of here before these policemen wake up."

"Are you able to walk, sir?" Merrick asked.

Aquinas climbed off the table and jumped to his feet. "Let us be on our way."

Merrick snickered. "We must first find you some clothes, My Captain."

Turning beet-red, Aquinas grabbed the sheet off the table and wrapped it around himself. "My apologies, ladies."

I noticed a stack of surgical scrubs on a nearby counter. Walking over to retrieve a pair, I found a plastic bag behind them, with the name "Dewhurst" written on it.

"Here's your personal effects and something you can wear."

Aquinas handed me the Sacred Stone and began dressing.

"You were dead." Dr. Webster said, eyes wide and still staring. "I'd stake my reputation on it. How is this possible?"

"Come with us, and we'll tell you," I replied.

When she hesitated, I turned to Aquinas. "When I shined the beam of light on her and the policemen, it froze them but didn't affect her."

Aquinas smiled. "You must come with us, doctor. You are part of the Great Work now."

Dr. Webster thought for a moment. "I can't believe I'm saying this, but alright, I'll go with you."

"Is there another way out?" Bob asked.

"Yes. Follow me."

Dr. Webster led us to a door at the end of the hall which opened to a second stairwell. Ten minutes later, we were aboard the DART, streaking across the sky at Mach 5 speed.

* * *

When we reached cruising altitude, I introduced Crystal and Dr. Webster to Ollie and Tim. When I announced Aquinas, Tim unbuckled his seat belt, climbed back into the cargo bay, and shook his hand like a giddy teenager.

"What an honor it is to meet you, Mr. Aquinas," Tim said.

"The honor is mine, Mr. McCurdy."

As Tim kept shaking his hand, Aquinas looked around, embarrassed.

"To think, I'm shaking hands with the man who eluded the largest manhunt of the 20th century."

"Tim's late father was an FBI agent who worked the D. B. Cooper case," I explained.

Aquinas smiled. "I see. Perhaps if we have time, we can chat about it."

"I'd very much like that," Tim replied, finally letting go.

During the rest of the flight to Groom Lake, we told Aquinas about the events transpiring during his "unending sleep." We also answered a multitude of questions from Dr. Webster about the Sacred Stone, the carmot, the Wordless Book, and the threat Lucas posed to the world. When Tim replayed the recording between Lucas and Gwendolyn, Aquinas, who'd been in deep thought, opened his eyes and spoke.

"Mrs. Alvarez, do you have the parables with you?"

"Right here." She handed him her phone. "Just use your finger to scroll down."

After reading through them, Aquinas' eyes slowly traveled to each of us.

"What is it, sir?" Merrick asked.

"Our centuries-long crusade to stop the Wanderer is nearly complete, my friend."

"What do you mean?"

"Look at us. Don't you see?"

I looked at each person, then back to him.

Aquinas chuckled. "Everyone on board this aircraft is of a different heritage."

It never occurred to me before, but he was right! Ollie was of Asian descent; Tim, African; Dr. Webster, Mid-Eastern; Bob, Hispanic; Crystal, Native American; Merrick, Nordic; Aquinas, Slavic; and me, Northern European.

"You might even say," Aquinas continued, "each of us are *heirs* to different races of human beings. The only race missing is the white, or Anglo-Saxon race."

"Madison is white," I offered.

"My thoughts exactly, George."

"Wait," Crystal interrupted. "Is that what the parable is talking about?"

"Precisely, Madam. The Almighty has brought us together to serve in the most important army in the history of mankind – the Army of Light. And once we rescue Maddie, we will be ready for the battle."

The Army of Light
must field nine as one.
Each heir taking part,
for the war to be won.

In a secret desert fortress,
they'll uncover the scheme,
to transform the world,
into a nightmarish dream.

Crystal Alvarez's interpretation of the third group of symbols in the last chapter of the Wordless Book

CHAPTER TWENTY: THE STRATEGY

Three Hours Later
Groom Lake Air Base
Area 51, Nevada

With their heavy-booted footsteps echoing off the cement walls, the ten-man security detachment escorted us through a hangar containing stacks of large round objects in open-faced shipping crates. Proceeding down a stairway, we made our way down a long underground passageway. The antiquated-looking overhead lights turned on in front of us and went dark behind us, making it impossible to tell how far we had walked. The further we progressed, the more the temperature dropped, the polar opposite of the triple-digit heat we'd left behind in the DART's hangar a short time ago.

When the walls widened into an unfurnished room, a door opened on the far side and the security personnel instantly snapped to attention.

Two people entered. The first, a middle-aged, silver-haired, gruff-looking man wore the uniform of an Army general, with the name "Lansing" on his nametape. The second, a much younger woman with jet-black hair and horn-rimmed glasses wore a red, expensive-looking business suit. An identification card clipped to the pocket of her jacket read, "Mrs. Atborne."

The two stood there for a moment, looking at us like scientists examining lab rats. Finally, the general walked up to Ollie and began chewing him out.

"Colonel Cheng," he barked, "just what in the hell were you thinking? Taking the DART to a major city? Landing on the roof of the CDC? As if that's not enough to get you court martialed, you bring civilians onto this base without authorization!"

"I can explain, General," Ollie replied, his shaky voice betraying his nervousness.

"I don't want to hear any explanations!"

"But sir," Tim said, "if you only knew…"

"As you were, Major! You're in as much trouble as he is."

Atborne chimed in. "Do either of you realize you've broken almost every security protocol in the book? At this facility, we cannot afford breaches in security!"

"If you're going to blame anyone, blame me," Bob said. "I was the one who..."

"As you were, Colonel!" Lansing shouted. "I'll get to you in a minute."

Aquinas signaled me with a nod, and I retrieved the Sacred Stone from my pocket. When the beam of light struck General Lansing, his speech slowed to a crawl.

"As flight commander, Colonel… Cheng… you… should've… known… bet…"

I turned and shined the light on Atborne and the security men. Like the policemen at the CDC, they froze in place.

Aquinas walked up to General Lansing and waived his hand in front of his eyes.

The General didn't blink.

"Remarkable." Merrick said. "The Sacred Stone has hypnotized them."

Aquinas whispered in the General's ear. "There's no need to be upset. Colonel Cheng, Colonel Alvarez, and Major McCurdy were simply following orders. *Your* orders."

With his eyes staring off into space, General Lansing nodded. "They were following my orders."

"Yes. They are to be commended for their bravery. Now take your men and go about your business."

As soon as the General and the security detachment were gone, Aquinas moved to Atborne and examined her identification. "Tell me, Mrs. Atborne, what do your duties entail?"

"I'm the civilian director over this base," Atborne replied, unblinking.

"I know you test new aircraft here, but what else do you do?"

"Conduct research."

"And where does this research take place?"

"In the SURFs."

"And what, exactly, are SURFs?"

"Secured underground research facilities. Government think tanks where scientists work in seclusion to develop new weapon systems for the military."

Aquinas thought for a moment. "Tell me more about these SURFs."

"They are self-contained living modules that can hold up to twenty people comfortably.

"How many SURFs are on this base?"

"Ten."

"Are all of them being used?"

Atborne shook her head, "At present, only six."

Aquinas smiled.

"Are you thinking of us using one of these facilities, sir?" Merrick asked.

413

Aquinas nodded. "We will need a place to confer."

"Good idea," Bob interjected, "seeing as how this is the most secure Air Force base in the world."

"Mrs. Atborne," Aquinas said, "we would like to utilize one of your SURFs for the foreseeable future. Please make the arrangements."

Atborne could only nod.

* * *

Atborne placed her access card on the reader, and the heavy, stainless-steel door with "SURF 7" stenciled on it slowly opened.

Proceeding in, we descended a stairway to a modern-looking kitchen, complete with a pantry stocked with cases of food and drinks of every variety. On the left side, two glass doors were marked with signs, one labeled "Lab," and the other "Bio Lab." Two more doors on the far wall were designated with single letters, "M" and "F," respectively. On the right, a stainless-steel door had a sign on it denoting "War Room."

"As you can see," Atborne said, "labs are to the left and right, living quarters are in the back."

"Show us the War Room," Merrick said.

As we passed the Lab, I looked in. It resembled a state-of-the-art metal fabrication shop with sophisticated looking machinery. Proceeding by the Bio Lab, I noticed there was another door inside, opening into what appeared to be a sterile room, furnished with an assortment of medical research equipment.

Entering the War Room, I was struck at how much it resembled the Airman Leadership School classroom I attended years before in the Air Force Reserve. Pads of tear-away poster paper adorned three walls. Below each pad, black markers, multicolored highlighters, and a roll of masking tape sat on a small shelf. A large flat-screen television monitor hung in the center of the fourth wall, its screen changing every few seconds to show a different part of the world.

The furniture consisted of five rows of four desks with matching chairs, arranged with a center aisle down the middle. On top of each desk sat a laptop computer, a standard-sized pad of paper, and various writing instruments. In the front of the room sat a long, modern-looking table, with ten chairs around it. The top of the table had a black glass covering. When I moved closer, I realized it wasn't black glass at all, but rather the background of a giant, built-in computer screen.

"I've never seen a computer this big," I commented.

"Ollie and I have," Tim said.

"With suspended, three-dimensional display," Ollie added.

Tim swept his hand across a corner, and the icons moved off the screen and hovered in mid-air *above* the table.

Merrick's eyes grew wide. "Are you a sorcerer?"

Tim laughed. "Everything works on motion-sensors. Try it."

Merrick touched one of the floating icons, and an Internet search page opened, also above the table.

"Magical."

Crystal and Dr. Webster reached out. When their hands passed through other icons, more programs opened.

"Wow!" Crystal exclaimed. "Now this is what I call a computer."

"It's like a sci-fi movie," Dr. Webster added.

Tim pointed to one of the icons. "Look, Ollie. We've got D-Web."

"D-Web?" I asked.

"Defense Interweb," Ollie explained. "It's like the G-Net we have on the DART but much more sophisticated. We'll be able to search anywhere, and our address will be encrypted."

"What do you mean by that?" Merrick asked.

"No one will be able to trace our searches. We'll be working in total anonymity."

"We'll also be able to monitor telemetry from every defense satellite," Tim added.

Aquinas smiled. "This is perfect."

"Sir," Merrick interrupted, "look there."

He pointed at a corner of the ceiling, where a swiveling camera panned back and forth.

Aquinas turned and addressed Mrs. Atborne. "Our research is classified far above your level. All monitoring devices are to be turned off, and no one is to know we are here. Do you understand?"

"Yes, sir," Atborne replied. She reached into her pocket, retrieved a cellphone, and punched in a number. "This is the Director. SURF 7 will be operating Security Code One. Turn off all surveillance. Confirmation code 1-1A-SF7."

Aquinas retrieved the nearest roll of masking tape and tossed it to Merrick, who immediately tore off a piece and covered the lens of the camera.

"Forgive me, Mrs. Atborne," Aquinas said, "but we must be cautious. Show me all the other monitoring devices in here."

While Atborne pointed them out to Aquinas, Merrick and Bob, who had also retrieved a roll of tape, followed behind covering the camera lenses. After finishing the other rooms in the facility, Aquinas thanked Atborne and instructed her to go about her duties. As soon as she had departed, Bob and Merrick secured the main door, and the eight of us assembled around the table in the War Room.

"Now that we are sequestered in a safe shelter," Aquinas began, "let us put our collective minds to work on locating Maddie. What do we know?"

"We know Lucas' plan involves using an atomic bomb enhanced with carmot," Bob said.

"And what better way to deliver it, than using a ballistic missile," I commented.

"But where do we look?" Crystal asked. "Pinpointing this Site Few is going to be like finding a needle in a haystack. It could be anywhere."

"How many missiles do we have?" Dr. Webster asked.

Tim thrust his hand into the floating D-Web icon. When the page came up, he typed in a search and examined the results. "There are currently four-hundred Minuteman III's in the U.S. inventory, located in silos scattered across Montana, North Dakota, and Wyoming."

"That's not counting the sea-launched ICBM missiles in our Navy," Ollie added.

"Do you think Site Few could be onboard a ship?" Crystal asked.

Ollie and Tim shrugged their shoulders.

"George, didn't you say Lucas knew Air Force terminology?" Bob asked.

"I'll say. He sounded like a seasoned maintenance group commander."

"Knowing Lucas," Merrick interjected, "he wouldn't have gone to the trouble of learning the lingo of one service, only to use another for his diabolical plan."

Bob smiled. "My thoughts exactly."

"I agree," Aquinas replied. "Let us proceed on the assumption that Lucas plans to utilize an Air Force missile."

"Probably one with multiple warheads," Ollie said.

"Or one big warhead with a lot of firepower." Bob added.

"Will we have to search four-hundred missile silos to find the right one?" Dr. Webster asked.

"Not necessarily," Ollie replied. "I started my career in missiles. At any one time, fifty to sixty are off-line for periodic maintenance."

"Oh, that's a game changer." Crystal commented, sarcastically.

We all laughed.

"Tim," Aquinas said, "you mentioned three states where the missiles are located. Can you plot them on the map?"

"Sure." Tim swept his hand across the table. A moment later, the areas highlighted in red. "As you can see, the U.S. land-based ICBMs are disbursed at three locations. Two-hundred at Malmstrom Air Force Base, Montana, one-hundred at Minot, North Dakota, and another hundred at Warren, Wyoming."

"If memory serves," Aquinas said, "isn't Warren Air Force Base named after a war hero?"

"Yes," Tim replied. "Francis Warren. He went on to become a state senator."

Ollie grinned. "How do you know that?"

"At Officer Training School, I had to write a paper about a Medal of Honor winner. I did mine on Senator Warren." Tim returned his attention to Aquinas. "What does he have to do with all of this?"

"Nothing," Aquinas replied, "but it does ring a bell. Pray tell, what was the senator's full name?"

"Francis Ermroy Warren." As the revelation came to him, Tim's voice trailed off to a whisper.

"Site Few!" Merrick yelled.

Aquinas smiled. "Not so fast, my friend. Let us be sure."

Tim typed in another command. A three-dimensional map of Warren Air Force Base appeared with the 90th Missile Wing headquarters and silos highlighted in yellow.

"What's this one?" Bob asked, pointing to a silo highlighted in red.

"Good question," Ollie replied. "Let's see if we can find out." He nodded to Tim, who immediately typed in another search.

"It's restricted," Tim said. "Let me try my military password." When he typed it in, a new page came up. "Missile silo Sierra 21. It's listed as inactive. Wait. Ollie, look at the designation. LGM-118-3."

"It's a Peacekeeper missile," Ollie said.

"I thought the Air Force replaced all the Peacekeepers with Minutemen?" I asked.

"According to the SALT II Treaty with Russia, we were supposed to begin scrapping all the Peacekeepers in 2005."

"But why is this one still here?"

"Maybe it's the last one, and they hadn't got around to scrapping it yet," Bob speculated.

"Or they kept it active and hidden," Tim said. "Let me see if I can find more information." He thrust his hand into the floating D-Web icon and began typing again.

"What is the biggest difference between the Minuteman and the Peacekeeper?" Aquinas asked.

"The Peacekeeper is a multiple independent reentry vehicle," Ollie replied, "which simply means you can load up to three atomic bombs, or one hydrogen bomb into one of them."

"Sounds like something Lucas would consider…"

"Wait," Tim interrupted, "look at this." He swept his hand across the table and a Warren Air Force Base newspaper appeared. On the front page, an article read:

Work to begin on modular Launch Control Facility.

Starting Monday, base personnel utilizing the south gate will need to add time to their commute. Crews from Phillips Industries will begin construction on a new, state-of-the-art Launch Control Facility (LCF). When finished, the modular LCF will be able to control up to twenty missiles from one hardened location. Currently, two Air Force officers, stationed inside each silo, are required to perform such tasks.

At a groundbreaking ceremony last Friday, the commander of the 90th Missile Wing, Colonel Dewayne Jensen, said, "It's the dawning of a new era in missile defense. The safer environment, coupled with the reduction of personnel in the field, will result in substantial cost savings to the Air Force."

In a statement, Miss Gwendolyn Phillips, the CEO of Phillips Industries, commented, "We at Phillips look forward to working hand-in-hand with the dedicated men and women of the United States Air Force in making this new launch facility the safest in the world."

If tests are successful, new LCFs will be built for the remaining missile inventory. Construction is expected to last two years.

"What is the date of this newspaper?" Aquinas asked.

Tim scrolled up to the top of the page. "September, two years ago."

Aquinas wrinkled his eyebrows. "How could I have missed this?"

"Maybe you had other things on your mind," I said, "like deciphering the Wordless Book."

"Perhaps."

"No worries, My Captain," Merrick said. "We know about it now."

Aquinas smiled. "Very well, let us get back to the matter at hand. If the work on this new launch facility proceeded on schedule, it will be completed *this* September."

"That's only three months away," Bob said.

"Conceivably the same time Lucas escapes from Antarctica," Merrick added.

"But if Lucas intends to use this new LCF to launch an ICBM, how can we be sure it's *this* Peacekeeper?" I asked.

"I've got an idea," Crystal said. "Can you bring up the government's contract with Phillips Industries?"

Tim typed in another search. In seconds, we were reviewing the contract.

"There's your answer, George," Ollie said. "The new LCF is being built adjacent to the Sierra 21 silo."

"I think we can safely assume Lucas plans on launching *this* Peacekeeper," Aquinas said.

"But how would he go about it?" Dr. Webster asked. "If I remember my chemistry, doesn't he need a lot of uranium?"

"You're forgetting his confederate, Gwendolyn Phillips," Merrick said. "With her contacts, we must assume they have all the materials they need to weaponize an inactive missile."

"Tim," Aquinas said, "Gwendolyn mentioned a Professor Davenport when she talked to Lucas. What can you find out about him?"

Tim typed in another search and read the results. "Dr. Laurence Davenport of Phillips Industries; holds a Doctorate of Theoretical Physics from MIT; joined the Defense Department in 1980; arrested for attempting to sell classified data to a terrorist group in 2003, but was later acquitted on a technicality."

"Exactly the kind of ilk Lucas would employ," Aquinas commented. "When Davenport worked for the government, what did he do, specifically?"

Tim scrolled down. "It says he worked under Edward Teller on the Strategic Defense Initiative."

"There's your answer," Ollie said. "Edward Teller is known as the father of the hydrogen bomb."

"And with Lucas spinning his web of lies to a man as knowledgeable as Davenport, a hydrogen bomb is not out of the realm of possibility," Aquinas added.

"What's the difference between an atomic bomb and a hydrogen bomb?" Crystal asked.

"Think of it this way," Tim replied. "The A-bomb is a cheap firecracker. The H-bomb is a stick of dynamite."

Her eyebrows raised. "Seriously?"

"I've seen videos of the destructive power of an H-bomb," Ollie said. "The Army detonated one in the Marshall Islands in the early '50s. It was estimated to be thirty times more powerful than both the A-bombs we dropped on Japan to end World War II."

"If Davenport gained the knowledge of how to build an H-bomb from Teller," Bob said, "and Lucas enhances it with carmot..." His voice trailed off.

"And let us not forget about what happens when carmot transforms objects into gold," Aquinas added. "Even if the exploding bomb vaporizes the missile or reduces it to atoms, the toxic residue from the transformation could poison the atmosphere for decades."

"But if the carmot changes the missile to gold, wouldn't it become too heavy to launch?" I asked.

"Under normal circumstances, yes," Ollie replied. "But this missile has a dash three designation, which means it is equipped with three extra solid-rocket booster engines. The three additional engines would provide more than enough power to launch a solid-gold missile."

From the deafening silence, I could tell I wasn't the only one with chills running down my spine.

"Doesn't the Air Force have safeguards to prevent a crazy person from taking over a silo and launching a missile?" Dr. Webster asked.

"Several," Ollie replied. "Like the article stated, two officers are stationed in each silo. To launch the missile, both must receive a top-secret email from the Pentagon. Each message contains a numeric code, which could be either a simulation or a launch order. The officers enter the code into the launch control computer. If the computer confirms it's an actual launch order, the missile will power up, but it still won't initiate a launch. The final safeguards are the officers themselves."

"What do you mean?"

"When the launch code is confirmed, each officer retrieves a key from a safe within the silo. These keys fit locks in the panels of their launch stations. The two panels are ten feet away from each other, making it impossible for one person to launch the missile by themself."

"Couldn't someone just unlock one and then the other?" Crystal asked.

Ollie shook his head. "The keys must be turned clockwise simultaneously. Successfully turning the keys starts a five-minute countdown.

"Once the countdown starts, is there any way to stop it?" Merrick asked.

Ollie nodded. "By turning the keys counterclockwise simultaneously."

"What about after the launch?"

"The missile can be aborted by turning the keys counterclockwise again."

"What about the warhead?" Bob asked. "I assume the missile doesn't take off armed."

"The computer arms the warhead when the missile is within fifty miles of its intended target. Once the warhead is armed, no electronic command in the world can turn it off."

"Thank you, Ollie," Aquinas said. "Very sobering. Hopefully, we'll be able to disrupt Lucas' plan before it goes that far."

"Amen to that."

"So how do we disrupt his plan?" Crystal asked.

"We know he still needs the launch codes," I said. "His entire plan depends on it."

"But why doesn't he just reprogram the launch control computer?" Dr. Webster asked. "I mean, wouldn't the old launch code numbers be outdated now?"

"I'm afraid not," Ollie replied. "The Peacekeeper's launch control computer has top-secret safeguards in place to prevent someone from hacking into it. It can only be deactivated when the entire platform is dismantled."

"Which explains why Lucas kidnapped Madison," I said. "She was on the team that developed the system for generating the launch code numbers."

Aquinas smiled. "Precisely, George. Since we now know, with a great deal of certainty, where Gwendolyn has taken Maddie, let us discuss tactics. Tim, could you find an image of what this new launch facility looks like?"

Tim swept his hand down, and the floating images of the government contract scrolled by. A moment later, he opened a diagram of the new LCF.

"Except for being circular-shaped, it doesn't look much different than where we are now," Bob commented.

"Agreed." Aquinas replied. "There's the kitchen and the living quarters, but I'm not seeing the launch control room."

"It's restricted access," Tim said. "Give me a second." He typed in his password, and a sketch of the room appeared.

"Those chairs sitting apart are the launch control stations," Ollie said. "It looks like two people are still required to turn the keys."

I pointed to a group of dotted lines "What are those?"

"The Security door," Ollie replied. "It isolates the control room from the rest of the facility."

"Where's the main entrance?" Aquinas asked.

Ollie pointed to the top of the image. "Back up a page, Tim."

When the diagram appeared, Ollie pointed to the area between the kitchen and the living quarters. "The elevator doors are here."

"Where does it lead to?"

"Probably a house or a barn. The Air Force tries to make them look as inconspicuous as possible, but it doesn't really fool anyone because they build fences around them and post signs telling people to stay out. Tim, see if you can bring up a satellite image of the exterior."

Tim moved his hand across the table, and the image of a farmhouse appeared. Except for a wide trail of dirt behind the house, obviously disturbed from the construction, the surrounding land appeared lush with green grass and trees. Approximately fifty feet from the farmhouse, at the end of the dirt trail, sat a circle of concrete, with a thick metal door covering the center.

"There it is," Tim said. "The Sierra 21 missile silo."

"What is that?" I pointed to what appeared to be a manhole cover situated near a line of trees, surrounded by a gated chain-link fence.

"It's the exit hatch for the emergency crew escape," Ollie replied.

"Is there another view?" Aquinas asked.

Tim scrolled down several pages, stopped and pointed. "It runs from the kitchen, down to a crawlspace, then over to the hatch."

"My Captain," Merrick said, "it appears we have found our entry point."

"The article stated this LCF will be state-of-the-art," I said. "Won't it be equipped with detection devices to prevent people from doing what we are attempting?"

"Yes," Ollie replied, "Motion sensors and video surveillance are normally placed in and around the facility."

"So how do we get into this crew escape undetected?"

Ollie smiled. "Easy. The DART is equipped with electromagnetic pulse technology. One burst will disrupt power on just about every electronic device within a five-mile radius."

"So, we'll be blind down there?"

"Not really. Once the main power goes out, battery power will turn on the emergency lights."

"What about the exit hatch?" Aquinas asked.

"The hatch is similar to those on submarines. Normally, when power is on, electronic locks are engaged to prevent anyone from entering. If the power goes out, it can be opened manually by turning a wheel on the hatch itself."

"If we use this pulse, how long will it last before the main power is restored?"

"Fifteen minutes, give or take."

"Excellent! It should blind them long enough for us to get inside. Once we do, we'll rescue Maddie, disable the missile, and contain Lucas once and for all."

Crystal raised her hand. "Mr. Aquinas?"

"Yes, Mrs. Alvarez."

"What if we are unable to rescue her? I mean, with what's at stake, I think we need to set our priorities."

"She's right," Bob said. "I'm all for rescuing Mrs. d'Clare, but in the overall scheme of things, our priority should be on saving as many lives as we can."

Aquinas thought for a moment. "As much as it pains me to say, I agree. We must do everything in our power to safeguard humanity."

Although I agreed, my eyes still welled up with tears.

Noticing, Merrick reached out and grasped my arm.

"Be brave, Lord George. My Captain is not suggesting we abandon your beloved wife."

"No, I'm not," Aquinas said.

"I'm not either," Crystal said. "I just don't think we should put all our eggs into one basket."

Merrick turned to her. "I beg your pardon, madam?"

"What I'm saying is, if we are unable to rescue Madison, we should have a back-up plan."

"Very well," Aquinas said, "let us take a closer look at the facility."

Tim brought up the sketch of the launch control room and enlarged it.

"Look at the thickness of the security door, My Captain," Merrick said, outlining the group of dots with his finger.

"And the exterior walls," Bob added, pointing to the drawing.

Aquinas leaned in. "Do we have anything at our disposal powerful enough to take out the entire facility?"

"A MOAB might be able to," Tim suggested. "If we rig it to detonate on impact, like a bunker-buster, it could conceivably destroy the LCF *and* the silo."

"What's a MOAB?" Dr. Webster asked.

"The mother of all bombs, or, in the official language of the military, Multi-Ordnance Air Burst. It's not an A-bomb or an H-bomb, but it's the biggest conventional weapon in the U.S. arsenal. We walked by some when they led us down here. They were in the hangar next to where we parked the DART."

So that's what those large round objects were in the shipping crates!

"Can your airship drop such a weapon?" Merrick asked.

Ollie nodded. "If we remove all the stretchers and medical cabinets from the cargo bay. But the MOAB is heavy. We'll need at least two men to push it out of the aircraft."

"Say we drop the MOAB. Will it set off the warhead?" Bob asked.

Ollie shook his head. "The Peacekeeper has some very efficient internal safeguards. The warhead must be armed to go off. But a MOAB has a blast equivalent to eleven tons of TNT. An explosion of such magnitude will breach the casing holding the uranium, so we're sure to have a radiation leak."

"Regardless of the radiation hazard, we now have a backup plan," Aquinas said. "If we are unable to rescue Maddie, we will use the MOAB and destroy the LCF and the missile."

"But sir," Merrick said, "with Lord George wielding the Sacred Stone, breaching the entrance and rescuing his wife shouldn't prove to be too difficult."

"I'm glad you said that, my friend. You reminded me of something. George, take the stone and place it in the freezer. Pack as much ice around it as you can."

I smiled. "I get it. The stone will produce more carmot."

"Precisely. In the event anyone gets hurt, we will need some."

"Wait," Crystal interrupted. "We're forgetting the Wordless Book." She retrieved her cell phone, quickly brought up the page of parables, and began reading:

A test of faith comes,
when the divine light fades.
On the altar of trust,
their hearts they must lay.

"Apparently, we are to wage this war *without* the Almighty's intervention." Merrick commented.

"So, when the stone dims, we'll be on our own?" I asked.

Aquinas nodded. "Pray continue, Mrs. Alvarez."

Returning to the parable, Crystal read:

As the battle draws near,
the great soldier must choose,
a learned companion
to enact the wind's ruse.

"To enact the wind's ruse?" Dr. Webster asked.

"I believe the parable is referring to an age-old discipline of hypnosis known as *The Ways of the Wind,*" Aquinas replied.

"But sir, how can we enact the discipline without the ancient text?" Merrick asked.

Aquinas smiled. "I discovered the text. I was trying to tell George and Maddie about it when I, um, temporarily left this world."

Merrick's eyes grew wide. "How? When?"

"Four years ago, archaeologists digging in the Judaean Desert uncovered the twelfth cave in the Qumran Region." He stopped and looked at the rest of us. "Forgive me. For those of you unfamiliar, the Qumran Region is an area of the world where the Dead Sea Scrolls were found. Up until four years ago, they had only uncovered eleven caves.

"When I learned of this I immediately traveled to the site, and using some hypnosis of my own, joined the excavation. A few days later, I uncovered a centuries-old jar containing a text written on parchment paper. Recognizing its importance, I absconded with the parchment, made my way home, and spent the next four years studying it."

"What is so special about this text?" Dr. Webster asked.

"Most disciplines teach four levels of hypnosis, all of which cover how to activate an unconscious response in an individual to achieve a desired outcome. *The Ways of the Wind* discipline teaches how to reach the fifth and sixth level, which involves reading a person's mind and projecting a hypnotic suggestion."

"*Projecting* a suggestion? I don't understand."

"Tricking someone into seeing people from their past, or things not really there. Lucas uses this skill to strike fear into the hearts of his adversaries, make them kill at his behest, or commit suicide."

"I'll vouch for that," I said. "He changed himself into a mannequin from one of my childhood nightmares."

"Many years ago, he made me believe I had fired the fatal arrow that took my beloved Bella from me," Merrick said. "I've been plagued by his trickery ever since. But pray continue, sir."

"While hiding in St. George, I devoted a great deal of time thinking about my situation. I came to realize every setback I have encountered can be attributed to Lucas using this ability."

"So what did you learn from the text?" Bob asked.

Aquinas smiled. "I now know how he does it and how to recognize it. More importantly, I learned the mindreading and projections can work both ways."

Merrick's eyes grew wide again. "Are you saying Lucas can be fooled?"

Aquinas nodded. "By the same hypnotic ability he uses on others."

"Then if the parable is to be believed, we must enact this knowledge for the upcoming battle."

"Correct, my friend. However, I must warn all of you, we are diving into very deep and dangerous waters. The actions we take could result in our deaths."

"How so?" I asked.

"If I condition your minds, and Lucas later captures you and uses his hypnotic ability, you could suffer a fatal stroke or an aneurism, like Maddie's parents. So, I must ask, will you trust me?"

Except for Dr. Webster, we all nodded.

"Doctor?" Aquinas asked.

She squirmed in her chair. "I trust you, but the others have skills or experience in military and police work. I don't know what I can do to help."

Aquinas smiled. "Oh doctor, you shouldn't downplay your gifts. You will be on hand to attend our wounds if we become injured. You will also play a very significant role in our ruse." He turned to Merrick. "What do you think?"

Merrick smiled. "Being a doctor, she is quite learned. And she looks to be the same height and general build. Add a blonde wig and…"

"My thought's exactly."

"Same height and build as who?" Dr. Webster asked.

"The influential woman with the black heart. Gwendolyn Phillips."

She looked at each of us, then back to Aquinas. "Surely you can't hypnotize Lucas into believing I am her."

Aquinas' eyes locked onto her. "Not only will you *look* like Gwendolyn Phillips, but you will fool Lucas into believing you *are* her."

"But where on earth am I going to find a blonde wig in this place?"

"There's a Base Exchange here," Tim offered. "Bigger than the ones on most Air Force bases."

"And if you can't find a wig," Aquinas added, "I'm sure we can find some hair dye. All we need is for you to vaguely resemble her. The hypnosis will do the rest."

I could tell from the decisiveness in Aquinas' voice he had been thinking about this for some time.

"What about the rest of us?" Merrick asked.

"I'd like you and Bob to go scout out the site. Ollie and Tim can take you in the DART. We'll also need strong leg shackles and handcuffs to contain Lucas."

"No problem," Bob said, "There's a police supply store in Cheyenne."

Aquinas turned to Ollie and Tim. "Once you drop them off, return here and load the MOAB weapon. If you have any problems with Mrs. Atborne or anyone else, let me know."

"What about Crystal and me?" I asked.

"I'd like you two to stay here and monitor McMurdo Station. Tim and Ollie can show you how before they leave. If anything happens there, anything at all, I want to know about it."

"Speaking of communications," Bob said, "what do we have?"

"I've got you covered," Tim replied. "The DART is equipped with the latest remoat, shoulder-mounted radios for ground personnel. Like what police wear, but much more powerful."

"How powerful?"

"A thousand miles, give or take. They also have Global Positioning, so we'll be able to pinpoint your position. But remember, if we use the electromagnetic pulse, or the LCF's electronic countermeasures come on, we'll lose communications with you."

"What weapons do we have?" Merrick asked.

"Handguns, assault rifles, small explosives, and stun grenades."

"Which reminds me," Aquinas said. "I'll check with Mrs. Atborne and see if there are any clergy assigned to this base. If the need arises, I want some holy water on hand."

"Holy water?" I asked.

"Yes. Lucas is an agent of evil, obsessed with destroying humanity. To win this war, we must be prepared for anything. We cannot show them any mercy." He locked his penetrating gaze on Merrick. "Including Gwendolyn Phillips. Do you understand, my friend?"

"Yes, My Captain. After what transpired at the Crater of Hope, I am fully aware of just how evil she is. Trust me. I am not one to repeat a mistake."

Aquinas smiled. "Good. Anything else?"

I raised my hand.

"Yes, George."

"You and Merrick have been trying to stop Lucas for almost seven-hundred years. How can we even hope to be successful?"

Aquinas rose to his feet. As he spoke, his eyes moved to each of us. "Where we were once two, we are now eight. Nine after we rescue Maddie. To succeed and survive, we must all have faith in each other. Now, shall we begin?"

* * *

For the next six days, while Aquinas conditioned our minds and practiced the hypnotic *Ways of the Wind* spells, Crystal and I took turns monitoring McMurdo Station. After dropping off Bob and Merrick outside of Cheyenne, Wyoming, Ollie and Tim returned and loaded the DART with one of the massive MOAB bombs. Rejoining Crystal and me, the four of us worked in shifts monitoring the station and receiving reports from Bob and Merrick.

In the past, when I had worked with others I didn't know, I would strike up conversations to learn more about them. This time, however, the casual talk was kept to a minimum because we were all worried about our loved ones. The added pressure of knowing the entire human race depended on the outcome of our battle with Lucas didn't help matters. Some days, we hardly spoke to each other.

Everything changed the evening of the seventh day. Taking a break from watching the Antarctic station on the computer, I made my way to the kitchen to get a bite to eat. While retrieving bread and lunch meat from the fridge, something brushed against the side of my head. Turning, I found myself face-to-face with Gwendolyn Phillips!

It can't be!

Looking much like I remembered from when she kicked me in the stomach, she wore a one-piece skin-tight leotard, showcasing her athletic build. Her blonde hair was pulled back in a bun, and pinned with a diamond-studded barrette. The wrinkle-lipped smug look on her face projected the unsettling aura of superiority.

It's really her!

I backed away, and my eyes lost focus of her face. A moment later, her features sharpened – her face had *transformed* into Dr. Webster's!

Aquinas stepped out from behind her, smiling. "What do you think, George?"

"Unbelievable," I whispered, awestruck.

434

Dr. Webster laughed. "You really thought I was Gwendolyn Phillips?"

Before I could answer, Aquinas' eyes locked onto the refrigerator behind me. When I turned, I noticed there was no longer a white glow around the freezer door. Investigating, I found the ice surrounding the Sacred Stone glowing violet, but the stone itself no longer projecting the beam of light. When I picked up the stone to examine it, the door to the male quarters opened and Ollie and Tim entered the room.

"What's going on?" Ollie asked.

Just then, the War Room door burst open, and Crystal came running in.

"I have Bob on the line. He said Lucas is at the launch control facility! How can he be in two places at once?"

We rushed into the War Room.

Aquinas examined the television showing McMurdo Station "Something seems familiar." He pointed to a man coming out the Pegasus Airfield Headquarters building. "That man there! If I'm not mistaken, he's going to be hit with a gust of wind and lose his footing."

We watched the scene unfold just as Aquinas described.

"How did you know that?" Crystal asked.

"The same thing happened five days ago."

"Lucas must have sabotaged the video feed."

"Precisely, Madam."

"But how did he manage to escape Antarctica?" I asked.

"Good question," Bob replied, his voice emanating from a speaker in the ceiling.

Aquinas motioned to Tim. "Do you have access to photos from around the world?"

Tim moved over to the computer. "Which ones? I can access thousands."

"The ship *Phillips 3*, moored at Easter Island seven days ago."

In seconds, photos of the ship projected across the three-dimensional screen. Chained to her deck was a black, sleek-looking helicopter.

Aquinas pointed to the ship's hull. "Just as I suspected. *Phillips 3* is an icebreaker."

"And the chopper looks like a modified version of a Lockheed 56-A," Ollie added, "It has the longest range of any helicopter, military or civilian."

So that's how he did it.

"Bob, tell Merrick we are on our way," Aquinas said. "Ollie and Tim, prepare the DART for immediate takeoff."

"What about me?" I asked.

"George, gather the stone and the carmot. There's a portable ice chest in the pantry you can use." Addressing Dr. Webster, Aquinas asked, "Are you ready?"

She nodded.

Aquinas' eyes slowly traveled to each of us before settling on Crystal.

"Mrs. Alvarez, please read the next parable."

The Army will face the Wanderer
deep in his lair,
sending four to the circle
and four to the air.

When the stone fails to shine
and the Day of Reckoning draws near,
the weakened man will face
the sum of his fear.

Crystal Alvarez's interpretation of the fifth group of symbols in the last chapter of the Wordless Book

CHAPTER TWENTY-ONE: THE INCURSION

One Hour Later
Approaching F. E. Warren Missile Range
Southeast Wyoming

A never-ending array of lightning strikes lit up the night sky, each flash emanating from the center of the strange approaching storm. Accompanying the light show, rumbles of thunder bombarded through the clouds like the grand finale of a fireworks show. The wind had also picked up speed, blowing across the panhandle in gusts nearing hurricane-velocity. What had first appeared on the DART's radar screen as a small blip, the freakish weather pattern had grown to gargantuan proportions. Several miles in the distance, some of the more pronounced thunderclaps still caused the high-tech aircraft to shake violently.

Although the aircraft had been designed with stealth technology, as an added precaution Ollie flew the DART at a low altitude to avoid being discovered by Warren Air Force Base's radar net. Homing in on Bob and Merrick's GPS signals, we landed amid a grove of trees, half a mile from the new launch control facility and the Sierra-21 missile silo.

I slid the door open. Fighting the strong wind, Bob and Merrick scurried over to meet us. When they reached the aircraft, I noticed each man was armed with an M-16 assault rifle in their hands, and a 9mm handgun holstered to their right hip. In addition to the guns, Merrick had a longbow and a quiver of arrows strapped around his left shoulder.

Aquinas laughed. "My friend, you never cease to amaze me. Where on earth did you procure the bow and arrows?"

"We visited the base's outdoor recreation office," Merrick replied. "I surmised we might need silence in our first attack."

"Excellent. Now tell me, what you have observed since your last report?"

"For over an hour, there's been a steady stream of Phillips Industries vehicles dropping off supplies at the launch facility," Bob said. "Then a few minutes ago, a refrigeration truck arrived at the silo and unloaded two large ice chests."

"The synthesized carmot, no doubt. What about Lucas?"

"We saw him enter the launch facility," Merrick replied. "When the refrigeration truck pulled in, he emerged and proceeded to the silo. But sir, one thing puzzles me. Lucas has undoubtedly ingested the carmot, yet he acted oblivious, as if he didn't know we were here watching him. Do you think his heightened awareness has faltered?"

Aquinas shook his head. "He wouldn't have taken the precaution of sabotaging the video feed from Antarctica if he didn't suspect someone may try to stop him. Remain vigilant. His ignoring you is nothing more than a ruse."

"Yes, My Captain."

"What about the crew escape?"

"The entrance is being guarded by two security men."

"Bob, I'll need your assault rifle."

Bob's eyebrows raised. "Don't you think I should come along?"

Aquinas shook his head. "If we are unsuccessful and lose our lives, I will need you to take over the Great Work."

What a brave man! He spoke of losing his life and didn't skip a beat!

"Why me?" Bob asked.

"Because you cannot be hypnotized, and therefore Lucas cannot exert his power over you. Also, if you deem it necessary to drop the MOAB, we'll need your muscles to help push it out of the aircraft. Crystal, Ollie, and Tim will also remain onboard."

"What about me?" I asked. "I could carry the rifle…"

"I'm sorry, George, but if Lucas or one of his men see you with a weapon, you'll draw their fire. We can't take the chance of you getting hurt."

I knew he was right, but I still wanted in on the action.

"There must be something I can do."

Aquinas thought for a moment. "I have two jobs for you. First, I want you to be our timekeeper. You'll need a watch."

Tim slipped his off and handed it to me. "It's spring-driven, so the EMP shouldn't affect it. And here, take these."

He handed Aquinas what appeared to be a pair of dark sunglasses.

"They're the latest in night vision technology. We only have two."

He handed the other pair to Merrick.

Merrick looked them over. "Surely you jest."

Tim smiled. "They come on when you wear them."

Merrick placed the glasses on and looked around. "Magical."

"Won't the EMP render them useless?" I asked.

Tim shook his head. "Not if they are off when the pulse hits. And remember to take them off when the lights are on. Otherwise, the brightness will blind you."

Aquinas put his night vision glasses on and smiled. "Ollie, the carmot please."

Ollie retrieved the ice chest. Taking it from him, Aquinas handed it to me.

"Your second job will be to carry the carmot. Dr. Webster, stay close to George. In the event one of us becomes wounded, you are to apply it sparingly to the injury."

"I understand," Dr. Webster replied.

"Why don't we all just eat some of it?" I asked.

Aquinas took the glasses off. "No, George. The higher the level of carmot we have in our bodies, the easier it will be for Lucas to detect us."

"But with the missile packed with carmot, won't that throw him off?"

"You are forgetting the carmot in the missile is synthetic. We have no way of knowing if it will have any effect on Lucas' intuition, and we have too few numbers to take such a chance. Now, as for the incursion, what do we have?"

"Two stun grenades, four small explosives, and a pair of wire cutters," Tim said. He placed the weapons and the wire cutters in a backpack and handed it to him.

"As for strategy," Aquinas continued, "we'll follow the instructions of the parable. Merrick, George, Dr. Webster, and I will proceed to the crew escape. Give us twenty minutes before engaging the electromagnetic pulse. Twenty minutes after that, if you haven't heard from us, you are to take off, climb to a safe altitude, and drop the MOAB. It doesn't matter if we are still inside. Under no circumstances can we allow the missile to launch. Are we clear on that?"

Everyone nodded.

"Let us not be late for our rendezvous with destiny."

DALE C. GEORGE
~ The Wanderer ~

Lucas stood at the rim of the Sierra 21 missile silo, watching the last load of synthesized carmot bricks being lowered into the shaft. Peering over the edge, he saw the element had already changed the nose cone and upper half of the missile to gold. Further down, Professor Davenport and another man, both dressed in full protective gear, loaded the carmot into the missile. On the opposite side of the missile, four men lay dead on the gangway.

Another flash of lightening cracked overhead, followed by a loud rumble of thunder. Shielding his eyes from the dusty wind, Lucas looked up at the sky.

Strange. I haven't seen a storm like this since the day I was punished. Could the Day of Reckoning finally be at hand?

Looking back down into the silo, Lucas cupped his hands around his mouth and yelled.

"Status report!"

Davenport stopped loading and looked up. "The residue from the transformed gold is more toxic than I calculated. It killed four of my men in fifteen minutes."

"Did you not warn them this phase of the operation might be dangerous, and that they should wear protective clothing?"

"Yes, but they wouldn't listen to me."

Lucas smiled to himself. *Excellent! My little experiment worked. The synthetic carmot is as lethal as the real carmot.*

"How much longer, Professor?"

"I'll need at least a half-hour to finish loading, and to close these access panels."

"Perfect!"

"But since we are not really launching the missile, what does it matter?"

Good! The suggestion I planted in his mind is also still working. He believes this is an extortion plot against the United States government, and that I am bluffing about launching the missile.

"If we are going to pull off this deception, we must make them *think* we are serious," Lucas replied. "When you are finished, report to me in the LCF."

"Yes, sir."

~ The Army of Light ~

At a sprint, Aquinas, Merrick, Dr. Webster, and I made our way to the emergency crew escape. Reaching the tree line, we found the entry illuminated by floodlights. Swiveling cameras were attached on top of the chain link fence surrounding it, one on each side. Two Phillips Security men walked slowly around the fence, assault rifles at the ready.

Aquinas motioned for us to hold our position. "George," he whispered, "how long do we have before the pulse?"

I checked the watch. "Less than a minute."

He turned to Merrick. "Take care of the guards. I'll get us through the fence."

Merrick set his assault rifle down and retrieved the bow and two arrows from his quiver. Loading one, he drew back on the bowstring, he took aim and fired. The arrow struck one of the security men in the chest. As the man crumpled, Merrick let loose the second arrow, dropping the other man in a similar fashion.

Following another flash of lightening and roar of thunder, the floodlights went out.

"That's the pulse," Aquinas said. "Let's go."

He placed his night vision glasses on and rushed to the fence. Retrieving the wire cutters from the backpack, he began snipping a hole in the chain link. Proceeding through, we made our way to the escape hatch. Following a few turns of the wheel, Merrick put on his night vision glasses and slithered inside. A few minutes later, he poked his head out of the opening.

"All clear, sir."

"George, hand him the ice chest."

Merrick took it from me and disappeared inside.

"Dr. Webster, you're next. Then George."

Once we were all down in the crawlspace, Aquinas whispered his instructions.

"Dr. Webster, take hold of Merrick's ankle. George, take hold of mine."

I felt around in the pitch-black darkness until I located him. For the next few minutes, we inched along through the cramped corridor until I heard Merrick whisper.

"We have reached the kitchen."

From above, I heard Gwendolyn Phillips screaming at the top of her lungs.

"Answer me! What has happened to the power?"

"I don't know," a man replied. "For some reason, the electrical grid is offline."

"Restore it immediately!"

"I can't. Nothing is working."

"This is insufferable! What could cause such a power outage?"

"Perhaps lightning from the storm hit a transformer?"

"How many times have I told you I *will not* tolerate incompetence?"

"Please, Miss Phillips, let me check the circuit breakers again."

"You are a fool!"

A shot rang out, followed by the sound of a body hitting the floor.

Merrick slowly opened the inside hatch. The red emergency lights illuminated his face in a dark shade of crimson.

"Sir," he whispered, "it appears Gwendolyn has killed a man."

"Are you sure he's dead?"

Merrick nodded. "He's lying between the launch stations, not moving."

"Is there anyone else?"

He looked around. "Six men, near the entrance to the launch control room."

"What about Maddie?"

"I don't see anyone else. No, wait. There is a woman in the launch control room tied down to a chair."

I heard the zipper on the backpack slide open.

"George, stay here with Dr. Webster. When it is safe, we'll come back and get you. Are you ready, my friend?"

"Ready, sir," Merrick replied.

"Stun grenades on three. One. Two. Three."

Seconds later, two loud booms reverberated from above. In a flash, Aquinas and Merrick were out of the crawlspace. A bevy of shots rang out. I reached out into the darkness and took hold of Dr. Webster's hand. When the gunfire ended, a deafening silence hung in the air – as if fate were awaiting our next move.

A long minute passed.

Still no sounds from above.

"George," Dr. Webster whispered, "what do you think is happening?"

"I'll take a look."

I slowly opened the inside hatch, stuck my head in, and looked around. From my position, I had a perfect vantage point of the interior of the complex. On the floor in the center of the kitchen lay the motionless bodies of six men. Aquinas stood on the right side of the threshold leading into the launch control room, aiming his assault rifle. Merrick stood on the left side, behind the thick security door. Just as Merrick described, the body of the man Gwendolyn had shot lay on the floor between the launch stations.

Catching my first glimpse of Madison, tears came to my eyes.

Tied down to the chair of the launch station to the right, she looked to be comatose; her face had a blank expression, and her unfocused eyes were staring off into the distance. Gwendolyn stood next to her, smirking confidently and pointing a revolver at her head.

"Whoever you are, drop your weapon or she dies."

She addressed Aquinas singularly. She doesn't know the rest of us are here!

Aquinas replied calmly. "No need for that. I will comply with your demands."

"Who are you?"

Aquinas signaled Merrick with a hand gesture and pointed to Madison.

Wait! Did I see that right?

Silently, Merrick knelt to one knee and examined the security door. Slowly withdrawing an arrow from his quiver, he pushed the razor-sharp tip through the crack on the hinged side of the door. Placing the bowstring up to the crack, he loaded the arrow and drew back.

"Answer me!" Gwendolyn shouted. "Who are you?"

Aquinas again pointed to Madison.

What's he doing?

Aquinas lowered his rifle and stepped out. The red emergency lights fully-revealed his face.

Gwendolyn's eyes grew wide. "Aquinas? By what magic are you back from the dead?"

Aquinas laughed. "Lucas is the magician. He orchestrated my return when he enlisted the aid of George d'Clare."

"Liar! He would never do that."

"Perhaps not willingly, but the fact remains I am standing here in front of you."

"We'll see if you can return from the dead again when I empty my gun into you."

Gwendolyn turned and pointed her revolver at Aquinas.

Merrick released the shot.

"Wait!" I screamed.

The arrow lodged in Madison's chest, grotesquely pinning her to the chair. At the same time, Gwendolyn fainted and fell to the floor.

Feeling nauseous, I frantically climbed out of the access shaft and ran toward Madison. When I reached the table, Aquinas and Merrick grabbed hold of me.

"Do you know what you've done?"

"Look again, George," Aquinas said. "It's not Maddie."

When my eyes met Madison's, her face contorted. A moment later, her features sharpened.

"Gwendolyn?"

Aquinas nodded. "And observe."

He pointed to the woman on the floor, whose blonde wig had fallen off.

"Madison!"

Incredible!

Making moaning sounds, I glanced back and saw Gwendolyn struggling to free herself. The tip of the arrow protruded out of the back of the chair – Merrick's incredible shot had traveled completely through her body!

As Gwendolyn's eyes moved to Merrick and back to Aquinas, the wide-eyed look of stunned surprise came across her face.

"How?" she gasped.

"It does not matter how, Miss Phillips," Aquinas replied. "What *is* important is you renounce Lucas."

"Never," she scoffed. "When he gets here, he will kill all of you."

"Need I remind you of your situation? Merrick's arrow has inflicted a fatal wound. You are dying."

"A temporary setback." Blood began dripping from her mouth. "I have eaten the carmot. It will save me."

Aquinas' eyebrows raised. "You cannot entrust your life to the carmot. It's too unpredictable."

Gasping for air, she looked around.

"Renounce Lucas and save your soul, Madam!"

Gwendolyn answered with a gurgling exhale. A moment later, her head dropped, eyes staring and motionless.

"Wicked to the end," Merrick commented.

Aquinas and I knelt to Madison. After checking her for injuries, he looked up at Merrick and me. "Go get Dr. Webster. Bring the carmot."

After helping Dr. Webster climb out of the access shaft, Merrick climbed in. When he handed me the ice chest, it felt like it weighed a ton! At the same time, tremors returned to my right arm and leg. Unstable, I lost my balance and fell over.

No! Not now!

"What's the matter?" Merrick asked.

Tears came to my eyes. "My Parkinson's symptoms are back."

Merrick's eyes grew wide. "Just as it was foretold!"

With Dr. Webster on one side of me and Merrick on the other, they helped me back to my feet and into the launch control room.

"How is she?" I asked.

"She's in a deep hypnotic spell." Aquinas replied.

"Can you break it?"

"I'll try, but it may take some time, which unfortunately is a luxury we don't have."

"My Captain," Merrick said, "Lord George's malady has returned, just as the Wordless Book foretold."

Aquinas looked at me. "So I see. Hand me a piece of carmot and give a piece to George."

"Are you sure, sir?"

"Quite certain. We must be mobile enough to move about."

Just then, the main lights flickered and came back on, brightening the entire facility. On the wall in front of the launch control stations, two large-screen televisions also came on, one showing the Sierra-21 missile silo from the outside, and the other, an interior view showing only the missile.

Merrick opened the lid of the ice chest and withdrew a piece of carmot. Aquinas took it from him and stuffed it into Madison's mouth. The violet-colored element instantly changed to a purple glowing gel. When he handed a piece to me, I quickly ate it. Expecting the same overwhelming reaction I'd had in the military briefing room, I braced myself, but nothing happened.

"Do you feel anything?" Dr. Webster asked.

I shook my head.

"The element is as unpredictable as it is magical," Aquinas said. "But be aware, it could begin to work at any moment."

"I understand."

Just then, Madison let out a moan, and I moved over and placed my arm around her.

"Madison?" I said softy. "It's me, George."

Her eyes focused. "George?"

"And look who else is here."

Her eyes traveled to Dr. Webster.

"Hello, Mrs. d'Clare."

Madison nodded. "Your hair looks just like Gwendolyn's."

Aquinas smiled and leaned in. "That's because she is *supposed* to look like Gwendolyn."

Her eyes grew wide. "Uncle Charlie? How can it be? George and I watched you die."

"It's a long story. Unfortunately, we don't have time to tell it."

Even in her lethargic state, she found the energy to light into him.

"You don't have time? You haven't had time to tell me a lot of things, like your real name and what happened to my parents!"

"Maddie…"

"If you had only asked, I would've helped you!"

Aquinas looked at Merrick and laughed. "Spunky, isn't she?"

"I'll say. A veritable firebrand, that one."

"Who are you?" Madison demanded.

"Merrick, at your service, madam."

Her eyes grew wide again. "Merrick? How is it possible?"

"Your husband, Lord George, brought me and Aquinas back to life with the Sacred Stone of Atlantis."

Madison looked at me. "Now I know I belong in a loony bin. All those weird science fiction movies you took me to have finally taken their toll."

I smiled.

"You are definitely sane, Maddie," Aquinas said. "Merrick and I are truly here. Right now, however, our focus must be on Lucas."

Aquinas and I helped her to her feet and over to a chair.

"Please remain seated and pretend you are tied down, hands behind you," Aquinas instructed.

"Oh no!" she gasped. "I remember Lucas hypnotizing me. He's going to launch an ICBM filled with carmot."

"We know," Dr. Webster replied. "We're here to stop him."

"Don't worry, Maddie," Aquinas added. "He cannot set off the missile without the launch codes."

"But Uncle, you don't understand. The pressure of his hypnotic suggestions were too strong. He *knows* the launch codes!"

"We must therefore move like swift water." He turned to Merrick. "Take Gwendolyn's body and hide it in the crawlspace."

Merrick quickly pulled the arrow out through the back of the chair, freeing her body. Effortlessly picking her up, he ran to the emergency escape shaft and dropped her in.

"Dr. Webster," Aquinas said, "I'll need you to lie down on the floor."

"On the floor?"

"Yes. I want Lucas to think Madison has overpowered you. Keep your head down for as long as you can. Once you've drawn him in far enough, Merrick and I will seal off his escape and attack him from behind."

As she knelt, Dr. Webster's face *transformed* into Gwendolyn's!

Merrick, Madison, and I stared dumbstruck at the sight.

"Maddie?" Aquinas asked.

She slowly turned and looked at him. "Did you do that?"

Aquinas nodded. "I'm going to project a suggestion for you too, so keep your head down. When Lucas is within arm's reach of Dr. Webster, I want you to raise your head and scream. Do you understand?"

She nodded.

Aquinas turned to Merrick. "Position yourself behind the door to the women's quarters. I'll stand behind the door to the men's. George, hide in the launch control room. Be ready with the Sacred Stone."

I moved behind the security door and crouched down. After wiping my sweaty palms on my pants. I retrieved the stone – still without the beam of light.

The elevator chimed and the door opened.

Lucas walked in.

When he saw who he thought to be Gwendolyn laying on the floor, he rushed over and knelt beside her.

"What has happened?"

Before she could answer, Madison raised her head and let out a scream reminiscent of a threatened teenager in a horror movie. Her face had taken the appearance of a hideous gargoyle!

The look of stunned surprise crossed Lucas' face. A split-second later, an arrow sliced through his right leg, followed by a shot striking his back. When he fell to the floor, his face *transformed* into Professor Davenport's.

"Hold your fire!" Aquinas screamed. "He's not Lucas!"

Before I could draw a breath, shots rang out – from behind me!

Aquinas and Merrick crumpled to the floor.

I turned to see who was shooting, and the man Gwendolyn had murdered was standing upright, holding a handgun! When our eyes met, his facial features contorted and sharpened.

Lucas!

He leaned over and pressed a button on one of the control stations.

The overhead lights went out, and the crimson-colored emergency lights came back on. The sounds of high-pitched sirens filled the air, and the heavy security door began to swing closed.

"George!" Aquinas screamed, "The stone!"

I held the stone out in front of me, but nothing happened. Realizing I was holding it in my left hand, I quickly switched it over to my right.

The stone remained dark.

Why won't it work?

Lucas slapped the stone from my hand and delivered a hard punch to my face, knocking me to the floor. Landing next to the ice chest, I could think of only one way to help Aquinas and Merrick: the carmot. Shoving the ice chest as hard as I could, it slid through the closing security door.

When the door clanged shut, Lucas moved fast. Touching the temple areas of Madison's and Dr. Webster's head, the women fell to the floor unconscious.

Lucas stepped toward me. When our eyes met, his face contorted. His deep guttural laugh followed, sending a cold chill down my spine.

Once again, I found myself face-to-face with my deepest fear – the mannequin!

* * *

Paralyzed with fright, and with my Parkinson's symptoms on overload, I sat on the floor shaking uncontrollably. Looking around the room, everything appeared cloudy and out of focus. A voice commanded me to stand, and I slowly rose to my feet.

Lucas has hypnotized me again!

Unable to resist, I followed his orders like a mindless robot. After pushing several buttons on one of the launch stations, he ordered me to turn the key. With all my might, I tried to resist, but to no avail.

The instant I turned the key, a loud artificial voice blared from the computer's speakers.

"T minus five minutes to missile launch!"

With the Wanderer near victory
the stone will shine again bright,
a divine adversary
becomes the Army of Light.

Like the brave knight's arrows
the soldiers must stand.
At the tip of the spear
the weakened man's right hand.

Crystal Alvarez's interpretation of the sixth group of symbols in the last chapter of the Wordless Book

CHAPTER TWENTY-TWO: THE COUNTDOWN

One Minute Later
Onboard the DART
Warren Missile Range, Wyoming

Like a blinking Christmas tree, a bevy of multi-colored lights suddenly lit up the sophisticated aircraft's instrument panel. High-pitched squeals of alarm bells followed, startling the two Air Force Reserve test pilots.

In the cargo bay, Bob Alvarez rose from his seat. "What's going on?"

"We're receiving an alert order," Ollie replied. He cupped his hand over his earpiece.

Tim looked at Ollie, then turned to Bob. "The U.S. military has just gone to DEF-CON One."

"That means we're about to be attacked. What's happened?"

"The Russians have detected one of our ICBMs powering-up to launch. They're readying their nukes for a counterattack."

"Anything from our team?"

Tim shook his head.

"Aquinas' plan must not have worked. Let's get this thing off the ground!"

A bolt of lightning flashed outside, followed by a loud crack of thunder.

"It's going to be a bumpy ride," Ollie said. "The weather is getting pretty ugly."

"Storm be damned! We've got to take out that missile!"

As the DART lifted off, Bob ducked back into the cramped cargo bay and came face-to-face with Crystal.

"What about the others?" she asked.

Bob could only shake his head.

~ Outside the Launch Control Room ~

As Aquinas spread the carmot on his and Merrick's bullet wounds, the artificial voice boomed from a loudspeaker.

"T minus three minutes to missile launch!"

The blonde archer opened his eyes.

"Are you with me?" Aquinas asked.

"Yes, My Captain. Thanks to you."

"I had nothing to do with it. George was the one who slid us the carmot."

"I must remember to thank him."

"You'll be able to, as soon as we rescue him from Lucas."

"But sir, when Lord George brandished the stone, nothing happened. What power continues to save our lives but hinders us from defeating Lucas?"

"We cannot question the ways of the Almighty. The only possible explanation I can think of is we have somehow misinterpreted the parable. Therefore, our only hope is to breach this door."

"How?"

Aquinas unzipped the backpack and withdrew the four explosives. "Shall we?"

Merrick nodded.

Placing the explosives at the base of the security door, Aquinas set the timer. Helping Merrick, they took cover behind the door to the men's quarters.

Seconds later, the explosion ripped through the facility, upending the kitchen table, chairs, and the refrigerator. When the smoke cleared, the door became visible.

Nothing had changed.

The door remained in place.

"It's useless, sir. What do we do now?"

"I wish I knew, my friend. I wish I knew."

~ Inside the Launch Control Room ~

Much like what happened in the briefing room, I felt the carmot go to work, restoring my brain's neuropathways and making my Parkinson's symptoms vanish. Now thinking clearly, I looked directly into Lucas' eyes.

I'm not afraid of you!

Just then, the artificial voice blurted out, "T minus two minutes to missile launch!"

Lucas' laugh echoed off the walls. While keeping his gun pointed at me, he checked several instruments on the launch control station.

"I know you have partaken of the carmot, Mr. d'Clare, and from the look on your face I can tell you are no longer under the influence of my suggestions. But I'm not going to kill you just yet."

"Why not?"

"Because I want you to experience the bitter taste of defeat, just as I did when you caused the military aircraft to crash. After this missile destroys Moscow, the Russians will respond. The world's governments will surely plunge into chaos, and when the Day of Reckoning arrives, I will be delivered from this existence."

Feeling emboldened, I laughed. "You've lived for so long, and you still underestimate the power of human beings."

"What do you mean?"

"How many plagues have we overcome? How many wars? Even if you launch the missile, it won't bring about the Day of Reckoning. We'll find a way to survive. We overcame Pearl Harbor and September 11th, didn't we?"

"You Americans sicken me," he scoffed. "Those events were retaliation against your pompous, morally corrupt government. Every layer of your democracy is riddled with crooked politicians or appointees that can be bribed."

"Our government may not be perfect, but people, for the most part, are good. Every day someone places their life in danger to save their fellow man. Unlike you, who just laid there and watched Gwendolyn die."

"She had served her purpose," he replied coldly.

The artificial voice began counting down the seconds.

"T minus thirty. Twenty-nine. Twenty-eight…"

~ Onboard the DART ~

"Are you ready?" Ollie asked.

"Ready!" Tim yelled.

Lightning flashed outside, followed by a violent, bone-rattling burst of thunder. One of the DART's tilt-rotor engines flamed out, and the aircraft lurched to one side. At the same time, alarm bells clanged in the cockpit.

"We lost rotor number four," Ollie said, "but I've got it under control. Arm the weapon."

Tim flipped a row of buttons inside the bomb, then slammed the access panel closed. "MOAB armed."

"Standby to deploy."

Another blinding flash lit up the sky. Ollie steered the DART into it, somewhat minimizing the shock wave. Bringing the aircraft over the silo, he opened the cargo bay door. "Now!"

Tim, Bob, and Crystal pushed against the weapon. The gigantic, wrecking ball-sized bomb slid only two feet along its guide rail and stopped.

"Again!" Bob screamed.

This time, the huge bomb moved only a foot.

The men placed their backs against the bomb and the heels of their feet against a bulkhead. Following their lead, Crystal moved between the men and placed her feet against the copilot's seat.

Pushing with all their might, the MOAB slid out.

Without the weight of the bomb, the DART instantly shot up, turned over, and went into a tailspin. Fighting the joystick as well as the wind, Ollie flipped the switch activating the airbrakes.

No effect!

Thinking fast, he took hold of the landing gear handle and moved it down. When the wheels locked into place, the DART immediately stopped spinning and he regained control.

"Let's get out of here!" Tim yelled.

Steering the aircraft away from the silo, Ollie engaged the turbojets, and the DART sped away at supersonic speed.

~ Inside the Launch Control Room ~

On the television screen, the launch door of the Sierra 21 silo slid open. On each side of the door, exhaust gases began spewing from the vent ports. At the same time, the artificial voice proclaimed, "Ignition sequence on. Six. Five. Four. Three. Two…"

A blinding flash of light suddenly appeared on both televisions, followed by the deafening sound of an explosion.

"No!" Lucas screamed.

A split-second later, a massive shock wave slammed into the facility, knocking me off my feet. The left wall and part of the ceiling instantly collapsed, and an avalanche of broken concrete and dirt poured in. The landside crashed into the security door, tearing it off its hinges, and violently threw Dr. Webster and me into the right wall under the still-intact part of the ceiling. At the same time, scrapes and cuts riddled my body, sending lightning bolts of pain to my brain.

As fast as it had started, the deluge of earth and cement ended. I opened my eyes, and the permeating cloud immediately filled my eyelids with bits of scratchy dirt and powdery concrete dust. Coughing and hacking, I spit several times trying to rid my mouth of the grit. Opening my eyes again, I noticed an emergency light had come to life, dimly illuminating what was left of the launch control room. Squinting, I looked back to where I had last seen Madison, and my hopes for her safety evaporated – the area was now covered with a mound of cement chunks.

No!

Hearing Dr. Webster struggling to stand, I reached out and helped her to her feet.

"Are you okay, doctor?"

She coughed several times. "I think so. What about you?"

I couldn't answer, but my eyes did, as a flood of tears began to cascade down my cheeks.

She looked around. "Mr. d'Clare, where is Madison?"

"I've lost her," I finally said, my voice cracking.

Just then, I heard Aquinas' voice.

"Maddie? George?"

"Over here!" Dr. Webster shouted.

Appearing through a thin opening, above where the security door used to be, Aquinas and Merrick climbed down and joined us.

"Where is Maddie?" Aquinas asked.

"We got separated when the blast hit," I replied. "She didn't make it."

"No! We *must* find her. Even if we have to dig out all this rubble."

Just then, I heard something move.

"Dr. Webster," Aquinas whispered, "you and George get behind us."

We peered into the cauldron of thick dust. When the cloud somewhat dissipated, I saw the vague outline of a big man standing right in front of us!

Lucas!

"Merrick, fire!" Aquinas shouted.

Shots rang out.

The bullets peppered Lucas' legs. Staggering, he fell to the ground. A moment later, with his wounds glowing purple, he stood back up.

Unbelievable!

"You cannot defeat me, Aquinas!" Lucas yelled. "The synthetic carmot is healing my wounds faster than the carmot found in nature."

"Continue firing!" Aquinas screamed.

Following another salvo, their guns clicked.

They're out of ammunition!

Lucas' deep laugh reverberated through the bombed-out facility. When his laughter finally ended, a surreal silence enveloped the room. Even the thunderclaps from the storm outside quieted, as if the earth had come to a complete standstill.

I had seen many incredible things during this adventure, but nothing could have prepared me for what happened next.

The mound of concrete chunks where I had last seen Madison began to glow!

What the...?

As the radiance *increased*, I glanced at the others and found them also mesmerized, wide-eyed and staring – including Lucas.

Like a blowtorch cutting through a pat of butter, the concrete began to *melt*. A moment later, Madison miraculously rose to her feet and stepped out of the rubble.

Tears rolled down my cheeks again.

She walked toward us and opened her left hand, revealing the Sacred Stone, still *without* the beam of light.

I tried to talk, but the lump in my throat made my words come out unintelligible.

"Maddie," Aquinas said, "place the stone in your right hand and hold it out in front of you."

She followed his instructions, and a dim flicker of light appeared in the center of the stone. Completely enthralled, we watched as the light grew brighter.

"How is this possible?" Dr. Webster whispered.

"Perhaps George can explain," Aquinas replied.

I cleared my throat. "Me? How would I know?"

"Think of the parable, and the nickname you gave to Maddie."

Nickname? What's he talking about?

Then it dawned on me. "Wait. I think I understand. The Wordless Book isn't talking about *my* right hand."

Aquinas smiled. "Precisely. I remembered you referring to Maddie as your *new* right hand."

"Are you saying Lord George's wife is the one who should be at the tip of the spear, sir?" Merrick asked.

"Correct! We must follow the parable and stand behind her."

As we moved into position, the light from the stone brightened to an almost-blinding intensity. Once we were set, Madison aimed the beam of light at Lucas. The instant it touched his body, he stopped moving and his face began to change, again and again. Each time his features sharpened, he appeared to be a *different* person. My element-enhanced intuition told me we were witnessing the faces of all the people he had murdered.

When the facial transformations ended, Lucas took a step toward Madison.

"Keep the light on him, Maddie," Aquinas said.

Using his arm to shield his eyes, Lucas reached out and took hold of Madison's right wrist. To avoid losing the stone, she closed her hand around it.

The sudden lack of light emboldened Lucas, and he pulled her closer to him.

"George," Aquinas whispered, "if we fire, we risk hitting Maddie. Draw Lucas away."

Not knowing what else to do, I charged forward and threw my left fist at Lucas' face. Letting go of Madison, he whirled around, blocked my punch, and grabbed me by the throat. I tried to pry his hand off me, but his fingers held me like a vice.

Images flashed in my mind of evil people throughout antiquity, including Adolph Hitler, Joseph Stalin, Pol Pot, and Genghis Khan, to name a few. In each instance, Lucas was standing by their side in a different disguise.

He had influenced them!

When Lucas spoke, the images stopped.

"Goodbye, Mr. d'Clare," he sneered. Squeezing my throat, his fingernails sliced through my skin, and a spray of purple, element-enhanced blood shot out of my neck. Tossing me aside like a rag doll, I landed on the ground, clutching my throat and gasping for air.

"George!" Madison screamed.

"Remain where you are, Maddie!" Aquinas shouted. "Dr. Webster will tend to George."

Madison opened her hand, but Lucas, shielding his eyes, again moved toward her.

Having reloaded their assault rifles, Aquinas and Merrick opened fire. Most of the bullets struck the invisible shield surrounding Lucas' body and fell to the ground. The ones hitting his extremities opened wounds, but they instantly turned purple and began to heal.

"Sir," Merrick said, "even with the light, the bullets are having no effect."

"Agreed. We must take a more drastic measure."

Retrieving a small bottle of water from his front pocket, he tossed it to Merrick. "Anoint your arrows."

"Anoint them, sir?"

"Have faith, my friend. I shall draw him away from Maddie."

Dropping his rifle, Merrick quickly twisted off the cap of the bottle and emptied it into his quiver. Snatching the longbow from his shoulder, he reached back and retrieved an arrow – its razor-sharp tip now dripping with holy water.

Aquinas stepped out and ran straight at Lucas. Once he was within arm's reach, he faked a move to the right, jumped to the left, threw his arm out, and placed Lucas in a headlock. His lightning-fast move completely surprised the Wanderer!

Letting go of Madison, Lucas dropped to his knees, leaned forward, and sprang up again. Upended, Aquinas lost his grip on the big man, and flew off his back. Landing on the ground, he quickly rolled out of the way.

Now unobstructed, Merrick drew back on the bowstring, took aim, and released the shot. The arrow struck the back of Lucas' left ankle, slicing his achilles tendon. A second arrow tore through his right forearm. A third impaled his left calf.

When the beam of light from the Sacred Stone touched Lucas' injuries, the wounds began to smolder! With a blood-curdling scream, he fell to the ground. Attempting to crawl away, he could only inch along.

Aquinas and Merrick moved in and blocked his way.

When he finally stopped crawling, Lucas looked up.

"How long, Aquinas?" he asked, his voice trembling.

Ignoring him, Aquinas addressed Merrick. "Let's get the shackles on him."

"Answer me!" Lucas roared. "How long must I remain a prisoner in this existence?"

Aquinas looked down at him. "What did our Savior tell you?"

Defeated, Lucas dropped his head down and began to sob.

I tried to stand, but Dr. Webster stopped me.

"You've lost a lot of blood, Mr. d'Clare. Don't try to move."

Taking a breath, fluid entered my lungs. I went into a coughing fit and soon became lightheaded.

I remembered what Aquinas told Madison and me about the carmot. "It's as unpredictable as it is magical," he'd said. "You can't rely on it to save your life or heal your injuries."

My vision blurred.

I'm dying!

Overcome with fatigue, I laid my head down. Before losing consciousness, I saw Madison approaching, and felt the warm, peaceful light of the Sacred Stone envelop my body.

CHAPTER TWENTY-THREE: THE AFTERMATH

Unknown Days Later
Inside Recovery Room #7
University Hospital, Salt Lake City, Utah

The flickering lights of the outside world created obscure shapes on the insides of my eyelids, each appearing as a different incarnation of the Wanderer. Around me, I could hear people whispering, but Lucas' deep laugh prevented me from understanding what they were saying. The combination of shapes and faint voices made it seem as if I was at a cheap horror movie, whose sound didn't match the movements on the screen.

When the laugh finally faded into the distance, I opened my eyes.

The vision in my right eye was blurry, but my left eye appeared clear. From the weakness I felt in my right hand, I could tell my Parkinson's symptoms had returned. I slowly looked around and realized I was in a hospital room.

I tried to move, but a sharp pain in my throat stopped me. I also felt a dull, throbbing ache in the top of my head. On the rollaway table next to my bed sat a cup of ice, but when I extended my arm, I couldn't reach it.

Strange.

I leaned up and stretched my arm out further, but the cup remained out of reach.

What's up with my depth perception?

Just then, Madison rushed in, wearing a surgical mask over her nose and mouth. When we embraced, I noticed a bandage on the inside of my right elbow.

"How do you feel?" she asked.

"My throat hurts," I replied, my voice faint and raspy.

She walked around the bed and handed me the cup of ice. "It's no wonder. Dr. Rowley said you tore your esophagus pulling the tube out."

"What tube?"

"The ventilator tube. During the procedure, you had trouble breathing, so Dr. Rowley put you on a ventilator."

"Wait. What procedure?"

"The procedure to implant the electrodes. You know. For the DBS."

It dawned on me: she was referring to Deep Brain Stimulation, a surgical option for Parkinson's patients to help control their symptoms.

"I've had brain surgery?"

From the way her cheeks turned up, I could tell she was smiling under the mask. "Yes, silly. And next week you'll have the second surgery to implant the battery pack in your chest. That is, if you promise not to pull out any more tubes."

"What about Lucas?"

She tilted her head. "Who?"

Handing the cup back to her, I noticed she also had a bandage on the inner side of her right elbow.

"What did you do to your arm?"

470

Her eyes stared off into space. "They are having a blood drive at the hospital today, so while you were in surgery, I donated a pint."

* * *

During the next few days, I talked with Madison numerous times about what had taken place in the Launch Control Facility and the Sierra-21 missile silo, but she had no recollection of the event. She also couldn't remember the abduction, or how we had joined with her uncle in his fight to stop Lucas. Each time we talked about it, her eyes would go into a stare and she would respond, "Your imagination is working overtime, George. You were with me when Uncle Charlie died in the hospital."

Feeling frustrated after one such discussion, I called Dr. Webster at the CDC, but she also had no memory of the events. Not stopping there, I tried calling Bob Alvarez and his wife Crystal, but found their numbers had been disconnected.

Turning to the Internet, I learned there had been an "incident" on the Warren Missile Range, which had taken the life of Gwendolyn Phillips and ten members of her staff.

In a statement, the Commander of the 90th Missile Wing, Colonel Dewayne Jensen, said, "Our investigators have determined a fault in the electrical system was the cause of the explosion that destroyed the Sierra-21 missile silo and the new Launch Control Facility. Although the public was never in danger, the Air Force has decided to seal the site with concrete to contain any residual radiation. Our condolences to Miss Phillips' family, and the families of the others who perished."

When I brought this to Madison's attention, she replied, "Why don't you do like you always do?"

"Write it all down?"

She nodded. "Your whacky story would make a great book."

* * *

I've often wondered why Aquinas drained the excess carmot from our bodies, leaving Madison with no memory of the events, and me with Parkinson's disease. Over time, I came to believe he must have had a good reason. I've also speculated why I could recall this story with such crystal clarity, as if the events had happened yesterday. I believe it might be from my exposure to the light of the Sacred Stone.

Merrick explained the stone was the *source* of the carmot. After the battle, just before I lost consciousness, Madison had shined the beam of light on me. I have no way of knowing how long I was exposed to the light. If it had been for an extended period, it's reasonable to assume light affected me in such a way it allowed me to remember.

Upon reflection, this adventure taught me the importance of having faith in God (or a higher power) and having faith in our fellow man. Before escaping Kaffa, Aquinas' father Augustus wholeheartedly believed if Aquinas had faith in the Almighty, he would be able to complete the Great Work. Later, when Aquinas experienced the devastating losses of Merrick and Sara, he heard Augustus' voice, and his father's words restored his faith and drove him onward.

As for having faith in our fellow man, the Army of Light proved human beings can work together for a common good. By looking beyond our differing ancestries, ignoring age-old bigotries, and trusting in each other, we defeated a threat to our very existence. I believe I survived this adventure so I could pass this message on to others.

Today, I no longer feel useless or irrelevant. The depression I had been experiencing has vanished. I now believe there must be a reason I was given the chance to help Aquinas and Merrick with such a monumental undertaking, and after I die, the reason will be made known to me.

Perhaps this will happen to each of us. As we age and our bodies falter, we will all have to take a journey into the unknown. And when we embark, our faith may be the only thing we have left.

English philosopher Gilbert K. Chesterton once wrote, "Courage is almost a contradiction of terms. It means a strong desire to live, taking the form of a readiness to die." Now, whenever I think of Aquinas and Merrick, I think of their faith and unwavering loyalty to their fellow man. For seven-hundred years, they protected us from Lucas. Through those years, they lost their loved ones, and had even (temporarily) lost their lives. The epitome of courage and heroism, they are the bravest men I have ever known.

So where did they go? I don't know, but I like to believe they are still out there, somewhere, keeping Lucas contained and watching over us.

As my Parkinson's journey continues, and Madison and I move together, hand-in-hand, into the post-DBS phase of the disease, I silently pray we never encounter another malevolent spirit like the Wanderer.

EPILOGUE

Unknown Days Later
On the Transantarctic Mountain Range, Antarctica

A sonic boom disturbed the quiet south polar night, not far from the skeletal, frozen wreckage of Aircraft 272. After a quick landing, the DART took off, but not before depositing three people on the barren, icy landscape. Once airborne, the jet turned north before disappearing into the starry sky.

A short time later, the Sacred Stone sat back atop the stalagmite of ice, lighting up the ancient Atlantean chamber in a bright hue of lavender. Reinvigorated, the thick ice surrounding it began to glow anew a pure shade of violet.

Outside the chamber entrance, Aquinas stood with Merrick. On the ground between them lay Lucas, handcuffed and with his ankles shackled. Retrieving the Wordless Book from his backpack, Aquinas set it face down on a small shelf of ice.

"Are you going to leave it there, sir?"

Aquinas nodded. "It served its purpose."

"My Captain, I must ask. Do you think it wise we subjected Lord George and Lady Madison to bloodletting?"

"We cannot interfere with their journey, no matter how much it pains us."

"But sir, to leave her with no memory, and him with such a malady ..."

"I know, but they still have lessons to learn, and we must respect the wishes of the Almighty."

They dragged Lucas into the chamber.

After a moment, a swirling mist appeared, and soon thickened into a dense fog. As the cloud moved around behind them, the chamber entrance disappeared – sealed by a thick wall of ice.

From out of the fog, a young woman emerged.

Smiling, tears streamed down Merrick's face. "Bella?"

"Yes, my love. It is I."

Shedding his longbow and quiver, he took her by the hand.

Another woman came forward.

"Sara?" Aquinas asked.

She nodded. "And look who else is here."

She moved aside, and Aquinas' father Augustus, Yuuto Tanaka, and his son Toshiro became visible.

Tears welled up in Aquinas' eyes.

"My son," Augustus said, "You have completed the Great Work."

"What of Lucas?"

"The Almighty will tend to Lucas. Your season is over, your work here is done."

Aquinas embraced Sara and the others, and they disappeared into the cloud.

A short time later, the swirling mist cleared, leaving Lucas alone and trapped in the chamber.

His screams echoed off the tall, icy walls of the Atlantean Cathedral, but there was no one left to hear them.

* * *

Outside the sealed chamber, the glow from the carmot illuminated the worn and weathered Wordless Book. The violet color highlighted several faded lines adorning the back cover. At one time, these lines were bordering edges of geometric symbols. which when deciphered, read:

With the Army of Light triumphant
and the Wanderer finally contained,
they'll banish him to the place of the stone
where the ice will serve as his chains.

Then the soldier and his knight
shall return home like doves,
carried by the wind
on the wings of love.

Dale C. George

During my Air Force Reserve career, nothing gave me more pleasure than documenting the actions of the men and women who wear our nation's uniform, and to subsequently see them presented with a medal or an award for their accomplishments. After my Parkinson's disease diagnosis, and a great deal of encouragement from those close to me, I decided to channel my skills toward a more-personal goal, and the first pages of The Device were born.

THE ELEMENT

After the success of The Device, I set my sights on writing a follow-up story, with Parkinson's patient George d'Clare and his wife Madison (once again) as my heroic protagonists. Rather than a sequel, The Element is a stand-alone companion piece to The Device – a high-octane adventure that blends fantasy, historical fiction, and science fiction into thrill ride for fans of those genres.

www.ingramcontent.com/pod-product-compliance
Lightning Source LLC
Chambersburg PA
CBHW061507020726
47502CB00006B/1968